If you love *The Magnificent Mrs Mayhew*,
discover Milly Johnson's other books,
available in paperback and eBook now

The Yorkshire Pudding Club

Three friends fall pregnant at the same time. For **Helen**, it's a dream come true. For **Janey**, the timing couldn't be worse. **Elizabeth** doubts if she can care for a child. But soon the women find themselves empowered by unexpected pregnancy.

The Birds and the Bees

Romance writer and single mum **Stevie Honeywell** has only weeks to go until her wedding when her fiancé Matthew runs off with her glamorous new friend Jo. It feels like history repeating itself for Stevie, but this time she is determined to win back her man.

A Spring Affair

'Clear your house and clear your mind. Don't let life's clutter dictate to you. Throw it away and take back control!' When **Lou Winter** picks up a dog-eared magazine in the dentist's waiting room and spots an article about clearing clutter, she little realises how it will change her life . . .

A Summer Fling

When dynamic, power-dressing **Christie** blows in like a warm wind to take over at work, five very different women find themselves thrown together. But none of them could have predicted the fierce bond of friendship that her leadership would inspire . . .

Here Come the Girls

Ven, **Roz**, **Olive** and **Frankie** have been friends since school. They day-dreamed of glorious futures, full of riches, romance and fabulous jobs. Twenty-five years later, things are not as they imagined. But that doesn't mean they have given up.

An Autumn Crush

Four friends, two crushes and a secret … After a bruising divorce, **Juliet Miller** invests in a flat and advertises for a flatmate. Along comes self-employed copywriter **Floz**, raw from her own relationship split, and the two women hit it off. Will they help each other to find new romance?

White Wedding

Bel, **Violet** and **Max** befriend each other at the White Wedding bridal shop as they prepare for their trips down the aisle. But is love the primary reason that these three women are getting married?

A Winter Flame

Eve has never liked Christmas. So when her adored elderly aunt dies, the last thing she is expecting is to be left a theme park in her will. Can she overcome her dislike of Christmas, and can her difficult counterpart Jacques melt her frozen heart at last?

It's Raining Men

Best friends from work **May**, **Lara** and **Clare** are desperate for some time away. So they set off to a luxurious spa for ten glorious days. But when they arrive at their destination, it's not quite the place they thought it was …

The Teashop on the Corner

Spring Hill Square is a pretty sanctuary away from the bustle of everyday life. And at its centre is **Leni Merryman**'s Teashop on the Corner. Can friends **Carla**, **Molly** and **Will** find the comfort they are looking for there?

Afternoon Tea at the Sunflower Café

When **Connie** discovers that **Jimmy**, her husband of more than twenty years, is planning to leave her for his office junior, her world is turned upside down. Determined to salvage her pride, she resolves to get her own back.

Sunshine Over Wildflower Cottage

New beginnings, old secrets, and a place to call home – escape to Wildflower Cottage with **Viv**, **Geraldine** and **Stel** for love, laughter and friendship.

The Queen of Wishful Thinking

Lewis Harley has opened the antique shop he always dreamed of. When **Bonnie Brookland** walks into Lew's shop, she knows this is the place for her. But each has secrets in their past which are about to be uncovered. Can they find the happiness they both deserve?

The Perfectly Imperfect Woman

Marnie has made so many mistakes in her life that she fears she will never get on the right track. But when **Lilian**, an eccentric old lady from a baking chatroom, offers her a fresh start, she ups sticks and heads for Wychwell. But her arrival is as unpopular as a force 12 gale in a confetti factory ... Will this little village in the heart of the Yorkshire Dales accept her as one of their own ...?

The Mother of All Christmases

Annie, **Palma** and **Eve** all meet at the 'Christmas Pudding Club', a new directive started by a forward-thinking young doctor to help mums-to-be mingle and share their pregnancy journeys. Will this group help them to find love, contentment and peace as Christmas approaches?

milly johnson

The Magnificent Mrs. Mayhew

**SIMON &
SCHUSTER**

London · New York · Sydney · Toronto · New Delhi

A CBS COMPANY

First published in Great Britain by Simon & Schuster UK Ltd, 2019
A CBS COMPANY

1 3 5 7 9 10 8 6 4 2

Simon & Schuster UK Ltd
1st Floor
222 Gray's Inn Road
London WC1X 8HB

Simon & Schuster Australia, Sydney
Simon & Schuster India, New Delhi

www.simonandschuster.co.uk
www.simonandschuster.com.au
www.simonandschuster.co.in

A CIP catalogue record for this book
is available from the British Library

Hardback ISBN: 978-1-4711-7844-3
eBook ISBN: 978-1-4711-7846-7
Audio ISBN: 978-1-4711-7848-1

Typeset in the UK by M Rules
Printed and bound by CPI Group (UK) Ltd, Croydon, CR0 4YY

For my mam and dad. For bringing me up fed well, safe and warm and raising me with love and care. I never fully appreciated how much you did until I became a parent myself.

Thank you xxx

Behind every successful man there is a woman.
Behind the fall of a successful man there is
usually another woman.

From: Len.Spinks@jfmayhewoffice.co.uk
To: Gina.Almonza@SouthCountiesMagazine.com
Subject: Sophie Mayhew Article – Editorial Control Suggestions.

Dear Gina

Thank you for the draft article on Mrs Mayhew entitled 'Sophie At Home'.

A few amendments, additions and deletions to consider then implement.

1. Mrs Mayhew smiles as she greets me; ~~warmth is perhaps not a word associated with her, but~~ **her handshake is firm and friendly.**
2. The reception room is wall-to-wall taste with its cool pastel walls and sumptuous carpet. ~~The furniture is more reflective of style than comfort. It is all too perfect, suggesting some deliberate artistic composition.~~ !!!!! **The furniture stylish and beautiful, rather like Mrs Mayhew herself.**
3. End the article after 'New York', see below.
   After the tour of her fabulous house, I ask Mrs Mayhew over tea what her dream is and she gives me a measured reply: to be by her husband's side as a support because she has put her dreams with his,

which reminds me somewhat sweetly of the lyrics of 'Fairytale of New York'. ~~I'm not convinced. There is more to Mrs Mayhew than as a mere appendage to her super-successful husband, much more I suspect but sadly I'm not going to get the true answer today.~~

And I think we will go with an alternative title: **The Magnificent Mrs Mayhew.**

Alliterative and entirely fitting to Sophie, the adjective 'Magnificent' has slightly old-fashioned yet fond and glamorous connotations see: Magnificent Obsession, Magnificent Seven, Magnificent Men in their Flying Machines. It is a word less used these days and for that reason stands out in the best way.

We are good to go once these have been incorporated into your article. Please send amended copy forthwith for final read-through.

Yours truly,
Len Spinks

Senior Communications Director and Press Officer to John F. Mayhew, Secretary of State for Family Matters.

Mrs Mayhew

Chapter 1

Doorstepgate, 11 a.m.

As Sophie stood in the middle of them all, the moment strangely crystallised for her, as if time had frozen solid and she was able to study everything at leisure, appreciate how odd it was to be surrounded by familiar people in the house she had lived in for eight years and yet still feel as if she had been dropped from a great height into a room full of strangers.

She saw her mother seated, holding a cup of tea in one hand and the accompanying china saucer in the other, talking to her father, who was standing, one hand slotted stiffly in his jacket pocket; his default pose, as if he were a catalogue model. Mother was talking to him and Father had a polite smile of concentration on his face. Standing next to him, her parents-in-law, Clive and Celeste, looking serious and focused as if they were building up to jumping out of a plane. Sophie's husband, John, deep in conversation with the top pick of his aides: Parliamentary Assistant (London) Rupert Bartley-Green; Senior Communications Director and Press Officer Len Spinks; Chief of Staff Edward Mayhew, who also happened to be John's eldest brother, and Executive Office Manager (Cherlgrove) Findlay Norris. Between his two governmental bases and the office that looked after his investment and property portfolio, John had more staff than the POTUS, although there was an opening for a Girl Friday (London) now, since his last one was currently enjoying her fifteen minutes of fame. The 'people' of breakfast and daytime TV, and every programme which attracted those the media chose to concentrate its temporary but brightest lights on, were no doubt already negotiating appearance fees with her 'people'. *Why was it always someone in that junior assistant/intern/researcher role who toppled the boss?* thought Sophie. Weren't there enough cautionary tales of littered corpses to warn any man in a high-profile position – who really should know better – what dark and treacherous waters he elected to dip into when he chose a pretty, young, ambitious swimming companion. A pond with a hundred signs around it, all lit up with massive red neon lettering and strings of exclamation marks: *Warning. Danger. Come any closer and you're a bloody IDIOT!!!!!*

It would have been easy for the other woman to fall in love with her husband, though; if that were what it was. John could sell ice to the Eskimos, coal to Newcastle, toys to Santa and all the other clichés. Charm personified, absurdly handsome, moneyed, intelligent, refined – oh yes, John F. Mayhew was the full package. Sophie could guess how quickly Rebecca Robinson would have become ensnared in his net, even thrown herself into it willingly, because she had done the same thing fourteen years ago when she was eighteen.

She'd met him at the Christmas Ball when she was in her

first year at Cambridge University, studying French, and he was in his last year studying Business and Politics. He'd been absolutely wrecked on champagne and told her he was going to marry her, before his friends dragged him off for yet more alcohol. She didn't think much about it until Valentine's Day, when their paths collided again at a private party. She spotted him long before he noticed her, which gave her the luxury of studying him unseen. He wasn't her dream type at all but he was extremely magnetic and from the way he held himself, it was more than obvious he knew what his best qualities were. Long-limbed and lean, she imagined him as a human equivalent of a well-bred racehorse, something pampered and valued. Greek-statue profile, mid-brown hair that flopped into his eyes – and what eyes they were: puppy-brown, intense, seductive. Eventually, as if detecting the heat in her gaze, his eyes swept around to hers, locked and she felt powerless, as if she were a hen and he a fox. He sliced through the banks of students that stood between them, mouth stretching into a killer smile, and when he reached her, said:

'Well if it isn't you again. Where have you been hiding yourself?'

And from that moment they were a couple. Sophie forgot all about swooning over the prop forward who was on her course, which was a shame because he would end up captaining England and was a thoroughly nice chap, but John F. Mayhew engulfed her brain and was all she could think about.

John F. was going to be richer than Croesus and prime minister, one day, he said and she didn't doubt that he would be. She could easily forecast his future: top of the tree in his chosen profession, women would adore him, men would want to be him, magazine reporters would queue up outside his door to take photos of the beautiful home he lived in. His children would be perfect and well-behaved. Maybe they'd be *her* children too. Maybe this was the man that her old headmistress Miss Palmer-Price told her would be the one to carry her along in the grip of his forcefield.

The F stood for Fitzroy, he told her post-coitus in bed on the night he took her virginity. His great-great-great-grandfather – Donal F. Mayhew – and his best friend, Patrick, had decided to escape the great Irish famine by emigrating to America in the late 1840s; but an Irish heiress fell hook, line and sinker for the strong and handsome – if impoverished – gypsy Donal and he changed his mind about going. Donal and his wife eventually moved to London where his determination both to shake off the label of male 'gold-digger' and to better himself drove him to build up a fortune in his own right selling property, metal, alcohol, ship parts; anything legal or illegal to trade in order to make a profit. Across the pond, Patrick's family's fortunes improved with every generation too. His great-grandson John F. Kennedy became president of the United States of America. The Kennedys, John said, had stolen the idea of using the F from the Mayhews, and in doing so had cursed themselves. As if he couldn't get any more fascinating, traveller magic was thrown into the mix.

By April Sophie could not imagine living without John F. Mayhew; then in May she found that she'd have to, because he dumped her for the fabulously rich wild-child, Lady Cresta Thorpe. Sophie was heartbroken. John graduated with a first and spent a year touring the world with Cresta, who had dropped out of uni, far preferring to indulge her habits of clubbing, cocktails and cocaine. His life, so she gleaned from gossip, was shining and golden as hers slipped further into the dark and depressing. Her coursework suffered and she started self-medicating with alcohol to blot out the pain. She also realised that the girls she'd thought of as friends weren't that hot in a crisis. She had never been good at gathering friends. The beautiful, insubstantial people were attracted to her, but the really nice people found her own good looks intimidating.

It took Sophie a long time to get over losing John F. Mayhew, partly because she didn't have a group of hard-core pals to help chase him out of her heart. She buried her true feelings deep as she had been taught to at school, threw herself into her studies, never let anyone see how wounded she was. Her heart had just about healed by the time she graduated, give or take the scar he had left.

Months later, Sophie had been working as a temp at the London headquarters of the glossy magazine *Mint* when she heard that they were to run a feature on a young successful investment banker, a high risk-taker and up-and-coming politician, at home in his recently acquired, stupidly expensive bachelor penthouse. His name was John F. Mayhew. Sophie's heart started to race. She wangled it so that she accompanied the reporter and the photographer, desperate to show herself off at her best to him: content, happy, preened and perfect – unattainable and indifferent. Or so she thought.

He was overjoyed to see her, ridiculously so, and she was gracious enough not to dampen his delight with a long-overdue rebuke for dumping her so callously. He asked her out to dinner and she accepted, merely for old times' sake. Sure that if he asked to see her again, she would politely refuse, walk away, having shut the door firmly in his face this time.

He had never forgiven himself for the caddish way he had behaved, he said in Le Gavroche. He'd been glamoured by Cresta's glitzy veneer, but it was mere infatuation. He hadn't realised how much he felt for Sophie until he lost her. Sophie was in love with him all over again before the dessert menus had been delivered to them.

Six months after the photos of his bachelor pad had been published, John F. Mayhew had moved out and into Park Court, a beautiful, if run-down, country residence – a wedding present from his parents for himself and his new bride-to-be, the sublime Miss Sophie Calladine. She ignored that little voice inside her that warned her about the speed of all this, the worm burying into her happiness. *Is this the real deal, Sophie, or are you just grateful to be loved?*

To a woman starved of affection, the full spotlight of his attention was blinding, disorientating – of course she knew this. She had gulped it like air seeping through a hole in a vacuum. For that reason, it would be too easy to let that worm convince her that genuine love was not her primary reason for accepting John's marriage proposal: but it was, it really was. It had to be said, though, that her heart was whooping considerably that she had also earned parental approval for her choice of husband and she could even hear the echoes of applause from her old headmistress, nodding consent from the afterlife: *I knew you'd be a credit to St Bathsheba's in the end, Sophie, like your sisters and your mother before you.* But she *did* love him very much. Enough to have sacrificed her own wants and needs on his altar for the past eight and a half years. Enough to be standing here with her heart ripped open in this room full of people who were looking at her to mend her marriage. Because by doing that, Sophie Mayhew would mend *everything*.

Chapter 2

Eighteen years before

'So can you tell me why you were engaged in such a vicious display of pugnacity that it took four members of my staff to separate you?' asked Miss Palmer-Price of the two girls standing in front of her desk. 'Sophie? Irina? Quiet now, aren't you? I did glean you weren't so silent on the playing field, unleashing all those invectives. Which one of you is going to speak first?'

Miss Palmer-Price knew it would be Irina. She was likely to have been the cause of this altercation and therefore would jump in first to give her account of the event, shifting pieces of evidence around to make them appear much more favourable to herself.

'I hit her in self-defence, madam,' said Irina, stroking her clawed and bleeding cheek for effect.

'And what do you have to say, Miss Calladine?'

Sophie coughed before answering. 'She's right it was self-defence, madam, because I did strike first.'

'And why was that?'

'Because she was attacking another pupil,' replied Sophie. 'One younger and more vulnerable . . .'

'You lying cow, you . . .'

'Miss Morozova, I will not have that sort of language in my office. You will lose thirty house-points for that outburst. Please see to that, Miss Egerton.'

Miss Egerton, standing behind the girls, nodded to indicate that she had committed the instruction to memory. The cane in her hand twitched hopefully. She was an ex-nun who had left the cloistered life because it didn't present enough sadistic opportunities. In a previous incarnation she had been sacked as a Spanish Grand Inquisitor for proving too hard-line.

'Miss Egerton, can you add anything based on what other girls have said?'

'By all accounts, Sophie did intervene to pull Irina off Magda Oakes. It did appear that Irina was intimidating—'

'I wasn't at—' interrupted Irina.

'Will you be quiet,' yelled Miss Egerton. 'I'm speaking about you, not to you. As I was saying . . . Magda has a friction burn on her arm—'

Sophie's turn to interrupt now. 'Which *she* put there,' she stabbed her finger at Irina. Before Miss Egerton could admonish her, Miss Palmer-Price held up her hand.

'All right, I've heard enough. Miss Egerton, please escort Irina to her room where she will remain until tomorrow morning. She will miss the Wednesday high tea' – punishment indeed for the food-orientated Irina – '. . . Sophie, stay here, please. Thank you, that will be all.' Miss Palmer-Price was careful to make the tone in her voice imply that Sophie was in for an equally harsh, if not worse, penalty. She always had to play a careful game where rich parents who over-indulged their daughters were concerned. Her ploy had obviously worked if the smug look which Irina flashed her fighting counterpart as she swaggered out was anything to go by.

When Miss Egerton and Irina were gone, Miss Palmer-Price indicated the chair at the other side of the desk and smiled at Sophie.

'Sit down, Miss Calladine. Please.' Sophie obeyed but remained stiff-backed, her body language signalling that she did not trust that this request was as friendly as it seemed. Miss Egerton smiled when she punished a pupil; Irina smiled when she terrified younger girls. Smiles were often no more than a mere deceptive flexing of muscles and, as such, to be viewed with caution.

'I understand that you interceded to rescue Magda from an unpleasant situation, would that be fair to say?'

'It would,' answered Sophie.

'I also understand it isn't the first time you and Irina have crossed swords over similar matters.'

She saw Sophie's jaw drop slightly open that she knew this. But Miss Palmer-Price was aware of everything that went on in her school: smoking, bullying, bulimia, so-called 'secret' assignations with local boys, and she moved to stamp such misconduct out always at the perfect time for maximum impact.

'Well?' she prompted.

'She's a bully, madam. One who only ever picks on weaker girls. She seems to derive particular pleasure from distressing Magda.'

Miss Palmer-Price leaned forward, rested her elbows on her desk, threaded her fingers together.

'Sophie, I think it's very noble that you stood up for

Magda. Magda, as you know, is here because of the Phyllida Grainger sponsorship that recognises excellence amongst the less fortunate girls in society. Phyllida Grainger girls always struggle here; their background is very different, too different for them to fit in, I've always maintained but . . .' She sighed resignedly before continuing. 'And Magda's accent is especially . . . alienating. That can exclude her from most friendship groups.'

'She's really nice,' said Sophie. 'She doesn't deserve to have Irina keep seeking her out to torment her just because she feels bored and needs entertainment.'

No one in the school had a family as rich as Irina's, but she couldn't truly look down on the other girls because they had what she never could: breeding, pedigree and a long association with money, which far outweighed newer fortunes at St Bathsheba's. Sadly, Magda didn't have any finesse, background or money — old or otherwise — and therefore was doomed. She'd been forced upon them thanks to a benevolent gesture by a former headmistress in her dotage: one girl per year from a working-class background joined the ranks of the senior school. It had been a disastrous initiative. Most had left somewhere between the first month and the end of the first year and the school had silently rejoiced about that, because they really didn't want them there. Magda, dumpy, plain, quiet and studious with a hideous (according to Miss Egerton) Liverpudlian accent, had acquired no friends and had been singled out 'for special treatment' by Irina's gang since day one.

Miss Palmer-Price studied the beautiful girl in front of her with her molten-sunshine hair and a defiant set to her full, dark-pink lips. Unlike Irina, there was an intelligence, a bright light behind her hazel eyes which fascinated the headmistress. She considered herself an expert at reading pupils but Sophie Calladine mystified her. She should have been one of her star students, yet there was a worrying spark of rebellion in her that showed itself rarely but never as spectacularly as today. Her two sisters had exhibited no such defect. Their ships had sailed calmly through the sea of their school years here, both achieving the highest status of head girl. Both characterless and instantly forgettable, it also had to be said.

Irina Morozova was at the school at the behest of her parents, who saw the value in their daughter being educated at one of the most exclusive and oldest private schools in the country despite the fact that she would never in life need the evidence of a single GCSE pass. Irina was destined for a life of luxury sailing on daddy's yacht, maybe having a role within one of his shady companies that involved her having a prestigious job title but not actually doing a lot of work. She would go on to marry another oligarch's son and come to rely on plastic surgery to reconstitute her fading looks; but a much different fate awaited Sophie. She would be nudged firmly towards a man who *needed* her. Not emotionally, because he would be cold, fixated on a career in industry, banking or politics – the top job, though. Sophie would be the power behind the throne, but never actually sit on the throne herself. The girls of St Bathsheba's were proud supporters, the oil in the family machines, wind beneath wings, lynchpins. Their men stood in the limelight that their wives enabled them to reach. St Bathsheba girls did not burn their bras.

'The reason I asked you to stay behind, Sophie, is to give you some advice,' said Miss Palmer-Price. She owed the Calladines some goodwill; after all, Angus Calladine had recently financed repairs to the east wing of the school, which is more than Mr Morozov, with his bank vault stuffed to the rafters had done. 'Answer this: the most important person in your life is whom?'

'My mother?' replied Sophie. Not the right answer obviously, she took from Miss Palmer-Price's unflinching expression. 'Father?'

'No. It's you, Sophie. You. And you need to remember that always and make provisions for it. The Irinas in life will be more useful to you than the Magdas. Altruism is an admirable quality, but it won't get you as far as you might think, because this is a dog-eat-dog world. A semblance of it is all that is required in this day and age. You must learn to hide your true feelings, Sophie. Play the long game in life. The girls here do not become nurses and social workers and shop assistants: they leave as soldiers, tough, adroit, capable and fully aware that self must be preserved at all costs. Kindness is a weakness and it will be used against you.'

Miss Palmer-Price saw Sophie's eyes blink as if there was a massive surge of brain activity behind them. And she was right, because less than an hour ago Sophie had been sitting in an RE lesson hearing evidence to the contrary.

'But Jesus . . .'

'Jesus taught us that kindness is a good thing, Sophie, yes. But there are different sorts of *kind*. Sometimes by being kind you interfere with fate, you do not let the recipient of your benevolence learn lessons, ergo that sort of kindness is actually a form of cruelty, do you see?'

She let that sink in, waited until Sophie answered with a slow nod of understanding.

'The time will come when you will need to put others before yourself; but not the Magdas of this world. Not them.'

She watched Sophie's eyebrows dip in confusion, trying to make sense of this apparent paradox: put yourself before others but not everyone. Who, then?

'You are looking puzzled, Sophie,' said Miss Palmer-Price. 'It is a tough world. Here at St Bathsheba's we have always recognised that its girls need to be prepared fully for life and all its complexities. There is no school like us: we are unique. You will leave us as intellectually accomplished young ladies, but our education goes far beyond that. We educate your soul at St Bathsheba's, Sophie. Our girls are polished jewels. Your inner strength and resilience will attract rich, powerful men and I'm sure you'd want one of those, my dear; which girl wouldn't? Trust me, love is no substitute for a private jet. Choose the most successful man you can find, put *him* first in your life and scythe to the quick anyone who stands in your way. But power does corrupt itself, so occasionally that will involve self-sacrifice on your part. Emotion will be of little use to you at these times. Get used to controlling it, not it controlling you; and that discipline starts with leaving kindnesses to the devotees of the Dalai Lama. Thank you for listening.'

That was an obvious cue for Sophie to go. And she did so, with bewilderment weighing down her features; but she would remember Miss Palmer-Price's advice and her words would come to make sense in time. More than she could ever guess at.

Sophie was the nicest girl that Miss Palmer-Price had taught in years, but 'nice' was no compliment, not in this singular school. She had high hopes for Sophie because she had the full complement of essentials: money, breeding, intelligence and beauty. If she could just learn to fight, claw and scratch on behalf of herself instead of underlings; not with nails and fists however, but with more guile than Black Ops could employ. That was why parents sent their daughters to St Bathsheba's. To learn skills from a forgotten era that the modern world scoffed at whilst envying also.

Chapter 3

Seven days before Doorstepgate

Something was different. Sophie felt it as soon as she woke up that morning even though it was an ordinary day with the alarm going off at the same time as it always did. A mere quiver of disparity, as if she were a spider sleeping soundly and a fly's leg had brushed across her web at the furthest point causing a low, low vibration, a tingle in her limbs.

The last time she had felt anything like this was four years ago. A strange prickle in the air, something amiss, something she had put down to the hormonal changes in her body, because she had nothing in her life to cause any anxiety. She had it all and the biggest adventure of her life was about to begin.

Then three days later Crying-girl turned up at the flat they had in Westminster. She marched straight in, unlocking the door with a key that John later said she'd stolen from his desk.

'Mrs Mayhew, my name is Malandra Moxon and I've been having an affair with your husband and I'm really really sorry,' Crying-girl had said, her voice starting off strong but losing impetus with every word, as she dissolved into sobs. 'And I wanted to tell you what a total and utter bastard he is,' she went on, her eyes dropping from Sophie's face to her well-rounded stomach. She gasped then, and she dropped the key onto the floor as she ran out. The sound of that gasp seemed to hang in the air as if it were loaded with many unsaid words that took their time to die.

Shaking and confused, Sophie rang John immediately. He was a fifteen minute bolt from her but it took him over an hour to get there and she knew, though it took her a long time to admit it to herself, that his priority would be rounding up his troops: Rupert, Edward, Findlay, Len – oh, especially Len.

Malandra was an intern who hadn't fitted in, and when she'd been caught taking photos of his diary pages, John had told her to leave the office immediately. She was angry and aggrieved and humiliated. It was textbook easy how to try and avenge yourself when you worked for a politician. Just accuse him of having an affair and watch the poison spread, said John. Malandra Moxon was blowing off steam but that's all it was because he was innocent of all charges.

'Do you think I would be so idiotic as to fuck an intern in my position?' he'd laughed. 'You really do have to believe me here, Sophie. When have I ever given you cause to doubt me?' She didn't cite Lady Cresta as an example because they weren't married then and he didn't have a political career to gamble away. He was too ambitious to be so stupid now. He then rolled out the Paul Newman line with his own twist, 'Why would I go out and shop for cheap scrag end when I have the best fillet steak at home?' Why indeed. It was a convincing argument when you wanted to be convinced.

Malandra Moxon's name had never appeared in any newspaper attached to a scurrilous story and that – said John F. Mayhew – spoke volumes, because if she'd had *anything* to take to the press, she would have, wouldn't she?

Malandra Moxon slipped into the background of their charmed existence and then further into obscurity. Sophie never wanted to hear her name again because it would for- ever be associated with the lowest point of her life. But a couple of months ago, for no reason she could think of, Sophie had googled her name and found a recent wedding notice in the *Kentish Herald*: 'Teaching assistant Malandra Rebelle Moxon and accountant Charles Andrew Edward Anderson'. The groom's parents were obviously fans of the Royal family, thought Sophie as she read it. It was definitely the same woman because there really couldn't have been that many twenty-four-year-old Malandra Rebelle Moxons in the UK. The accountant was forty-five, so clearly Malandra still had a thing about older men.

Four years ago John had been a junior minister, fully proficient in the art of expert schmoozing and oiling his way around the corridors and people of Westminster. He had a gift for playing people, saying the right thing at the right time, flattering in exactly the correct dose so there was no suggestion of toadying. It helped that he had a Hollywood smile, a mesmerising oratory style and looked shit-hot in a suit. Women loved him and men liked him, even those in the party who envied him. He had a Midas touch with life as well as with money: he was unstoppable, a political super- hero. In the last cabinet reshuffle, John had been made Secretary of State for Family Matters. With his own parents and in-laws solidly behind him every step of the way, John F. Mayhew epitomised the core strength and values of family – immediate and extended. Nowadays it was the turn of others to grease around him. And boy, did they.

'I could really do without this today,' said John, as he and Sophie drove past the queue waiting outside the cricket club in Cherlgrove for his political surgery. He hated mixing with the hoi polloi but it was a necessary evil and he'd managed to avoid doing one for nearly two months. A rare space in his midweek diary had to be filled and he might as well load himself with brownie points, so Len Spinks said.

He knew that most of the waiting constituents were going to be whingeing about the plans for a new housing estate in the town and/or the decimation of a square of green in order to widen a road, because he always insisted on an appointment-only system with advance warning on what people needed to consult him about. Sophie dealt with most of the constituency correspondence, though John F. publicly maintained he did it himself. She'd even perfected his signature for letters. John F. preferred the thrill of Westminster life and playing with the high-value cards. He considered Cherlgrove business the twos and threes in the pack: required in order to play the game but annoying to be dealt them.

It was a beautiful bright day, no breeze, clement temperature – in other words, perfect golfing weather. As soon as John had finished his business here, he was heading off to the course with Sophie's father and their Pringle-jumpered 'Old Lions' cronies. It was Sod's Law that the sun had brought everyone out today in order to moan at him, hoping he would deign to see them despite having no appointment (fatter than fat chance). *Didn't they have anything better to do than prattle on about traffic?* he grumbled.

'Let's just make a lot of promises and get out of here,' said John, as they parked up. *'I'll find out and get back to you* is the order of the day, okay, Sophie?'

Unlike her husband, Sophie enjoyed mixing with people of the town and she got a buzz from the fact that John trusted her so implicitly to manage this side of things, which she did to the best of her ability. But the surgeries brought out the worst in John and highlighted that with him it was always ambition before people, self before others. He was driven to win at everything and primed to snow-plough all opposition out of the way with ruthless speed. The perfect man, according to the dictates of St Bathsheba's. Sometimes she wondered if he would have been such a good family boy if family hadn't been so instrumental to his success. His father and father-in-law both threw a lot of money at the Conservative party. The husbands of Sophie's sisters were useful business contacts, John's eldest brother worked for his office in London, the middle brother was his solicitor. The families of others were much less impor-tant to him. In saying that, John had a vested interest in getting that housing estate vetoed because it was going to be built on green-belt land adjacent to Park Court. Luckily this allowed him to make a song and dance about it for personal reasons whilst also being a champion of the people at the same time.

'Morning, Mr Mayhew,' some women said as he walked past them and into the club, swinging his important-looking carried-to-impress briefcase.

'Morning, everyone,' he trilled back to them, pearly-whites on full display.

'Morning, Mrs Mayhew.' Delivered politely but with less flirtatious eyelash-wafting.

'Good morning.' Sophie's smile was smaller and infinitely more genuine, but size is deceptive in so many areas of life.

The caretaker had a tray of tea and biscuits waiting for them as always. John rubbed his hands together gleefully.

'You always make the best tea, Mrs Farley,' he said and Mrs Farley did that little shoulder-judder of joy at the compliment. Mrs Farley always served John before Sophie. Mrs Farley barely ever looked at her.

'All right then, let's get started,' said John after a quick glug from his cup. A rough-looking woman was first in, carrying a toddler with bright red cheeks, a small army of followers in her wake.

'Oh God, it's Mrs Sillycow,' growled John through gritted teeth, for Sophie's ears only. 'Ah, Mrs Sillitoe, please take a seat. Now, the last time you were here you were concerned about the closure of the green, I believe.'

That disarmed her slightly, that he'd remembered.

'Er, yeah, yeah that's right. Last time you were here, you said that you'd do your best to stop it happening and as far as we know it's still going ahead.'

'I had a word with the council,' replied John, tapping his finger which was his prompt for Sophie to come in.

'You have a note in your diary, John, that there is a meeting next week in the Town Hall for residents to discuss their concerns.'

'Yes, they changed it to an open and well-publicised forum. I made sure they did that,' said John, taking the credit for the email that Sophie had written in his name.

'It'll do no good,' said one of the women standing in a group behind Mrs Sillitoe. 'They hear but they don't listen.'

Sophie scribbled on her pad, then pushed it into John's eyeline.

John, glancing over at her words, was mopping them all up and processing them at speed. 'You need to go to the meet—'

'But they don't need that road widening,' Mrs Sillitoe interrupted him. Cardinal sin, because that was John's pet hate.

'I'm afraid they say they do,' he replied and Sophie noticed his change of tone: it was subtle, but she picked up his annoyance. 'As it stands, children going to Cherlgrove primary school are not safe. The council have asked that people attend the meeting so this can be explained. They only want to take away a slice of the green, a small price to pay for children's lives, wouldn't you say? There is no other way it can be done. Trust me, Miss Sillitoe, I have done all my homework on this one.'

He hadn't at all. Sophie herself had done the legwork and it had been painful because the leader of Cherlgrove Council was a florid misogynist who was better suited to appearing in a seventies sexist sitcom than he was to objective analysis.

The fire had left Mrs Sillitoe's voice as she continued:

'I heard that in time they were going to close down the whole park. Use some for the road and then build on the rest.'

Sophie wrote: *Old rumour. No go. Ground not fit for building.*

'That is a very old rumour with absolutely no foundation to it,' said John. 'None at all. For a start the land isn't suitable for building houses on.'

'The council do what they want when they want,' said a woman popping out from behind Carol Sillitoe. 'There's no point going to one of their bloody meetings. They just feed you bullshit.' A murmur of agreement and nods ensued.

'I would not be doing my job if I did not encourage you

to engage with the council at a public meeting when you have the chance. The more questions you ask, the more answers you will be given,' said John. 'Go, and then if you aren't happy with what they tell you, email me immediately. I so want to be there at this meeting with you.' He turned to Sophie. 'Did you try and switch things around so I could attend?'

'You have a meeting with the PM. It can't be done.'

'Oh damn,' said John. 'Sometimes in this job I really do wish I could be in two places at once.'

'Okay, we'll go to it then,' said Carol Sillitoe.

'Good. Thank you for coming and please . . . you know where I am if you need any further help. Phone, email, I'll answer always,' said John, standing, holding out his hand. He was a master of dismissal; politeness and piss off balanced perfectly at either end of the see-saw.

'You are amazing,' said John to Sophie after she had helped him appease more people complaining about the green, a burly man who wanted to hang a bus driver for not accepting his Scottish ten-pound note and three people complaining about the new housing estate. Last in the queue was a student asking permission to use John as a case study for his project as he had to write about an influential modern-day politician.

'Absolutely,' said John, throwing up his hands, genuinely proud, feeling the sun shine on his ego. 'We might even be able to get you down to Westminster for a visit. Log your details with my parliamentary assistant Rebecca on this number,' and he whipped a business card out of his pocket.

That was the first time Sophie had heard the R word.

She questioned him about it in the car, who Rebecca was.

'I've mentioned her, haven't I?' said John, surprised she'd

asked. 'She started about . . . a month ago. Girl Friday position really, does filing and makes tea. So far so good.'

No, he definitely hadn't mentioned her.

'Why do you need another assistant?' asked Sophie. He
had half the cast of *Ben Hur* working for him.

'Because Rupert blows a fuse every time I want a drink
and he thinks it's beneath him to stick a kettle on. So a Girl
Friday was needed, or a boy, but a girl simply happened to
come along first. She's a graduate who wants to absorb the
essence of Whitehall for a few months and she makes a very
good Americano and files efficiently. Is there a problem
here?' A brittle tone had crept into his voice and so she didn't
say that after the Crying-girl episode, he'd told her he would
only employ male aides because then he wouldn't leave
himself open to *that* sort of situation again.

'No.' What else could she say?

Chapter 4

Seven days before Doorstepgate ... continued

En route to the golf course John dropped Sophie off at the Cherlgrove Manor Hotel where she was due to meet a friend for lunch, although 'friend' was pushing it really because she'd known Elise Penn-Davies for over two years and yet she didn't really *know* her at all. Her friends now were the wives of John's friends (who weren't friends either but party members, clients, movers and shakers, bum-lickers). She craved a friend, someone to whom she could open up wholly. There was no one like that in her life at present, but there was Elise.

Elise was fifteen years older than Sophie and married to the MP for Cherlgrove North, Gerald Penn-Davies; a seasoned, efficient politician made entirely of fat who bore more than a passing physical resemblance to Winston Churchill and encouraged the comparison. Elise, by her own admission, was not to be trusted. 'Never tell any female in our circle anything in confidence', she had warned Sophie at their very first meeting. 'Knowledge is power and

currency and any one of them would use words like knives
if they had to. Don't even trust me, I absolutely insist.' She
was a Jewish princess, full of quotes and mantras and expan-
sive gestures and she made Sophie laugh without meaning
to with her words of wisdom: *A stranger is just an enemy you
haven't met yet.* Which was true, in their world at least. This
present Tory party was a nest of vipers, all residing amicably
in a low-alert swirl but ready to bare fangs and bite jugulars
in order to survive.

Elise was already seated at the table, which was a first
because she was always fashionably late, and there was a glass
in front of her with a dribble of wine left in it. She looked
pale and drawn, despite the attempt to disguise that with
make-up. She'd lost weight since Sophie had seen her a
month ago. Her skin was stretched more thinly over her
cheekbones and the corners of her mouth were sunken as if
pulled down by a weight of depression. She stood at the sight
of Sophie and they air-kissed. Elise sported her usual fra-
grance, which was Gardenia and, on this occasion, a hint of
bar-room floor. A waiter greased over and handed Sophie a
menu, told her that the soup of the day was asparagus and
that the fish of the day was turbot. Then he took their drinks
order: a sparkling water for her and bottle of Pinot Noir for
Elise. Sophie waved away the offer of a second glass. She
sensed an undercurrent, a whirlpool of activity below Elise's
customary composure.

'Everything all right?' Sophie dared to ask.

'Totally,' smiled Elise. 'I'm worn out today already and
sick of the sight of bloody coffee after spending an excruci-
ating morning with Dena Stockdale and her hangers-on.
Feel your ears burning, did you?'

So, they'd been bitching about her then.

'Why, though?' asked Sophie.

Elise had laughed then. 'Because Dena looks in the mirror and sees her and not you, darling.'

The compliment was lost on Sophie; she felt only a deep pang of disappointment, especially because she'd seen a potential friend in the milkmaid–plump Dena, wife of the Chief Whip, who was heiress to the Daisy Shoes fortune. At functions Dena always greeted her effusively and said that they must do lunch, though they'd never managed to fix a firm date. Sophie had decided that the next time they met, she would pin her down to a meet. Maybe not, then.

Elise had no compunction about being brutally candid. Sophie was in no doubt, thanks to her revelations, how she was perceived by people in John's circle. *She says she wouldn't have your figure if someone paid her,* Elise had once told her about Cordelia Greaves, who was married to the leader of Cherlgrove Council. *Apparently you're too thin and pasty.* The treasurer's wife, Eileen Eveleigh: *She said you looked very cold, very unapproachable, boring. Remember when she apologised for forgetting to invite you to the ladies' lunch – she didn't forget.* Yet to her face, they were full of fawning pleasantries. So, for now, Elise was the only person she socialised with for any amount of time and out of all the women in their world, she felt as if Elise was the least likely to stick a knife in her back. She might not have trusted her as far as she could throw her, but Sophie liked her nonetheless.

'So how was the surgery?' asked Elise.

'Busy,' replied Sophie. 'John was keen to get it over and done with as quickly as possible, as he had a date with eighteen holes.'

'I don't know how you put up with all those whingeing people, Sophie. I mean John has to listen to them all moaning on about roads and schools, but you don't.'

'I enjoy it.'

'Do you? Or does it give you a purpose that you feel is lacking from your life? You can so easily become a shadow of your partner in this job,' sniffed Elise. 'Take Eileen Eveleigh. I've seen more personality in a dead moth. If she didn't bitch, she'd have nothing to say.'

True, thought Sophie, though she didn't say that. Having a conversation with Eileen was excruciatingly hard work. 'So, how are you?'

'Builders have gone, extension is finished, thank God,' said Elise with a weighty sigh of relief.

'Oh, that's good.'

'Bought myself a grossly expensive sports car this week which I'll pick up on Monday, and I do believe Gerald is having an affair.'

She said it so matter of factly that Sophie didn't absorb the enormity of her words at first, not until Elise picked up a roll of bread from the basket and ripped it roughly in two as if it represented something more flesh and blood and connected to her husband via his groin.

'Are you . . . are you joking?' It wasn't delivered like a joke but the idea that Gerald would even dare to try and do the dirty on the formidable Elise was surely not to be taken seriously.

A small, barely discernible shake of the head from Elise, as if dismissing her last words. The matter had opened and been closed down immediately.

'Cherlgrove Ball tomorrow. Should be very good. I'm looking forward to it immensely.'

'Yes, so am I,' said Sophie, respecting Elise's choice not to talk about Gerald's alleged affair further.

'I think I'll have the lamb today. Then again, *Welsh* lamb. No, I don't think I'll bother. Let me reconsider that.'

The airspace around them felt unpleasantly charged with whatever was going on inside Elise's head.

'I shall have the stroganoff,' Sophie said eventually, her voice crashing into the silence between them as if it were a hammer on ice.

'Good choice. Me too.' Elise snapped the menu shut as the waiter arrived with the wine. He rotated the bottle, showing it off.

'Just pour,' she commanded. 'I don't need to test it.'

When he had gone, Elise snatched up her glass immediately and drained half of it in one.

'Ever felt another female straying onto your territory, Sophie?' she said, dabbing at her mouth then with the stiff white napkin.

A bubble of Crying-girl drifted across the front of her brain but Sophie ignored it. 'No.'

'Bloody annoying.'

'You can talk to me in confidence, Elise,' Sophie said gently.

'I shall talk, don't you worry. I'll go mad if I don't tell someone and I wasn't going to spill to the fucking Witches of Eastwick this morning.' Her face remained immobile, but then she'd just had a course of Botox that would have smoothed out a whole adult male African elephant. But she didn't talk until she had drained her glass of the rest of the wine and poured herself another.

'Do you know who she is?' asked Sophie.

'She's Welsh,' answered Elise, imbuing the word with all

the worst qualities she could muster, 'and is renting a house in his constituency. Quite attractive if you like that frumpy, face-scrubbed-with-a-Brillo-pad look. Twenty-five.'

'Twenty-five?' Sophie couldn't help the exclamation which came out louder than she'd anticipated and she quickly tweaked the volume down for the third syllable. How the hell had the portly Gerald Penn-Davies managed to pull a twenty-five-year-old, even if she was desperate? If Gerald sat in the sun and burned, he'd turn into a pork scratching.

'Yes, twenty-five. It's obvious what you're thinking, Sophie, but power is a sexual lure; haven't you realised that by now? We have husbands who are riddled with it, soaked through with it. Of course they're going to be prey for libidinous harlots. I've had to shoo off a couple in my time before they got too close to their goal. Yes, even fat fucker Gerald has his groupies. Power can turn a frog into Hugh Jackman.'

Sophie stopped another interjection of disbelief escaping her, even if she did have difficulty believing that anyone could ever equate Gerald with Hugh Jackman. She was also astounded that, after everything Elise had told her about spilling secrets, she was opening up to her like this. By Elise's own admission, secrets could be used to dismantle; disclosures were mallets and chisels. Gerald and John, for all their outward camaraderie and joint obligation of party loyalty, both had their eye on the leadership and might have to resort to gladiatorial measures if that particular throne became vacant.

'A pretty face coupled with ambition has the power to divert men's brains from their heads into their underpants, darling,' said Elise. 'Even the most holy of them are susceptible. I really thought Gerald might have learned his lesson.'

'There have been more?' Sophie almost squeaked.

'Just one, and I'm sure of that. No one else knows. I extinguished her totally, it's the only way. They have a tendency to get nasty, you see, attempt to haunt you seeking vengeance, drill into your brain like a bug that can't be reached or excised. It's no good wounding them, you have to slaughter them where they stand.'

'We are talking figuratively here aren't we?' Sophie thought it best to check.

'Of course. But it probably would have been kinder if I had murdered her. I was rather brutal. But once she was gone, we could get on with our lives again.'

'What about the trust, Elise?'

Elise smiled. The long stretch of her mouth had little humour to it though.

'Personally, I've never really put trust on a pedestal to be worshipped. Not fidelity within marriage sort of trust anyway. I trust Gerald to be loyal to the party, I trust him to keep within confines that allow him to progress in his career and keep us in the style to which I and our sons have become accustomed, but I do not trust him to remain impervious to womanly wiles. If, however, the woman to whom those wiles are attached poses a danger to his career or my comfort, then I will see her off without a moment's consideration. And did. And will again, though it really is a bore and a drain on my energy having to deal with an infatuated silly cow who actually believes he would leave me for her.' She blew out her cheeks. 'Was it Abraham Lincoln who said that if you wanted to test a man's character, give him power?'

*

Sheila Crabtree was Gerald's long-term secretary. She was drab and dumpy and had been in love with him for years, Elise disclosed. Her internal organs must have exploded with joy when one night, after four fingers of malt whisky downed whilst he was writing a speech, Gerald's hand extended towards her substantial bottom and slowly caressed it. Five minutes later he'd had his wicked way with her on the ingrained leather top of his oak partners' desk. He didn't realise it would result in releasing her inner bunny boiler.

'She had her hair permed, face waxed, dropped thirty pounds, walked into work wearing lurid eyeshadow and glossy lipsticks,' Elise told an enthralled Sophie. 'Gerald's "top-ups" to Sheila's wage resulted in a complete personality change. She started behaving like his wife in the office, guarding him like a German Shepherd with a pig's ear. It was when she would not allow me to speak to my own husband that I was moved to act. For all Gerald's public reputation as a hardliner, he was terrified to confront Sheila, so I did it for him. She was a very stupid woman to under-estimate a Jewish mother.'

'What happened?' If this had been the theatre, Sophie would have been on the edge of her seat. This was unashamedly more exciting than a James Herbert novel.

'Always do your homework, Sophie. Come to the table armed with information and as many hidden knives as you can secrete about yourself – figuratively speaking again, of course. Sheila Crabtree had a history of fixations, stalking, I discovered. I told her to be a good girl, grow back her moustache and I'd find her another position within Whitehall, or she'd never work again. Conveniently she had a sick mother in a nursing home owned by a business associate of my brother. The mother was very happy there and a move could have been catastrophic for her.'

Sophie gulped, in much the same way as she imagined Sheila Crabtree gulped.

'I also had some very unflattering photographs of her sprawled on my husband's desk, thanks to an excellent private detective I employed. Sheila really wouldn't have wanted the people at her local church to see them. She went away without a whisper.' Elise paused for more wine. 'For some reason no one expects the wife to be so full of guile. The public see us standing behind our husbands and think we are vacuous and flimsy. More so if you are beautiful. I was modelling for *Vogue* when I met Gerald, therefore I was automatically stupid.' She smiled softly. 'My dear Sophie the Trophy, be Marilyn Monroe on the surface and Sherlock Holmes underneath it. The element of surprise can be your best friend.' Then she sighed and said quietly, 'Oh what a bloody week. Awful, absolutely awful,' the words riding on her breath. Sophie saw a single tear slip down Elise's face and realised just how seriously she was affected. Elise had said before that 'tears were only for the weak and manipulative' and 'tears were a waste of vital fluid', maxims that could have come straight from the ideology of St Bathsheba's. Elise Penn-Davies did not do tears. Sophie's hand moved across the table, closed over Elise's, gave it a gentle squeeze.

'You and Gerald will be all right. I'm sure of it.'

'Gerald?' Elise guffawed. 'I couldn't give a toss about him. One of my horses had to be shot yesterday, that's the only pain I need to blot out,' and she removed her hand from underneath Sophie's before the sympathy burned her.

Chapter 5

Six days before Doorstepgate

Sophie picked up John's discarded shirt from the bed and before she deposited it in the laundry basket, she lifted it to her nose and inhaled. It smelled of a day's work and his strong, spicy, expensive Italian aftershave with no notes of a woman's perfume intruding upon the scent. *You're being stupid, Sophie, get a grip*, said a reprimanding voice in her head. The trouble was there was another voice that was telling her to watch out for herself. That one was quiet but knowing, a whisper with a vigilant eye. A part of her that cared for herself more than anyone else ever had. She'd last heard it four years ago and dismissed it; she wouldn't this time.

She didn't want to turn into the sort of woman who searched pockets or went snooping in desks, prying open locked drawers with a paper knife, but her radar had picked up something. There had to be a reason why Crying-girl had been in her thoughts recently. Then again, John's focus was purely on work, not women. His adrenaline levels

were in overdrive at the moment because there were rum-
blings of discontent within the party. The PM Norman
Wax had enemies in the ranks whose consciences would
not let them support his stance on some heavy issues: the
contentious lifting of an ivory ban, unpopular stealth taxes
on the middle classes and the one John was most excited
about – the PM's intention to renege on a large chunk of
investment that he'd promised to the NHS. A death knell
was ringing on his career and the party was already fur-
tively gathering behind John, ready to lift him onto their
shoulders and deposit him in number ten. He wouldn't risk
all that for an affair now, would he? '*Do you think I would
be so idiotic as to fuck an intern in my position?*' he'd said to
her about Crying-girl. '*Even the most holy of them are susceptible,*' Elise had told her.

The gown Sophie had chosen for the Cherlgrove Ball was
beautiful and very expensive: matt satin in a shade of pale
grey-blue that shimmered like lake water when light caught
it. The cut showed off her slim shoulders and long neck, her
tiny waist, the gentle curve of her hips below it and her
small, pert breasts above. Sophie hadn't liked the way it sat
on her waist so she had unpicked the seam there and res-
titched it so it fitted perfectly. It wasn't a difficult job and
she'd done tweaks like this more times than she could
remember. She could quite easily have designed and made
her own dress but John had vetoed such ridiculousness
before. A home-made dress? Who did she think she was –
Maria von Trapp? She was the wife of the future prime
minister, he'd barked, and she could make all the clothes she
liked in her little sewing room but she would not wear them
in public. He had never heard anything so preposterous
in his life.

As she sat at her dressing table putting in her earrings, John emerged from his en suite, towel covering his modesty. He smiled at her in the mirror, walked towards her, put his hands on her shoulders, kissed the corner of her jaw with a butterfly touch of his lips.

'You look absolutely beautiful, darling,' he said. 'I should get a move on, shouldn't I?'

'You've got plenty of time before the car arrives,' replied Sophie.

'That's good. By the way, we have an engagement on Monday so don't make any arrangements,' he called casually over his shoulder as he strode into his dressing room.

'Do we?' She couldn't remember anything in the diary for Monday.

'Last-minute appointment.'

She paused then from fixing some tendrils of hair which had worked loose from their pins.

'Where?'

'The hospital.'

He was being sketchy on the detail and that triggered off an alarm inside her.

'What department?'

Please don't say it.

'Geriatric.'

Her climbing nerves relaxed. For a moment there, she'd expected him to say the neonatal unit because she wasn't an idiot, she'd been following the news. It had only just reopened after a refurbishment and already it looked as if it might have to close. She had been pushed into duties before that she had stoically undertaken when she really hadn't wanted to, but she couldn't have gone in there. Even after four years, it was too soon.

'I thought . . .' she said, almost laughing with relief, then closed her mouth. There was no point in putting an idea there for him to harvest.

'What? You thought what?'

'Nothing.'

'It's important you're at my side. Norman is kicking the NHS in the balls. I . . . *we* . . . have to show that we are supporting our local hospital.'

'Absolutely. But isn't that going against Norman?'

'I've considered that. Len thinks that looking after our local constituents should be our priority on this occasion. Norman won't be in the job much longer. I . . . we have a wonderful opportunity here to make a mark. Damned if I do and damned if I don't, so I might as well do something that will benefit me . . . us.'

'Yes, of course.' Sophie liked old people. She enjoyed talking to them, hearing their stories, seeing the light in their eyes and imagining all that learning and wisdom behind them. It broke her heart sometimes to think of the still ones, to see the shells of the once young and lively waiting for nothing because even hope had deserted them.

John reappeared from the dressing room fastening up his shirt. 'Thank you. I'm so lucky to have you, Sophie. Sometimes it hits me just what a great team we are. You are going to make a magnificent prime minister's wife,' and he smiled at her and though she smiled back, the feeling persisted that all was not as it seemed.

They arrived at the venue looking fabulous enough to attend the Oscars. There were quite a few cameras clicking and a TV news team was present because the ball was a big, *big* event in the county calendar, thanks to the newsworthiness of its sponsors: the young, hip and enviably rich Duke and Duchess of Hawshire had invested an obscene amount of money into this evening to raise money for disabled servicemen, and in the process had attracted a whole shedload of celebrities because everyone was keen to be associated with such a charity, whether for purely altruistic reasons or to enjoy the glitz and mingling, or to take advantage of such a shiny bundle of PR opportunities. Robbie Williams, a few minor young royals, David Walliams were all rumoured to be attending, along with glamorous reality TV stars snatching their moment in the spotlight before it waned and Simon Cowell's latest boy band. The cameras burst into action as soon as Sophie and John had alighted from their car. The lens loved them; sometimes Sophie looked at photographs of herself and marvelled how beautiful she appeared in them even though she never equated them with a true image of herself. She felt as if she was looking at a different person, an imposter. The woman in the magazines was stunning but also too self-assured, unreachable, distant, cold, as if she lived life behind an impenetrable barrier. No wonder people felt about her the way they did if she felt that about herself.

'Sophie, darling.' A woman waved across – the council leader's wife, Cordelia Greaves, grinning like a hyena on a good drug trip. The one who thought her too thin. She was standing with Eileen Eveleigh, who had adjudged her to be boring – as if that weren't a case of pot calling kettle. Sophie waved back but a smile could not be coaxed. She might as well live up to what they thought of her.

She spotted Elise standing with Gerald, over whom she towered. He was wearing a kilt and looked far more attractive from the knees down than he did from the knees up.

They were conversing with Dena and Christopher Stockdale, the Chief Whip, who'd graced them with a visit from London. They all looked very jolly and friendly together despite Sophie knowing that neither couple could stand the other. Gerald had got even fatter since the last time she had seen him. His neck had disappeared and his chin was puffed over his collar. Sophie tried to imagine him in a clinch with a young woman of twenty-five and couldn't. Elise waved over. She seemed cheerful which was good because Sophie had been quite concerned for her after their lunch yesterday. She had texted her last night to check how she was, but she hadn't replied. That was nothing new. Elise did things when she wanted to, not when she was summoned to.

Handshakes were exchanged between the men, cheek kisses between men and women, air kisses between women.

'You're looking absolutely gorgeous, Sophie,' said Dena.

'That's very nice of you, thank you. And your dress is beautiful, Dena,' Sophie replied. Politeness and smiles successfully masking the insincerity. Dena's dress would have cost a fortune, but the price tag would always be more important than the object with Dena, so Elise had informed her in the past. The dress was stunning but Dena didn't suit it at all. It was dark purple, which made her skin look sallow and the cut made her waist appear thicker than it was. Sophie had a true talent for instinctively knowing what shades suited people's colouring, what necklines they should wear, even what cloth would make the best of their attributes. Some people rocked linen, others looked as if they'd been dragged through a hedge backwards in it. John suited linen. John suited everything. He looked more model material than many of the professionals in the glossy magazine shoots. He could throw a photoshopped David Beckham into the shade.

Dena flicked her eyes up and down Sophie again. Sophie suspected she was hoping to find faults to make herself feel better, a slick of lipstick on her teeth, a stain in the watery satin. She almost wished Elise hadn't told her about Dena's true feelings towards her. She'd really hoped they could have been friends. But she didn't want friends who were nice to her face but ripped her to shreds as soon as her back was turned.

'Excuse me,' butted in Elise. 'I wonder if I could have a private word with you, Sophie. I do apologise, Dena.'

Elise steered a surprised Sophie a few steps away from the group by the elbow.

'I'm guessing you wouldn't mind me rescuing you from that insincere bitch, Sophie. What I told you yesterday about Gerald, please keep it to yourself.'

'Oh of course,' said Sophie. 'You didn't need to say that . . .'

'Sophie, none of us are to be trusted. I blame the fucking menopause for my indiscretion. As I've already told you, knowledge is currency in our world. I'm not such a fool that I'm not aware that your loyalty is more with John than it could ever be with me, so I appreciate your silence more than you can know.'

'You can trust me, Elise. I haven't told John, nor would I.'

Elise's eyelids dropped for a split second as if pulled down by the weight of the sigh of relief whistling past her lips. 'I'm not sure I could have afforded you the same courtesy, Sophie. Gerald would love to have something on John, something to savour and use to bring him down if he needed to. You're naïve if you think otherwise.'

In the background Gerald guffawed and clapped John on the back as if they were the best of buddies.

'Look at them, all pretence,' said Elise. 'All gamesmanship. Everyone enjoys the thrill of cutting down a tall poppy.' She shrugged her shoulders. 'Anyway, I had to say it. I can't stop you using the information but—'

'I won't. I promise,' Sophie interrupted her. 'It's forgotten.'

'Thank you,' said Elise. 'Best get back to the throng.'

'I messaged you. To see if you were okay,' said Sophie.

'I am. I went to see another horse this morning. Onwards and upwards eh? I feel much better.'

They returned to the group. 'We must do lunch, Sophie,' said Dena.

'We must,' returned Sophie.

She looks in a mirror and sees her and not you. Elise's words came back at her. Was that really the reason why Dena Stockdale bitched about her, because it couldn't be anything else, could it? Miss Palmer-Price had once warned a selection of girls, whom she deemed to be the ones who might encounter such a problem, that beauty brought its own particular set of complications. *Pulchritude will make people hate you for no other reason than that they can. Avoid those who envy because they can only destroy, never construct,* she said. *They are to be pitied and despised.*

But Sophie had never seen beauty in her reflection. She could recognise that she had all the requirements in place to look well on photographs: hazel eyes (two of) perfectly symmetrical, thick dark lashes, straight nose with a slight tilt at the end, full lips (also two of), bottom one fuller than the top. High cheekbones, golden hair that streak-lightened naturally as soon as the sun found it. She was above average height, willowy with gentle curves; her legs were long, her skin a shade or two darker than her parental genes dictated. She was a possible throwback to an Italian great-grandparent on her father's side that no one spoke of, because it was an extra-marital scandal. All the other Calladines were pale bordering on pasty, with light-brown hair and a no stand-out shade of blue-grey eyes. Yet all the most attractive people Sophie had seen had more imperfect features, their personalities adding more to their auras than a straight nose ever could. Sophie saw bland when she looked in the mirror.

Her attention was drawn from this reverie seeing John's brother Edward working his way across the room to them, a woman in tow behind him that was not his fiancée Davina. Sophie was linking John's arm at this point and felt a muscle in it spasm slightly as Edward entered their circle.

'Hello, all,' he said, shaking hands, smiling broadly, sparking a round of kisses. The woman stood behind him, wearing a smile that didn't slip. She had a headful of wild fire-red curls and huge brown eyes shown off to their best with expertly applied smoky eyeshadow. Her mouth was a scarlet slash, the same colour as the dress she wore. A look-at-me colour, at odds with the understated style that still managed to accentuate her shapely figure. Just a hint of cleavage showing, delicate silver necklace at her throat, small silver studs in her ears.

That feeling visited Sophie again, the image of herself resting on a quiet web but on her radar, a disturbance, a tweak to her silken threads sending a tingling feeling to her extremities. A line from *Macbeth* floated past her ... *By the pricking of my thumbs, something wicked this way comes.* This woman had dressed very carefully: the most unshowy showy gown possible, her ensemble a perfect balance of modesty and swank. Very clever. A statement. Edward looked understandably pleased to be escorting her, which was no surprise considering Davina acted like a burst cold tap on everyone's mood. Still, she hoped that Edward wasn't doing the dirty on her. She didn't deserve that. No one did.

'Mrs Mayhew, how delightful to meet you at last,' said the woman, smile still held, hand extended.

Sophie's hand stretched forward to meet it, hoping for some sort of introduction, which she presumed Edward would supply.

'Ah, Rebecca, glad you could make it,' said John. 'Sophie, this is Rebecca, the newest member of our staff.' He didn't miss a beat before saying to Rebecca, 'I didn't know you had a ticket.' The statement had a flick at the end, turning it into a question and Sophie picked up the hint of something reproachful.

'Edward's plus one let him down at the last minute so I stepped into the breach.'

'Davina and a woman's thing,' said Edward, pulling a face. 'Didn't ask any questions.'

'Nice to meet you, Rebecca. Beautiful dress.'

'Thank you. I bought it ages ago for another function. Didn't have time to go shopping for a new one,' replied Rebecca, with a click of her tongue.

Oh but that is a new dress, thought Sophie. An expensive new dress bought for this evening, perchance, she recognised it as part of a very current collection. Sophie's interest was piqued by this colourful creature in their midst and the game she was playing.

Sophie had been fascinated by psychology all of her life, the hidden language that bodies gave up. This woman had dressed to impress tonight. But an individual rather than a group, she considered, catching a glimpse of those very glamorous fuck-me shoes. Someone that she hoped to lure back after the evening maybe? The jewellery chosen to give out a message also, subtle and non-competitive. To throw a woman off the scent?

'And how long have you been working for Sophie's husband,' Elise asked her, choosing the possessive phrasing as carefully as Rebecca had chosen her dress, Sophie thought.

'A couple of months or thereabouts,' answered Rebecca. Her smile hadn't dropped yet, it appeared to be super-glued on.

That was longer than John had said. Strange then how he hadn't mentioned her, thought Sophie. She'd known about the male staff he'd employed, but not Rebecca.

'I hope my husband isn't being too much of a demanding monster,' said Sophie, mirroring that smile. She had a flashback to a lesson she'd had at St Bathsheba's which taught them, basically, how to behave when threatened by a rival bitch on heat, although it wasn't exactly called that but *Confrontational Resilience.* Not the case here though because she hadn't worn those shoes for John. Edward maybe, who was much warmer and kinder and possibly vulnerable, considering the amount of pressure the dreadful Davina had put on him to get engaged recently.

'Not at all,' said Rebecca. 'I'm enjoying it. Learning so much from a true master.'

'People are making their way to their seats,' said John, his arm a bar against Sophie's back now, ready to steer her forwards. 'Anyway, have a good evening, Rebecca, Edward.'

'Thank you.' Rebecca appeared to answer for them.

Edward and Rebecca were not seated on their table. They were with similar less important people in the middle of the room; John and Sophie were on the next table to Robbie Williams, whom Gerald called Robin when Elise forced an introduction upon him.

'Is something going on between Edward and your new assistant?' asked Sophie as John pulled out the seat for her.

'I have no idea. I don't get involved in the personal lives of my staff,' he said. 'Though who could blame him, tied to that miserable fish-faced shrew,' he added for her ears only. 'I suppose we will find out on Sunday if he brings her to the party, won't we?'

As Sophie was refreshing her make-up in the ladies' powder room, after coffee and before the entertainment began, she was joined by Dena Stockdale.

'We can't get the chance to chatter across the table,' Dena said to her via the mirror.

'We must set up that lunch,' said Sophie mischievously, in the sure and certain knowledge that it would never happen.

'We must. Lovely evening, isn't it?'

'It's fabulous, yes.'

Dena fished a Chanel compact out of her bag and dabbed the pad into the powder before sweeping it across her cheeks.

'I didn't know John's brother worked for him,' she said eventually, taking out a Chanel lipstick now. She clearly had a favourite brand.

'That's right,' replied Sophie, with a smile she didn't feel like giving out.

'But that wasn't his partner with him as I understand it?'

'No.' Sophie was determined to make Dena work for this conversation.

'Striking-looking girl with that red hair and red dress. Stare at that colour combination for too long and you're bound to get a migraine.' Dena dropped a tinkly laugh, but

Sophie didn't grace it by joining in. She wasn't going to bitch about someone she barely knew, to a bitch she barely knew. In fact, she found herself coming to Rebecca's defence.

'It's brave, but I think she carries it off perfectly. You have to be so careful with bold colours as it's too easy to look ridiculous, don't you think?' There, a little snide comment of her own, which Dena didn't pick up on.

'Personally, I insist on being part of the employment process,' Dena went on. 'Christopher doesn't take anyone on without me vetting them first.'

'Oh, why's that?' asked Sophie. 'Don't you trust him?' *Another barb? My, Sophie, you're on a roll tonight.*

'Lots of ambitious people are drawn to Whitehall hoping to fast-track one way or another, if you know what I mean,' said Dena. Her lipstick was dark wine-coloured and gave her the appearance of a heart problem.

'No, I don't know what you mean,' said Sophie, feigning innocence, forcing her to explain.

'I prefer Christopher to have men working for him. Removes any temptation,' said Dena, with a stressed softness in her voice that smacked of sympathy and annoyed the hell out of Sophie. What was she trying to intimate?

Sophie dropped her lipstick into her bag and closed it with a snappy gesture that indicated her mood perfectly.

'I don't think there is automatically any temptation when you employ female staff, Dena. As John has always said, "Why go out and buy a cheap cut of scrag end when you have a fridge full of fillet steak at home",' said Sophie. It might have sounded up her own backside, but she knew what Dena was trying to imply and she needed shutting down. She took a step away before being halted by Dena's hand on her arm.

'Some men – and I'm not saying John is one of them – have a taste for different cuts of meat, Sophie. Even fillet steak gets very boring after a while.'

She was smiling, a nasty, patronising smile that wrinkled up her nose. *The bigger the crocodile, the bigger the smile* said Elise once.

'I'll bear your wisdom in mind,' said Sophie with a pearly-white smile in return that could easily have blinded that crocodile.

Chapter 6

Four days before Doorstepgate

Two days after the Cherlgrove Ball, Sophie spent the morning decorating their baroque-style dining room with flowers and candles, confetti and bunting, which she had stitched from gold cloth to celebrate John's parents' golden wedding anniversary. The long dining table had been set for both his and her side of the family. Outside caterers had been engaged to cook a five-course dinner for them all. Sophie added a finishing touch to the flowers with a spray of gold paint. John coughed as it hit the air.

'Overkill, Sophie, is that really needed?'

'It's gold, John, so yes, I think so.'

John's eyes strayed upward to the bunting. Sophie had embroidered the number 50 onto many of the triangles. 'And what's with all that stuff? Have you ever heard the expression *less is more*?'

In private she received his approval less and less, and that didn't mean more.

'I think they'll appreciate the effort.'

He made a noise that intimated they wouldn't.

'Not going to spray yourself gilt are you? Like that woman in *Goldfinger*?'

'No, I'm not.'

She went upstairs and changed out of her jeans and came down again to await the arrival of their relatives. She'd made a fifties-style full-skirted dress in eau-de-nil for the occasion.

'You look beautiful, darling,' said John. She knew that he wouldn't be able to tell she had made it herself because it was more tailored to fit her than anything she could ever buy.

The doorbell rang.

'Goodness, they're early,' remarked Sophie. Her in-laws and parents were sticklers for time, neither arriving early nor late. Usually.

John checked his watch. A Rolex, obviously. Even at leisure, he wore the best.

'That'll be the photographer,' he announced.

'Photographer?' Sophie felt the first stirrings of panic. She hadn't figured on the fact that John wouldn't have missed a PR opportunity, even for a private gathering – and both sides of the family would have encouraged such a move. They were all hanging onto John's coat tails because as he rose, so would they.

'I'll go and change,' she said hurriedly.

'No, you look perfect.'

So she posed with John for the photographer by the French windows. The late afternoon sunlight draped them with a deep golden light and he wouldn't need to add a filter in his studio. Single shots of Sophie next. Then the photographer pulled a notepad out of his pocket.

'Who's the designer of the dress, Mrs Mayhew?' he asked.

Sophie's heart kicked a beat.

'I don't know, I can't quite remember.' She should have pulled any old designer's name out of the hat. The magazine might have had a few complaints that they'd got the editorial wrong, but because Sophie Mayhew was caught on the hop, she didn't.

She tried to wave the question away. 'I just bought it.'

'They'll want to know,' said the photographer, pencil tapping on his pad. 'They always want to know.'

'What's the problem?' asked John, walking over from the other side of the room.

'I need the name of the designer of your wife's dress,' said the photographer. 'For the copy.'

'Tell the man, Sophie,' said John with a little laugh, 'What's wrong with you?'

Sophie felt her cheeks begin to heat.

'I don't really want to.' Well that was lame, said a voice inside her.

'Excuse us a moment,' said John, taking Sophie's arm none too gently and steering her out of the door into the hallway. There, he whirled her around so her back was facing him and forced down the collar.

'There's no label,' he said, releasing her roughly enough for her to have to take a step forward to steady herself.

'Look, it's second-hand, vintage,' she lied. 'I saw it and I fell in love with it and—'

'Go and change, Sophie,' said John, his face suffusing with colour. 'Second-hand? Are you stupid? What the fucking hell are you playing at?'

'What's wrong with that? Vintage, upcycling . . . it's all the rage these—'

'Our image is not vintage and up-fucking-cycling, Sophie, in case you haven't grasped,' said John, managing to concentrate a scream into a whisper and it being none the less harsh for the lack of volume. 'Put something else on and do it now. The fucking photographer will have to take all the shots again now, you stupid bitch.'

John's hand made a furious comb through his hair.

'Take off that rag before I rip it off here and now in the hallway,' he said again, grabbing her arm and pushing her forward by it towards the staircase and she winced audibly which infuriated him more, because the photographer would have heard her. She and her idiocy had made him do that and turned him into the bad guy, was his thought process. Sophie knew this because she had been here a couple of times before and he'd told her as much then. He'd never hit her, but sometimes his words hurt as much as if he had.

As Sophie scurried up the stairs, she had a sudden vision of the scene in *Rebecca* where the girl turns up dressed as Caroline de Winter and Maxim barks at her to go and change before the ball. She was angry at herself as she blasted through their bedroom and into her dressing room. What madness had possessed her to wear one of her own creations and then choose a lie that probably made matters worse? She could have avoided that scene if she'd put on something in her wardrobe made by someone else. Didn't it even cross her mind that John would plunder the occasion for a PR opportunity? He had a point, she thought as she slipped out of the dress, screwed it up, never wanted to see it again because it would be forever tainted with the memory of him handling her as he had just done. How ridiculous it would have read: 'Mr Mayhew in Hugo Boss, Mrs Mayhew in a dress she'd made herself.' John would be laughed at. *His wife reduced to making her own clothes.* He was right, she was wrong. She could have argued that Victoria Beckham made her own clothes but John would have argued back that she was not Victoria Beckham. She would never win an argument with him; there was no bend in his soul.

So she pulled out an olive green dress she had worn once before, paused momentarily to study if that would be a good match in photographs for what John was wearing. His suit was a strong dark blue, it was fine. She put it on, then swapped her jewellery and altered her hairstyle because pinned up it looked too severe with this much plainer dress. She slid in two combs above the ears. The reflection that stared back from her mirror was now photo-ready again, but she certainly didn't feel it.

John was talking to the photographer when she walked back into the dining room. Charming him to forget anything he might have heard that jarred with the image of the Mayhews as the perfect loving couple.

'We were about to send out a search party,' he chuckled. 'I know you didn't feel comfortable, so you did the right thing to change. We didn't mind waiting.' He turned back to the photographer. 'Now I recognise this one instantly. Stella isn't it? Stunning.'

'That's right,' said Sophie. 'This one is a Stella McCartney.'

'I'm such a lucky man,' said John F. Mayhew, folding his arms and tilting his head in order to admire his wife. 'Now, let's take those photographs before the others arrive.'

As the last pose was being staged, the doorbell sounded. Extra staff had been employed to serve and a butler had been engaged to answer the door, a needless expense thought Sophie, but she'd had no say in the matter. Someone in

John's office had sorted it all out. Rebecca perhaps? She had looked like the sort of person who might enjoy pomp and ceremony, or at least be fascinated by it.

The clan Calladine had arrived by the sound of the voices. Sophie prepared to greet them like official guests rather than family. It was odd that she'd had a conversation with Magda Oakes at school once about siblings. Magda didn't have any and was asking Sophie to explain the family dynamics when one had them. All Sophie could tell her was that they were people who shared her parents and her home yet she felt no real connection to them. Magda said she found that odd. Didn't they play together? Or help each other when they felt they needed it? No, said Sophie. 'Well that's rubbish then,' Magda had said. 'Yep,' was Sophie's reply. She hadn't thought about it much until then, until she'd analysed it so she could explain it to Magda. That triggered a phase where she became a little obsessed by families and how they interacted with each other. She made notes in a book about it, how Irina's mother and father rang her every Saturday and they spoke for at least an hour, how much she looked forward to hearing from them. How Polly Rice's grandmother sent her letters and cards, how Joanna Falstaff's sister, who lived quite close, would take her out for tea once a week. Fatima Ghazi was terribly homesick and cried a lot because she missed being in the bosom of her family. So much so that she'd eventually had to leave and attend a non-boarding day school – none of these things Sophie experienced. She rejoiced when the end of term came to go home because she missed the family dogs and couldn't wait to see them, but there were no human arms waiting for her to rush into.

Victoria was seven years older than Sophie, Annabella six years older. None of the sisters ever socialised outside family occasions, they were three very separate entities. Annabella arrived first into the dining room, followed by her squat little husband Pearson who was a merchant banker which, in his case, was both his profession and what he was in Cockney rhyming slang. That he would inherit a title one day had been the attraction for Annabella, because his monosyllabic line in conversation and his ability to look down on everyone from a great height, despite being five foot five, most certainly wasn't.

'Oh my, this looks fabulous, you have been busy,' said Annabella, eyes flicking everywhere. Annabella was the queen of one-upmanship; Sophie knew she was hunting for an opportunity to brag, and she always found one. 'You've had the floor re-polished, I see. We've just changed the whole of our downstairs to Spanish cherry. I can't tell you what it cost.' Even though she would within the half-hour.

Victoria followed behind with her parents. Victoria's marionette lines looked particularly deep today, telling of her misery. Her glass wasn't only always half-empty, but it had a crack in it and there was a person with their hand out ready to steal it and then smash it with a hammer. She made Eeyore look like Tigger. 'Have you any ibuprofen in the house?' were her first words. Her husband Giles didn't join in the ritual of air-kissing because he had a thing about germs. He didn't do physical contact. Not surprisingly they didn't have children.

'How are you, Daddy?' asked Sophie, seeing him drop rather heavily onto a chair.

'Mustn't grumble. Now then, John, I see Wax is making rather an idiot of himself with his proposals for the NHS.'

'Oh don't get me started, Angus.'

Sophie should have been used to witnessing how inconsequential she was to her own. It still gave her a skin-twist
of hurt, although she never let it show but today, because of
what she had endured, it pinched extra hard. She'd been a
disappointment to her father by arriving into the world as a
girl and not as the son he coveted – the son he'd eventually
found in John F. – and she knew this because he had written
and told her so in a letter that he had sent to her when she
was fourteen explaining why she would not be coming
home for the summer holidays. Then she had failed to
become head girl at St Bathsheba's, thus spoiling the clean
sheet of her mother and two sisters. She had redeemed herself by being beautiful enough to hook the king fish in the
pond, so she did have some value, but little more than a
maggot in a bait box.

Strangers fawned over her, the press were fascinated by
her, but to her family she was a mere add-on to her husband.
An accoutrement, a golden key to a treasure vault. If the
Calladine and Mayhew families combined were a Christmas
tree, she would be a very small decoration buried deep in
the branches. John, of course, would be the showy star
on the top.

The doorbell again: the Mayhews had arrived now in a
fleet of prestigious cars, Celeste and Clive heading the
almost presidential convoy in their Bentley; the middle son
Robert and his new girlfriend, who wouldn't last very long
because they never did, and Edward and his fiancée Davina
who made the hairs on Sophie's neck rise. They flooded
into the room to be greeted by the Calladines who con-
gratulated Clive and Celeste on being married for fifty
years. Celeste Mayhew was resplendent in a new mink that
Sophie couldn't acknowledge as being as admirable as

everyone else thought it was. John's political stance on fur was very publicly anti, but there he was asking his mother to give him a twirl in her new animal-suffering monstrosity. Sophie wanted to rip it from her back and give it a decent burial.

A waitress in a black dress and white starched apron appeared with a tray full of champagne. Giles took two glasses, both for himself. Giles drank a lot. Being married to Victoria, that was understandable. He obviously had no qualms about germs in champagne.

Sophie stood amongst them, as she had so many times, feeling like the central post in a merry-go-round, watching everything whirl around her without feeling part of them at all. Today, she felt it more than ever. Snippets of conversation drifted to her. Giles: 'Is this the real stuff then, Mayhew, or one of those sparkling wines?' Victoria: 'They can't get my medication right. I put on a stone with the last lot of tablets. That did wonders for my anxiety – not.' Clive Mayhew: 'I didn't expect all this. The bunting is a little overkill though.' Alice Calladine: 'I do hope we get the same treatment next year for our golden wedding celebrations.' Celeste (to the photographer): 'Gucci. And don't forget to mention that it's female mink, they're far superior: lighter, softer and it takes more of them to make a coat so ultimately that makes them more expensive.' Sophie had a sudden vision of herself tearing across the room and jumping through the picture window like a superhero into the garden, galloping over the grass like one of Elise's horses and running away from them all. But to where? Where would Sophie Mayhew go where she wouldn't be recognised? She was more famous than Madonna in Britain. The newspapers already referred to them as the new JFK and Jackie. Ironic considering that the antecedents of both the Kennedy and the Mayhew clans had once been so close.

Edward waved over to Sophie. So Rebecca the redhead had not supplanted the vapid Davina then. Sophie found herself a little disappointed by that. Rebecca looked infinitely more fun and a much better match for a genial personality such as Edward's.

The gong sounded for them to go through to the dining room. Thank goodness there were place names because without them, everyone would have rushed to be seated near John at the top end of the table. Sophie was lumbered with germ-free Giles and Victoria, who didn't eat the lobster starter as she feared her tablets were exacerbating a sensitivity to seafood. Giles talked to Edward at his other side, Victoria chattered to Davina. Sophie thought that if she walked off and disappeared, no one would even notice she had gone.

'Elspeth Bryant is moving house, did I tell you?' Alice Calladine called down to the bottom of the table.

'Who?' asked Giles.

'Neighbours on the left,' Annabella explained. 'The house has been in the family for three generations. Not as large as Elm Manor but still a substantial pile. I thought the Bryants would only move from there if they were carried out in a box.'

'Where are they going to live, Mother?' asked Victoria.

'Phoenix, Arizona. They have an estate there and prefer the weather. Morris was telling me they've used a new estate agent who usually deals with sales of houses for Saudi royalty. Very good by all accounts. Excellent service.'

'Haven't you ever thought about selling up, Angus? Moving to somewhere smaller?' asked Robert, the middle Mayhew brother.

'Whatever for?' said Angus. 'Elm Manor is perfectly manageable.'

'Perfectly manageable when you have three live-in staff, Daddy,' chortled Victoria.

'Edward always wanted to be an estate agent,' said Robert, with a laugh that bordered on the derisive. He was the biggest snob in the Mayhew stable and, considering the competition he had, that was quite an achievement.

'Oh yes, you did, didn't you, Eddie?' said John. 'I'd forgotten about that. Used to sell us Lego houses complete with the deeds.'

'Aren't you a sort of estate agent with your "property portfolio", John?' Edward put to his brother.

'Hardly the same, Edward,' said their father. 'You can't equate a few terraced houses with the sort of property your brother buys and sells.'

Robert snorted at the mere suggestion that John, in Edward's eyes, was a glorified estate agent.

'I'd love to have a job looking around houses. They fascinate me,' said Sophie, sensing the start of a familiar 'Edward-goading' episode and moving to nip it in the bud. She loathed bullies and Robert Mayhew was a bully of the highest order when he was allowed to be.

'Me too, Sophie,' agreed Edward, smiling at her. Out of all of the people around this table, Sophie felt that Edward was by far the kindest. He was the one who had always tried to include her, bring her into conversation. He considered other people. Probably that was why he seemed to be at the bottom of the family pecking order.

Beef Wellington for the main course, the beef served too rare for Sophie to stomach.

'You're not eating much, Sophie,' Edward observed.

'She can't eat, she'd lose her figure,' said Victoria, with a habitual wry twist to her mouth. Victoria had never quite forgiven Sophie for being beautiful so if any opportunity presented itself to stick a pin in her sister's side, she grabbed it.

'I do eat and well,' replied Sophie. 'But I run. You should try it. It'll release some endorphins in your system, then you wouldn't need all those tablets.'

Victoria raised her eyebrows at her youngest sister.

'Thank you, Doctor Mayhew. Running can't cure the storm happening in my brain.'

Maybe not, but it would reduce the size of your enormous bottom, Sophie wanted to say but it would have been unkind, so she didn't.

At the other end of the table, her father and father-in-law were guffawing loudly at something John had said. He was entertaining them royally, but then he was a brilliant raconteur. As prime minister, he would hold everyone in the palm of his hand, she was sure. Even the monarch. He was an amazing orator, he'd have gone down a smash in the Roman senate.

'How's Stanley doing, Annabella?' Victoria asked after her nephew. 'Settled yet?'

'Not really, but he will. Can't soft-soap them at that age.'

Sophie opened her mouth to say something to that but Davina dived into the conversation first.

'What's this?'

'My son's at boarding school,' said Annabella. 'Can't settle. Being a bit of a cry-baby.'

'He'll adjust,' said Robert. 'We did.'

'Precisely,' agreed Davina. 'They need to learn.'

'We've told him no phone calls at weekends until he pulls himself together,' Annabella went on.

'He's seven years old. Of course he's going to cry. He's virtually a baby.' Sophie stabbed at her horrible beef. She'd asked Margaret to make sure it wasn't too rare and if anything it was even more rare than she'd expected. It was almost mooing.

'He isn't a baby at seven, Sophie,' countered Annabella. 'We had to go away to be educated and it didn't do us any harm.'

'We didn't go until we were eight, if you remember,' Sophie threw back. 'And as I recall hearing, you cried so much you hospitalised yourself, nearly choking to death.'

Oh, she really shouldn't have said that, judging from how Annabella coloured and pursed her lips. Annabella did not like to be corrected or reminded of her shortcomings.

'What's happening down at that end of the table?' called John.

'Sophie's just telling us how to live our lives,' said Annabella, with a tinkly laugh to offset any humiliation. Her mother's laughter joined it and Angus Calladine muttered something which Sophie didn't hear but Robert evidently found amusing. Something sarcastic about Sophie, that much was clear, and something that her husband did not jump in to quash. In a moment of astounding clarity, Sophie realised that, with the possible exception of Edward Mayhew, she was in the midst of people who never put the feelings of others before themselves. She wasn't even sure if she liked any of them enough to miss them if she were to get up from her seat, walk out of the door and never return. She loved John, but at the moment she was still smarting from being told to take off her dress and change, as if she were a child. Life ran smoothly when things were going well for him: when they weren't, he could be volcanic. The higher up the political ladder he rose, the more the yes-men gathered and the more used he became to having his own way without exception. It had been drilled into her at St Bathsheba's that in order for a man to fulfil his true potential, it was often necessary for him to be totally self-centred. He would achieve success both for himself and for his own much more expediently if he worshipped at the altar of his ego. It was a quality to be admired, so Miss Palmer-Price had taught her.

Annabella, emboldened by the response to her comment, decided to capitalise on it.

'So if . . . when you become prime minister, John, are you going to ban boarding schools, is the question?' she asked her brother-in-law with a smirk.

'Why on earth would I do that, Bella?' asked John.

'All children should be sent away to school,' said Robert. 'Teaches them discipline and independence.'

'Absolutely,' said Giles. 'As Davina has so rightly put it, they need to learn.'

'Is that what you did at boarding school, Giles. Learn? Is that why you're such an advocate for them?'

The words were out before Sophie could stop them. Despite speaking through an orchardful of plums, Giles had attended a rough comprehensive in the East End of London until he'd received a scholarship for a local grammar school. After completing a degree at Oxford he wrote his family out of his life because they didn't fit in with this new grand(iose) version of himself. They hadn't even been invited to his and Victoria's wedding. Sophie had found that disgusting. She had never liked him, but managed to like him even less for that.

Giles spluttered.

'Go on then, because we'd love to hear what your experience of them is.'

'Sophie?' John's use of her name was delivered with a smile but it was loaded with warning.

Ordinarily, Sophie would have heeded that warning and remained silent now, but something long pushed down inside her was inching upwards like a jack-in-a-box with a rusty, yet determined, spring. He had called her beautiful dress a rag. A flume of anger was building inside her and she didn't know if it was more directed at John for the insult and his manhandling of her, or towards herself for not standing her ground. For *never* standing her ground.

'I'm sure we'd all love to hear Giles's take on sending small children to boarding school. Small children who miss their parents and so naturally cry, even though their parents are glad to be rid of them for the inconvenience that they so obviously are to them,' said Sophie sweetly.

Now it was Annabella's turn to splutter.

'What . . . how . . . what do you mean? Pearson. Say something.' She nudged her husband hard.

'I say, what's going on over there?' called Angus Calladine.

'What would she know?' Victoria to her sister, feeding her a line.

Annabella, smug now: 'You don't have children, Sophie, so how could you possibly know what being a mother means.'

A silence fell on the room like a blanket, like a deluge of water so big that it engulfed a fire without allowing a single swirl of smoke to escape. Sophie felt her sister's words like a knife slicing through her breastbone and finding the centre of her heart. Inside she crumbled like a dynamited building, but outside Sophie barely flinched. Because that was what

St Bathsheba's had taught her to do. The inner was a separate animal to the outer. The two could function independently from one another.

Annabella's triumphant grin bled out and she paled into immediate embarrassment.

'My apologies ... John ... Sfff...' Sophie's name was reduced to a low hiss.

Victoria leapt in with, 'I don't think you started it to be fair, I think—'

'Enough,' said Pearson, his tone hard, slicing off the head of the conversation. Pearson Briggstaffe was near the top of the list of wanting to keep his brother-in-law on side.

'A toast,' said John, reaching for his glass, spinning the topic back onto safe ground with a skill that would impress Len Spinks. 'We are all here to celebrate fifty wonderful, happy, golden years of marriage. All of us around this table with our differing views ...' He made a point of scanning everyone with an accompanying twinkle in his eye, totally diffusing all tension, except from behind the calm, composed façade of his wife, '... are united in wishing my parents our heartfelt congratulations, respect and love. *The most wonderful love is that which submits to the arbitration of time.* Mum, Dad, may all of us follow in your footsteps and be sitting with our loved ones, in time to come, being toasted as we toast you. Happy Anniversary.'

'Happy Anniversary' echoes rippled around the room, together with applause; chatter exploded, enmities were put aside for now. Glasses were filled, plates were taken, dessert and cheese were brought out. At the bottom end of the table, talk veered expertly away from the slightest of contentious issues, but still resentment simmered under the surface of their lightly delivered words like a latent poison. By the time their guests had started leaving, there was a headache drilling into the side of Sophie's skull so fierce she could barely keep her eyes open. She craved restful darkness and quiet.

Sophie and John stood on the doorstep waving off the cars; the doorstep where, in a few days' time, she would be standing, facing the full glare of the press.

'You look worn out, darling,' said John. 'That bitch of a sister of yours had no right to say that to you. She knew she had overstepped the mark and had it not been my parents' day, I would have shot her down.'

Sophie hadn't expected him to say that. She'd thought that as soon as the cars were gone, as soon as the hired hands for the evening had left, he would have torn into her. She was relieved because she felt ill, worn down by the pain in her head, felled inside. Annabella's words had stung like a scorpion. No, she didn't have children but still she knew she would never have let her own go to a cold, faraway boarding school, such as the one young Stanley was attending. What parent gives a child a puppy for his birthday, then a week later, without any warning, dumps him in a school in the highlands of Scotland?

John kissed her head. 'Have an early night,' he said. 'Be rested for tomorrow.'

Sophie didn't resist. She was tired, so incredibly tired. Tired from maintaining a smile that she wanted to drop like a hot rock, tired from dredging up small talk, tired from feeling as if she were living half a life.

She stripped off and laid her head on her cool pillow, knowing that sleep was inches away. Oblivion, she needed that tonight. She'd always wanted a house where family gathered around a table, chattering, passing bread, laughing, loving. That ideal was a solar system away from what she had.

Have an early night. Be rested for tomorrow.

The hospital. The old people. Her last thought before she drifted off was again that she really hadn't expected John to be on her side after everyone had gone.

Chapter 7

Three days before Doorstepgate

Vintage Alexander McQueen if anyone asked: pink dress and jacket. Shoes Valentino, as was her handbag. Sophie loved this outfit and she'd pushed the boat out to be colourful for the old people in the hospital. She had worn it once before, when she opened the new retirement village in Cherlgrove and one of the gentlemen there, who had been a tailor by profession, had told her that she should wear that colour more often because it added a freshness to her skin tone. And she needed to add some freshness to her complexion today because she felt drained. The headache hadn't been blasted away by the two ibuprofen she took before bed and she'd had to get up at dawn for two more and a warm cloth to hold against her temple. John hadn't been disturbed by her moving around. He could sleep through an earthquake, thought Sophie, remembering that he'd done so once in Crete. He had a solid seven hours sleep every night, no nightmares or tossing and turning, but proper, deep rest, no matter what was happening in his life: *the Devil's sleep*, some called that ability to collapse into a restful void as soon as his eyes were closed. He was never groggy in the mornings; he was bright and alert from the moment he became conscious. Sophie often took tablets to sleep and even then, she was accustomed to waking up in the early hours. She'd read once somewhere that *sleep doesn't help if it's your soul that's tired*. Sophie Mayhew always felt tired yet always slept badly and she had no idea why.

'Sophie, help me with this damned tie,' said John. 'I'm all fingers and thumbs today for some reason.'

'Of course.'

The tie needed completely redoing. She felt his eyes on her as she unknotted it. His brown chocolate eyes that could melt hearts if they chose to.

'Windsor or ordinary?'

'Ordinary. Don't want them thinking I'm a posh twit,' he said, grinning. He was so ridiculously handsome. Age had only added to his appeal, accentuating his bone structure; in ten years he'd make George Clooney look like Quasimodo by comparison.

'I love you, you know,' he said, his voice tender, soft.

Sophie's eyes left his tie, found his, went back to the tie.

'I love you too,' she said.

'You're an amazing wife, a beautiful woman. I'm so lucky. I hope you know how much I value you, even if I don't say it as often as I should do because I'm working so intently to secure our future.'

'I know you work hard. Damn.' She'd made the tie uneven, started again.

'The knives are out though. Norman's toppling and his old guard are rushing to his defence. The backbenchers

who've been snoring have suddenly woken up and are rat-
tling their fists at the prospect of change.'

'Nothing you can't handle,' said Sophie.

'Might be some waves in our waters. Dirty tricks brigade.'

'There.' She stood back to admire her handiwork. 'What
sort of waves?'

'You tell me, Sophie. Politics can be evil. But with you
at my side, I think we have all bases covered. I'm under a
lot of pressure, which is why yesterday I blew up at you.'

'I know,' she said. It was his way of apologising without
saying the actual 'sorry' word, which he never did, but she
appreciated the acknowledgement that he'd overstepped
the mark. Every day brought more rats, deserting the sinking ship of Norman, leaping onto John's deck. Norman
had scuppered his own vessel with his obdurate disdain for
the NHS.

John's phone vibrated. He answered it quickly, said just
the one word – 'Okay' – and then switched it off again.

'Car's here.'

Sophie picked up her bag and gave herself a quick check
in the cheval mirror that stood by the door. She looked
perfectly colourful for the old people, a flash of brightness
and glamour to cheer up their day.

There was quite a welcoming committee waiting for them
at the hospital. Lots of press, both local and national TV
vans. Slightly over the top for a casual visit to the geriatric
unit, thought Sophie, but then Len was an expert at
drumming up interest in anything the Mayhews were
involved in.

'Thank you for coming, Mrs Mayhew, because we need
all the publicity we can get,' said the chairman of the

hospital trust, shaking her hand warmly. 'You especially being here will send out a loud message.'

Sophie's returning smile was one of confusion. She opened her mouth to reply but John took her hand, threaded it through his arm, held it firm. And she knew. She knew that she had been tricked into coming here under false pretences. She knew that she was not on a visit to talk with old people and she knew where they were heading instead. How could she not have guessed why this had all been arranged?

She was going to the neonatal unit which was on the verge of closing down. Prickles of anxiety formed in her hands, her scalp. Inside she was screaming *No, no, no,* as her feet walked towards that lift, each step as if she were moving through treacle.

'The neonatal unit should be the jewel in our crown ...' the chairman was saying in the lift but his words were drowned out by swirling memories, awful, traumatic ones she'd done her best to suppress.

'Mrs Mayhew more than anyone knows how important this is,' John was saying, as if from underwater, his voice sounding far away. 'If my wife and I can help ...'

The lift doors opened. Smiling nurses there in their scrubs, newly delivered women in their dressing gowns peering over goldfish-tank boxes with babies inside. Tiny babies hooked up to machines that bleeped, wires and equipment everywhere.

A sister in a dark blue uniform holding out her hand, a woman she recognised. She'd had a lighter blue uniform on when Sophie had been admitted at twenty-three and a half weeks. Four years ago, in the old unit, her own baby had been in one of those incubators.

She was in a blur, listening to them speak but only absorbing snatches of phrases.

Means so much ... your support ... you know how important ... thank you.

Sophie felt her legs weaken, a chair was pushed under her, a glass of water pressed into her hand. John talking to the chief executive. 'We knew it would be emotional.' *A flash of a camera.* She didn't cry. But inside she was weeping floods, and fearing that she would never stop.

Sophie recalibrated, aware that her weakness was on display. She waved away the fuss, completed her duties. She walked along the corridor, eyes locking with a woman at the side of an enclosed incubator: her face was full of pain and worry. The baby inside it was tiny. *A bag of sugar baby,* that's what Henry had been. Sophie turned away from her, carried on, tried to listen to the information from the chairman about investment and figures and value to the community. *I'm sorry, Mrs Mayhew, Henry was too poorly. We tried, we tried everything. We gave him all we could.*

She shook hands with the executives, the nurses, though she couldn't even remember what she said to them, but the look of concern on their faces was seared onto her retinas. So many of them were witness to John's gallantry as he helped her into the car when the visit was over. She didn't answer his 'Are you all right, darling?' She let him hold her hand, was aware that the driver's eyes flashed to her in the rear-view mirror and she would not give him anything to gossip about.

As soon as the door to Park Court had been opened and closed behind them, Sophie let rip, as much as Mrs Mayhew could.

'You crossed a line today, you bastard, John,' she said.

'Sophie, I couldn't tell you,' said John, looking as contrite as John F. Mayhew was able to. 'I wanted to, but this was too important. This was *everything*. This is what you signed up for. This is what we do. Today you have just put me into number ten. Sky was there and the BBC, did you see? You were magnificent, darling. You have just . . .'

She turned from him, walked up the stairs, kicked her shoes off in her dressing room, stripped off her jacket and dress, tights, everything. She unpinned her hair and wiped off her make-up whilst sitting at her dressing table without looking at herself in the mirror because she did not want to stare into her own eyes and see the sadness there. Sophie the Trophy. Never had she been more of a trophy than that day. Never had she been less of a person, more of a shell, scooped out, used, empty.

Chapter 8

Two days before Doorstepgate

Sophie felt exhausted that night, but still sleep cruelly eluded her. At three a.m., she went downstairs to try and reset her body clock. She poured herself a brandy, felt the burn on the back of her throat as she tossed it down in one single smooth movement, but nothing could have burned her more than the sight of those tiny babies each fighting for life.

The alcohol worked its magic and, going back to bed, she fell into a sleep that was solid and surprisingly dreamless. She would have slept for longer had it not been for the commotion downstairs: doorbells, door knockers, doors opening and shutting, men's voices, laughter.

Sophie rose, put on her running gear, brushed her long caramel hair into a jog-friendly ponytail, ventured downstairs, followed the sound into the dining room to find not only John and Findlay, but Len, Edward and even Rupert, all of whom had come up from London. The top half of the dining table was covered in newspapers. Findlay was sitting in front of his MacBook. At the sight of Sophie, all the men stopped conversing, turned to her as if synchronised and smiled. John came bounding over, embraced her.

'Sophie, my darling. You are the brightest star in the universe.' He kissed her head. 'Well done, Sophie,' added Len, in his gravelly voice that always made Sophie want to cough for him.

She was about to ask well done for what, then her eyes drifted downwards onto the newspapers. The headlines: *Sophie's Tears. Sad Sophie. Sophie the Trophy's Sadness.* She picked up the *Mail*, saw the photo of herself, sitting on the chair, hand to her head, John kneeling at her side, the Chairman holding a glass of water for her. She looked punctured.

> *Sophie the Trophy's composure crumbled yesterday when she and her husband visited the beleaguered neonatal unit at Cherlgrove Hospital. Mr and Mrs Mayhew, whose own child was born and died in the unit four years ago . . .*

She put it down and picked up the *Telegraph*:

> *Sophie Mayhew showed her human side yesterday. . .*

The *Guardian*:

> *Sophie Mayhew, wife of popular Tory Minister John F. Mayhew, broke down yesterday at the prospect of the closure of the neonatal unit in Cherlgrove Hospital. The specialist unit, a centre of excellence in care for premature babies, has become a symbol of the split in the Tory party as Prime Minister Norman Wax plans to introduce*

*into Britain an American-style privatised health system
whilst John Mayhew champions the NHS ...*

There was a picture of her face and an insert of a close-up
of her cheek, a single tear sliding down it as if it were every
bit as spectacular an occurrence as a weeping statue of the
Virgin Mary.

'This is it, Sophie. Norman is edging closer to the
moment when he has to fall on his sword.'

'He can't retreat because he will look weak, so his only
option is to push forward and hardly anyone is behind him,'
said the rubbery Len. *So much for the good of the party*, thought
Sophie. Maybe that was true of the lower echelons of it, but
once you reached a certain level, it really was every man
for himself.

'Sky!' exclaimed Findlay, twisting his laptop around. On
the screen was footage of Sophie and John in the hospital.
Sophie, straight-backed and beautiful in the pink suit that
she had put on for the old people.

'You look like Eva Peron,' gasped Len.

She jumped as behind her John popped a bottle of
champagne.

She turned to go.

'Oh, stay, Sophie, celebrate with us,' said Len. 'Get her a
glass, Rupert.'

'No, I'm going for a run,' said Sophie. *I need to run.*

On the screen now, a SAVE OUR NHS demonstration.
Norman walking to his car, an egg hitting him squarely
between the shoulder blades.

'When was this?' asked John, his delight evident.

'It's live,' replied Findlay.

'Anyone got a miracle on them to save Norman?' said

John, leading the guffaws which followed Sophie out of the room as she left them to their quaffing and mutual back-slapping. She went into the kitchen and filled up her water bottle, then she slipped out of the door and started to run, down the garden, through the field at the back and towards the sun. She felt like running until she caught it.

*

That afternoon Clive and Celeste Mayhew graced them with their presence. Sophie walked into the hallway to find Celeste instructing the housekeeper on how to hang up that dreadful mink, on a long padded coathanger and not by the hook sewn into the collar which was merely for decoration, she insisted.

'Isn't it wonderful news,' Celeste greeted her. 'I'm so proud of John. I mean, I'm proud of all my children, but particularly proud of John today.'

'What have I missed?' asked Sophie. Had the POTUS resigned, the country been declared a republic and John taken over the running of an UK/USA alliance? John had such a Midas touch, it wasn't beyond the realms of possibility.

'Well, it's in the bag isn't it?' said Clive, in that impatient way he had as if everything was obvious and questions were superfluous. 'No one has any confidence in Wax any more. The British public need a strong leader with their best interests at heart. Haven't you seen the newspapers today, Sophie?' His tone indicated annoyance that she wasn't fully clued up.

John came out of his office, arms opened like a goose spreading its wings to embrace his mother and shake his father by the hand.

'Master-stroke yesterday,' said Clive. 'Master-stroke. Rescued the Tory party single-handedly.'

John raised his hands to bat back the compliment. 'It wasn't just me, Dad,' he said. 'It was Len's idea. He has to take some credit for this.'

So it was Len's idea to smash her heart to get brownie points. He'd sold her tears to the British public for a handful of headlines. She hated the slimy weasel more than ever.

'Very brave going there, Sophie, very brave,' said her father-in-law.

'I didn't know that's where I was going,' snapped Sophie. 'I thought I was going to the geriatric department.'

Celeste's head swivelled around to her.

'I suppose John didn't want to upset you by fore-warning you.'

Sophie wanted to laugh then. Was this normal? Was this really normal?

'Maybe John should have given me the choice to make up my own mind instead of pressuring me into doing some-thing that upset me,' Sophie parried, using a tone that shocked Celeste, judging by the way her pencilled-on eye-brows shot up her forehead.

'No harm done, was there,' jumped in Clive.

'Not to John, obviously. He's already mentally moved in to number ten and you're practising your Sir Clive and Lady Mayhew signatures, aren't you?' said Sophie, registering Edward and Findlay passing glances to each other. 'Because that is all that matters isn't it?'

'I say, steady . . .' began Clive, adopting his *I mean business* stance of hands behind his back.

Sophie turned from him, left the room, hearing her mother-in-law's huff of outrage that she had spoken so disrespectfully to a senior member of the family. She took the stairs two at a time to their bedroom, not realising that John was at her heels until she tried to slam the door behind her.

'What the fuck is wrong with you, Sophie?' he demanded.

She turned. 'Do you really have to ask that, John? After what you did to me yesterday? Humiliated me in pub—'

'I didn't humiliate you at all. You ... *you*' – he stabbed his finger at her – 'made yourself human in front of the whole country for the first time. You needed to crack, Sophie. People hate you.'

A gasp rose in her throat like a bubble.

'You are too distant, don't you see that? I turned you into Princess Diana yesterday, darling. People are going Sophie-crazy. Now the BBC want to interview you about the impact that the hospital—'

'No,' she said, dashing away that idea with a double-handed gesture. 'No. I will not talk about Henry.'

'I'm not asking you to talk about him. Well, not exactly him *per se,* but our experience of losing a child. To help other women.'

'Not even you believe that bullshit, John. This isn't for other women, this is a PR exercise for you and your career.' She took a step in the direction of her en suite but he grabbed her arm, pulled her back.

'So what if it is? Don't you want to be the prime minister's wife? Don't you want to dine with presidents, be at the next royal wedding? Norman will resign, and you know I'm clear favourite to succeed him. I expected him to go this morning, we all did. The polls on my popularity have gone through the fucking roof, Sophie.'

His grip on her arm relaxed and he caught her hand instead, his voice softening.

'Come down and celebrate with us. This is what we've been waiting for, Sophie.'

'I know,' she said, to appease him because an argument would have been futile; he would not let her spoil this day for him. So she would go downstairs and watch them smiling and congratulating each other on a job well done, but she would not rejoice with him that the tragedy of their son's death had been a contributory factor in bringing him what he wanted most.

That night, when everyone had gone, John and Sophie sat in their soulless drawing room each with a large brandy. Sophie thought the house would never empty. There had been a constant stream of visitors to it all day, none of whom she wanted here. It wasn't a home, it was an extension of John's office and a place that her in-laws considered their property as much as Glebe Hall, the hideous manor house they owned in grounds as large as Cherlgrove public park.

'Can you feel the changes in the air, Sophie?' said John, grinning. It was his fourth celebratory brandy and his words were slurring.

She could. She was still that spider and there was an electricity thrumming through the web, stronger now. This is what she had felt last week, these changes already on their way.

'Let's make love,' said John.

Sophie felt about as keen to make love as she did to empty the sewage tank with her bare hands.

'I'm tired,' she said.

'Come on.' He bounced off the sofa, picked up her hand, pulled her to her feet. John only heard words he wanted to hear. He always had.

Chapter 9

One day before Doorstepdate – morning

Sophie awoke the next morning in an empty bed. Like the previous day, there were sounds coming from downstairs, doors opening and shutting, Groundhog Day for politicians. More good news, no doubt. More back-slapping, hand-shaking and champagne corks popping.

She had been manipulative herself the previous evening, insisting on a shower before bed. A long shower and John was fast asleep by the time she emerged from her bathroom, as she'd hoped. She didn't want to make love with him. She didn't even want to sleep with him. Then again she did, but not like this. She wanted him to tell her he needed her, loved her as a woman; not just as someone who answered all his letters, prompted him on local government issues, who looked good on his arm as Sophie the Trophy. He was so handsome: perfect even – at least in looks. She remembered staring at him so many times over the years as he slept and marvelling how she couldn't keep her hands off him, gently touching his face, hoping he would awaken and reach for her, pull her into a lazy embrace. When had he started banishing her to the sidelines of his life, still wanting her there to cheer him on but not to join him on the pitch? When had she started not minding that he stayed in London for most of the week? When had she started being grateful that he hadn't initiated sex? She couldn't remember. The changes had drip-fed themselves into her marriage over the years, altering the DNA of their relationship. The last time they'd had sex was after his triumph on *Question Time*, when he'd ripped apart the Shadow Education Secretary months ago and he'd come home to the flat in London so full of himself and pumped up with testosterone that it was inevitable intimacy would occur. But she'd felt even then as if that session on TV were the real sexual act and their liaison was the celebratory post-coitus cigarette.

Swearing, she heard swearing. Not laughter. The sounds were different to the ones she'd heard the previous morning, the voices harsher, louder. She padded to the door, opened it up slowly, listened.

'No, do not open those bloody gates.' John's voice echoing in the hallway below. 'Tell him to come around the back.'

Sophie dressed quickly in her running gear. Whatever was happening, she was best out of it, she thought.

They were all there again: Findlay, Edward, Rupert, John darting around like a mad thing. She caught Rupert's eye as she came down the staircase but he dropped contact and scurried off. Len appeared in a drenched raincoat, walking out from the kitchen, the housekeeper trotting behind him ready to take his coat and his umbrella.

'Morning, Len,' Sophie said politely, but tightly, as she passed him.

'Sophie, I wouldn't go out if I were you.'

'I'm used to running in the rain, Len.'

'No it's not ...'

John strode towards her. Something was very wrong because he opened his mouth to speak and not a single word came out. Not one. And John had words for every occasion.

Sophie was conscious of her head tilting to one side, like one of the family Great Danes was accustomed to doing when he was trying to understand what was going on and drawing no conclusion that helped.

'John, what is it?'

'Sophie ...' The words stopped at her name as John's hands came out to rest on the top of her arms, then Edward interrupted them, holding out his mobile phone.

'PM's on the line, John.'

'Shit.' John turned from her, took the phone. 'Norman,' he said breezily, moved into the dining room.

'Edward? What's happening?'

The atmosphere couldn't have been more different from yesterday morning. Not Groundhog Day after all, then.

'Er, I think that maybe ... John needs to ...' Edward pointed behind him at the dining room.

'Edward?' Her tone insistent.

'Wait for John, Sophie.'

Sophie had had enough of this nonsense. This was her house and yet she was the only one who didn't know what was going on in it.

'Edward, I will not—'

She felt a hand on her shoulder from behind her. Len.

'Let's you and I go and have a coffee, Sophie, whilst we wait for John, hmm?' He steered her into the kitchen. At least Len wouldn't be afraid of whatever it was that seemed to be petrifying Edward.

'Sit down, Sophie,' said Len. 'Coffee? Tea?'

Sophie didn't really want either but she said, 'Coffee, please.' There was a percolator full of it in front of him so he wouldn't need to wait for a kettle to boil.

Everything Len did was measured. She watched him take two mugs from the rack, pour coffee, take the milk out of the fridge. He knew this house as well as she did, where everything was.

'I'm presuming Norman hasn't resigned,' she remarked, leaping to the obvious conclusion.

'Sadly not,' said Len. 'He should have but ... something has ... interrupted the process. Something none of us saw coming.'

Sophie's brain spun on the possibilities, jumped from stepping stone to stepping stone. Family illness? Some terrorist attack? Death of the monarch? Every eventuality crossed her mind except one – the one it actually was.

Len's movements were slow, every word he uttered drawn out, buying time.

'Sophie. John has been under an inordinate amount of pressure, as you know.' Len smiled at her as he carried the mugs over, encouraging her to understand.

Sophie sipped the coffee; it had been left too long and was acrid, bitter.

'As you found out yourself, only yesterday, our flaws are what make us human. Many people think that John is super-human; hence his popularity, in the face of the PM's incompetence, but he isn't, he is a man, with human frailties. Remember that word, Sophie, *human*.'

Sophie had no idea what he was talking about.

The kitchen door swung open and in burst John.

'Sophie,' he said, the word imbued with a quality she

didn't recognise. He had never said her name in that way before.

'I'll leave you two alone to talk. Everything will be all right, don't you worry,' Len said, getting up. He paused on his way out to place an avuncular hand once again on Sophie's shoulder. 'Nothing to worry about at all, my dear.' As he passed John, Sophie noticed him give a small shake of his head as if answering a silent question. John threw himself into the chair which Len had just vacated.

'Oh, Sophie.' He reached for her hands across the table, held them tightly. He had narrow hands with slim, long fingers. She'd always thought he had hands that might have belonged to a concert pianist.

'Is someone going to tell me what's going on?' said Sophie. 'It's like being caught up in a giant puzzle.' She laughed, a sound of confusion, not humour.

John kissed the back of her hand, a reverent gesture. His eyes were closed as his lips touched her skin. He sighed.

'Sophie, there's no other way of saying this . . . I've made a mistake, a big one. A really, really stupid fucking big one.'

'What sort of . . .' Three words into the question and she self-answered it. There was only one sort of stupid mistake that would warrant this whirligig of activity. Sophie tried to pull her hand back, but John held firm.

'Sophie, darling . . .'

Sophie stood, tore her hand away successfully this time. She needed to move, spend this sudden injection of nervous energy. Even if it was to pace up and down her kitchen.

'Who is she?'

'No one . . . I . . .'

'Obviously she's someone, John, unless you've screwed a ghost.'

John exhaled a long, laboured breath of resignation.

'I'm going to tell you everything, Sophie. I shan't leave a detail out, okay?'

Sophie's hands and feet were tingling, as if her body were filled with nails. Dena Stockdale's smirking face drifted past the front of her mind, '*Some men – and I'm not saying John is one of them – have a taste for different cuts of meat, Sophie.*'

'Who knows about this?' she asked.

'Well ... us ... for now. The story will break in the papers tomorrow. We're trying to contain it. Norman knows ...'

'Who is she?' Sophie demanded the name.

John pinched the top of his nose. 'Rebecca. Rebecca Robinson.'

The Girl Friday with the red dress and the red hair and the red lips at the Cherlgrove Ball. She had been the fly hovering near Sophie's web, making her presence felt, touching her spider thread, whispering, '*I'm here.*' It had been John she had worn those fuck-me shoes for, the scarlet to flaunt at him, the subtle jewellery to throw *her* – the wife – off the scent; how could she not have seen what was in front of her face? She was stupid *stupid stupid*.

Sophie stumbled back to the chair before her legs gave way. Pictures worthy of a porn film bombarded her brain from all directions: that red hair splayed on a pillow, John kissing Rebecca's body, the pair of them slithering around on black satin sheets like oiled eels feasting on each other. Sadness swamped her, she felt sick, barely able to breathe.

'Oh, my darling, Sophie ...' John was kneeling at her side now as if about to propose. Tears felt closer than ever before but not close enough to show because they were always diverted; like an underground river they plunged down further, seeking a cave to hide in, rather than out towards the surface.

'How long has it been going on for?'

'A few weeks, if that. It only happened a couple of times. In hotels.'

Every clichéd phrase in the book followed. *It was a mistake. I was flattered by her attention. It meant nothing. It had ended before it begun.*

Sophie heard the doorbell ring, more people arriving. The familiar tones of her in-laws reached her.

'The bitch has timed this to cause total devastation because I rejected her. Because I told her it was over. Because I love my wife. Sophie, I am begging you for help. Throw everything you have at me.' He picked up her hand, slapped his face with it. 'Hit me, do anything you can to make yourself feel better but stand by me here. We can make this go away. Norman doesn't want me to resign.' John laughed. 'Oh, the irony of it all.'

Sophie was flung into panic. The whole fabric of her life was about to be ripped to shreds by a woman she had met only once; everything she knew, everything she had, everything she'd been made and trained for was at stake. There was chaos inside her, confusion, hurt, humiliation, disgust, fear, all vying for supremacy. She felt as if she'd been cast into unknown waters that threatened to drown her. Her defences short-circuited to the best course of action: she wouldn't flounder; she would get back on board and steer this ship. *Keep the ship level. Hold the wheel steady, Sophie.*

Sophie felt all her rage being wrested from John, repacked into a laser-like beam ready to launch in the direction of that red-haired tart.

'What do we need to do?' she asked, feeling his arms close around her in relief and gratitude.

Chapter 10

Eighteen years ago

Miss Palmer-Price's words struck home after the tête-à-tête in her office. Sophie did want to make her parents proud of her, she didn't want to let the family down. She'd never felt as saintly as her two sisters who had never once received a reprimand at St Bathsheba's and gained more house points than a Gryffindor full of Harry Potters. Like a pair of weak, watery ghosts they had glided through school, handing in their homework punctually, never contributing to any acceleration of the greying-hair process of their housemistresses. They were the ones who earned extra house points for reporting girls for smoking behind the sports pavilion, snitching on the ones who paid others to do their homework. But they'd had to slog far harder than Sophie to achieve their grades of success because she was much more naturally bright; something else that engendered their resentment. They hadn't been blessed with Sophie's lithe frame, her clear skin, her flawless features either. Annabella resembled their mother with her naturally pallid skin, shapeless form and hair that refused to grow past her shoulders, not ideal for a girl with secret Rapunzel ambitions. Victoria was the female double of their father with his long face and large features. She'd had her nose surgically altered but now it looked oddly too small sitting in the middle of her face like a lost island. She had mannish hands and thick shapeless legs that she always kept covered. To have such a perfect-looking sister to hold herself up against for comparison had made Victoria especially bitter, enough to cause frown lines that an Olympian could have bobsleighed down.

For the following five weeks Sophie blocked out Irina's presence from her life as much as was humanly possible. She sat as far away from her as she could at mealtimes, ignoring any little aside comments intended to inflame. She mastered the art of overcoming her desire to shut Irina's foul mouth by blocking it with her fist. It was surprisingly easy with a concerted effort. Even when she happened upon Irina and her cronies throwing stones at Magda Oakes as she swam in the outdoor pool and poking her with a stack of garden canes, Sophie remained indifferent. Fat Fiona Coates-Duff was blocking the steps so Magda couldn't get out and she was panting and gulping and bleeding from a cut to her head and calling between gasps of breath for help. Sophie remembered what Miss Palmer-Price had told her about it being a dog-eat-dog world, because the words had branded themselves onto her brain and she understood them a little more after much cogitation. Magda would just have to get out of this one herself and learn a life lesson, so she thought as she put her head down and continued on her way.

Chapter 11

One day before Doorstepgate – afternoon

Despite even Len's best machinations, the story could not be halted. Rebecca Robinson's exposé was due to hit the front pages in the morning and it was dynamite. Even though John F. Mayhew's position as chief promoter of family values meant that he would be mercilessly lambasted, Len wasn't unduly worried; he was firmly in his comfort zone. *Human* was the word he had zoomed in on. Whatever life threw at 'the family', it could be weathered. John F. Mayhew was a good man, he cared about his constituents, who should in no way be affected by a regrettable mistake in his personal life. His values were solid; he put others before himself always, but personal tragedy had taken its toll. This gross error of judgement stemmed from unresolved grief. *Forgive him*, would be Len's pitch. He was at this very moment ensconced in the Mayhews' dining room writing a speech that would be worthy of Julius Caesar.

John had found out that the PM had been having a dalliance himself with his long-standing secretary. The affair had been a closely guarded secret for years – and not a sniff of scandal had reached anyone's attention until very recently. One tiny indiscretion on the lady's part had put John on her trail. He had been planning to leak it to the press and knife Norman squarely in the back once he could present irrefutable evidence. *Ironically,* because he still thought his secret was safe, Norman did not want to set a precedent of anyone in his government abandoning a post because of an extra-marital indiscretion and that was why he was coming out in full defence of John. He had no idea of John's scheming, still thought he was the golden boy – despite their obvious disagreement over the NHS. The price of getting John out of the mire by lending him his support would be John's absolute loyalty going forward. The PM had him bound up in knots and he had no alternative but to be a good boy and wait a little longer for the top job. It would come, eventually, but he could cancel the champagne order for now.

Sophie's own parents arrived after lunch cross about the trouble they'd had to get in through the gates. The word had spread that something big was about to break around the Mayhews and a few journalists with long lenses and flasks of coffee had arrived to camp out. Edward had arranged for a locally based security firm to be in charge of letting people in at both the front and the back of the house, and already there had been a kerfuffle as one journalist had been forcibly thrown back over the hedge under which he had crawled and the police had been called. Things would get uglier, they all knew.

Sophie's mother's head started shaking as soon as she had taken her coat off.

'What a terrible situation,' she said. 'Are you bearing up?'

Sophie wanted her mother to open up her arms, but they didn't do things like that in the Calladine family.

'Yes, I . . .'

Her mother strode past her and towards John. She'd been addressing him.

'Can this be rescued? There's an army of press outside. An army. John, whatever possessed you to be so stupid?'

Not cruel, not thoughtless, but stupid. Not for the first time this week did Sophie wonder if she was cut from a different cloth to these people who were supposed to be her family.

'Come through,' said John, leading his mother-in-law into the dining room, or the new Office HQ as it was fast becoming, leaving Sophie and her father alone in the hallway.

Sophie's father gave her a small smile.

'Men make mistakes, Sophie,' he said. 'That's what you have to remember.'

Sophie didn't know what she'd hoped for here but it wasn't that everyone thought that John was a casualty of his own balls.

'He's broken my heart, Daddy,' said Sophie, the disclosure surprising her. She couldn't help it, she needed to feel someone holding her and she crashed forwards into her father's chest, but he didn't embrace her. Awkwardly, his hand came out, gave her a pat on the back.

'There's too much to throw away for a bit of silliness,' said Angus Calladine. 'You must be strong now, Sophie. Strong and sensible and loyal.'

Sophie stepped back, burned by his coldness.

'Loyal?' she echoed. She was being asked to be loyal? Was this national irony day?

'Teamwork,' went on Angus. 'A lot at stake, Sophie.'

Miss Palmer-Price's words came thundering to the front of her brain as if riding on one of Elise's Arabian stallions.

One day you will most likely have to call upon what you have learned here. The training to remain faithful to someone who has kicked you in the heart, the training to 'do the right thing' when it feels like the wrong thing. The training not to throw everything away when you temporarily refuse to see the bigger picture because emotion is blinding you.

This was that time.

'Come on,' said her father, stepping towards the dining room, encouraging her to join him. 'United front. Remember your marriage vows: *for better, for worse.*'

Yet there was no mention of *'forsaking all others for as long as ye both shall live'*.

Sophie and John made love that night. Or rather had sex because it was wild and animal-like, clinging, possessive. Desperate. Sex that had something to prove, and in Sophie's case that was that John was hers. They had never made love that way before; it was almost animalistic, primal. He said that he loved her and that he had realised what he had done and could have lost and how much he valued her, but she knew deep down in her heart that this was a façade. He wanted her to feel desired because he needed her onside. She knew this but still she clung to him and she faked a climax for him because she felt numb and dead inside and couldn't have managed a real one. Not once that day had he said the two words that she wanted to hear from him more than any others; words which had never been part of his vocabulary: 'I'm sorry.'

Maybe they would have made all the difference.

Chapter 12

Doorstepgate, 5 a.m.

Sophie was awake at a ridiculous hour, yet again. She show-
ered and wished she could have taken a run but peeping
through the curtains informed her that would be an absolute
impossibility. Reporters were banked against the gates and
beyond them, vans from various radio and TV companies
lined the road. John had told her not to look on the internet
because the internet lied. Rebecca Robinson was ambitious
and vengeful and though the indiscretion (not an 'affair',
which implies some level of affection rather than just
straightforward lust, he said) had happened, Robinson
would have embellished and woven an elaborate tapestry
around the bare bones of what could only be described as
inconsequential at best. The detail would torture her, he
forewarned and he did not want to see her hurt. Sometimes
there was an awful lot of smoke from a little fire, he said – a
line right out of the book of Len. Think how much money
Robinson was going to make from this, plus the fame. What
decent woman wanted that sort of attention? Think, Sophie,

think – one with no shame, one with hate in her heart because she had been rejected, because she had been dismissed as a mistake. Her ego would be trying to redress the balance by portraying herself as wronged and used. Incredible, considering that it is *I, John F. Mayhew who has been exploited, manipulated, targeted.*

But still Sophie looked.

She crept downstairs into her sitting room and fired up her laptop. The news headlines were suitably tacky: *Mayday for Mayhew. From Hero to Zero. Government Minister not Keeping it in the Family. John F... ive Times a Night.* There were clear pictures of John and Rebecca standing facing each other in public and smiling at one another, or sitting on a park bench sharing a picnic lunch. Len could throw these into the camp of innocence, but not the others which showed the pair of them kissing passionately in a shop doorway. Grainy, but unmistakably John and *her.*

Every newspaper seemed to be carrying the story on the front page but it was the downmarket *News of the Day* that had obviously written the biggest cheque, because they had the full exclusive. Sophie pressed on their link and a long teaser opened.

> *Seven hours after I got the job last October, I was bedding the boss. John couldn't keep his hands off me. That first night we made love five times which became our record to beat and we've done so over and over again.*

She slammed the laptop shut and then opened it up again as quickly. She didn't want to read these salacious details, but it was as though she felt compelled to. Then she read something that made her heart stop.

We made love so fervently that the condom split once. John F. was furious when I revealed I was pregnant six weeks later. He told me that he didn't even want children with his wife, never mind his mistress. He said that Sophie wanted to adopt a child but he could never have accepted a baby fathered by another man. I even offered to have our child and let her bring it up as he said she was desperate to be a mother and had almost lost it totally after their son had died, but he didn't think she would make a very good one. She was "emotionally frigid", he said. She thought more about her sewing machine than she did him. He loved that I was uninhibited, affectionate and sensual. Sophie was an ice-maiden, someone whom he felt was ideal for career reasons but he needed love and affection and he was not getting that in his marriage. To read more, buy the News of the Day today.

Read all about 'sewing-loving Sophie' the boring, frozen-solid woman with the ineffectual womb who would have been a crap mother, so maybe it was a blessing that she couldn't have kids: those were the words between the lines.

She knew he had said this about her and she felt as if something had reached into her chest and punched her. John had rubbished his wife and his marriage to make Rebecca feel as if she were the only one who could nourish him. And they had talked about Henry together. How dare they even imply she wouldn't have loved her son. Her heart would never heal from the pain of losing him. Never.

She heard stirrings within the house. Len was in one of the bedrooms; he had stayed over. He had been working with Sophie until past ten o'clock the previous night, because she was pivotal to the success of what was going to happen today. The public were going to be looking at her more than they were John and would take their lead from her, he had told her.

Rebecca Robinson would be on Breakfast TV giving an interview soon and at eleven o'clock John F. Mayhew would be standing on the doorstep with his wife, parents and in-laws. John's speech would be short and sweet because Len needed to see what would be appearing in the newspapers over the coming days so he could build the most effective counter-offensive. John would merely say that he would give a more detailed statement in time, but that he had always been stronger for other people than he had for him-self, wanting to be more than human, when in fact that's all he was – just a man – and now he needed some space to tend to his *core priorities*. Len's speech was masterly crafted to mirror the 'back to basics' philosophy: start with the hub of the family and work outwards. In time he would make John sound like a saint and Rebecca like a deranged harpy but for now, less was more.

The speech he had written for Sophie was equally skilful. Quiet and dignified, she would say that she understood that John had been working under enormous pressure and that, as a wife, she had maybe not been there for him as much as she should have been. Grief had cast a long shadow over their lives and this incident had made her realise how much distance had grown between herself and John, resulting in an emotional wilderness in which they were both wan-dering lost.

In short, Len was blaming her. John F. had to be kept as clean and blameless as possible and so it would be Sophie's job to bear the tarnish; after all, this week the public had witnessed first-hand how damaged she was. A great sweep of sympathy from them for her would help to push this matter neatly under the carpet.

At nine o'clock Sophie, her mother and mother-in-law sat in the kitchen taking tea, away from the others watching the Rebecca Robinson interview in the drawing room. They made no mention of the woman but she was there with them all the same: the red-haired, red-lipsticked elephant in the room with the red dress and the fuck-me shoes. Sophie was expected to forgive and forget, get up and get on; John was her husband after all. Her mother's favourite word was 'rally'. No point in dissolving into a pool of self-pity when strength was what was needed. *Time to rally, Sophie.* Sophie hated that word.

'Un-fucking-believable,' declared John, when the men filed into the kitchen after the interview. 'Lie after lie after lie. How can someone spin a whole relationship out of a couple of encounters. I was set up. How else can anyone explain a photographer being in exactly the right place at the right time to capture key shots. He was employed by that bitch.'

'We can pour water on nearly all of her flames,' said Len.

'I'll go and change,' said Sophie, getting up from the table.

'Remember – wear something mid-blue,' said Len. 'Keep your hair down, it makes you look softer and more approachable.' *Because she said you were frigid*, Sophie added to herself.

She had the perfect dress, summer blue, with a matching shrug. Party loyalty colour. One that 'sewing-loving' Sophie had made. She wondered if John would force her back upstairs this morning to *take that rag off* if she wore it. It was a beautiful dress and she had no idea why she had made it. Maybe she knew on some psychic level that she might need it one day to help save her husband's political life; but she couldn't risk it. She chose another, a plain unspectacular dress that would be ideal for a coffee morning and wondered, as she zipped it up, if her husband and his lover had laughed about her 'little hobby' as they lay in bed wrapped in sex-soaked sheets. Did they call her Julie Andrews behind her back?

She picked gold earrings rather than silver – gold for a winner, not a runner-up. A gold necklace with a small cross suggesting piety and purity; she knew psychology. Low heels in a neutral fawn; her bracelet which had been featured in several magazines and newspapers, full of charms that she had collected all her life representing things that were important to her: a small Notre Dame for the time she lived in France, a number one for her first at university, wedding bells for her marriage, a small sewing machine for the rags she stitched. A teddy bear for when she had found out she was pregnant with Henry . . .

She applied a pearly pink eyeshadow, blusher to her colourless cheeks, mid-pink to her full lips, her favourite shade. She brushed her hair, nudged the waves into position, sprayed it. She studied herself in the mirror: Sophie the Trophy, who was so blank and impassive that she had made her husband go elsewhere for the affection he craved. The unfeeling wife.

She was ready.

Chapter 13

Doorstepgate, 10.45 a.m.

Len Spinks took a quick call before returning to the knot of men to share something with them. Whatever it was, it made them all smile. Len 'the Spink doctor', a PR toolbox essential, whitewasher-extraordinaire, whatever you wanted to call him, could make the Pope look like Al Capone and the Great Train Robbers look like the Osmonds. John was patting him on the back now, Rupert shaking his hand in an 'I don't believe it' delighted kind of way.

Through the window, Sophie could see the TV vans, people milling with cameras perched on their shoulders, iPads and long, furry 'dead-cat' microphones. They were held back behind the grand iron gates for now, but soon they would open and those people would pour forward like extras from a zombie film and though the lens would be trained on John, the real attention would be on her – *Sophie the Trophy.* Women especially. Millions of them, raking over her every word, studying her for clues. Body experts would be taking notes, her clothes would be dissected: *Why has she chosen this outfit, what does it reveal about her feelings?* Every involuntary facial tic would be analysed; they would zoom in to see how far her pupils were dilating, even if there was any tell-tale change in the colour of her ears. She would be adjudged either a frozen bitch or a weak and fragile shell – nothing in between, because where was the fun in that? If the latter, Britain would be waiting for her to crack and reveal what was really going on behind her large hazel eyes. What did Sophie the Trophy really think about her husband John F. Mayhew's dalliance with his twenty-four-year-old Girl Friday, Saturday, Sunday and every other day of the week? They were all desperate to see if there was a real woman with real feelings behind the Stepford Wife mask that she presented to the world.

Sophie's eyes panned across everyone in this room, people she knew so well but then again hardly at all. Not even her husband. Not even her parents, who were here to show how much they supported their famous in-law, the brilliant, charismatic son they never had. They were here to prove that the Mayhews and the Calladines were united as one family unit, bonded. Bonded by what? Not love, of course, because that came much further down on the list than duty, unless it was part of a phrase: *love of* prestige, *love of* power, *love of* money. Oh my, they were all bound by affection for those things.

Sophie had never liked Park Court. Despite living in it since the week before her marriage, it had never once felt like home. It had been thrust on her, a wedding present from her in-laws. It was cavernous and full of ornaments and furniture that the interior designer had procured for them, décor that looked stunning in the high-end thick-paged magazines, but was without character and bland.

North-facing, wind seemed to rush at it, unheatable. It was a showy pile but the market price had been cheap, thanks to the list of work it needed in order to make it habitable. Her own parents had paid for a substantial amount of it as their wedding present. Other couples got toasters and sheets; Sophie and John were gifted a total rewire and new plumbing throughout. Sophie had tried to make it her own, but the house seemed to resist her at every turn. She'd hoped she and John would choose the furnishings together like other young couples but John had employed a designer of his choice. He wanted Park Court to surpass its original Edwardian splendour. He shunned carpets for cold marble and polished oak, cool colours. He wanted grand, he wanted expensive, he wanted statement furniture; he overrode her choices at every turn. Part of his political success came from his inability to compromise when he felt that his course was the right one, she understood that. It had always been the case that she bent to his will rather than he bent to hers.

She had insisted on getting her own way as far as the ladies' sitting room was concerned, which would be her own personal space. Even then, the designer had arrogantly defied her preference for pale duck-egg-blue walls and had them painted a regency *terra di sienna* whilst they were on honeymoon. She'd been absolutely furious to find that out when they returned. One of the first things she had done as a married woman was buy herself some undercoat and bury that awful colour once and for all.

Her sitting room was the only place in the house where she felt remotely at home. It had its own fireplace and, despite the generous size of the room, a small fire in the grate warmed it up in a way that the ineffectual central heating couldn't. It was not over-stashed with furniture, just a serpentine writing desk in the corner and, by the massive east-facing bay window, a long table which Sophie had found in an antiques shop, stripped down and polished, where her sewing machine had a permanent place. An old display cabinet from a gentleman's outfitters that she had bid for and won in an auction housed all her sewing equipment and bolts of material and there was a chaise-longue sofa in the corner where she sometimes sat and read books. This room was her happy place. She spent a lot of time in here whilst John was in London, and he was there most weeks Monday to Friday.

The plan had always been that Sophie would be part of Team Mayhew. Sophie had been on board with that, expecting she would have an integral role in building up his parliamentary profile, even helping to run his investment company; then, when the babies came along, she would be a total hands-on mother. Except that John had no intention of encouraging her to go out to work or of considering her input, further than doing some of his constituency home-work and answering a few letters. Then, when the babies didn't come along, Sophie realised that her function was primarily to be a mere ornamental wife. She had carte blanche to go and lunch with ladies, spoil herself in spas, shop for designer clothes. What woman wouldn't want that, said John.

But Sophie didn't want the life that women like Elise lived, hopping from café to restaurant, nail to hair appoint-ment. She needed a role and she'd hoped it would be as a proper support for John. She had known nothing about politics at first, but she learned it all, from three-line whips to white papers. She studied Cherlgrove itself, its people and its problems so she could accompany John to his surgeries clued up to the eyeballs – because Cherlgrove did not really interest him that much; London was where all the excitement lay. She wanted to show John that she could be both ornament and use, and she did so, but not enough for him to put her on the payroll and give her a desk next to Findlay's. It wouldn't work, he said. *Enjoy, do some gardening, Pilates, embroidery.*

John's principles centred on the home and the importance of it as the most stable piece on life's chessboard. Some thought his views were dated, some thought that his policies were dystopian rather than utopian, but acclaim for the stand he took far outweighed any criticism. The breakdown of society could be reversed, he insisted, and it started with what went on in the home. John F. Mayhew was making people think. His country was like an out-of-control dog, he said, and someone was needed to bring it to heel. Someone charismatic and strong who wasn't afraid to beat that dog into submission, for its own good and future happiness. (Someone who would end up making *The Handmaid's Tale* a reality, said his outspoken female counterpart in the Labour Party, Lena Sowerby.) Back to Basics as it should have been done the first time, in the 1990s, without all the sleazy political scandals staining the ideology.

Oh, the irony.

Chapter 14

Doorstepgate, 11.02 a.m.

'Ready?' said Len, turning from the men, addressing the family elders first before sweeping his eyes over to Sophie, the afterthought.

'As we will ever be,' sighed Alice Calladine, putting down the cup and the saucer on the drum table at her side. She stood and took her husband Angus's arm. Rupert walked forward to open the drawing room door out into the hallway, John took a step and Sophie noticed how he turned then, realising that something was missing, something essential. Her.

He looked across at her and smiled. Once that smile had melted her heart as it had been designed and refined to. It still did, a little. A complete full ghost-heart that lingered in the space where her real shattered heart sat, pumping dutifully, sending a pulse of pain through her with its every beat.

'Sophie, are you ready?' John asked, which alerted the others to her presence. *Ah yes, we need Sophie, don't we. How silly of us to forget.* The least important person in the room and yet paradoxically the most crucial, because she held John F. Mayhew's balls in her perfectly manicured hand.

John crooked his arm and she had a sudden flashback to their wedding, when they first walked down the aisle together as man and wife after their vows to love each other for richer or poorer (it was always going to be richer with their pedigrees), for better for worse (he'd had it significantly better), forsaking all others for as long as we both shall live (the least said about that the better).

She threaded her arm through his.

'So, Sophie, you're totally clear about everything, hmm?' cut in Len, in that annoying condescending tone he had, with the patronising *hmm* that an adult might use to a small child, '*You are going to be well-behaved, Sophie, aren't you, hmm? You aren't going to make a fuss and show us all up, hmm?*'

'I'm quite clear,' replied Sophie, hearing a faint playing of Tammy Wynette singing 'Stand by Your Man' in her mind.

They moved, as a battle-ready phalanx, out of the front door of Park Court, synchronised and solid in support.

Ahead of them the electric gates opened, interminably slowly. The press, drip-wet through after waiting in the rain for a good half-hour longer than they'd expected to, surged forwards, questions tumbling greedily from their lips.

'Minister, can you . . .'

'Mr Mayhew, what do you have to say about . . .'

'Mrs Mayhew, what do you make of Rebecca Robinson's suggestion that she was giving your husband something he wasn't getting at home?'

Behind Sophie her mother made an 'ugh' noise. 'Tabloid,' she said. 'Lowest of the low.'

John began. 'Thank you all for coming here today and allowing us, as a family, to give our statement . . .'

'Quiet,' Len hushed the baying crowd.

John stuck to the brief, adding a little postscript of his own in which he managed not to say that Hell hath no fury like a woman scorned whilst also implying it heavily. Genius. '. . . And that is all I have to say.' A smile: self-assured and self-congratulatory.

Attention streamed to Sophie.

'Mrs Mayhew . . .'

'Over here, Sophie . . .'

'Sophie, are you standing by your man?'

Sophie. Sophie. Sophie.

Sophie geared up to admit her part in all this. But there was a familiar uncomfortable weight sitting inside her. That sense of wrongness catapulted her back to that day standing by the swimming pool when Magda Oakes was splashing exhausted and she, Sophie Calladine, had walked past. *It was wrong, wrong, wrong . . .*

'Answer them, darling . . .' John prompted, whispering now, 'remember what Len told you.'

But she couldn't remember a word of what Len Spinks had told her, not a word. She opened her mouth to speak and felt air rush from her lungs, past her vocal cords, vibrating them like a stringed instrument, but she hadn't a clue what she was about to say until she said it.

Chapter 15

Eighteen years before

Her own voice was screaming at her in her head. *'This is wrong, wrong, wrong, Sophie. Do something.'* And she had tried to supplant it with Miss Palmer-Price's dog-eat-dog world analogy and being cruel to be kind but it wasn't working. She had made it as far as the sports pavilion, her heart feeling heavier in her chest with every step she took, the image of Magda's frightened, gulping face growing more and more lurid in detail like a fast-developing Polaroid photo. She was going to get in real trouble for this, she knew, but she turned on her heel and sprinted as speedily as she could back to the pool, her adrenaline levels spiking so high that she couldn't have stopped herself if she tried.

She barrelled straight into Irina and the pair of them thudded into the water. Irina spluttered and struggled as Sophie grabbed tightly on to her hair and pushed her head down under the surface.

'Fiona, get your fat backside off those steps or I swear I will drown her.'

She raised Irina's gasping head. Fiona, who was too stunned to move initially, began to scramble madly up the steps when Irina's head went under the water again. Irina was a poor swimmer and started coughing up swallowed water in panic.

'Magda, get out of here,' commanded Sophie. 'Any of you lay a finger on her and I will kill this bitch, trust me.'

Irina's cronies – Beatrice Fallowes and Lady Selina Montford – edged back from the sides of the pool to give Magda space. Just for good measure, Sophie ducked Irina again, which set Fiona off screaming. Sophie felt surprisingly powerful for a few seconds and experienced the sadistic rush that Irina must enjoy. Intoxicating.

'There, she's all yours,' Sophie said, when Magda was clear of them, stumbling away.

Sophie let go of Irina's hair and swam effortlessly to the steps. Fiona and the others leaned over the side to try and reach their leader and help her out. Irina was sobbing pathetically. When she was safely on terra firma, she screeched at Sophie, who was now trying to catch up with Magda.

'You'll be sorry for this, you cow, you total bitch, you . . .'

She hadn't bargained on Sophie still having plenty of that temper left inside her, which she was only too happy to dispense. Sophie whirled around, came at her again, knocking both Irina and Fat Fiona into the pool. Fiona grabbed at Selina to stop herself falling and ended up pulling her in too. Beatrice, who stood petrified at the side of the pool not knowing what to do for the best, was too easy a target for Sophie not to push in as well. After all, she didn't want her to feel left out.

'Any time you are ready for more, bitches, come and find me. I'll take the lot of you on single-handedly. Again.' And, because they all believed that Sophie could do exactly that, they never did come and find her for more.

Sophie caught up with Magda in the changing rooms. She was shivering and upset and jumped when Sophie entered.

'You okay?' she asked, sitting down beside her.

Magda nodded. But she wasn't. Her throat was sore from coughing and there were cuts on her shoulders and her head where the canes had stabbed her.

'I'm sorry I walked past at first. I hate myself,' said Sophie.

'You came back, though,' said Magda. 'Thank you.' Her hands were shaking so much, she couldn't unfasten her bag to get out her towel.

'You look frozen, Magda.'

'My skin looks like corned beef, doesn't it?' Magda remarked, but Sophie had no idea what corned beef was so couldn't comment.

'I'll run a shower for you, a warm one,' said Sophie. 'I won't leave you. I'll keep watch. They won't dare come in here, trust me.'

She waited for Magda to emerge from the shower, adrenaline still pumping around in her system ready for another showdown if necessary, and felt quite disappointed that Irina denied her the opportunity.

'You've got a bit more colour to you now,' said Sophie when Magda had dressed. 'I've got some antiseptic cream for those cuts in my bedroom. Why don't you come back with me now? I've got a very large bar of chocolate in my cupboard and I'll share it with you. Chocolate is very good for cuts.'

'Is it?' said Magda, then realised it was a joke. She smiled. 'I'd like that, thank you.'

'It's shit sharing a dorm in the first year isn't it?' said Sophie.

'Totally shit,' replied Magda.

'I like your accent.'

'You're the only one who does.'

'I wish I had it. It's so full of joy. *I come from Liverpoo-il.*'

Magda laughed. 'I'll teach you Scouse in exchange for the chocolate.'

And they walked back to the school following a wet path made by four soggy bullies.

Chapter 16

Doorstepgate, 11.11 a.m.

. . . *Wrong, wrong, wrong,* being dictated to, being told what to do when it wasn't the right thing. When her heart told her that it was unfair, when it was screaming at her that she should not compromise her values to follow the directives of others whatever the consequences.

He called my dress a rag.

She had absolutely no idea why, out of everything that John F. Mayhew had ever said or done – or not done – why that insult reigned over them all, but it did. She saw herself walking up the staircase, head bowed with humiliation, to change her eau-de-nil dress as clearly as if she were watching a film. And now that person who made her feel like that was expecting her to heap all the blame for his misdemeanours onto herself until she was drowning in it. Drowning like Magda almost did until she was rescued.

'This is my statement,' Sophie began. 'My husband works incredibly hard . . .' Pins dropping everywhere could be heard. 'Politics is his life . . .' So far she had adhered to Len's instructions. 'This job is one full of pressure and that pressure occasionally causes one to act irrationally. My husband . . .'

Aaand, mentally at this point, she screwed up the script and threw it in the air. Mentally she was at the sports pavilion hearing a cry for help, but this time it was her own voice calling out and not Magda's. Mentally she was a woman standing tall in a beautiful hand-made dress who was not prepared to drown in a pool of anyone else's mess.

'. . . My husband . . . my husband has been an absolute selfish shit of the highest order. And no, I will not be standing behind or beside him. Thank you.'

And with that Sophie nodded to the crowd, turned and walked back into Park Court. The assembly was so smothered by shock that it did not immediately react; then all hell was unleashed as cameras clicked and reporters pushed forward; the Calladines and Mayhews piled into the house, slamming the door behind them.

'Sophie, what the fuck . . .?'

'Sophie.'

Sophie, Sophie, Sophie.

'God, I am so SICK of my name,' she screamed as she headed up the stairs. 'Leave me alone, all of you. Do NOT follow me.'

No one did, which led Sophie to think that Len had orchestrated their inaction. His brain must be spinning so much, his head was in danger of whizzing off his shoulders. The thought of it made Sophie giggle and she wondered if she might be going slightly mad.

Then, as she flung herself onto her bed, the panic set in, the enormity of what she had done hit her. She could have destroyed John's career.

No, he did that, said a voice inside her. *Not you. Him.*

But fear continued to hold her in a vice-like grip because she was now in unchartered waters. *What have you done, you wretched girl?* Miss Palmer-Price's voice. She'd said that when she found out about the Magda Oakes incident and how she'd pushed a Viscount's daughter, the Chairman of ICI's daughter and the Bishop of Pontefract's daughter into a swimming pool and, worst of all, nearly drowned the apple of a Russian oligarch's eye. She'd never regretted her actions then, but she was already starting to regret this one.

She had no idea how long she was lying there for before the door cracked open and John appeared. She sat bolt upright, waiting for a verbal onslaught. He had a mug in his hand.

'Hi,' he said, his voice full of concern. She hadn't expected that.

'I've brought you a drink. Hot milk.'

'Thank you.'

He put it down on the bedside table.

'I obviously haven't realised how much strain you've been under.' His voice was uncharacteristically gentle.

'I have,' she agreed stiffly.

'I just wanted to say I register that. You couldn't have slept well last night.'

Unlike yourself.

'I didn't.'

He stood. 'I'll go back downstairs and try and sort . . . you get some rest now.' He gave her a small smile, bent to kiss the top of her head, closed the door softly behind him and Sophie continued to stare at it, expecting him to burst back in and tell her how he really felt about what she had done.

She knew John and he would be livid. So why the gentle voice? Why the considerate milk?

Sophie lifted the mug to her lips and sipped, even though she had no idea why because warm milk didn't appeal to her at all. It was the sort of drink they gave you in films when they were trying to drug you. She pulled her lips from the edge of the mug, looked down into it with a cynical eye. *Surely he wouldn't?* Well, she wasn't about to take any chances. She poured the milk carefully down the sink, all too aware of how low a spot she was in even to contemplate that her own husband might be attempting to sedate/poison her.

She opened the bedroom door then, stole down the landing towards the end room, which was directly above the dining room. No one used it; it had once been the designated nursery. It was devoid of all furniture: the pale blue walls had been painted over with white, the curtains with the yellow chickens taken down, the blue carpet had been lifted and discarded four years ago. When the house was quiet, it was possible to hear in there what was going on below. Len *et al* always gravitated there to rant rather than to John's office, which he liked to keep totally private to himself.

Sophie laid flat and pressed her ear to the floorboards.

John's voice: 'Strain . . . understandable . . .' She could only hear the odd word. Then Celeste Mayhew's voice, twittering like a high-pitched really angry bird. Her mother's now, calm, measured but too quiet to make out actual words.

Len's: 'Extreme step . . . but . . . might . . . work . . .'

Her father: 'Sectioned? . . . a bit far.'

John's voice: '. . . Short time . . . obviously ill . . . need . . . rest.'

Sophie's pulse started to beat in her ears. *Sectioned?* Were they discussing having her sectioned? Is that how they were going to explain her outburst: by implying she'd had a breakdown and having her locked away? Her heart was galloping. If that were so, how long before a white van arrived? *This could not be happening. But this was happening.* Paradoxically, she *should* be sectioned for such paranoia. *Oh God, help me.* God. No point in beseeching him. Not after what he'd done to her. She was on her own in this.

Sophie tiptoed back to her bedroom, blood pounding in her ears. She pulled a mid-sized suitcase from her dressing room, wildly started throwing in the nearest clothes to hand: jeans, sweatshirts, underwear, her make-up bag. Her handbag was at the side of her bed, phone inside, purse. *What else?* She needed to get away for a few nights, what would she need? Bank cards, driving licence; her passport was in the safe downstairs so she'd have to leave that. Her head was a whirl. She needed to get out of this house and soon. *Think, Sophie, think.*

As quickly as she could, she tied her hair up into a pony-tail, pulled a knitted bobble hat on, changed into her running gear, trainers. They'd hear her if she tried to leave via the main staircase, but not if she went up to the attic, out of the window there and down the fire escape steps. If they were still attached to the wall, that was.

She opened the bedroom door, heart bouncing like a mad ball in her chest, trod as lightly as she could to the door leading up to the attic. It hadn't been opened in ages and had to be centimetred away from the jamb to stop it squeaking. Then up the stairs. The old sash window was stiff but it gave after three tugs. She climbed out. She couldn't be seen from anywhere here, not by cameras, yes to drones and helicopters, but she'd have to take a chance on that.

The fire escape rattled and shook and she wasn't convinced it wouldn't collapse on her because some of the bolts fastening it to the wall had worked loose and her breath caught in her throat a couple of times as she ventured down. Then she was at the bottom, dragging air into her lungs as if it were in short supply, and wondering what the bloody hell she was going to do now.

There was only one thing she could do: garden-hop. There would be reporters outside the back gates and the front. But if she could find a way over the wall into the neighbour's garden, she could get to the main road and then . . . she didn't know. But at least she was now out of the house.

Using the hedge for cover, she scurried along the length of the boundary wall between Park Court and Fernlea hoping for a convenient hole, without any luck. There was nothing for it but to climb over it. Sophie looked around for a rock or something to stand on and found only ones which were too far away and too heavy for her to lift. There had to be something. She looked again, found a discarded wheelbarrow covered in foliage. *Lazy damned gardener must have seen this and not bothered to shift it. Blessed wonderful lazy gardener.* Sophie wrestled with it until it was in position against the wall, hefted the suitcase up, over and onto next door's land and then put her foot into the wheelbarrow, testing that it would hold her weight if she stood in it. She felt the rusty metal give slightly, but it held. She pulled upwards with everything she'd got, swung her leg up, found purchase with her foot enough to lever herself up over the top. Now just to let herself down on the other side without impaling herself on a pitchfork or breaking her neck, whilst hoping that there were no Rottweilers on guard duty. She didn't know the neighbours, they were

American and rarely over here but she'd spotted a security van patrolling sometimes, checking in to make sure everything was tickety-boo.

Fernlea's garden was perfect for subterfuge, full of trees and bushes. Sophie took a breather for five minutes whilst planning what to do next.

Elise. The word came to her in an inspired rush. She pulled her phone out the side of her bag and switched it on. Then wished she hadn't because it began to buzz as email after email and text after text came through. Dena Stockdale:

Dear Sophie, what terrible news. Can I help in any way?

'No you can't you horrible cow,' said Sophie to that.

A message from Elise in insistent capital letters.

WHAT IS GOING ON, RING ME IMMEDIATELY.

Sophie's hands were shaking. As if in a nightmare, she couldn't negotiate her way around the phone and had to force herself to calm down. Elise picked up after two rings.

'Sophie. Are you all right?'

'Elise, are you alone?'

'Yes, I'm in Waitrose.'

'I need your help. But you have to swear to me that you won't ring John or anyone. I really really need to trust you.'

There was silence. Sophie had a mental picture of Len standing by Elise's side at the checkout prompting her what to say, like a hostage negotiator.

'Elise?'

'Sorry, I'm loading my halibut onto the conveyor belt. What do you want me to do?'

'Can you pick me up from Church Lane as soon as you can. There's a passing place for cars, I'll be hiding behind the wall there.'

'Hiding behind the wall? Whatever for?'

'Please just go with this. And swear to me that you won't tell anyone.'

'I swear on my new horse's life. There, will that do?'

It would. That was the ultimate in swears.

Twenty minutes later, Sophie was sitting in the back seat of Elise's new Maserati GranTurismo, filling her in with the story so far and wondering how the hell she'd had the luck not to be spotted by the Sky News van. It had whizzed around the corner at the same time that she had darted across the main road. The driver had given her an enraged blast on his horn and, thinking on her feet, Sophie had flipped him the bird. They wouldn't think it was Sophie Mayhew doing that.

'Drugged?' repeated Elise. 'Sectioned?'

'I can't swear to any drugs, but I know what I heard, Elise,' replied Sophie.

'Ruthless bastards, politicians,' harrumphed Elise. 'Although I have to say at this point that Gerald isn't having an affair after all. He's probably the only one in the party who has learned to keep it in his trousers. I confronted him. Long story but the woman is his long-lost daughter. I'll save the details for another time, I doubt you are in the mood to listen to that one now. So what are you going to do?'

'I don't know,' said Sophie. 'I need some time to think. Away from here. Where no one can find me.'

'Don't tell me where, then I can't tell anyone else.'

Sophie smiled. 'If you want to do me a massive favour, you can lend me some money, please. I'll write you a cheque to cover it.'

'I can manage that. How much?'

'Ten thousand pounds.'

'Certainly. Pay me later. Cheques can be traced.' Change in her back pocket, Elise didn't even flinch at the amount. 'And so can bank cards. Don't use them.'

'I don't plan to.'

'There's a little guest house in Otterly St Philip. Dreadfully impersonal, not very savoury, cheap and don't eat there. After the Sheila Crabtree incident I had a revenge fuck in it. Probably shouldn't have told you that but, there you go. Big mistake, hated myself. I'll have the money for you in the morning. Totally secret squirrel – on Monty's life.'

'Do you think you could pull in at the next supermarket and get me a few bits and pieces en route?' asked Sophie.

Elise nodded. 'I was surprisingly relieved to find that Gerald wasn't being unfaithful, Sophie. I wasn't even sure if I loved him any more but I find that I do. Very much. Sometimes idiocy can bind you together with very strong glue so I don't know if I'm presently helping you preserve your marriage or aiding you to destroy it.'

'I don't know either,' said Sophie.

An hour later, Sophie was ensconced in a grotty room in a guest house and wondering who Elise had bonked in this awful place. She'd been right, though: the man on the desk didn't even seek eye contact with her, he only wanted his cash up front. She opened up the bag of shopping that Elise had acquired for her and prepared to un-Sophie herself. First, the hair had to go. She stood in front of the bathroom mirror, put the blades of the new scissors around the initial hank and without thinking about it too much she cut. There was a horrible crunch and her eyes widened at the sight of the unsymmetrical hairdo she'd inadvertently created. There was no turning back now. The front was harder to do, especially with scissors that were more suited to cutting wallpaper than an accurate fringe but she made a decent job of it. Then she mixed up the black dye.

Three-quarters of an hour later, a combination of Cleopatra and Claudia Winkelman was staring back at her via the distressed glass. Sophie the Trophy was no more.

Chapter 17

'Good grief,' said Elise when she walked into the room the next morning. 'I didn't recognise you.'

'Perfect,' replied Sophie.

'You look French,' said Elise. 'Here, I bought you some *petit déjeuner. Un café, un sandwich et une pomme.*'

Pom.

How odd she should use that word. One happy summer she was known as Pom and not Sophie. She took the bag and said, '*Merci bien, Elise. Tu es très gentil.*'

It was a sign. That's where she needed to go. Back up to Yorkshire.

'Ten thousand pounds cash. How the hell I didn't get mugged in this area is anyone's guess.'

Sophie took the packed envelope. 'Thank you so much. Will you drop me off at the train station, please?'

'You're travelling somewhere by train with all that money on you?'

'I don't look as if I'm the sort of person to be carrying ten thousand pounds cash, to be fair.'

Elise sighed. 'We'll go to Allerwich. It's a bigger station

and you can get a direct train to London there. Or wherever you're going, though I insist you don't tell me. And if you really do not want to have the police searching for you, you'd better send John a text to say that you are going away for a while and to leave you alone. Otherwise he might say that you're a vulnerable person and have all the country looking out for you.'

'I did that whilst you were in the supermarket yesterday. Then I stamped on the phone and dumped it.'

'Good girl. Did you put my number in your new phone?'

'Yes. I'll ring you so you have mine.'

'I'll save you as *Farrier*. I won't tell a soul that I've helped you escape, I promise,' said Elise, giving Sophie a small, sad smile.

'You do believe me... that John was thinking about having me sectioned?'

'I don't disbelieve you, Sophie. Gerald has always said that John was the sort of man who would do what he had to when the chips were down.'

Sophie shivered.

Elise dropped her at the busy train station. Elise didn't hug her because she wasn't the type, but she told her to be careful and her concern was evident.

Sophie boarded the 13.45 to York. The train was quiet and she drew no one's attention. She kept her head towards the window, staring out at the scenery but seeing none of it because her head was a maelstrom of thoughts. When she arrived there, she tried not to look at the front pages of the newspapers as she passed a kiosk but couldn't help it. Her outburst was lead story in all of them, the headlines a variation of the sentence: MY HUSBAND IS A SHIT. She felt sick. John could easily have got away with having her committed to a psychiatric unit for evaluation after her behaviour. She'd probably helped drive public sympathy to him more than if she'd read out Len's words. People would presume they had witnessed a glimpse of the real Sophie Mayhew, a foul-mouthed harridan, so vile her husband had sought solace in the bosom of a much kinder, softer woman. No wonder she hid behind a mask, if that was what lurked beneath it.

She walked into the station café and ordered a tea, picking up a leaflet from the stand to give her something to read whilst she drank it. It had a detailed map of North Yorkshire in it. She found the village of Winmark, where St Bathsheba's was, the school now abandoned and not featured as a point of interest. She traced the road down to the coast with her finger and smiled. *Briswith.* The year of Pom. That wonderful summer that changed everything for her. She followed the coastline upwards, her mouth moving over long-forgotten names she recognised. *Ren Dullem, Slattercove.* Ren Dullem was tiny; Slattercove was larger, she'd head there. No one would think of her returning to Yorkshire, they'd all presume she would lose herself in London and be staying in a swanky hotel that she'd foolishly pay for with her bank card and then they'd find her. She took off her wedding and engagement rings and popped them in her purse, rubbing the groove away. It felt strange looking at her ringless hand and weirdly like a betrayal, pretending to be single when she was very much married. She wondered if John had kept his ring on whilst he had been screwing Rebecca.

Once on the train to Slattercove, she started to think about what she was going to do and then decided that the best thing she could do was *not* think and just go with the flow.

She needed to recalibrate, she needed to strengthen, she needed time out of the madness of the situation. If she thought of everything that must be going on behind her back, she would go insane. *Wouldn't that be too funny.* She needed some rest most of all. She was tired: mentally battered and physically weary. The bed in the guest house had been lumpy, the quilt stained and smelling of damp. She decided that she would hole up in the first hotel she came to, climb into bed and sleep.

Slattercove was a pretty town with a long street of independent shops but only one hotel, which was full. The hotelier recommended two guest houses down the road but they were both full too. 'There's an inn in Little Loste,' said the landlady in the second guesthouse. 'It's about a ten-minute taxi ride from here. There's a rank around the corner.'

There was a group of people behind Sophie waiting to check in so she didn't ask for a phone number so she could ring ahead. She'd just have to take a chance.

Little Loste. She couldn't remember the place. Maybe it was a sign, because no one felt more than a little lost than Sophie did at the moment. Maybe she was being guided by something that had helped her so much already. Not God, though. Not Him.

Pom

Chapter 18

Sophie was soaked by the time she got into the back of a taxi and she'd barely been waiting above five minutes. Packing an umbrella as well as a coat might have been a good idea, but hindsight was a wonderful thing. The taxi driver had to go slowly because his windscreen wipers were working at full pelt and still his vision was impaired.

'Coming down a treat tonight,' he said in his broad Yorkshire accent.

'Yes, it is very wet,' she said, trying her best to sound authentically French; anything to further disassociate herself from the posh politician's wife in all the newspapers. Elise had said she looked like a Frenchwoman, maybe she could convince other people that that's what she was too.

'You're not from round here, are you?'

'No. I am from France.'

'I love France. Me and the wife have a little holiday home over there. In Barfleur, do you know it?'

'I know it, yes.'

'Bloody hell, what a small world.' And the driver chattered on until they reached their destination.

Little Loste looked tiny: a couple of streets full of houses and three-quarters of the way up a hill, the Little Loste Inn with a car park to the side.

'Here you go, love. Four pounds fifty please.'

The rain wasn't letting up. Sophie darted from the car into the building hoping that the black dye on her hair wasn't leaving rivulets all over her face. The woman behind the darkened bar seemed more than surprised to see her. It looked as if she had started to close up.

'Oh, am I too late?' asked Sophie.

'No, not at all. Let me put the lights back on,' said the woman. She had mid-length curly brown hair and pretty blue eyes and was roughly the same age as herself. 'I didn't think anyone would be in tonight, what with the weather, so I was going to shut up early, but happy to serve you.'

'I don't suppose you sell food?'

'Got some crisps and nuts, that's it.'

'Just a glass of red wine in that case, please.'

'Coming up.'

'Do you have any rooms available?'

'Sorry, no.'

Sophie's heart sank. She'd have to get a taxi to Whitby then. As if able to see into her brain the woman then said:

'You'll not find anywhere around here if you haven't booked. There's a massive music festival on in Whitby and everywhere's been booked for a while.'

'I didn't know I would need to find anywhere.'

'Oh that's a shame,' said the woman. 'Five pounds sixty, please.'

Sophie's hands were shaking as she took the money out of her purse, which the woman assumed was because she was cold. Sophie picked up her glass and went to sit next to the small fire burning out in the grate in the corner of the pub. The woman came out from behind the bar and put another log on it from a basket at the side.

'You look frozen,' she said.

'I am,' replied Sophie. Frozen and beat and more than a little lost, a big lost. A huge fat enormous massive lost.

'Where've you journeyed from?'

'London,' lied Sophie.

'What for? I'm presuming not the music festival, seeing as you didn't know it was on.'

'I ... er ...' *I've run away from my husband who is trying to have me committed to an asylum.* A sob escaped her, shocking her with its suddenness.

'Sorry, it's none of my business,' said the woman, looking embarrassed.

'I 'ave left my 'usband,' said Sophie, sounding less subtle and more like Fifi from *'Allo 'Allo.* 'I didn't have the chance to think ahead.'

'Oh, bless you,' said the woman.

The tears were raining down Sophie's cheeks now. One Yorkshire accent and a bit of sympathy and the dam walls had crumbled. She didn't have a handkerchief and so mopped at her face with her sleeve, which was soaked from rain so not the best item for drying.

The woman went back behind the bar then, brought over a wine bottle and tilted it over Sophie's glass, filling it to the top. 'Here, get that down you. I'll be back in a minute.'

She disappeared into a room to the right of the bar whilst Sophie sipped the wine. How could so much have happened in thirty-six hours? Yesterday morning she was a blonde English woman living in a huge house. Now she was French, black-haired and homeless.

The wine wasn't the best but it was palatable and warmed her inside. She had no idea what she was going to do now. None at all. When the barlady came back she'd have to ask her if she could recommend somewhere that would have a vacant room, however far away. She should have stayed in York, she thought. There had to be a room free somewhere in the North of England. She was so tired she was starting to hallucinate. The smell of toast curled up her nostrils.

Then the woman reappeared with a stack of buttered toast which she set down in front of Sophie.

'Here you go,' she said. 'I couldn't see you starving. And I've got you somewhere to stay for the night or the weekend if you need it. Don't get too excited. My brother is the local vicar and there's an almshouse. It was left to the church by the old lady who owned it. I've rung him, he says it's okay, there's hardly a rush for the place.'

No, she'd misheard, she couldn't be that lucky.

'Really?'

'Yes, really.' The landlady smiled gently.

'Oh my goodness. Thank you, thank you, I can pay,' gushed Sophie. 'Tell me how—'

'It's a church house,' said the woman. 'You don't pay. Trust me, when you see it, you'll be asking me to pay you for staying in it.' She laughed. 'I'm Tracey by the way. Tracey Green.'

'Pom,' said Sophie, without even having to think about it. She was Pom again. Pom who had no surname. It was like finding an old favourite coat in a wardrobe, slipping it on and realising it still fitted.

'Isn't that a potato in French?'

Sophie smiled. 'An apple. But I'm a P-O-M. It's spelled differently.'

'Unusual, does it mean anything?'

It meant a lot.

'It's just a name that my mother liked.' Another fib.

The toast was delicious and Sophie gobbled it all up whilst Tracey bustled around closing up the bar. Eventually she came out of the room at the side with a carrier bag and a set of keys.

'There's some newspapers in here so you can start a fire if you need to warm the place up. It's been standing empty for a while so I imagine it'll be quite cold tonight. And I've made you up a flask of soup.'

Her kindness humbled Sophie, who felt weakened by it.

'Thank you,' she said, her voice scraped dry with emotion.

'Let's just say I left my husband in much the same way, so I have every sympathy,' said Tracey. 'Come on, I'll take you there.'

Whatever Sophie was expecting was not this. The alms-house was enormous. A huge double-fronted building with deep bay windows.

'This is it,' said Tracey, opening the sort of front door that would have featured happily on the Addams' Family residence, complete with haunted-house creak. 'It's a shame it's so run down, but it would cost a fortune to do up and the church doesn't have the money. There's only the front left part of the house that is liveable in. Don't go up the stairs, they aren't safe. We should seal them off really but – again – money. So fall and break your neck at your own peril. Plus none of the lights work anywhere but in the bedsit.'

'I will stay in the bottom,' said Sophie. 'I am so grateful.'

The sight that greeted her when they stepped inside was of a grand staircase and a white-and-black tiled floor that had seen much better days.

'My brother has some photos of the house in its heyday,' said Tracey. 'There was a massive chandelier that hung there.' She pointed to a gaping wound in the ceiling. 'And the tiles shone like a dance floor.'

'What happened to the last owner?' asked Sophie.

'It's quite romantic in a tragic way. Kitty came to the house seeking sanctuary on a very stormy night after being thrown out of her maid's position. She'd been used and abused by her boss, turfed out pregnant and Mr Henshaw, who lived here – a confirmed bachelor surgeon – nursed her back to health. Sadly she lost her baby and couldn't have any more, but he fell madly in love with her and married her. They were incredibly happy for many years until he died. It sent her slightly mad and she was convinced that he was still around, which is quite a nice sort of mad, don't you think? It's said that she . . .' Tracey cut off her words and made an awkward face.

'She what?' asked Sophie, taking in the hallway, not finding it difficult to imagine the former grandeur of the place despite its present state.

'Oh, er, that she . . . er . . . loved this place so much and didn't want to . . . er . . . leave it . . .'

'She haunts it? Is that what you are trying to say?'

Tracey cringed. 'Sorry, I shouldn't have said anything. I didn't want to freak you out.'

Sophie smiled. 'You haven't freaked me out. I don't believe in . . .' She shut up. Maybe not the best time to say that she didn't believe in ghosts, ghoulies or gods. Not when it was the church who had come to her rescue tonight.

'You'll be okay, anyway. She likes having guests. No one who has stayed here has run off screaming. Not yet, anyway.'

'I am happy to make your acquaintance, Kitty,' Sophie spoke into the air. There was no response, as she expected.

'Come through,' said Tracey, unlocking the door to her left.

What used to be a parlour was now a bedsit. It had a single unmade bed in the window bay, a wooden ottoman standing at the bottom of it; a couch facing an open fireplace, complete with grate; a table and two chairs in the middle of the room and, against the far wall, a run of cheap kitchen units. An old Baby Belling oven sat on the work surface.

'Bathroom's through there,' said Tracey, pointing to a door in the far corner. 'Those two switches to the left of it, one is for the light and the other's for the immersion heater. It turns itself off after an hour but that'll give you enough for a nice bath. There's towels and bedding in the ottoman there. They'll be clean but lord knows the last time anyone stayed here. Must be at least a year so they might smell a bit musty.'

'It's very trusting of you.'

'Ha! There's nothing to nick,' laughed Tracey. 'The kettle maybe. We've had to replace a couple of those over the years, which is why it's a ten quid thing from Argos and not a Smeg.'

'I won't steal your kettle,' smiled Sophie. 'I promise.'

Tracey handed over the carrier bag. 'There's a couple of teabags in there too, although if you're French you probably prefer coffee.'

'No, I like English tea,' replied Sophie. 'Thank you. Again.'

'It's Yorkshire tea, the best sort,' said Tracey. 'Right. Here's the key. I'll call around tomorrow and check on you. Have a good night. Don't let the bed bugs bite. Do you say that in France?'

'Not really. We say, *bonne nuit, dors bien, fais de beaux rêves*. Sleep well, sweet dreams.'

'Sleep well, eh?' replied Tracey. 'I hope you do. Oh and the only stipulation if you stay here for any length of time is that you attend the church service on Sunday morning. You won't find it a hardship, even if the vicar is my brother.' She gave Sophie a wonky grin as she turned to go, but no explanation of what she meant by that.

Sophie made up the bed and considered waiting for the water to heat up for a bath, but she was too tired even to brush her teeth. She slipped off her tracksuit bottoms and snuggled down under the quilt. She was asleep in minutes, the deep restful sleep of someone who felt safe.

Chapter 19

Sophie awoke the next morning with a brass band playing in her head, a throbbing painful drum beat in her temple. A class A bona fide stress headache that had taken up residence in her skull with the sure and certain knowledge that it had the right to be there. She had no tablets to combat it, so she decided to see if she could try and run it off. The rain hadn't let up and, judging from how the trees were blowing, the wind was pissed off about something. Perfect weather for blasting a headache to smithereens.

She put on her tracksuit and her running shoes and it was only when she reached the end of the front garden that she realised how close the beach was. There was a curling path that led down to the sand. The beach was deserted, but then no one but madmen and women pretending to be French would be out in this.

Her 'spidey senses' picked up that something had changed when she got back. Something wasn't quite as she left it. She leapt to her suitcase in a wild panic, angry at herself that she hadn't secreted the money somewhere, but it was still there in the zipped compartment. Nothing seemed to be missing, but there was an imprint on her bed as if someone had sat down on the quilt and it hadn't been her. She didn't know if ghosts made bottom prints, though she doubted it. Maybe her imagination just needed to calm down, but then again, she was sure she hadn't left her make-up bag on the edge of the table like that. She walked into the hallway. 'Hello,' she called. She tried the door on the opposite side, but it was locked securely, as were all the other downstairs doors. The one underneath the stairs wasn't, however. She opened it and peered down into the inky darkness because the light switch didn't work. A shiver rippled down the full length of her back. It wasn't ghosts who could hurt her though, it was people who did that.

She stripped off her tracksuit and changed into dry jeans and a sweatshirt. She needed to buy some clothes if she was going to be away from Cherlgrove for any length of time, because her packing had been panicked and absolutely rubbish: tracksuits, too many bras, not enough pants or socks, no coat, smart trousers, a silk shirt that was hideously creased, and a pair of Christian Louboutins – as if she'd need those. Then she knelt by the grate in order to make a fire. She reached into the bag of newspapers, pulled out yesterday's *News of the Day* and was confronted by her own face. And John's and Rebecca Robinson's. She felt a sudden physical ache inside her as if her heart had been pinged with an elastic band.

She didn't want to read it, but she couldn't stop herself. Rebecca's story. This was the newspaper she had given the exclusive to, sold her soul for.

This is not all the truth, said that voice inside her. But some of it was. John had slept with this woman. He had trashed their wedding vows, ridden roughshod over their marriage for sex. Sex that he could have had with his wife.

John liked risky sex. He loved the idea that we might be seen. We once had sex in Cherlgrove woods near his house. I was screaming with delight with my back against a tree whilst his wife was less than half a mile away arranging flowers ...

Was this true? She didn't know.

He said he loved me and that we would be together. He told his wife he had to go to Germany on business but instead we went to Italy for a long weekend. She rang him when we were on a gondola and he had to pretend he had lost the signal ...

She had rung him when he had been in 'Germany'. He had said that the signal was weak and he would ring her back.

I picked his wife's birthday present for her. Sapphire earrings. In the same shop he bought me diamond earrings. That should tell me all I needed to know about who he loved the most, he said.

Sophie swallowed. He had bought her sapphire earrings for her birthday. How would Rebecca Robinson know that?

I wangled an invite to the Cherlgrove Ball last week. I wore the expensive red dress he bought me and no knickers. He was so angry that I was there because he thought his wife might smell a rat, but it didn't stop him dragging me into a cubicle in an upstairs toilet.

Sophie felt sick. He had taken a strangely long time to come back from the toilet at the very end of the evening but blamed it on being caught up with 'some dreary tosser droning on' to him. How could she even hope to unpick the truth from the lies?

She heard a pulsing noise and it took her a long few seconds to realise that it was the noise of her new phone. Elise's name was on the display.

'Hello, can you talk?' said Elise in her brisk no-nonsense way.

'Yes, I can. Hello.'

'I shan't ask where you are but do you know what's going on?'

'No, I haven't got a TV and—'

'The official line is that you had a mental aberration and you're being looked after for the poor, sick thing you are in the bosom of your loving family.'

'Am I?' asked Sophie.

'Yes you are. Gerald told me, so I immediately rang John and asked if there was anything I could do. He told me that the doctors had decided you should have no visitors and plenty of rest. So, you're in seclusion. That's what the papers will report when you eventually get to read one. Your wonderful husband is tending to your every need.'

'It's good to know I'm being so well cared for,' said Sophie, with a snap of sarcasm.

'I think he did suspect initially that I might know more than I did but I'm very good at lying when I need to. I do hope you are holed up in the Ritz or somewhere, darling. They're very discreet there.'

Sophie looked around her and thought that she was about as far away from the Ritz as it was possible to be.

'What are you going to do, Sophie? How long do you think you'll be away?'

'I don't know and I don't know,' answered Sophie with a long outward breath. She couldn't go back at the moment, that was for sure. They'd take one look at her hair and conclude that she must be mad after all.

Sophie made a fire out of the newspapers and some of the logs and sticks stacked up at the side of the hearth. Her headache had gone now, thanks to her run in the very unsummery weather, and she thought it would be a shame to waste the wind once the rain had stopped. There was a washing line outside the house and she'd found a few wooden pegs in the cupboard underneath the sink so she hung her tracksuit out to dry and the bedsheet for airing. It snapped impatiently on the line as if it wanted to fly free like a kite and was frustratingly tethered. Half an hour later, she spotted raindrops on the window and went to bring them in.

She was folding the sheet when she heard a small voice.

'Hello lady. Whatcha doing?'

She looked around but couldn't see anyone. Then she detected a movement behind the picket fence separating the almshouse garden from the neighbouring one. A small boy was peering through the slats.

'Hello there,' she said. 'I've been drying some damp things.'

'What's your name?'

'My name is Pom. And what is your name?'

'Luke,' the boy replied. 'Luke George Peter Bellringer.'

'Goodness,' said Sophie, suddenly remembering to put on her French accent. 'That is a mouthful.'

'I've been on my swing,' said Luke.

'You have a swing in your garden? That's nice. I always wanted a swing.'

'I live there.' He pointed behind him, at a house where a man had just appeared on the doorstep, arms akimbo with annoyance. 'I haven't gone to nursery today because it's Saturday. I'm four.'

'Luke Bellringer, what have I told you about going outside and not telling me,' called the man.

'That's my dad. Oh boy, I'm in big trouble now,' said Luke, in such a theatrical tone that Sophie had to bite on her lip to stop herself from laughing aloud.

The man walked down the garden towards them. He was wearing jeans and a black T-shirt, showing off a pair of arms that hinted at being no stranger to weights. He had thick, straight dark hair, combed to the side and geek-chic framed black glasses. Very Clark Kent, thought Sophie, Christopher Reeve version. Tall, wide-shouldered, the handsome-but-didn't-know-it type, totally unlike her husband. As he approached the fence, she could see his smile widen in greeting.

'Once you start talking to my son, that's a day gone,' he said and held out his hand. The breeze lifted his scent, carried it to her: notes of cedar. 'Elliott Bellringer, nice to meet you. I hear that we are possibly going to be neighbours for a little while.'

Sophie hoped this wasn't a gossipy village, otherwise she'd have to leave immediately.

His hand engulfed Sophie's when hers came out to meet it.

'Hello,' she said, warily.

'I'm Tracey's brother,' he clarified. 'I'm the local vicar.'

Surely not, she thought. Vicars didn't look like this. The vicar at Cherlgrove looked like the first Doctor Who. He had cotton wool for hair and drank more of his communion wine than he administered.

'Oh.' *Wow.* 'I am very grateful for your 'ospitality,' said Sophie.

'Sleep well?'

'Like an 'orse,' replied Sophie.

Elliott Bellringer grinned. Sophie thought she saw his lips move over the words 'like an 'orse' and then he reached down to take the hand of his son just as there was an ominous rumble of thunder above their heads.

'Come on then, Lukey. Let's get you inside before the skies open. Nice to meet you . . . Pom.'

'Nice to meet you both too,' said Sophie. It was good to be Pom again. It had been too long.

Chapter 20

Eighteen years ago

Sophie's disgraceful exhibition at the poolside was an offence that would earn her a heavy punishment, namely a massive chunk of Petronius's 'The Millionaire's Dinner Party' to translate from Latin, which was nothing compared to the penalty she received from her parents. As her father said in his furious letter, he had never once had a daughter put on a full report before and he was beyond incensed. Victoria and Annabella were the Mother Theresas to her Anti-Christ. This was not the sort of behaviour with which a Calladine was associated and it would be stamped out absolutely.

Sophie and her parents were due to spend that summer in the Far East: Cambodia, China, Thailand, Vietnam, Korea; along with Saint Victoria and Saint Annabella, both home from Oxford University. Now, Sophie would remain at the school instead. A sole pupil, undergoing two and a half months of extra academic lessons. Maybe then she might learn how to behave and respect her fellow pupils.

As it happened, her parents ended up committing their

errant youngest daughter to the best summer of her life. Miss Gateley, who had been given the job of running the one-girl summer school, was dumped rather unceremoniously by her boyfriend and begged the school cook for help whilst she tried to sort out her chaotic love life.

Mrs Ackroyd, the school cook, had felt extremely sorry for Sophie having to stay by herself all summer. So, between them, they arranged it that Miss Gateley would pay Mrs Ackroyd to look after Sophie for her. Sophie was to stay with Mrs Ackroyd in her house in Briswith instead of at the horrible, freezing, lonely school. No one would ever know. No one did ever know.

Catherine Ackroyd lived in a beautiful olde worlde cottage with deep window seats and uneven floors. She was a widow with a grown-up daughter, Lucy, who lived in Australia, and thirteen-year-old twins Charlie and Tina. This would be her last summer in Britain because they were all going to join Lucy, so she was willing to take the risk that Miss Palmer-Price would find out what had taken place. She was kindness itself and a wonderful cook. It was lucky that Sophie had discovered running by then because if she hadn't she would have been as rotund as Fat Fiona from all the lovely baking she mainlined that summer.

Sophie shared a bedroom with Tina and after an initial awkwardness, they were soon chatting about boys and bonding over make-up techniques. On sunny days, Sophie joined Tina and Charlie and their friends down on the beach, where they sunbathed whilst listening to music or combed the beach for treasure. They played hide and seek in Briswith Woods and held a car boot sale of all the things the Ackroyds weren't taking to Australia. On rainy days they stayed in and talked and watched TV, helped Mrs Ackroyd with cleaning or did some baking. Tina showed Sophie how to make pom-poms and Sophie made hundreds of them, stitching them onto a jumper. 'This will be a fashion one day,' she insisted: she was totally convinced of it, and she stitched pom-poms on everything she owned. 'We'll have to call you Pom,' laughed Mrs Ackroyd, and the nickname had stuck. 'Pom' told them of her plan to open up a clothes shop full of all her own designs, except she'd only mastered how to make an A-line skirt so far.

So Mrs Ackroyd taught her how to sew and knit, because she was a dab hand at making clothes. She'd knitted jumpers for her children and made their school uniforms because the stuff off the pegs never fitted them right and she was a stickler for a good fit. She taught Sophie how to measure properly, put in zips, fit sleeves, do ladder-stitch and darts. She taught her about inverted pleats and scalloped edges and Sophie soaked it all up like a sponge. Now she could make all those wonderful clothes she had seen in her head.

Then Sophie had to go back to school with Miss Gateley and pretend that she had been studying with her all summer. Miss Gateley was a happy bunny now that she had been reunited with her boyfriend and didn't push Sophie too hard before term started.

Magda didn't come back after the summer holidays. Sophie never heard from her again in fact and she reasoned that Magda wanted to put the whole St Bathsheba episode behind her and forget everything and everyone associated with it, and she couldn't blame her for that. The Ackroyds left for the Antipodes and no one called Sophie Pom any more. And even though Sophie thought she might never see that happy, free, wild and wonderful side of herself again, Pom stayed curled up inside her, waiting.

Chapter 21

Sophie was inexplicably tired and dropped off to sleep that afternoon. She was woken by the sound of someone knocking loudly on the front door.

Tracey was standing on the doorstep with a large shopping bag, hair plastered to her face from the falling rain.

'Sorry, did I wake you up? I brought food and wine,' she said. 'I thought you might like some company but if you don't, I'll leave you to it. Fish and chips. Best in the area.'

'No, please, come in.' Company would be nice. And some food.

The last time Sophie had eaten them from a fish and chip shop was in Briswith with Tina and her friends. They'd sat on a wall outside the shop and talked about rubbish but soaked up each other's company just as much as the chips soaked up the salt and vinegar.

The smell was making Sophie's stomach grumble with anticipation. Was it the sea air working its magic? And why did they taste so much more delicious out of paper than on a plate? Sophie broke off the greasy tail of the fish and popped it in her mouth.

'I have some money, I can pay you for this,' she said.

Tracey waved it away. 'It's only fish and chips and cheap plonk. I figured you hadn't managed to get out to do any food shopping with the weather being so vile today.'

'Not yet, no. Thank you.'

They polished off the food and a glass of wine each whilst the rain pelted at the windows.

'When you get a storm up here, you get a proper storm,' said Tracey, looking at the clouds boiling in the sky.

'It's beautiful,' said Sophie. 'Can I make you some tea?' She was enjoying Tracey's easy company and didn't want her to rush off.

'That would be nice, thank you. I'll make you a fire.'

'I had one burning earlier but it went out when I fell asleep.'

'I thought it was warm in here when I came in.'

Sophie put the kettle on. Tracey screwed up the fish and chip paper and put it in the grate, rested some kindling on it and a log, then lit a match to set it alight. 'Ells Bells said he'd met you this morning. Elliott, my brother.'

'Ells Bells.' Sophie chuckled. 'Oh, that is a wonderful name for a vicar.'

'Couldn't make it up, could you? Everyone calls him Ells Bells. Plenty of women around here would like to be Mrs Ells Bells, let me tell you. Well, when he manages to rid himself of the present Mrs Ells Bells that is, the . . .' Tracey bit off her words and shook her head as if annoyed at herself. 'Sorry. Sore subject. Like you want to hear about this sort of stuff!'

'I don't mind at all.'

'She left him soon after Luke was born. Couldn't take the responsibility, she said.'

Some women threw away what others would kill for, thought Sophie.

'And what is your story?' asked Sophie, stirring the teapot to hasten the brewing. *Mashing*, that's what Mrs Ackroyd used to call it. Mashing the tea.

'You really don't want to hear my story when you've got your own problems,' said Tracey. 'I came here to see if you wanted to offload, not to offload onto you.'

'Sometimes hearing the stories of others helps you put things into perspective.' *And as long as I'm listening to somebody else, I'm not being asked about myself,* thought Sophie.

'Okay then. I was with Barry for seven years. I was a bit of a fatty when I met him: not much confidence, aimed low, didn't think I was worth much. And that's how Barry treated me, as if I wasn't that valuable. I made his dinner, which he ate silently before he went out to the pub with his pals, then on Saturday nights we had the obligatory bonk but even that died off. It was all very boring and unfulfilling. Then, three years ago, a free day's pass to join the new swanky gym in Slattercove landed through the letterbox and I have no idea what made me do it, but I went, by myself in monster-sized tracksuit bottoms and a top that Billy Smart could have used as a circus tent. And I enjoyed it. So I signed up for the whole year. It's testament to how much Barry looked at me because he only asked me if I'd lost some weight after I'd shifted four stone. I got thinner and fitter, he got fatter and balder. My confidence grew and I packed my bags. He didn't even see it coming. I didn't even see it coming if I'm honest. I woke up one morning expecting a normal day and by eleven o'clock I thought, "Go, leave now." So I did, before I could change my mind. It was like I had a voice inside me, another person lending me some strength: I know that sounds bonkers. He couldn't believe I'd done it. Then it all got a bit nasty. Sometimes you don't realise you're on a leash until you try and walk off further than usual.'

Sophie could empathise with that.

'Yes. That's true.'

'If anyone had told me when I first went into that gym that within two years I'd have a waist, my own business and a decree absolute, I'd have laughed them out of town.'

'And where is your husband?'

'Ex-husband if you don't mind. He's still in Whitby, he'll be there till he dies. In the same house, stuck in the same routine, getting even more boring with every day that passes. But not me, I want more. I want to make up for lost time. I love having my own business. It's not exactly a Hilton but it's mine and I want to grow it and do it up. I've got loads of plans. So what about you, Pom? Do you want to talk about anything?'

No. Even if she did want to, she wouldn't know where to begin. How could you find a starting point in that big ball of mess?

'Sorry,' said Tracey, answering her silence. 'I didn't come here to pry. I really didn't.'

'No, it's all right,' said Sophie, handing her a cup of tea – black because she didn't have any milk or sugar to offer.

'I think I'd have left Barry a lot sooner if he'd been unfaithful. I almost wanted him to be unfaithful so it would galvanise me into action, because I couldn't have forgiven that. But he was too bloody lazy,' Tracey went on. 'I wasn't "me" with Barry. I was . . . an add-on, some-one in the background who oiled his wheels. Okay, so I might run the smallest inn on the planet now but it's all mine. I'm independent and free and in control, even if you do need a magnifying glass to see my profits, but what I have now is worth all the money in the world. I tell you, I wouldn't change places with that poor cow married to that Tory minister in the papers, for all her fancy house and fortune.'

Sophie went cold and hoped the alarm didn't show on her face. She tried to look blank, hoping Tracey hadn't seen her involuntary gulp.

'I don't know her,' she said, hoping to shut that subject down, but the opposite happened as Tracey started to fill her in on the details.

'Sophie Mayhew, she's married to that slimy git politician John Mayhew, who's just been caught with his trousers down. It's massive news, you'd recognise them if you saw a picture. Anyway, on Thursday, they're outside their big posh house and he's making one of those statements trying to undo all the damage – fat chance – and she ends up calling him a shit. On live TV. Go on, girl. She ... Pom, are you okay?'

Tracey thought Pom was about to faint. She seemed to slump forward, her eyes fluttered, then her spine snapped straight again, as if an emergency reboot had been triggered.

'I ... yes. I'm fine.'

'As I was saying ...' Inside Tracey's head was a clear picture of Sophie Mayhew and as her eyes settled on Pom's face, she quickly became aware of an odd congruence between the two.

'That's weird, Pom, you look like ...' She laughed at the absurdity of what she was about to say because it was madness, but ... 'You look like her – Mrs Mayhew.'

It was said half-jokingly, but Pom's reaction turned any

attempt at humour onto its head. Sophie stood up, panicked. 'I have to go,' she said, dropping the French accent abruptly.

'Whoa.' Tracey leapt to her feet, put her hands on Sophie's arms, held her steady. 'You absolutely do not have to go anywhere.'

'If you guessed, others will . . .'

'Please, Mrs . . . Pom . . . sit, please.' Tracey pushed her back down. 'Flipping heck. Look, I have excellent facial mapping skills, no idea why God gave me that as a gift because it only ever comes in handy when I'm watching films and trying to work out where I've seen actors before . . .' She was waffling; she took a deep breath to stop herself. 'I'm really good at remembering faces is what I'm trying to say. I know it's weird. But please don't worry, Pom, this house is a sanctuary and what sort of person would I be if I gave you up after what I've just told you about crap husbands? And trust me, you haven't heard the half of what I went through. You're safe, I promise. I'll stick with calling you Pom for consistency. You are totally and utterly in the best place here with us.'

Sophie's heart was racing like Red Rum closing in on the Aintree finishing line. 'Blimey,' Tracey said. 'I didn't expect this when I brought the fish and chips. You're supposed to be resting in a hospital, aren't you?'

'I would have been if I hadn't run away,' said Sophie. 'My husband was going to have me sectioned.'

'You're joking?' gasped Tracey. 'No, you aren't joking, are you?' That much was obvious from Sophie's expression. 'Sod the tea.' She poured out two more glasses of wine. Sophie lifted hers with a shaking hand.

'You poor thing. Well, that's settled. You are staying in the almshouse for as long as you need it. And for the record, that French look really works for you. You'd have anyone else fooled. I suppose you can speak French?'

'Yes, fluently. I lived there for a year and studied it at university.'

'How many people know where you are?'

'Just you,' replied Sophie. 'I have a friend who lent me some money to get away but she doesn't know where I am.'

'Right, right,' said Tracey. 'Oh my. Think, Tracey, think. Now, I'll have to tell Ells Bells, but he's a man of God. He is incapable of spilling a secret.' Then Tracey answered Sophie's horrified look. 'Really, if he knows and there's any problem, he'd be able to throw people off the scent. I can't lie to him. You'll be fine. Blimey, this is bonkers.'

'I know. I feel as if I'm in a bad dream with no chance of waking up.'

'You say your husband was going to have you put away? For saying that he was a shit and you wouldn't stand by him?' Tracey huffed. 'I think you should have been put away if you had stayed with him after what he did.'

'I don't know why I said it. I've never believed in washing dirty linen in public.'

Tracey let loose a dry laugh. 'I imagine it was dying to come out of you and you couldn't stop it, that's why you said it.'

Sophie covered her face with her hands and winced. If only she could have turned the clock back. Her life would have been so much less complicated now.

Tracey clicked her fingers as she remembered something. 'Hang on, Sophie Mayhew went to St Bathsheba's didn't she . . . you?'

'I did.'

'That's why you've come back here?'

'Yes. Because I hated it so much. I don't think anyone would guess this is where I would hole up.'

'I went to Liverpool uni with a girl who went there, Magdalena Oakes. She'd be one or two years younger than you though so I don't suppose—'

'Magda Oakes?' Sophie's head lifted.

'Yes, Lena Sowerby as she is now.'

Sophie was gobsmacked. 'Lena Sowerby is Magda Oakes?'

'Did you know Magdalena then?'

'Yes, yes, I did know her. And I liked her very much.'

She didn't have to ask what Magda was doing these days if Magda Oakes and Lena Sowerby were one and the same person. Lena Sowerby was the Shadow Secretary of State for Family Matters, a very big thorn in her husband's side. But Lena Sowerby was an Amazon: tall, stately, formidable, glamorous, eloquent, nothing like the pudgy, plain, stammering Magda.

'I haven't seen her for years but we keep in contact by email every so often. Ages ago it cropped up in a conversation that she knew you from school,' Tracey went on. 'Told me you once saved her from drowning. That true?'

'Well, I tackled some bullies that were giving her a hard time,' said Sophie.

'She said you taught her how to style herself and stand up to people. The school might have done nothing for her but you certainly did.'

'Me?' Sophie found that hard to believe.

'Yep. She wanted to get back in touch with you and say as much but she didn't think it appropriate. Not with her being so anti your husband.'

Sophie wanted to laugh. How ironic that she'd been

partly responsible for the rise of Lena Sowerby. As if her life couldn't get any more insane.

'You will be okay here, I promise,' said Tracey. 'If anyone needs the sanctuary of this almshouse, it's you. Only Ells Bells, you and I will know about this.'

'Thank you. I really appreciate it.'

The fire in the grate had taken hold and was already warming the room.

'I wish I were staying in here instead of going out there,' smiled Tracey, nodding towards the window whilst she drank the rest of her wine. 'But I have a bar to open. I've always loved this house. It's got a wonderfully cosy feel to it, hasn't it, for such a big place.'

'I think I might have had a visit from Kitty yesterday,' said Sophie. 'Some of my things had been moved.'

'She likes to tidy up, so I've been told. I think if she's listening to this she'd tell you that she won't blab your secret either,' said Tracey, blowing out the full capacity of her lungs. 'Wow, just wow.'

Chapter 22

The next day was Sunday and Sophie was duty-bound to go to church. She didn't want to arouse any suspicion by not going, as it was a condition of staying at the almshouse, although she didn't have any smart clothes other than a Versace silk shirt and Louboutin shoes, which could possibly draw unwanted attention and even her jeans were a bit posh, so she went in tracksuit bottoms and a sweatshirt. No one would have ever guessed they had the infamous Sophie Mayhew in their midst. Village gossip circulated that a French woman had moved in, but nothing more. No one had any reason to think she was other than someone at rock bottom who needed sanctuary, and they would have been right in that.

Sophie walked into St George's church and shuddered. The spirit of the building would be able to see into her heart and how much she instinctively hated everything about it, even a church as beautiful as this one with its fabulous stained-glass window of the saint himself, sword pressed against the breast of the dragon. It couldn't have been more indicative of what the church had done to Sophie, mortally wounding her and then passing it off as a holy act. She knew how that poor dragon felt.

Out of the corner of her eye, she detected a rapid movement: Tracey waving her over. Sophie walked down the central aisle, aware of how very underdressed she was because all the women over fifty were wearing hats and anyone under fifty was wearing a lot of make-up. She wondered how many women were here for the sermon and how many were here to flutter their eyelashes at the Reverend Elliott Bellringer.

Even Sophie had to admit that 'Ells Bells' could rock a cassock and surplice. He was possibly the most handsome man in the British clergy. He had large blue eyes and a strong jaw and, as he was welcoming them all, she found herself wondering why Mrs Bellringer had abandoned him. Then again, John Mayhew was the most handsome man in politics, proving that looks weren't everything. She wouldn't immediately load all the blame onto Mrs Bellringer for the failure of her marriage, as many would load it onto Sophie for hers.

He was very different from the school chaplain at St Bathsheba's, who smelled of snuff and had a monotonous delivery of uninspiring preachy sermons, plus he had been a little too touchy-feely for her liking. Sophie attended church nowadays when she had to, when duty called: Remembrance Sunday, Easter, funerals, weddings. Christmas services were the worst of all. Hearing carols tore her heart to pieces; watching a nativity was torturous. People mistook her unsmiling demeanour for lack of interest and it did her no favours, especially when her husband was smiling at baby kings and angels, but they could not know what it did to her to think that her child should be amongst them: an inn-keeper, a donkey with wonky ears, a shepherd with a tea-towel on his head.

Elliott Bellringer spoke from the pulpit the way that John did in the House: passionately, convincingly, entreating people to believe what he said. Sophie didn't actually want to believe the Reverend Bellringer on this occasion because he was retelling the parable of the lost sheep. She had a vision of John, holding a crook, tenaciously tearing Britain apart to find her and bring her home so he could lock her up in a padded cell. It all felt too close for comfort and if she could have left without drawing attention to herself she might have.

'Got any plans for lunch?' asked Tracey at the end of the service. 'Fancy joining my brother and my brat of a nephew for a Sunday roast? He's a great cook. Okay, good, that's settled.' She didn't leave any space for an answer. Sophie just wanted to get out of church as quickly as possible because people were glancing at her, the stranger in their midst. Smart old couples were smiling at her, younger women giving her the once-over as a possible rival for the reverend's affections – even in tracksuit bottoms and hacked-off hair. The only person who had totally ignored her presence was an auburn-haired teenage girl with a moody pout. An outer petulance masking something troubling her within; Sophie recognised that look.

The reverend was shaking everyone's hands at the door. Sophie hoped he wouldn't blow her cover when it was her turn.

'Ah, Pom, *enchantée*. I hope I've said it right,' said Elliott.

'*Oui*,' answered Sophie, keeping it brief because she felt a bit of a fraud now. Acting French in front of someone who knew she was from the Home Counties.

'Pom's joining us for lunch,' Tracey told her brother.

'You won't be sorry,' said Elliott. 'I'm a brilliant cook.'

'Pride is a sin, Ells Bells.' Tracey winked then turned to Sophie. 'I need to pick up Luke from the Sunday school. Come with me if you like.'

They walked round to the back of the church and Sophie waited outside whilst Tracey went in through a heavy arched door, returning a minute later with her nephew. A plump woman with too-dark eyebrows scuttled out behind them, smiling at Sophie whilst sweeping her eyes up and down her at the same time. *Just like Dena Stockdale*, was Sophie's immediate thought, because that smile didn't reach her eyes. She stood there angling for an introduction, which Tracey felt obliged to make.

'Pom, this is Miriam, Luke's Sunday School teacher.'

''Allo,' said Sophie.

'Settling in?' asked Miriam.

'Yes, *merci*.'

The young woman's eyes didn't stop raking over Sophie; she really was going to town with her scrutiny.

'Hello, Pom,' said Luke, with a grin on his face that did light up his eyes.

'Ah, you remembered my name,' said Sophie, rolling her 'r's for all they were worth.

'Look what I made.' He held up a twist of brown pipe-cleaners.

'Give me a clue what it is, Luke,' said Tracey, squinting at it as if that might help.

'It begins with *li-o*,' replied Luke.

Not even that helped.

'It's a lion,' said Miriam. 'We've been discussing Daniel in the lion's den today.'

'Is it a lion from Chernobyl?' asked Tracey, taking it from her nephew and examining it. She had thought it might just be a little squashed, but that would not explain its eight legs and no head. Sophie might hardly know Tracey at all, but she suspected she enjoyed winding up Miriam.

'Do you like him, Auntie Tracey?' asked Luke.

'He's fantastic. He's my favourite surrealist lion of all time. Let's call him Salvador. Anyway, come on Luke, we have work to do. Pom's coming to have lunch with us, so we need to get out another knife and fork,' said Tracey and Sophie wondered if that was for Dena Mark II's benefit. If so, and the aim was to make Miriam's lips contract over her teeth, then she'd certainly achieved it.

'Yesss,' said Luke with a fist–pump.

'Are you sure this is okay?' asked Sophie, as they walked towards the vicarage, Luke running on ahead.

''Course. Ells makes far too much every week. His quantity control isn't honed. Plus we like to drag someone else along.' Then Tracey lowered her voice. 'Miss Bird has been angling for an invite for months.'

'Miss Bird?'

'Miriam Bird, the Sunday School teacher. The one who was away on the days they did art lessons at school.' She thumbed behind her. 'The one who's just been analysing your every feature. I have to whisper, because Luke has ears like a bat. Miriam considers Ells her own personal property. She'd be in like Flynn if she knew that he was in the process of getting a divorce.'

Tracey unlocked the vicarage and the smell of roast beef greeted them as warmly as an old friend. *A gentleman's residence* is how an estate agent might have described the house. There was lots of dark wood on the walls, thick blue carpeting and cast-iron radiators pumping out heat. The ceilings were high with period coving and an impressive staircase with a chunky wooden bannister led up to the next floor. This was the sort of house where you kicked your shoes off at the door and were instantly at home, thought Sophie.

'Come through,' said Tracey, leading Sophie into a kitchen which was large, square and light. Whoever had made the curtains at the windows had attempted elaborate swags and tails and shouldn't have, Sophie noticed. A well-meaning or keen-to-impress parishioner, she guessed.

'Ells likes to cook. This is his kingdom – Ells' kitchen,' said Tracey, hooting at her own joke as she switched on the heat under various pans. 'He prepares everything before the sermon. I'm only allowed to turn on knobs. He goes ape if I do anything else. He's a total control freak in here.'

'Thank you,' Sophie was suddenly moved to say. 'For this, for the use of the almshouse. It's so very kind of you.'

'Oh, don't be daft,' said Tracey. 'We'd be shit Christians if we didn't help people who needed it. I wish we had the money to do something with the almshouse. Or, plan B, we could sell it to someone who did, then we could do some-thing useful with the cash for the community.'

'You must have had interest.'

'Yes, from builders who've offered peanuts because they want the land, until they find out they can't pull it down because it's a listed structure. It would be nice to see it restored to its former glory, as it was when Kitty had it. I think she'd like that.'

The sound of the front door opening, and a man's cheery voice calling, 'Hello, hello.' Then Elliott Bellringer strode into the kitchen. 'Okay, I'm here, back away from the stove, sister.'

'See, told you,' said Tracey.

Elliott checked the stove knobs. 'Give me five minutes to get changed. Don't touch a thing.'

Sophie smiled. 'He really does take it seriously then, you weren't joking.'

'He's the sort of control freak you could easily live with, though. Come and help me lay the table.'

Elliott reappeared as Tracey was putting Luke's special cutlery out with the Thomas the Tank Engine tops. He had changed into jeans and a camouflage T-shirt that showed off his toned arms and Sophie was reminded why women of the parish might wish they were in her position right now. Oh my, if they only knew what her position actually was.

'Tracey, horseradish please,' said Elliott, slipping on an oven gauntlet.

'He makes his own,' said Tracey with a fond tut. 'And look what's for afters.' She opened the fridge and pointed to a raspberry Pavlova on the second shelf. 'Proper little Mary Berry. Luke calls it crunchy pie and it's his all-time favourite.'

Elliott swung a sizzling roasting tin out of the oven, put it down on a trivet to rest and covered it with a square of foil. 'Lunch will be served in twenty-five minutes exactly, after the Yorkshire puddings come out.' He then began to madly whisk the contents of a bowl before spooning the batter into hot tins in the oven.

'Who's looking after the inn?' Sophie asked Tracey.

'My second in command. An atheist,' said Tracey. 'I always have Sunday off. Sundays were always precious to us. My mum wasn't well for years and Dad coped best he could but somehow on Sunday, just eating together and talking around the table set us up for everything life threw at us.'

'I'll call Luke,' said Elliott, stepping out of the kitchen to shout up the stairs and summon his son.

'I think we were both trying to replicate the happy family thing with our respective partners, but it never happened,' said Tracey, quietly. 'I also think we are both closet Italians, wanting that whole barking across the table at each other and waving garlic bread around scenario. Like they do in *Goodfellas*. Do you know what I mean?'

Sophie had never seen the film but she could imagine, and nodded.

'Do you think you'll ever take the plunge again, Tracey, given the chance?'

'If Gerard Butler comes a-calling, I may consider it, yes,' said Tracey. 'Okay, I jest. There is . . . someone. He's a local builder, solid and lovely, a widower – lost his wife nearly two years ago and he's got a teenage daughter who's still hurting and she won't let me in, so we're taking it slowly and carefully. It's a shame because I lost my mum at the same age as Jade was when Jenny died and so I know what she's going through more than anyone else in this village, but . . . she misses her mum and she has a lot of healing to do. She was at church today, you might have seen her. Long dark-red hair and very serious expression disguising a lot of tears. She doesn't go much, but it would have been her mum's birthday yesterday so I know she was feeling raw. Wanted to light a candle for her. Funny how the simple act of lighting a candle used to work for me too when we lost Mum.'

Luke charged into the room at that moment and threw his arms around Sophie's legs. Sophie stood stiff like a tree, not knowing what to do, whilst Tracey peeled him off.

'Pom, do you like eating?' Luke asked then.

'I do, very much,' Sophie said, with just the lightest touch of a French accent.

'Do you like crunchy pie?'

'It is my absolute favourite pudding.'

'Are you my daddy's girlfriend?'

'Er . . . no . . . I am a friend.'

Elliott rubbed his forehead. 'Luke Bellringer, go and wash your hands please. Pom, I apologise.'

'Out of the mouths of babes and sucklings,' laughed Tracey. 'That rumour didn't take long. Lock your door tonight, Pom. You'll be having late-night female visitors armed with machetes.'

Lunch was delicious, served with home-made beetroot wine made by a parishioner, though it tasted nothing like beetroot. Luke had Ribena and after a portion of crunchy pie he went off to play and conversation could leave the banal and enter the realm of the more entertaining.

'So, you've set the cat amongst the pigeons it seems, Pom,' said Tracey. She turned then to her brother. 'Wait until Mrs Braithwaite gets back from her cruise.'

Elliott stabbed a finger at his sister. 'You are a minx, Tracey Green.'

'Mrs Braithwaite is the flower lady,' explained Tracey. 'Totally fixated on Elliott, despite being married for forty years. Mr Braithwaite has long accepted that if Ells happened to declare undying love for his wife, he'd be turfed out of the house immediately.'

'It won't happen,' Elliott said, twinkle present in his eye, 'just in case you were wondering.'

'An incumbent vicar is a special prize. The bishop warned him how possessive some members of his flock could become. Especially about an unmarried vicar who looks like him.'

'A rare compliment, sister,' said Elliott, viewing her with wonder.

'Don't get too used to the phenomenon,' Tracey batted back.

'By the way, it's not me, it's the uniform. I'm under no illusions,' Elliott explained for Sophie's benefit. 'It's not an uncommon problem amongst the clergy.'

Sophie couldn't imagine anyone getting so possessive over the horrible old vicar who was allied to her school. She was pretty sure that looking like Ells Bells had something to do with the amount of mascara and lipstick on display in church that morning.

'The role is not without its complications,' added Elliott. 'Especially when you're relatively young and move into a community used to an old church that sadly does not exist any more, and reluctant to move with the times. I had to drag Little Loste into the twentieth century before I could even attempt the twenty-first.'

'He should write a book,' said Tracey. 'He has the best stories. Tell Pom about the nativity when Miriam cast the Dobson twins as Mary and Joseph and they had a fight and pulled baby Jesus's head off.'

Elliott threw up his hands. 'Well, there's nothing left to tell now, is there? But yes, Pom, my sister is right, I have some great stories. And one day I just might write a book.'

'How long have you been the vicar here?'

'Five years. And in that time I think I've seen it all. Drunken godfathers at christenings, fights at funerals, a mother of the bride trying to stop a wedding. But I've also officiated at some wonderful and moving occasions, met some brave and fabulous people. Little Loste is a special village. Somewhat old-fashioned but its heart is in the right place.'

'We lived in Whitby when I was married, but I'm a village person at heart. So is Ells, aren't you, bruv?'

'Yes. I'm very happy here. And so is Luke.'

'He's getting a kitten next week from the rescue centre and is beyond excited,' said Tracey. 'Imagine the visitors you're going to have, Ells, all those female visitors wanting to stroke your animal.' She gave him a very exaggerated wink.

'You're absolutely incorrigible,' he tutted, a grin pulling up one corner of his mouth.

'It's odd because Luke has an aversion to furry things. Furry toys freak him out and so do dogs, yet he loves cats with a passion.' Tracey cut herself another sliver of crunchy pie and put it in her mouth whole.

'I've never had a cat,' said Sophie. 'We had dogs when I was growing up. Great Danes. I missed them so much when I was at school.' *I had to stay there one summer and when I went back home at Christmas they'd both died and no one even told me.*

'I've got a cat,' said Tracey. 'Old, deaf and white. When I lived in Whitby, the neighbours moved house and left him behind, which was nice of them.' She made a face that indicated exactly what she thought of them. 'He's more or less an extra sofa cushion but I love him dearly. Deaf Jeff. Luke adores him. Oh heck . . .' she looked at her watch and then sprang from her seat. 'I promised Dave he could leave early today to watch the darts. I'd better shoot off. Pom can help you do the dishes. Sorry, folks. Must dash.'

'I'm perfectly capable of doing the dishes,' said Elliott, 'I wouldn't ask our guest.'

'I'd be delighted to help,' said Sophie.

Tracey gave her brother a kiss on the top of the head, mouthed 'got to go' at Sophie and then called up the stairs to her nephew on the way out. 'Lukey. I'm rushing off, if you want a kiss shout now or forever hold your peace.'

'Auntie Tracey, I want a kiss.'

'Okay, I'm coming up.'

Footsteps thundering up stairs.

Elliott raised his eyebrows at Sophie. 'Why do I always feel as if she got more than her fair share of the family energy?' he said, pushing his Clark Kent glasses back up his nose.

Sophie smiled and stood to collect the plates.

'No, no,' he protested.

'I insist,' she protested back. 'You've both been very kind to me. Let me help in some small way.'

'It's not necess . . . okay, I relent.' Elliott held up his hands in surrender and walked across to the dishwasher. 'Do you usually do the big Sunday lunch thing at home then?'

'Not really. My husband often plays golf on Sunday. And if my parents or in-laws come over, our housekeeper does the cooking. I'm not a great cook, I'll be honest, all that co-ordination . . . so I leave it to the expert. It's not my strength.'

'And what is your strength then, Pom?'

'My strength?' Was being an ornament a strength? Or a weakness. She wouldn't have admitted that anyway, it was pathetic. 'I'm not sure I have one.'

'Everyone has a strength.'

'I don't know if it's a strength, but I love to sew and garden. If anything, sewing is what I'm best at. A hobby rather than a strength, I would have said, though.'

'My mother loved to sew when we were little,' said Elliott, with a soft smile of nostalgia. 'Where did you learn, school?'

'No, you have no idea how bad the homestyle and domestic science teachers were there.' Sophie puffed out her cheeks, thinking about horrible Miss Branchester who took flower arranging and whipped your hands with thorny rose stems if your Oasis crumbled. 'One summer I had to stay behind, as a punishment. A whole summer of extra school and – long story, but – I ended up staying at the cook's house in Briswith instead. I had some wonderful weeks beachcombing and hanging around with kids my own age and in the evenings the cook, Mrs Ackroyd, taught me to sew and crochet and knit, but sewing was my thing. I wish I'd had time to grab my sewing machine when I left, but it might have been a bit damaged by throwing it over the wall.'

She laughed then, even though it wasn't really anything to laugh about. Elliott wasn't laughing, his mouth was a serious line.

'Have you any plan of action?'

'Absolutely none,' replied Sophie, certain at least about her uncertainty. 'I have no idea what to do at all. I remember Mrs Ackroyd once saying to me' – and she imitated her heavy Yorkshire accent as she quoted her – '*as we say rahnd here, if you don't know what to do, do nowt.* So that's my plan of action for now: do nowt.' Sophie didn't even want to open the door to her options. It felt as though if she did, what lay behind that door would fall forward and bury her.

'Mrs Ackroyd sounds a very wise woman. Let me get you a coffee. Tracey bought me a machine for my birthday. It's very good. She gives cool presents.'

'Thank you, Elliott, I'd like that.'

She watched him pick out a coffee pod from a rack, press a button on the machine and then, when nothing happened, consult the book that stood behind it.

'I haven't used it very often,' he explained. 'Ah, here we go. Might help if I switched it on at the mains first.'

The machine sprang into life then made a strangled noise of pain.

'Is there any water in the reservoir?' Sophie prompted.

'Oh bollocks . . . No. Good point.'

Now she did laugh. 'Are vicars allowed to say *bollocks*?'

'I shall deny I did so if you decided to quote me,' said Elliott, a smile in his voice, as he filled up the reservoir. He pressed the button again and gave a finger snap of victory as a stream of coffee hit the awaiting cup. He brought the two cups over to the table and set them down. 'Wait. I have hot milk as well.' He darted back to the machine to empty some custard-thick froth into a jug. 'Be impressed,' he said.

'I am.'

'I was a policeman for three years before I joined the club,' he said. 'I always wanted to serve the community and I think I managed that, even though I was very young. I considered myself a fair cop and I enjoyed it, but there was something missing for me. It wasn't enough.' He proffered the sugar bowl, she refused it.

'So what made you change professions, because that's quite a leap?'

'Dad was very ill. I was sitting with him in the hospital, holding his hand. I didn't really have a lot of time for God back then because I didn't think he'd particularly done much for us. But you grab at any passing straw sometimes so I prayed, prayed really hard that Dad would have a gentle passing because he'd had a hard life and I didn't think he deserved a hard death too. And just before he died he opened his eyes and he said to me, "I've loved it, son. I've loved it all." He was so lucid, more lucid than he'd been for weeks, and I was filled with this incredible feeling of . . . love, joy even: I know that sounds strange because my father was dying, but it was so powerful. I hadn't considered that my father could have enjoyed his life as much as he did, because he'd struggled so much, but love had made it all worthwhile and at the moment he passed, it was as if I had a glimpse into a . . . magnificence beyond the realms of any human understanding. And trust me, Pom, I tried to rationalise this, pigeonhole it into hysteria or grief, but it wouldn't fit neatly into any slot. What I had been put on earth to do is what I'm doing now and it is exactly where I belong. Tracey was worried I was mad, deranged . . .' He closed his eyes, aware of what he was saying. 'Oh goodness, I'm sorry. Not the sort of terminology you need to hear. I apol—'

'Elliott, it's fine. I know I'm okay up here,' and Sophie tapped her forehead.

'I'm sure you are. Are you a Christian?' Elliott asked.

'I was raised as one,' she replied.

He mused for a moment. 'A careful answer. It's conversation, not a judgement call.'

She swerved it. 'I think it's wonderful that you've found your place in life. I envy people who have done that. I always felt as if I was on the sidelines, cheering other people on but never actually joining in on the game. Some people never do find their place though. Maybe I'm one of those.'

She smiled at him, looked into his blue, blue eyes and something stirred inside her. Something that had no place stirring. She drained the coffee cup and stood.

'Thank you for lunch, it was really lovely of you to invite me.'

'Happy that you came. I have an appointment in

Winmark tomorrow morning. Would you like to drive in with me, see St Bathsheba's again?'

Her first reaction was *absolutely not*, but what came out of her mouth was 'Yes. Yes please.' She had no idea why she would to revisit it because she could still remember the euphoria of ripping up her blazer on her last ever day there. She'd torn it apart with her bare hands.

'If you can be here for quarter to nine, I'll drop Luke off at the nursery on the way.'

'I will be here on time.'

At the door she remembered to ask, 'Elliott, do you have a torch I can borrow, please?'

Hanging up on a coat hook was a monster-sized torch.

'Another present from Tracey. She is the queen of practical gifts,' he said, handing it over.

Chapter 23

John slammed down the phone. 'Bloody ridiculous,' he announced to the six people sitting around the dining table. 'The police cannot trace someone who does not want to be traced, they say.'

'Well they do have a point, why waste their resources?' asked Edward.

'Because Sophie clearly isn't sane?' suggested Davina.

'She was sane enough to pack a suitcase, climb out of the attic window and escape over the neighbour's wall,' countered Edward. They'd found the CCTV footage and in his eyes, Sophie had been very resourceful. She was probably the most sane amongst them all.

John rattled a newspaper. His face was front page again. Rebecca had decided to reveal even more sexploits. Most of them true but some of them – such as that he had worn her leopard-print thong whilst arguing with Lena Sowerby in the House of Commons – were grossly mendacious.

'Why isn't there a terrorist incident when you need one?' he screamed heavenwards.

'John, what a terrible thing to say,' remarked his mother.

'He means, to bury that bloody woman,' said his father.

There was no other scandal, no bombs, no volcanos erupting, nothing – the playing field was clear for Rebecca Robinson's bedroom shenanigans with John to monopolise the headlines. The only thing that could rescue him was Sophie standing at his side, dismissing the red-haired whore for the piece of flotsam she was. Trivialising her as mere human error on his part. Len had devised a counter-blitz from Sophie 'in her own words'. The tragedy of their son dying, bottling up all that emotion in public, though in private it poisoned their marriage, had made John lonely enough to turn to a woman he thought he could trust as a friend. A woman to talk to, but one who manipulated the situation in order to use him for her own personal gain. Len had done a terrific job in preparation but they needed Sophie to blow Rebecca out of the water. John wished above all that they had a child because that could have saved them; Rebecca would have looked extra-vicious for trying to break up a family. When he found Sophie, he'd suggest they adopt; that would make her happy and he supposed he'd get used to the idea. To get him back on course and into number ten, he'd do it. He'd shag Lena Sowerby if that's what it took; that's how far he was prepared to go.

'Where can she have gone to?' John directed this at Sophie's parents. 'Isn't there some place in her childhood that was special to her?'

'Not that I can think of,' said Alice. 'We holidayed in the Far East mainly and you said she hadn't taken her passport.'

'And you're sure she hasn't contacted her sisters?' asked Celeste Mayhew. Edward made a loud 'huh' sound and all heads turned to him so he tried to pass it off as a cough.

'Friends?' asked John's father. 'She must have told someone.'

'There's only Elise Penn-Davies and she hadn't a clue,' replied John. 'Elise couldn't keep a secret if her life depended on it, she'd have blabbed in an instant.'

'What about that girl at school?' asked Angus Calladine, as something flagged up in his hippocampus. 'The one she saved from drowning.'

'Oh, her.' Alice's disapproval was obvious. 'That Birch girl? Elm? Oak? Beech? Some tree name. It's so long ago now.'

'She saved someone from drowning? I didn't know that,' said John.

'She was lower working class,' said Alice, 'and I wouldn't be too impressed because Sophie almost murdered another girl in the process. A Russian oligarch's daughter, no less. She was severely punished for that episode and quite rightly so. Any *friendship* was nipped firmly in the bud.'

Again Edward muttered something and John, who was operating on the cliff-edge of his nerves anyway, had had about enough of his brother's asides.

'If you have a contribution to make, Edward, please make it an audible one so that we can all share in your razor-sharp powers of observation.'

'I don't. I was simply wondering how she was punished.'

'What's that got to do with anything?' asked Davina.

'I'm just curious.'

'She stayed at school through the summer,' said Alice. 'She was denied a marvellous trip with us visiting Cambodia and Thailand, Japan, China, et cetera at the pleasure of various members of the diplomatic corps.'

'I would have thought a much more horrible punishment would have been to come home for an extra term,' said Edward. Davina elbowed him sharply.

'Nonsense,' said Angus Calladine, not quite getting what Edward was intimating. 'Sophie hated St Bathsheba's so it was a very fitting castigation. She didn't go around saving anyone else's life after that, let me tell you.' And he guffawed in a 'so there – point proved' manner.

Edward sighed. 'No wonder she buggered off.'

'That really helps, Edward. Thank you,' said John, turning to his brother and giving him his best withering glare.

'So she wouldn't have gone up to Yorkshire, then?' asked Davina.

'Quite categorically the last place on earth she would venture,' said Alice.

'Or maybe' – John clicked his fingers – 'the first place she'd go, presuming that we would think it would be the last.'

'Trust me on this,' said Alice, with a strange level of pride. 'I think St Bathsheba's scarred her enough to stay away from the North of England for ever.'

Edward removed himself from the table. 'Going for a smoke,' he said, using his habit as an excuse to head outside, although really he wanted fresh air in his lungs and distance from all the people in the room without exception. If that was sanity, he would prefer to be as mad as they all thought Sophie was. He hadn't fully realised until she had left just how little she was valued. Seeing the footage of her hoisting her case over the wall whilst her own family *and her husband* conspired against her had given him a pain in his heart and he wanted no part of any discussion about having his sister-in-law committed to a hospital in order to get John F. Golden Bollocks out of a scrape of his own making.

He hoped dear Sophie was holed up in a very luxurious hotel with a copious amount of champagne and access to the best solicitor John's money could buy her.

Chapter 24

Sophie had only been asleep for a short time that night when she was awakened by a noise deep in the bowels of the house. She sat up abruptly, listened hard, dragged on her tracksuit bottoms, slipped her phone into the back pocket and reached for the giant torch which she had borrowed from Elliott Bellringer that same day. She heard the squeak of a door opening slowly somewhere and the tinkling of a bell.

There was a ghost at St Bathsheba's that was rumoured to manifest itself as a cold shock of air outside the first-years' dormitory. She didn't believe in ghosts (though she might have had she ever seen one) but something had definitely set the hairs on the back of her neck standing to attention on many an occasion there. A ghost would not have been her first conclusion on hearing a noise in this house though.

Sophie stole outside into the hallway then stood still and silently there until she was rewarded by more sounds. Someone or thing – but more likely some*one* – was in the cellar. She padded across to the door under the stairs that led down to it, placed her hand over the round brass knob and as she was about to turn it, it turned from the other side. *Here goes*, she thought, taking in a fortifying breath. She switched on the torch, ripped open the door.

'Hello Kitty, nice to meet you,' she bellowed and caught sight of someone in black thundering back down the stairs, until the sound changed to someone falling down them to the musical accompaniment of a bell and 'Shit, shit, shit.' A female voice, she reckoned. Her first thought was Miriam Bird.

Sophie walked down the steps towards the crumpled figure rolling around in pain at the bottom.

'Who are you?' she demanded, shining the torch at the intruder. Whoever it was was wearing a dark woolly hat and was a totally different shape to Miriam Bird, but definitely a woman, a tall, slim one who was now trying unsuccessfully to struggle to her feet.

'Okay, if you won't tell me you can tell the police,' said Sophie, reaching for her phone.

'Don't, I'm really sorry. Shit, my leg.'

Sophie saw dark red hair underneath the hat. 'I recognise you,' she said then. The girl in the church, the one whom Tracey had told her about who had lit a candle for her mother. 'Jade, isn't it?'

'Who?' said the girl.

Nice try. Sophie picked up the bell from the bottom stair and tinkled it. 'Pretending to be a ghost by any chance?' she asked, remembering to add in a touch of French accent.

'I can't get up.' Jade gave a pitiful cry of pain.

Sophie bent to the girl. 'Put your arm around my shoulder.'

'Ow, ow, ow,' Jade said as she attempted to stand.

The stairs were wide enough for them both to go up side by side, Jade forced to rely on the support of a woman who was obviously stronger than she looked. Sophie led her into the bedsit, switched on the light, plonked the girl on a chair, then with one fluid movement, pulled off the hat so she could fully see her face.

'Right, now, *mam'selle*, if you could tell me what the hell you are doing here I'd be much obliged.' Sophie stared hard at her: the girl shrugged and avoided eye contact but, as she had no chance of running off, the impasse became increasingly uncomfortable.

'Well? Your father is the builder, isn't he? Shall I give him a call to come and fetch you?'

Now the girl did answer. 'No,' she said. 'Look, I'm sorry, okay. I used to like to come here sometimes. It's usually empty. I didn't realise someone was staying here when I came in yesterday.'

'Ah, it was you who moved my things around?'

'I didn't take anything. I just looked. I wasn't going to come back when I knew someone was here.'

'But you did – at midnight, tinkling a – how do you say – *une cloche*? A bell? How did you get in?'

'There's an unlocked window in the cellar.'

'Why? Were you trying to scare me?'

That shrug again.

'Okay, I am ringing Tracey and asking for the number of your father.'

'No, please. It's . . . because. Look, it's best if you went.'

'Went? Why? What 'arm am I doing to you?'

Shrug.

A flashbulb lit up in Sophie's head. It couldn't be that obvious, could it? It would be ludicrous if it were.

'Please do not tell me that you fancy the vicar and are trying to—'

'Ugh – gross,' protested Jade. 'Not me. I mean, really . . . that's not what . . . Oh, shit.'

'Well what, then?' Sophie raked her hand through her hair in frustration. She liked it this length, but it did need a proper cut. 'Oh my!' Then the penny dropped. 'Someone asked you to scare me away pretending to be *une fantôme.*'

'I didn't say that . . .'

But Sophie was laughing now. How was it that with the world's worst haircut and a single visit to church dressed in her running gear, she was still engendering hostility? Was that what her purpose in life was? Was that what her *strength* in life was: being a complete annoyance to everyone? Her laughter turned hard and then in a trice to a hiccup, a sniff, a dangerous skirmish with sadness which she reined in very quickly.

'I feel crap now if that helps,' said Jade.

'It doesn't,' said Sophie.

'I'll give the money back.'

'Money? What money? *Mon dieu,* someone paid you to do this?'

Jade clammed up.

'You'd better go home,' said Sophie wearily. 'It's the middle of the night and you really shouldn't be out trying to scare people climbing through cellar windows. What if you had fallen down the stairs and broken your neck?'

'I wouldn't have. I know this house like the back of my hand,' said Jade. 'My mum always said that if she won the lottery she'd buy it and do it all up. Have you had a good look around it? I know they lock up the downstairs rooms now but the bedrooms are fantastic. I like to sit up there and stare out at the sea.'

Sophie was horrified. 'You shouldn't be going there, the stairs aren't safe.'

'Oh, they are. Tracey tells everyone they're not so no one's tempted to snoop.'

'Where is your house?'

'Down the lane a bit.'

'Come on, I'll help you.'

Jade leaned on Sophie and together they hobbled out of the house. About halfway down the hill, she could put some of her weight on her foot, indicating that if it was a sprain, it wasn't such a bad one.

'This is where I live,' said Jade, pointing towards a white-painted house. 'My bedroom is at the back. I climbed through the window. If I go in that way, Dad won't know I snuck out.'

'You are joking.'

'I have to. It's okay, it's on the ground floor.'

They moved as quietly as possible through the side gate.

'You won't say anything to anyone, will you?' Jade whispered, after Sophie had helped to hoist her inside. 'Not even to Tracey?'

'I promise. But I shall be locking the cellar window in the house. If you want to come and visit, please knock on the front door in future.'

Jade smiled at her, which pulled a smile unwittingly from Sophie.

'I'm sorry again. And thank you.'

''Ow much did Miss Bird pay you?' asked Sophie, craftily.

'Twenty qui— Oh shit.'

'Keep the money and tell her that I was terrified. Goodnight, Jade,' said Sophie with a twinkle in her eye.

Chapter 25

Sophie was awake early the next morning and the first job of the day was to venture into the cellar and close off any point of entry that she might find. The basement was cavernous: surprisingly dry, too. There was a door to the outside which had been nailed up and a window beside it which was wedged open. Sophie closed it and shut the bolt and hoped that would hold off any more would-be *fantômes*. Shame her late-night prowler turned out to be human, as she'd rather liked the idea of encountering Kitty Henshaw. She would gladly have been proved wrong on the ghost front and seen one in the flesh, or lack of. She didn't think she would be afraid of Kitty, if she manifested herself. They both had similar tales to tell, both experienced the worst kind of loss, except that Kitty had found a happy ending of sorts. That's where their stories differed. Besides, old houses like this one should have a resident ghost, she thought. Park Court didn't have one. Park Court was too boring and characterless to be interesting to a spectre. Plus it would have been more spooked by the Mayhews than the other way round.

She gave in to the temptation then to visit the upper floor, and just as Jade had reported, the bedrooms were unlocked. There were six of them and a huge bathroom, all in a very tatty state, but the original features were still present and waiting patiently for a day when they could be restored: picture and dado rails, ceiling roses, elaborate cornices. And the view of the sea from up there was stunning, Jade was right about that too. The window framed the vista like a picture that she would never get tired of looking at: pale blue morning sky, a rising sun, a grey sea awakening, stretching towards the beach – nothing and yet everything.

Sophie could have stood there for much longer, taking in a landscape that soothed her soul, but time was ticking and soon she would be visiting a place that would do anything but that. As she was locking up the front door, she noticed the original name of the property, chiselled into the lintel. *Seaspray.* There was something about the house that gave her shivers, but in a thrilling way. The house had a character all of its own, that wasn't in dispute: it was fitting it should have a beautiful name.

She walked round to the vicarage wondering if any curtains were twitching, especially the curtains of Miriam Bird, who had paid Jade to scare her away with *Scooby-Doo*-style tactics. It would be funny if it weren't so tragic.

The door opened before she had even rung the bell. Luke was doing an excited dance on the doormat.

'Well, someone's pleased to see me,' chuckled Sophie. *Which was a change*, she thought.

'Luke has been standing by the window waiting for you,' said Elliott.

Boy, you look good in a dog collar, Sophie just stopped herself from saying.

'Pom, will you take me into the nursery?' asked Luke.

Sophie looked at Elliott for direction.

'No, I'll do it. It would take a lot of explaining why someone whom the teachers don't know is dropping you off.'

'Aww . . .'

'Another time,' said Sophie.

'Yesss,' said Luke, which seemed to appease him.

Luke turned four times to wave to Sophie on the short journey from the car to the nursery door.

'Seems as if my son has taken a shine to you,' said Elliott when he returned.

'That's nice. I'm so used to the opposite reaction,' she said.

'The spotlight can be a very cold place, for all its bright-ness, I imagine.'

'I hate it,' said Sophie. 'Being away from it, if only for a couple of days, has been liberating.' The thought of going back to it, as she would most likely have to in order to undo all the damage, made her feel more than slightly sick. She had made herself into a very tasty morsel for the cameras to devour.

'I wonder if you'd drop me off in Slattercove afterwards,' said Sophie. 'There's a few things I need to buy. I can get a taxi back.'

'No problem,' said Elliott.

St Bathsheba's, despite being redundant, still managed to conjure up the feeling of dread in her that the start of every new term had induced. The building itself was beautiful, quite Hogwarty with its castle-like structure, but she had been part of it, and would never be able to appreciate its splendour objectively. There were too many sour and miserable memories attached to it for her.

'It's quite something, isn't it?' Elliott commented, after they had got out of the car. 'No one really knows what to do with it, though.'

She'd expected it to appear smaller than she remembered but the opposite was true. For a second, she was a girl again, being dropped off for the New Year term in the cold, depressing dark. She shuddered the memory away but St Bathsheba's had become part of her, she would never be able to escape it fully.

Sophie counted along the broken rectangles of glass.

'See that window, fourth from the end, three up. That was mine. The first years share a dormitory but after that you are given your own cell.'

'Interesting choice of word,' said Elliott.

'It was quite nice actually, once you got used to the cold, but the bedrooms were referred to as "cells". In a monastic way rather than a criminal one, that is. Although the whole place sometimes felt like it was a prison.'

A picture flitted into her mind of Magda sitting on her bed with a pen and a notebook entitled 'grooming'. They were both wearing Dead Sea salt facemasks, Magda to clear up her spots and Sophie just to keep her company. Magda was madly scribbling down all the fashion tips that Sophie was dictating to her: everything from how to stop getting lipstick on your teeth to how to stand in order to look extra slim on photographs. She'd forgotten about that until now. She'd really liked Magda. Despite the two-year age gap and coming from worlds apart, they were fundamentally similar. She'd been totally gutted when Magda hadn't come back after the summer holidays.

'They had some very strange doctrines there. You could be a good Samaritan but only in exceptional circumstances. For example you could help out a Russian oligarch's daughter, but not one of the girls who came from a much poorer background on a scholarship as they were merely to be tolerated. Kindness was viewed as weakness; emotion was banned.'

'I see why it was closed down in the end,' said Elliott.

'I have no idea how they got away with functioning for so long. I think Ofsted must have been bribed for years to keep it open.'

'We live in a very corrupt world.'

'You're telling me.'

They walked on, around the high wall that was now topped with razor wire. Anyone who knew the place wouldn't have broken in, only out.

'Outside the first-year dormitory was a staircase that didn't lead to anywhere: it was very odd. We thought a door at the top must have been bricked over. If you went up a couple of steps, sometimes a coldness would descend, a freezing sensation that was very scary. There. You can see where there once was a window.' Sophie pointed upwards. 'There was a story circulating that a pupil had died in there and the icy spot was where her ghost sat. Something angry and trapped and dead.' The thought of being held in that place forever made Sophie shiver. It was bad enough being there for a snippet of time, never mind eternity. 'The rumour was she was beaten to death by a teacher and her body hidden in the walls. The school explained her disappearance by saying she had eloped with one of the gardeners. Despite the lack of any evidence to support that story, we all believed it.'

'Did they hit the pupils there?' asked Elliott.

'They still used to when I first went there, right up until I was thirteen, when it was finally made illegal in independent schools,' said Sophie tightly. 'There was one teacher in particular who would whack you with a cane at any opportunity. Miss Egerton. She'd been a nun once. We all hated her with an absolute passion. She was cruel. I thought she was a shrivelled-up old woman when I was there, but I suppose she must have been not more than ten years older than I am now. Even when she couldn't hit us any more, she still carried her cane with her everywhere and would whack the furniture instead. The sound of it whistling past your ear set your nerves on edge. Not being able to use it made her even more frustrated and vicious. And Miss Branchester used to smack us with thorny rose stems if we didn't arrange our flowers properly. It doesn't sound very brutal but it really hurt.'

'There was a big scandal when the school eventually closed, wasn't there? Huge. A lot of parents said that they had no idea what was going on within the walls,' said Elliott.

'I doubt that,' huffed Sophie. 'Most girls were sent there because their parents knew exactly what was going on within the walls. Centre of academic excellence of course, but with an added hidden curriculum. It was run like some warped Swiss finishing school. They were determined to quash my spirit.'

'I don't think they quite managed,' said Elliott.

Sophie disputed that. Sophie the Trophy was hardly known for being her own woman. If anything, she was the enemy of strong women. She existed in the shadow of her husband, she was good enough to work for him but not good enough to be given a wage for it. She bowed to his will and for her pains he humiliated her in the worst way possible whilst lecturing the British public on keeping their own houses in order. And that same British public now believed that Sophie the Trophy was presently being massaged and pampered back to health, following a mental anomaly, so that she could stand up and tell them all how she had forgiven her very silly husband, that she must learn from this, take it on the chin because it was entirely her own fault that this episode had occurred. She really must learn to be a better wife.

St Bathsheba's had made her cold and controlled, unspontaneous and overly cautious, apart from one wonderful summer when she had run wild with a pack of sun-painted kids and leapt in lakes and laughed.

'I've seen enough,' said Sophie, turning her back on the building. 'I hope they knock it down and build something modern where people can have fun. It was a terribly grim place and I think unhappiness can stain a building indelibly.'

'I agree,' said Elliott. 'Or people can colour it with their happiness. Kitty Henshaw loved the almshouse which is why it has such a merry feel to it. Has she visited you yet, Pom?'

'I thought I heard something moving around last night but I must have been dreaming,' said Sophie, with an inner chuckle.

Slattercove had a weird mix of shops on its High Street, such as The Knit Nurse woolshop, the Whitby Animal Welfare charity shop, a handmade sweet and chocolate emporium, a very expensive jewellers next to a European mini-mart, a gift and card shop and a very beautiful old-fashioned toy shop from a bygone age, called Nancy Kringles. There was a massive blue teddy bear in the window sitting on a ride-on toy train. He was wearing a guard's hat and waistcoat and wore both a whistle around his neck and a hefty price tag. The selection of clothes shops in Slattercove wasn't great either: a couple of ladies' dress shops – Veronica's and A la Mode – Girly Girl, which catered for female teens; Patsy's Pants; Cazual which catered for middle-aged people who favoured the jumble sale look and Seconds Out which sold chain-store rejects. Sophie bought some clothes and underwear, a waffle dressing gown and some sneakers. Then from Bob's Bits and Bobs, she bought bubble bath and washing powder and then walked into a hairdresser's and asked for a trim. She sat in the waiting area for twenty minutes and read the most downmarket tabloid newspaper of them all. The headline was 'MY REBECCA DUMPED ME FOR MP'. Rebecca Robinson's ex-boyfriend was telling the story of how they'd often had threesomes with both men and women, as if there wasn't enough sleaze surrounding the saga. She flicked to the letters page but couldn't escape mention of herself even there. The title of the letter intrigued her. *Blame the Husband, not the Wife.*

It seems to be a common occurrence that in high-profile affairs, the partner of the erring spouse is tarred with an unfair level of blame as seems to be the case with John F. Mayhew and his wife Sophie. Often when this happens, the partner has no idea there is anything wrong in the marriage and that is because there isn't. Opportunity presents itself to said erring spouse who wants to have his cake and eat it so it is grossly unfair to assume that Mrs Mayhew is at fault. I wish her a speedy recovery.

That heartened her, someone coming to her defence. She hadn't considered anyone would do that.

'Ready for you now, love,' said the junior, holding out a nylon gown for Sophie to put on.

'Bloody hell, who's cut your hair? Ray Charles?' asked Betty of Betty's of Slattercove when Sophie was seated.

'My sister,' lied Sophie. 'She's a trainee.'

'A trainee what – butcher?' scoffed Betty. 'I hope you didn't pay her.'

Forty minutes later, Sophie's bob was sleek and even and shiny as a beetle's back. She did look very French and nothing like Sophie the Trophy. In WH Smith, she noticed that John's face didn't appear on the front of the *Telegraph* or the *Guardian*, which would have pleased him, she thought. Apparently there had been a terror attack in Spain and she could imagine him sinking to his knees in gratitude for it. His priority would be that a nutter had gone mad in a van and diverted the heat from him rather than that innocent people had been injured; she knew how his brain ticked.

Tracey was knocking on her door when Sophie's taxi pulled up in front of the almshouse. She has the same cheery blue eyes as her brother, Sophie thought as she walked towards her with her carrier bags.

'Been shopping? Dolce and Gabbana?'

'They were shut, I had to settle for alternatives.'

Tracey grinned. 'Nice hair.'

'It needed a tweak. Betty of Slattercove.'

'Ah, the famous Betty of Slattercove. I bet she's a change from your usual.'

'She was slightly cheaper,' said Sophie. 'Come in, I've

bought some coffee and biscuits.' She unlocked the door and invited Tracey inside.

'Thanks but I'll have to pass as I can't stay for long. Oh, I lied about the staircase being unsafe, I meant to tell you,' said Tracey. 'Now I know you're trustworthy, go and have a poke around the upstairs rooms if you like. The view is quite something.'

'I will. Thank you.'

'It's very warm in here,' said Tracey as they walked into the bedsit. 'Did you make a fire this morning or is Kitty making sure you're comfortable?'

'It's all down to Kitty,' smiled Sophie, dumping her bags. At the mention of her name, a draught blew down the chimney sending a puff of ash from the grate into the room.

'She heard us talking about her,' Tracey said with a soft chuckle. 'Listen, I'm here to ask you a favour. A massive favour, but I totally understand if you wouldn't want to. I haven't got anyone to look after the bar tonight. Dave can't do it and it's Steve's birthday – the builder I told you about. He wants to take me and Jade out for a meal. Hoping to build some bridges and . . .'

'You want me to look after the bar?'

'In a nutshell. I'll chuck in as many bags of nuts and crisps as you can eat.'

'If you give me a quick lesson, I'll be happy to.'

'Really?' Tracey raised her eyebrows. 'I thought you'd say no. I mean I know you're in hiding, so I was expecting that, but I would like to go. Elliott's taking Luke for his swimming lesson and I didn't want to ask him to cancel it because he's hoping to get his first badge tonight and there's no one else I would trust. I know we've only just met but . . . well, I'm pretty sure you wouldn't rob me blind and drink all the vodka. Have you ever ... no don't answer that, of course you haven't.'

'Have I ever run a bar? Surprisingly enough yes. At a charity event last year. I can pull a pint and I can work a fancy till.'

'Nothing fancy about my till,' Tracey assured her. 'But there won't exactly be a rush on and I'll be back before closing. It's a really simple system, no cocktails or anything like that. The most complicated thing you'll be asked for is a bitter top. Old Marshall from down the hill calls in at seven p.m. for a pint of it every night and he'll leave at eight. He sits in the corner and analyses that day's racing results. It's that exciting. Anyone else is a bonus.'

'It's the least I can do for you,' said Sophie.

'If you want to run any clothes through my washing machine whilst you're there, you're welcome,' Tracey offered. 'It's a washer-drier and it's in the room to the side.'

'That would be brilliant, thank you. I bought some washing powder today.'

'Oh for goodness sake, I wouldn't expect you to supply that ... Ells said that he'd taken you to St Bathsheba's today. How was it?'

'Stirred up a lot of memories,' said Sophie. 'Ninety-nine per cent of them awful.'

'Magdalena said the same the last time she was up in this neck of the woods, which would be about seven years ago I think. She lives in London now, you know.'

'I didn't. We sadly lost contact, like you do,' said Sophie. 'I regret that. We had some nice chats. She taught me Scouse and I taught her how to put blusher and false eyelashes on.'

'She'll be PM one day. I hope she is. But she does say that she wouldn't be who she is today if it weren't for that school;

she took a lot of positives from the negatives. And she gives you a lot of credit too. Right, must go. I have to try and make myself beautiful for a man and approachable to a teenage girl. I hope to get a few words out of her tonight that have at least two syllables. If you come over in about an hour that would be grand, Pom.'

'I'll be there,' said Sophie, though she was feeling less and less like Sophie with every hour that passed and more like Pom, who tackled ghosts, charmed young boys and whom people talked to as if she were a real person and not a statue.

Chapter 26

'Here's a price list,' said Tracey. 'There's ice in the freezer next to the washing machine in the side room, but you probably won't need any. Barrel's changed so you don't have that to worry about. Now, what else?'

'Nothing,' said Sophie. 'Go and enjoy yourself. After you've adjusted your eye make-up.'

'Why, what's wrong with it?' Tracey looked at herself in the mirror behind the bar. 'Oh shit, I've gone for smoky and ended up with spooky.' She foraged in her handbag for a tissue.

'Where's your make-up bag?'

'Here,' said Tracey, reaching underneath the counter. 'I always put my make-up on down here, the lights are brighter.'

'Sit on the bar stool,' Sophie commanded. Tracey did as she was told and Sophie poked around inside the pouch.

'Eyes or mouth, not both, that's the rule. I'd go for eyes in your case because they're lovely. Your lipstick is too dark and makes your lips look thinner than they are. Now this rose pink is a much nicer shade.'

'I don't wear a lot of make-up,' said Tracey. 'I don't know what I'm doing with it. I end up looking like a clown.'

'You won't when I've finished with you. Let's start again on the lips. And where's your blusher?'

'I never use blusher.'

'Blusher is an essential,' said Sophie with a tut. 'Next time you go into town, buy blusher. I'll use a little of this pink eye-shadow in the meantime. And some of the white to highlight.'

A few minutes later and Tracey was looking at herself in a mirror with a rose-pink mouth agape.

'Bloody hell, I'm gorgeous,' she said. 'You've given me cheekbones. And kissable lips. Hopefully. Did you learn how do to this at St Bathsheba's?'

'Nope. I just always loved messing around with make-up.' Her childhood masterclass had obviously gone down well with Magda. She wondered if she'd impressed Tina Ackroyd as much and she'd become a make-up artist to the stars, as she'd said she would when her dream was born that summer they spent together. Sophie hoped so.

Old Marshall came in for his pint at the allotted hour.

'How do,' he greeted her, totally unmoved by a new face behind the bar. Or by a French accent. He sat silently in the corner and took out his newspaper. Her own face was on the front of it, her Sophie face. Talk about hiding in plain sight. It was wonderful not being recognised. She'd felt at ease today strolling around Slattercove, no one staring at her, virtually invisible. For the first time in years she felt able to breathe freely, as if fame had somehow constricted her chest.

She busied herself tidying behind the bar for something to do, then when the washing cycle was over, she moved her clothes into the tumble drier. It would be so good to have everything clean. She heard the bell above the door tinkle and went back into the bar to find Miriam Bird and another woman newly arrived. Someone must have told the Sunday school teacher that she was in charge that night and Miriam had come to check her out. Sophie felt a mischievous thrill trip down the length of her spine. She gave the brace of women her widest smile.

''Allo, ladies, can I 'elp you,' she said, shovelling on the French.

'We'd like two gin and tonics, ice and lemon please,' said Miriam. She had a small mouth gathered into a tight little moue, like the top of a draw-string bag.

'Cerrrrtainly,' said Sophie.

'Can you put the lemon underneath the ice please?' asked the other woman.

'Cerrrrtainly,' replied Sophie again, as if her sole aim was to please. 'Do you 'ave any preference as to what jjjjin? Gordons? Bumbay Zaffir? Barf-hitter?'

'Oh, I think we'll have the Bumbay,' said Miriam, a glint in her eye, smirking at her companion.

Sophie held the glasses up to the optic, then put in the lemon, then the ice and popped the tops off two small bottles of tonic.

'You can put the whole tonic in,' said the other woman, also pursing her mouth. They looked very alike as they pursed. Sisters, Sophie guessed. Actually they could have been sisters to Annabella and Victoria as well, because they were partial to a purse and had the resulting lip lines too.

'It always tastes bettair with the lemon under, I think,' said Sophie, handing over the glasses. 'Seven pounds eighty pence, *s'il vous plaît.*'

Miriam fumbled in her purse, counted out the exact money and then went to join the other woman, who had chosen the table by the window.

'Settling in, are you?' Miriam called over.

'Oh yes, thank you very much. Tracey and Elliott 'ave been so kind.'

Another round of compressed lips.

'I can't imagine that almshouse being very warm or comfortable,' said the other woman.

'*Au contraire*, it is lovely and warm. And ...' Sophie leaned over the bar as if about to divulge a secret, 'it 'as a ghost. I have 'eard it in the middle of the night, ringing a bell, moving about, knocking on the wall. At first, I was afraid ... I was petrified.'

'Oh, I couldn't live with a ghost,' said Miriam, patting her chest. 'I have it on good authority there's a malevolent poltergeist in that house. It cut one man's head open by flinging a plate at him.'

Sophie wanted to snigger. 'Oh no, I love the ghost. I say to eet, "Come out and show yourself and say hello, you are welcome. We will share." It is so exciting. I want to see Miss Kitty 'Enshaw so much.'

She saw the two women exchange a quick glance with each other. Did she detect a flash of annoyance?

'Ah – I recognise you. You are Miss Turd the Sunday School teacher, aren't you?' Sophie asked, innocent to the last, as she wiped down the bar top with a cloth.

'Bird. Miriam *Bird*,' said Miriam Bird. 'And my sister Josie here is a teacher at Slattercove Nursery.'

'Very pleased to meet you,' Sophie smiled. 'So you both teach little Luke Bellrin-gurrr? One through the week and the other on Zunday.'

'That's right,' returned Josie Bird. 'Lovely little boy.'

'And zuch a lovely far-ser – *zut alors*! He has the face of *un ange*.' Sophie pretended to fan her face. Which prompted Miriam to snap, 'And he's a married man.'

'Even more attracteev, because he is unattainable, *n'est-ce pas?*' said Sophie, after a split second of thinking *dare I actually poke this fire?* And then deciding, *oh, why not.*

That switched up Miriam's lip-pursing to max. She must only be in her twenties, thought Sophie, yet she was going to have a face like a hessian blanket if she didn't stop frowning and doing that ridiculous thing with her mouth. Sophie would never have mentioned anything like that to another woman, but Pom was a different animal.

'Can I just give you a little advice, Miss Bird?' Pom did not wait for permission. 'I notice that you do ziz . . .' she gathered her lips into a cats bum. 'You 'ave to stop crumpling, because you will get ze smoker's lines and will look so much older than you are.'

'Well!' Miriam's jaw dropped open.

'I am sure that it might be all right for you to say such things in France, *miss,* but it isn't done in Yorkshire,' said Josie.

'But you Yorkshire people are straight-talking, so I have 'eard. And, ladies, my advice is kindly given. If you want to attract a man, you should smile, be 'appy. Not have the face of a *cul de chat*.'

The glass in Josie's hand banged down onto the table as if she were an auctioneer closing a sale.

'Drink up, Miriam, we're going,' she said. 'I haven't come here to be insulted by a *barmaid*.'

'Oh, mademoiselle, please do not take my words the wrong way . . .' Sophie was starting to turn into Poirot now. Her accent was getting stronger with every word. She would be calling for Captain Hastings and Miss Lemon soon.

Miriam and Josie Bird stood, picked up their handbags and stormed out, slamming the door behind them. Marshall looked up from his newspaper, gained eye contact with Sophie, said the immortal line, 'If you put lipstick on a pig, lass, it's still a pig,' and then returned to his newspaper.

From behind Sophie a snort made her whirl round and there, standing in the room to the side of the bar, was Elliott Bellringer.

'Sorry,' he said. 'I came in the back door to check that you were all right. I didn't want to interrupt the floorshow.'

Sophie felt herself colouring. How long had he been there? Had he heard her talking about him having the face of an angel and being even more attractive because he was married?

'I couldn't resist,' she whispered, dropping the accent. 'I don't know what got into me.' Well, clearly Pom had gotten into her.

'It was very funny. I shouldn't laugh, but I did. What was that about the ghost ringing a bell?'

Sophie did a quick track back: she had been talking about the ghost before discussing Elliott's attributes. Aarrgh. He must have heard the face-of-an-angel line.

'Oh, I made that up,' she said.

'Luke's having an hour at his friend's house tonight, in case you think I'm a bad parent and have left him home alone. He earned his badge for swimming a width of the baby pool and he's totally hyper. It's a one-off late one for him,' said Elliott. He was wearing jeans and a leather jacket and looked as if he had just stepped off a motorbike.

'I never thought anything of the sort,' she said. 'Is he happy about his achievement?'

'Er, you could say that. Nice hair, by the way.'

'Betty's of Slattercove.'

A silence fell between them that was charged with a strange energy. If the tumble drier hadn't ended its cycle prematurely and buzzed, it was possible the pair of them would have been standing there forever, held in its grip.

'Washing,' explained Sophie. 'Tracey said I could wash my things here.'

'You're always welcome to use the facilities at the vicarage.'

'Thank you.'

'Do you need any help?'

'Nope, I'm enjoying myself.'

'Okay. I'll be off then if you're in control of everything. There's always some paperwork to catch up with in my job.'

'Good night, Reverend.'

'Elliott's fine. Or Ells Bells. I answer to both.' He smiled, suddenly looking more like Superman than Clark Kent and Sophie felt a kick in her chest. That shouldn't be happening. It really shouldn't. She obviously wasn't in control of everything at all.

Six more customers came in after Marshall had left and were themselves leaving by the time Tracey returned.

'How did it go?' asked Sophie, after she had bolted the door behind them.

'Just pour me a glass of wine, will you?' Tracey said by way of reply.

'Shiraz or . . .'

'Any. Red, white, green, blue, preferably pink though . . . the higher alcohol content the better.'

'That bad?'

'No, it was a lovely evening. Jade actually initiated some conversation . . .'

There was a big pregnant 'but' hanging in the air.

Sophie handed over a large glass of rosé which Tracey almost dived into head first, then asked, 'But?'

Tracey gave a low growl of frustration. 'But ... I have done the most idiotic thing ever to impress.'

'Go on.'

'Jade bought a prom dress on the internet and it doesn't fit. It came from China and there isn't enough time to send it back and change it for a smaller size, so I said I'd alter it for her.'

'Oh, you sew?'

'I do. I told her to give it to me and I'd sort it. I'll have to unpick all the seams though and put them back together again ...' She made an anguished noise. 'Why oh why did I say that?'

'Because you care and you want to help, perhaps?'

'Because I am a total big-mouthed dick, that's more the truth.'

'I can sew if you need any help,' said Sophie.

'Bless you, but I have to do this myself. I promised and I will do it. I'll take it really slowly and carefully and I'll come up with the goods. I've got plenty of time. It's doable. Get yourself a glass and join me.'

'Bless you. I'll have a small one.' Sophie poured herself a glass of red.

'And thank you for standing in for me this evening,' said Tracey. 'I started to feel pretty rotten for asking you when I thought about it. I know you need some space. When people have stayed in the almshouse before, we've always said, *we'll leave you alone to sort out your head and you know where we are if you need us.* I promise, I shan't be asking you any more favours.'

'I really didn't mind,' Sophie replied.

'Yeah, but still. You came here for peace and quiet and the least we can give you is that.'

That night Sophie lay in bed and listened to the old house settling down for the night with the odd creak as it cooled, and as she thought about the Miriam Bird scene, she started to giggle to herself. The more she thought about it, the funnier it got. She couldn't remember the last time she had lain in bed and laughed like that. Indeed had she ever lain in bed and laughed like that? No wonder her own face was so free of lines, because no emotion ever enlivened it. The press wrongly reported she had overdosed on Botox, but that wasn't true. Not much in her life made her smile, and all her sadness was pushed down, hidden. A neutral mask was what she wore; indifference confused people, put them on the back foot. Indifference was control and control was power. *Do not let anyone read your expression.* That's what she had been taught at St Bathsheba's.

She'd enjoyed smiling tonight. She'd enjoyed serving people with drinks and being a teensy bit mischievous. She'd enjoyed being Pom.

Chapter 27

She went for a run early the next morning after being awoken at a ridiculous hour by cacophonous seagulls. She filled her lungs with salt-fresh air and felt exhilarated and liberated. She passed a man with a frisky Golden Retriever and they exchanged good mornings; he didn't have a clue who she was, just a woman on a beach running and that's all she wanted to be to him. She didn't want to think about real life outside this little bubble, but it was there, ready to break in at its earliest convenience. She couldn't live in one room of an old house for ever. She couldn't pretend that Sophie Mayhew didn't exist, because she did; it was Pom No-Surname who didn't exist, and yet out of the two personalities, Pom felt the most real.

As she jogged back to the house, she heard her name being carried on the wind but couldn't see anyone. *'Pom, Pom.'* Then she saw a small hand above the fence at the bottom of the vicarage garden. She ran across to find a grinning Luke.

'Morning, Luke. And how are you today?'

'I got my width badge at the swimming pool yesterday.' The Cheshire Cat had nothing on that grin.

'I heard. Congratulations, you are a real superstar.'

'I'm getting a kitten,' said Luke. 'Will you come and see him?'

'I'd love to,' said Sophie. 'Have you got a name for him yet?'

'I'm going to call him Pom,' replied Luke.

Sophie smiled. 'Really?'

Out of the corner of her eye she detected a movement. Elliott on the back step, waving also.

'Luke Bellringer, get your coat on for nursery now. Good morning, Pom.'

'Good morning, Rev . . . Elliott,' called Sophie.

'Been running?'

'Yes.'

'Bye, Pom,' Luke was walking three steps and then turning round again to wave.

'Go on, Luke, hurry up. I will see you later. Have a lovely day.'

'See you, Pom.' Luke scurried towards his father, who picked him up and carried him into the house and Sophie felt a pang of something painful deep in her chest.

She didn't think about Henry much because it was too raw, even after four years, but whenever she wanted to, she could pull up the picture of his wisp of fair hair and his tiny hands, her lips against his soft little cheek as she kissed him goodbye. She tried not to let herself think about what would have happened had he lived, thrived, grown, because there was no point. There was no, 'Well, Mrs Mayhew, just go back and try again', because there never would be another chance to have a baby. It was a wonder she had conceived at all, the doctors told her. Her uterus was heart-shaped, less romantic than it sounded. Her womb malformed. Inside she was as imperfect as the outside was perfect.

She had never really grieved for her son. Not properly. There had been a 'formal period' of grief for both families until after the funeral and then John had returned to work and it was business as usual, as if they all clicked back onto a 'normal' track, as if their grieving had been scheduled into a diary – but that wasn't how it was for her. Newspapers had commented on the fact that she hadn't been seen to cry in public. One of the broadsheets had carried a story about it, debating the public showing of sorrow, and though the editorial had been sympathetic, the photo they chose to use depicted her with a composed, almost bored expression in the front pew at her son's funeral service, 'inspecting her nails' and she'd never forgiven them for it. How had they even got a photographer into the church to take it? She'd been looking at her bracelet, the teddy bear charm, remembering all the hope in her heart when she'd chosen it; not inspecting her bloody nails.

She'd made the mistake of reading some of the comments under the story:

Hard-hearted bitch . . .

Has she chipped her nail varnish? Quick, get a doctor . . .

Leave her alone, she's just lost her son. Who are you to tell people how to grieve?

She'd spoil her make-up if she cried . . .

She should of cryed. It was her son FFS!

They were right, she should have cried, but she couldn't and she was as disgusted at herself for it. For months, she had felt scooped out and hollow but she had hardly cried.

'It's a terrible thing for a man to lose a son,' said Angus Calladine, when he came to visit her in hospital.

'If it's not meant to be, there's no point in worrying about things you can't control,' said Celeste Mayhew. 'Having children is a privilege, not a right.'

No one had held her, no one had put their arms around her – except for John, briefly – in the days following their son's passing. 'We'll get through this,' he had said, in the same breath as, 'the press want to interview me. I've told them you're not up to it. I'll shoulder it, for us both. I'll make sure they're fully aware of how upset you are so there's no misreporting.'

When she reached the almshouse, she found a bag on the doorstep. Someone had left her a packet of croissants, half a pound of butter and a small jar of jam. A French breakfast from an anonymous well-wisher. That made her smile. She heated up a pastry in the oven and had it for breakfast with coffee whilst she sat at the window and looked out at the view; the sun sparkling on the waves, the clouds scudding across the sky driven by a strong sea breeze. One of them looked like a horse. In the 'summer of Pom' she and the others had lain on the beach and stared up at clouds, finding shapes in them. She hadn't done it since.

That afternoon, Sophie walked down the hill into the centre of Little Loste which consisted of the inn, a knot of houses, a general shop ('Loste Things') that served them all and a post office. A delivery of bread had just landed at the shop and she bought two still-warm rolls as well as some tins of soup and three newspapers, hoping that the shopkeeper wasn't wondering why the Frenchwoman in the tracksuit had exactly the same facial features as the posh woman plastered across the front page of one of them.

'I've put you an extra breadcake in the bag,' said the shop-keeper matter-of-factly, expecting neither praise nor thanks.

'Thank you, you are so kind,' said Sophie, touched by his consideration for the stranger in the almshouse. She smiled at him. No one would recognise her if she smiled. She went back to the house and locked the door on the world – for now. She needed to be alone, to have the luxury of time to think, recalibrate. She didn't want to read any more about John's affair, but she thought she should in order to find a way through the whole mess. Before she opened up the first of the newspapers, she warned herself that any story would be a barrel of chaff and it would be her mission to find the odd wheat grains of truth in amongst it.

Her eyes dropped to the page and she read all about herself, her husband and his mistress. She read hoping to find holes in the story, holes that Rebecca Robinson would slip through and disappear. 'A friend' said John was infatuated with Rebecca, her earthiness and hot-bloodedness. A columnist drew on the polarisation between the wife and mistress: the ice-queen and the hot raunchy lover. There was a comparison chart of ten points: Beauty, Intelligence, Sexiness, Wealth, Wit, Warmth, Class, Education, Fashion Sense, Exes (Rebecca's list was as long as Sophie's was short on that last one). 'Warmth: Sophie the Trophy has the expression of a frozen fish. Is she even flesh and blood?' She stopped reading because she was torturing herself; it had been a bad idea, not a helpful one. She lay on the bed and closed her eyes, tried to drift off. She never counted sheep but instead imagined she was making a dress from scratch: a bright yellow silk gown today. She fell into unconsciousness at the point of tacking in the first sleeve, then dreamed that she was at a family lunch and her own parents had made her sit by herself whilst they welcomed Rebecca into their midst.

She barely moved for the two days after that and knew that she was in danger of sliding down into a pit of depression and self-recrimination. Thank goodness for the voice that spoke up occasionally when she needed it. The voice that resided somewhere in her core and chose not to interfere with her life except when she was teetering on an edge. It had made itself heard the day when Magda was half-drowning and the day in the hospital when she was standing at the side of her baby son in an incubator. *This is not your fault, Sophie.*

The voice was a survival mechanism. There had been no one around for Sophie to turn to, so it had invented itself. A sensible, caring inner being ensuring its own preservation by protecting the whole. It knew that she was a good person, that whatever her outside seemed to show, inside she wasn't cold or unfeeling at all. And now the voice was saying, *Let's go for a nice run, shall we? Let's stop thinking about the opinions of people who don't matter and lies written in newspapers. Let's forget all about Sophie Mayhew and enjoy being Pom No-Surname today.*

She forced herself to take that run and felt better for it. She came back to find a bag on the doorstep once again, this time containing a cottage pie in a dish and some instructions for heating it up. On the back of the note was written: *From Mrs Wilson. Please leave dish on doorstep in a bag when you've done with it and I'll pick it up when next passing.* She imagined Mrs Wilson, whoever she was, making the pie, taking it up in the rain for the poor woman in the church charity house simply because she wanted to. Neither Mrs Wilson, she thought, nor whoever had left the croissants a couple of days ago, would realise just how big an effect their small considerations might have: how they cheered her up when she most needed it, how they highlighted just how much kindness was lacking from her world. Miss Palmer-Price had got it wrong: kindness was not a weakness, it was an essential part of being a human being, a gift to be bestowed upon others, a strength.

She had taken the pie out of the oven and was about to serve it up when she saw Tracey pass by the window en route to the front door, a fully-stuffed carrier bag in her hand.

'Am I being a pest?' she said, when Sophie invited her in.

'Not at all.'

'I said I'd leave you alone.'

'I could do with the company.'

'Really? That makes me feel better then. Something smells good.'

'A cottage pie from Mrs Wilson. There's plenty if you'd like some.'

'I can't take your food,' protested Tracey. 'That would be ridiculous.'

Sophie smiled and took an extra plate out of the cupboard. 'Go on, it's fine.'

'Mrs Wilson's cooking is really good. Had it come from anyone else but her, I would have stood firm. I shouldn't really share it, she made it for you. I'll bring something over to replace it because that would have done you two meals and—'

'Tracey, take this fork, sit down and eat with me,' insisted Sophie. Tracey obeyed her.

'In case you're wondering what's in the bag, Mrs

Braithwaite, the flower lady with the monster crush on Ells Bells, dropped something off at mine for you. One of those snuggle blankets that you put your arms into. She didn't want to disturb you, she said, and asked if I'd deliver it instead.'

'That's very kind of her.'

'I've checked it for poison. If you ever did Greek myths at school you'll know the story of Nessus and Hercules.'

Sophie smiled. 'I know all about the poisoned shirt. Is Mrs Braithwaite a vengeful centaur then?'

'Blimey, you do know your myths.' Tracey spooned mince and potato onto her plate. 'It's still got the price tag on, so she's not palmed you off with any old tat. I'm probably being mean, but she is the sort that would like you to appreciate how much it cost. It wasn't cheap.'

'It doesn't make me feel very good to know that people are spending their money on me when I don't need them to,' said Sophie, pouring out two cups of tea from the pot.

'You being rich enough to buy and sell them all is not the issue here. You need sanctuary and some kindness and that's been freely given.'

'Now the music festival is over, I could go and stay at a hotel somewhere,' said Sophie.

'You could indeed, but you're safe here and established as Pom with no suspicions surrounding you. Plus it's nice to have the almshouse aired every so often.'

'I could pay you some rent.'

'No one stays at the almshouse and pays, Elliott wouldn't allow that. If Richard Branson turned up needing to use it, Elliott wouldn't take his money. Look, just accept some help with no strings. Now eat your pie.'

Sophie sighed and stuck her fork through the buttery mashed potato. Mrs Wilson's cooking really was very good.

'I promise as soon as I've eaten this, I'll go home and leave you alone. I expect you're doing a lot of thinking,' said Tracey.

'Too much,' came the answer. 'I read some newspapers and I feel as if my life is being picked apart.'

Tracey nodded. 'I won't lie to you by telling you that you're wrong.'

'That bad?'

'Well, it's more that the other woman is drip-feeding the press with more and more revelations and rubbishing your husband. If I'm at all representative of the British public, then most of it is thinking that your husband is a top-class idiot and his mistress is a vindictive cow who can't keep her knickers on. Some of her exes have come out of the woodwork to say what an ambitious and ruthless piece of work she is.'

Sophie closed her eyes and let loose a sigh so long that her whole body seemed to deflate. 'I don't even know how to start processing all this.'

'Maybe you shouldn't, then,' suggested Tracey. 'Maybe you should just let things wash over you, pretend that nothing exists outside this patch of Yorkshire. Let your head breathe.'

Sophie considered that and nodded unconsciously. Tracey was right. Let the fire die, let Rebecca tire herself out with her vitriol, let the press get so bored with the taste of the Mayhew name that they turn to something else to refresh their jaded palate.

Let her head breathe.

*

One thing she could plough her energies into whilst she was here was doing something about the garden, because it was a mess and badly in need of some TLC. She loved to garden; it relaxed her, so it seemed the perfect solution, a mutually beneficial project. Sticky weeds were choking the flowers, brambles needed cutting back, dandelions were having a wild party. She'd noticed a shed in the garden and presumed it would either be locked or empty, but further investigation revealed it was neither. It was full of rusty tools hidden behind a thick veil of cobwebs but there was a helpful can of WD40 on a shelf, so Sophie got stuck in to spraying and grappling with the secateurs and shears until they smoothed open and shut and then attacked the overgrown foliage with zeal. She discovered a pair of gauntlets and after bashing them against a wall to remove all the dead insects, they proved handy for pulling at stubborn roots. She ripped and snipped well into the afternoon, energised by Mrs Wilson's pie. It was so much better than carrying on marinating in gloom.

She worked on the garden until it was too dark to see, then she took a bath, slipped on her waffle robe and tried to do something about the state of her nails. Gone were her lovely long talons, and in their place were short, neat ones – at least, they were after she had used her new emery board and buffer on them. But all the better for getting down and dirty with. Her arms were criss-crossed with welts and scratches from all the prickly foliage, but she didn't mind. There were no photocalls on her horizon, no reason to keep herself perfect for the cameras.

It was bliss.

Chapter 28

For the next two days Sophie continued attacking the garden, determined to bring it to heel as if it were somehow representative of her whole life. It helped to think of the brambles as the Mayhew family and dandelions as the Calladines. Chopping them down and pulling them out was psychologically cleansing and she exhausted herself battling with them and winning – in a good way. On the Saturday night, she was just about to strip off her very muddy tracksuit, rest her weary bones in the bath, slip into her dressing gown and then toast herself a breadcake for supper when there was a knock on the front door. When she looked through the window to see who her visitor might be, she saw Jade smiling meekly, holding a carrier bag in one hand and a bunch of flowers in the other.

'Hi,' she said, when Sophie opened the door. She thrust the flowers out. 'These are late. I wanted to come before but I felt a bit . . . awkward.'

'Thank you. Are you coming in?' asked Sophie.

'Don't want to intrude.'

'You aren't.'

'Okay. If that's all right.'

Jade followed Sophie into the bedsit.

'Can I get you a cup of tea or coffee?'

'If it's no trouble I'll have a cup of coffee, please. Can I have it really milky? Oh and this is for you, from Dad.' She put the carrier down on the table. 'It's a curry. Dad made extra so he could send you some, it's his speciality. I said I'd bring it so I could give you the flowers at the same time. They're from our garden . . . to say thank you for not telling on me, not that he knows that's the reason.' She was blushing so furiously that Sophie feared if she didn't stop, her head would blow clean off her shoulders.

'Take a seat,' smiled Sophie. 'It was our secret. There was no harm done.'

Jade sat down on a chair at the table whilst Sophie put the kettle on.

'Feels different in this house when someone's staying in it. Warmer,' said Jade. 'I don't think it likes being empty.'

'It's a very nice house.'

'It's a nice house for thinking in. That's why I used to come here,' said Jade and she let loose a loaded outward breath that signified whatever she needed to think about was deep and serious.

'I see.' Sophie didn't coax her, just made it clear she was listening if Jade wanted to expand on that. Whilst the kettle was boiling, she took a vase out of the cupboard under the sink, filled it with water and put the flowers into it.

'They are very pretty. Thank you, Jade,' said Sophie, setting the vase down in the middle of the table.

'They came from Mum's flower garden. We've tried to keep it as lovely as she did, but she had green fingers. Do you know what I mean?'

'Ah, yes. Magic. I know this,' said Sophie, bringing over two mugs of coffee then. Well at least she had Jade convinced that she wasn't English.

'I read that things get easier when you've been without someone a year ... you know, when you've had the first anniversary of their birthday and Mother's Day and Christmas and their ... when they left you, but it hasn't. Not really. I still miss her so much.' She coughed, shifted in her seat, embarrassed by her show of emotion.

Sophie was in no position to grief-counsel. Not when her method had been to block everything out, keep function-ing, *rally*. She wouldn't insult the girl by passing on the advice she'd been given.

'You've lost your mother. The most significant woman in your life,' said Sophie gently, feeling more than hypocritical because the most significant woman in her own life was the school cook that she'd known for only a short while. 'There is no set time for your heart to stop grieving, Jade. Your feelings don't fit into a schedule, whatever anyone might say.' *Three months is more than enough, Sophie.*

'The principal at school said I should focus on making Mum proud because she'd want me to look forward. Do you think that sounds right?'

'I think your principal is very wise. I think your mother would want you to be the very best you can be – for your-self, though. When you find something that you enjoy doing, the rest ... somehow it falls into place. Do you have any idea what you want to do in life? University? Or look after animals? Be a burglar – or a *fantôme*?' Her voice had a twinkle of mischief in it and Jade smiled.

'I'd love to go to university and do something arty. Not quite sure what course yet.'

'You have to follow your dreams. Make them happen.' Which was rich coming from her, since she was hardly a shining example either as Pom or Sophie. Pom was destitute, relying on charity and Sophie was a pale shadow of the woman she aspired to be.

'I know, I've got two years before I'd go to uni – three if I take a year out. I've got a job in a café in Slattercove at weekends and I'm saving up like mad. Wage is rubbish but the tips aren't bad. I'm determined to go, one way or another.'

Jade could teach her a thing or two about following her dreams rather than the other way around.

'What did you want to be when you were my age, Pom?' asked Jade.

'I always wanted to be the owner of a beautiful dress shop,' came the reply.

'That's doable, isn't it?' said Jade. 'If you could get the money together.'

How ironic that it wasn't so doable in Sophie's world. She easily had the money to open one; it wasn't that which was stopping her.

'I love beautiful clothes. You might not think it to look at me now,' – she gestured towards her muddy garb, and then patted her heart as she went on – 'but in here, I'm like the Fairy Godmother in the Cinderella story. I'd want to make people feel like princesses in my dresses. And princes. I'd have a special section for boys in my shop.'

'You should do it then. Follow your own dream,' said Jade.

'One day, maybe.'

Jade stood up, went over to the sink to swill out her cup and then put it upside down on the draining board. 'Thank

Milly Johnson

you for the coffee, Pom. I hope you enjoy the curry. And thank you for the talk, it helped me.' She smiled. A smile that had real depth to it.

'Did it?'

'Yeah, it did. I do want to make my mum proud and I don't think I am by crying all the time. I think I'd be getting on her nerves.'

'Oh, Jade.' Sophie stood up and put her arms around the girl, pulled her into a tight hug and felt Jade hug her back as if she really needed a woman's embrace. Then Sophie held her at arm's length and spoke directly to her with emphasis.

'Then you have a plan. People who love you want the best for you: to be happy, fulfilled. You will make your mother proud of you by being those things.'

There was a bounce to Jade's step as she walked out that hadn't been there when she walked in. Why was it so much easier to give advice than to take it, thought Sophie as she waved goodnight to her through the window.

*

Sophie honoured the obligation to go to church on Sunday but she was the last to arrive and sat at the back. The Reverend Bellringer's sermon was close to the bone again today and Sophie wondered if he had written it especially for her. It was about trusting God and the example he gave was of a woman crushed by the infidelity of her husband. 'Life happens,' he said. 'God gave us freedom of choice and will and we cannot control our partner's behaviour. Don't blame God for what has happened to you but let God take the wheel. He will direct you. It may be that the right thing for the woman to do is to stay and forgive her husband or maybe she needs to move on. Let him guide you and he will.'

She thought he looked over at her once or twice but she didn't seek eye contact. It felt as if he could see into her head and she might have blushed had she not been so adroit at disguising her true feelings – in public, at least.

As soon as the final prayer had been said, Sophie was first out of the church. It was good that Elliott Bellringer had his faith and he spoke of it convincingly but God had taken the steering wheel of her life and driven her into a ditch. She felt a fraud even walking through the doors here because if He existed at all He would see only darkness in her heart.

Chapter 29

She didn't see another soul until Tuesday. She was hacking at the long grass with a scythe when a scruffy white van pulled up outside and a man she hadn't seen before got out. He was dressed like a scarecrow and she wondered why he was here. She edged slightly towards the rake which was resting against the hedge.

'I passed you earlier on,' he said. 'It'll take you for ever to cut the grass with that scythe even if it were sharp.' He walked to the back of his vehicle and took out a strimmer. 'Do you want to strim or mow?' Then he hoisted out a petrol mower as well. 'I'm Marshall's son, Roger. My dad said you made him laugh last week.'

Sophie's face broke into a smile.

'Oh, thank you,' she said. 'I'd prefer to mow, if I have a choice.'

'Aye, I was going to say as much. This madam is a bit keen,' he said, slipping on some large plastic safety glasses.

He zuzzed around the edges of the garden and Sophie fired up the petrol mower which was ancient and battered but cut through the long grass with ease. Then she went over it all again on the short cut setting. Even halfway to finishing, the difference was incredible and there was now a high compost tip in the far corner. Sophie insisted on knocking up some lunch and they sat on the wall in the sunshine munching on fresh bread rolls from the Loste Things shop, dipped in mugs of soup.

'Thank you, this is so kind of you,' said Sophie.

'My dad used to look after this garden for the church but his back's not been too great,' said Roger. 'He's been proper depressed having to slow down. He says you were a tonic, you didn't half cheer him up putting them Bird sisters in their place. He says it was better than the telly.' He smiled at Sophie. He had three teeth in the top set and three in the bottom, all strangely bright white. Roger actually looked older than his father.

'My dad volunteered me to come down and help you but this is the first quiet day I've had. We passed you earlier on in the car when I took him to the doctors, but you were hard at it. Don't think you'd have noticed him waving at you.'

'I didn't, or I would have waved back to him,' said Sophie, wondering how a buttered bread roll and a tin of soup could taste so damned delicious.

Roger wiped his sleeve across his mouth and put down the mug. 'Come on then. Part two. I'll get the hedge trimmer out of the van and you do a bit of raking.'

Just over an hour later they had finished. Roger stood back to admire their handiwork and nodded approvingly.

'That's better. In fact it's better than it's been for years, but don't tell my dad that. Now, I ought to get back to the missus. I don't want her thinking you've stolen me away.'

Sophie smiled again. 'Thank you for helping me, Roger. The garden looks wonderful after an 'aircut.'

'They don't let anyone stay here who doesn't really need it,' said Roger, picking up the strimmer. 'We count our blessings and help where we can, lass.'

That was more than evident. She'd had more doorstep gifts left recently: a bag of Mills and Boon books, a home-baked loaf, a jar of pickled onions and a block of cheese and a bottle of Radox bubble bath. One night she had lounged in a foaming bath and started reading one of the books but, as dashing as the Italian billionaire hero was, romance was the last thing on her mind.

She wheeled the mower to the back of Roger's vehicle, noticing that in the dirt someone had written with their finger: 'I wish my wife were as mucky as this van' and she laughed.

'If you haven't heard that line before, you must have been living on Mars,' said Roger.

Maybe not Mars, but Sophie certainly felt as if she had been living on a different planet to the one she was inhabiting now.

She was putting the tools into the shed when she heard a familiar voice.

'Hello lady. Pom. Pom. Lady.' She looked over at the fence and saw Luke peering through. She walked over.

'Hi, Luke. How are you?'

'I've got my kitten. Are you coming over to see him?'

'I'd love to,' she said. 'I'm a bit dirty at the moment because I—'

'Oh come now, please . . .'

She saw Elliott appear on the back step, hands going to his waist, head shaking again.

'How did I know where you'd be, Luke Bellringer,' he

said. 'Sorry, Pom, is he making a pest of himself?' He was smiling.

'No, not at all. He was telling me that he has a new kitten.'

'Come and see, Pom, pleeeease.'

'I will, soon, I promise,' said Sophie.

'Pleeeease.'

'You're going to get absolutely no peace until you do, Pom, you do realise this,' called Elliott, lifting up his hands in a *you're stuffed* gesture.

'Maybe later. I've been gardening.'

'Tracey's here. I've made a huge pan of celebratory pasta and you are welcome to share.'

'I don't want to impose on you,' said Sophie.

'You really wouldn't be imposing, there's more than enough to go round.'

Luke started to jump up and down in excitement, repeating the word *please* on a continual loop.

There was no way that Sophie could say no after this onslaught. 'Okay, give me five minutes to scrub up,' she said.

Elliott stuck up his thumb. 'Luke, come and help me lay the table for another person.'

Luke Bellringer ran back up the path like an Olympic sprinter.

Inside the almshouse, Sophie changed into jeans and a T-shirt and the sneakers she'd bought in Slattercove. She had no reason for dressing to impress, which was just as well with the current wardrobe she had to call upon.

She knocked on the vicarage door and it was opened seconds later by Elliott. Behind him a grinning Luke stood holding a tiny black kitten.

'Come in and meet the new addition to the family,' said

Elliott. 'We picked a black one because they're the hardest to rehome, allegedly.'

'Oh my goodness, what a cutie,' said Sophie, bending down to the little boy and his pet.

'He's called Pom,' said Luke.

'Er, no, he isn't,' corrected Elliott. 'He's called Plum. We decided, didn't we, Luke, that it would be unfair to have two Poms living next door to each other: it could cause all sorts of confusion. So Luke chose a name that was close, but not too close.'

'Plum is a wonderful name for a kitten. Much better than Pom,' Sophie nodded in agreement as Luke held the kitten up for her to take.

'Blimey, you're honoured,' said Elliott. 'He wouldn't even let Tracey hold him.'

Sophie had never held a kitten before and she was surprised at how incredibly fragile Plum felt. The kitten pushed his head against her neck, his whole body vibrating with a purr as he snuggled there.

'It was either Plum or Bomb,' said Elliott.

'Oh, right,' Sophie chuckled.

'Me now,' said Luke, reaching for his kitten. Sophie gently extricated Plum's claws from her top and placed him into Luke's waiting hands.

'Come through,' Elliott's span touched her back lightly, to guide her forwards but as soon as it made contact it left her again. She imagined he had to keep his boundaries defined, especially with all the women in the congregation thinking they were his minders.

The kitchen smelled of basil, garlic and tomatoes; a huge pan was sitting on the stove emitting Italian aromas.

'Tracey, Pom's here,' said Elliott.

'In here,' Tracey called from another room.

Elliott pointed to the open door in the corner. 'Go and say hello whilst I dish up. Luke, put Plum down and wash your hands, please.'

Sophie stepped into the next room, a study, she guessed. A dark-green leather Chesterfield sofa sat underneath a picture window – more dodgy swags and tails sat above the curtains – and shelves of books filled two whole walls. The room was dominated by a large mahogany partners' desk, now covered in a chaos of material.

'Hi, Pom,' said Tracey. She both looked and sounded stressed.

'What a beautiful room,' Sophie remarked.

'Ells' study, but I've taken up temporary residence in it. Welcome to prom dress HQ.'

'How's it going?'

'So far, so good.' said Tracey. I've dismantled it all and I'm now in the process of altering it and then putting it back together.'

'Great. Taking the seams apart can be really tricky.' Not as much as reassembling it, but Sophie didn't want to sound like a harbinger of doom.

'And I've blown the dust off Mum's old sewing machine. *Ta da*.' Tracey pointed to the other side of the room where a vintage treadle sewing machine stood.

Sophie's breath caught in her throat. It was almost identical to the old Singer that Mrs Ackroyd had, the one that Sophie learned her craft upon. 'Oh my, that is a thing of beauty.' She rushed over to admire it. 'Does the machine fold down into the table?'

'It does indeed.'

'It's in fantastic condition.'

'It used to be my granny's before it was Mum's. It's been well used, but also very much treasured.'

Sophie pulled open the long square drawers. They were full of cotton reels and pins, needles wrapped in tissue paper, embroidery threads, scissors, buttons.

It meant a lot for Tracey to do Jade's dress, Sophie knew. It would bond them, ease the way forward for their relationship to sprout leaves. There was a lot riding on Tracey getting it right. A true labour of love.

'Tea's up, ladies,' said Elliott.

'Good because I'm pigging starving. So what have you been up to the last few days then, Pom?' asked Tracey as they walked through into the kitchen. 'I noticed you at church on Sunday but I kind of presumed because you were sitting where you were that you wanted to be left alone. Plus you might have felt as if Elliott's sermon about the wronged woman was directed at you. I cringed heartily.'

'It wasn't, for the record,' said Elliott, making a discomfited face. 'It didn't strike me until halfway through that you might think it was and I must confess I had a moment of cringing heartily myself then.'

'I didn't at all,' lied Sophie, taking her place at the table, 'and to answer your question, Tracey, I've been gardening. I thought I'd tidy it up a little and earn my keep. Marshall's son came around today and helped, which was very sweet of him.'

'Worzel?'

'Roger,' said Sophie.

'That's who I meant,' replied Tracey. 'Wouldn't think it to look at him would you that he's a millionaire. Scrap metal merchant. Rich as Croesus. But uses string for a belt.'

'Appearances can be deceptive,' said Sophie, indicating her own clothing, which caused Tracey to hoot.

'Absolutely, take my brother there. Mild-mannered man of God or ninja?'

'Auntie Tracey, what's an nininja?' asked Luke.

'Oh, Tracey,' tutted Elliott bashfully, passing around a plate of garlic bread covered with cheese.

'Someone who does all this sort of stuff,' said Tracey to Luke, chopping her hands everywhere and making noises like a very badly dubbed Japanese film.

'You do martial arts?' asked Sophie, raising an impressed brace of eyebrows.

'I do.'

'He's a black belt in karate.'

'Throwback from the police days,' Elliott tried to explain his skill away.

'And what's that thing with the stick?' asked Tracey. 'He can do all that fancy stuff with it.'

'Kendo,' said Elliott, clearly not comfortable with being bragged about. 'Anyway, tuck in.'

'He goes running on the beach sometimes too, he's very fit,' added Tracey, as if she were selling her brother at a slave market.

'It is permitted for vicars to exercise, surprisingly. *Mens sana in corpore sano* and all that,' said Elliott, with a faux-serious nod. 'We also feel the cold and visit McDonald's occasionally like normal men.'

'And I once came in and found him watching *TOWIE*,' said Tracey.

'No way.' Sophie gave a faux-gasp.

'Yep, all the stuff that other people do,' said Elliott, scratching his neck. An unbidden picture of him about to do something very temporal slipped into Sophie's mind and she chased it off quickly because it had an X rating.

Elliott shifted the conversation away from himself and onto his son. 'Luke does baby judo. He should have been going tonight but ...'

Sophie and Tracey both gave an understanding nod.

'... there was no way, not with a new kitten on the block,' Elliott carried on.

'No way, José,' said Luke, stuffing a huge forkful of pasta into his mouth.

'How do you manage to juggle it all, Elliott?' asked Sophie. 'I don't imagine the job is nine to five.'

'Well, like any other single parent family, you just do. Tracey helps; Luke's best friend's mum picks him up and drops him off from nursery sometimes. People *muck in*, as we say here.'

'Little Loste might be small, but there's plenty of community spirit,' added Tracey. 'Although I wish they'd centre it around the pub a little bit more than they do. I might actually make some money then.'

'Slattercove is becoming more attractive to holiday-makers,' said Elliott. 'They've spent a fortune cleaning it up, building a funfair, restaurants. The death of the fishing industry hit this area hard; it's taken an age to recover and reinvent itself, but it's getting there.'

'And Ren Dullem has become quite a popular spot,' said Tracey. 'Once upon a time it was like the Forbidden City.'

'How come?' asked Sophie.

'No idea,' Tracey answered, through a mouthful of pasta. 'Very odd place. It was dying on its arse until a few years ago ...'

'Auntie Tracey, that's a naughty word,' said Luke, giggling.

'Yes, *Auntie Tracey*,' said Elliott with emphasis.

'Sorry, Lukey. Naughty Auntie Tracey,' said naughty Auntie Tracey, slapping her own hand. 'Ren Dullem was a really unfriendly place, you never felt welcome when you went there ... so no one went there. It was like something off one of those horror films where all the locals are nutters. Then a couple of years ago, it threw open the doors and said, "Come on in, folks." It's a sweet little place now with a gorgeous café. Luke and I go sometimes for ice-cream. Oh and here's something I bet you didn't know, this area was renowned for sightings of mermaids. Apparently – and listen carefully, Lukey, because this will probably come up in your History A-level and you heard it here first – a lot of the ships from the Spanish Armada were blown off course and were chased up the east coast by English ships and they mysteriously sank in these waters, though the English ships didn't.' She pressed her face close to Luke's. 'Mermaids scuppered them.'

'*Reines de la Mer*,' said Sophie. 'Queens of the sea, that's what they used to call them in the place in France where I lived for a year when I was doing my degree.'

'That must have been a nice experience. Did you enjoy it?' asked Elliott.

'I did.' She'd often wondered why she didn't go back after she'd graduated. Worked in a French fashion house and not taken the temporary position at *Mint* in London. *It must have seemed the right idea at the time* was the best answer she could come up with. 'I enjoyed living by the seaside.'

'My mummy lives in France,' announced Luke.

'No, she doesn't,' said Tracey. 'Whatever makes you think that, Luke?'

Luke shrugged. 'I've had enough tea. Can I go and play with Plum?'

'I suppose so,' said Elliott, 'though it looks as if Plum is asleep. He's only a baby so don't wake him.'

'I'll tell him a story,' said Luke, heading for a stack of books piled in the corner.

'Where's that idea come from?' asked Tracey quietly. 'Joy isn't in France. Is she?'

'No,' said Elliott. 'Wigan. I think maybe Elliott is fusing her with Pom here.'

'Oh my. I don't want to mix him up . . .'

'It's not your fault. If he gets things confused, we correct him when we need to without making a fuss,' Tracey insisted. 'Have you sent the divorce papers back, Ells?'

'Not yet,' replied Elliott.

'Bitch from hell. I never did see what you saw in her. Joy. Huh. The name couldn't suit her less,' Tracey said with a huff.

'One of the teachers at St Bathsheba's was called Merry Egerton,' said Sophie. 'You couldn't meet a more horrible woman ever.'

'Elliott could.'

'Tracey, behave yourself,' said her brother. 'Stuff some more bread in your mouth.'

'Don't mind if I do,' she chuckled and reached for a hunk of it. 'I hope when you get divorced she goes back to being a Wisbey and leaves our surname to nice people who deserve it.'

'I have no control over that, have I?' said Elliott.

'It's a perfect name for someone who belongs to the church,' Sophie commented.

'But not so much for a murderer,' put in Tracey. 'One of our Bellringer ancestors was shipped over to Australia for slitting someone's throat. Got off lightly in my opinion.'

'Yes, don't be fooled.' Elliott grinned. 'The Bellringers have a chequered history.'

'Why didn't you go back to being a Bellringer, Tracey?' asked Sophie.

'She's hoping she'll soon be a Darlow, that's why,' said Elliott.

'Oy, that's a lie. Well . . . okay, maybe it's a little bit true; but there are so many forms to fill in, is what I'll admit to,' Tracey replied. 'Oh bloody Norah, look at the time. I've got a bar to open. I'll have to wolf this down.'

'You'll get indigestion eating your food at that pace,' tutted Elliott, watching his sister load her mouth with pasta and chew quickly.

'Yes, Mum. Okay, I'm done.' She grabbed another slice of bread to take with her.

'I should leave you to it, too,' said Sophie. 'You'll want to enjoy your time with Luke and Plum on his first day here.'

'No, you stay,' said Tracey. 'We can't both desert him. He'll feel rejected. Besides, you haven't finished.'

She leaned over her brother's shoulder, planted a kiss on his cheek and then went to give her nephew a hug.

'See you soon, Pom. I'll give your love to Marshall. He's been asking when you're next in. You've got yourself a fan there. I'll see myself out.' And with that she was off.

Elliott raised his eyebrows. 'Bossy, isn't she.'

'Very.' Sophie smiled. 'In the best way.'

'She's right, though, I would feel very rejected if you left straight after her. No emotional blackmail intended.' He nodded mock-seriously.

'Of course not,' she replied with the same expression.

'I've made enough pasta to feed the five thousand,' said Elliott. 'Please, dig in.'

Maybe it was because of the heavy-duty gardening, maybe it was the sea air, maybe it was this lovely house and this kind man and his son and their new kitten, but Sophie's appetite was demanding that she scoop another spoonful of pasta onto her plate, sprinkle it with shaved parmesan from the dish, grind some black pepper over it and savour.

'Have you made any plans?' asked Elliott, quickly adding, 'And that isn't me asking you how long you intend to stay for, because the almshouse is there as long as you need it. This is simply me asking if you've made any plans.'

'Not yet,' replied Sophie. 'I don't even know where to start making them, Elliott. I don't know what to do. I'll have to do something eventually – obviously – but I just feel . . . numb. If that makes any sense.'

Elliott got up from the table, took two glasses out of a cupboard and brought them and a bottle of wine over to the table.

'Mrs Cherry's parsnip, or it could be Mrs Parsnip's cherry, I can't remember.'

It was silly but Sophie burst into a disproportionate giggle at that. She apologised, blamed it on stress.

'It's my delivery, I think . . . *The way I tell 'em*,' he said, in a terrible impression of a TV comedian. He smiled and she thought again, what a handsome man he was. No wonder all the women in the parish were waiting for him to become single again. She tried not to notice his strong *nininja* arms covered in dark hairs, the shape of his chest pressing against his T-shirt as he stood pouring the wine. The lecherous old vicar at St Bathsheba's had definitely not been contoured like that.

'Take the time whilst you have it to find some

perspective – and answers. You're safe here. There's still a lot of heat in the newspapers.'

'I know. I bought a couple. Masochistic of me really, especially to read the insinuations that I brought all this on myself.'

'That certainly isn't the general opinion from what I've read,' countered Elliott. 'There's a lot of support for you out there.'

Sophie shrugged, grateful for his gallantry, even if it wasn't true. 'It's been wonderful not feeling as if there is a great big eye in the sky watching everything I do. Although I suppose you must feel as if you're being watched all the time too.' She glanced upwards.

'I'm sure God's not concentrating solely on me,' said Elliott, taking a sip of wine, coughing and then setting the glass back down on the table. 'My, that's a pungent parsnip . . . Not quite the same as your situation, I think.'

'I'd hope not. For your sake,' said Sophie. She took a sip also and started coughing, then laughing then nearly choking.

'You okay?' he asked, quickly fetching her a glass of water.

She nodded but couldn't speak. It set Elliott off grinning. A grin that reached up to his eyes and made them shine.

'Daddy, I'm tired.' Luke's head was resting in the cat bed, the kitten snuggled up to his face.

'Look, I'll go,' said Sophie.

'Please, stay. Finish off your wine or let it finish you off. I'll put Luke in bed. It's good to talk to someone who isn't my sister, in the nicest possible way.'

Luke sprang into animation when his father picked him up.

'Will Pom give me a goodnight kiss?'

Sophie stood. She gave Luke a kiss on his butter-soft cheek. He smelled of garlic and soap and a little bit of cat wee. He waved wearily at her over his dad's shoulder as he was being carried away. Sophie sat back down, speared another forkful of pasta and thought what a friendly kitchen this was. Clean, tidy, but not too much so. There was a corner heaped with toys and books and a very large floor cushion next to the furry cat bed where the sleeping kitten lay. The shelves of an oak dresser were filled with framed family photographs, pots of coloured pens, ornaments, letters, a small vase of garden flowers. The dining table was scrubbed antique pine, distressed, the heads of clout nails clearly visible, the chairs around it different styles and woods: a beech fiddleback, Lancashire slat, bullseye, a mahogany carver at the end. A mix of new and old. So different from the décor of Park Court with everything matching, everything precise, everything house rather than *home.*

She took the plates over to the sink, rinsed them, placed them in the dishwasher. She looked at the photos on the dresser: Elliott as a much younger man in a police uniform standing with a stick-thin Tracey sporting a punky-short hairstyle. Elliott and Tracey as children with their parents presumably: a plump blonde woman in a wheelchair and a big strapping man with thick dark hair standing behind; Elliott was so very like him. A bride and groom – their parents, much younger – standing outside a church with men in suits and women in hats. Elliott holding a baby, a delighted curve of a smile on his face. Sophie heard a creak on the stairs and threw herself back into the chair at the dining table, not wanting him to find her snooping.

'I'll have to get him a kitten every day,' said Elliott. 'Out like a light. Mind you, he hardly slept at all last night, he was so excited.'

'He's very sweet,' said Sophie.

'He is, if I say so myself,' agreed Elliott. 'I have tiramisu for dessert. I apologise in advance as I can be quite heavy-handed with the rum.'

'I couldn't squeeze another ... oh, all right, maybe a little,' said Sophie, deciding that she had better go for a very long beach run tomorrow morning.

'You don't have children, do you?' asked Elliott, beginning to serve out the tiramisu from a large glass trifle bowl. 'Was that from choice?'

'I can't carry babies,' said Sophie. 'Everything inside me is the wrong shape.'

Elliott froze in position, spoon buried in the dessert.

'I'm so sorry, I didn't know. I shouldn't have asked. That was really clumsy of me.'

'Don't worry. I had a couple of very early miscarriages and then I became pregnant again and everything was going great. But I went into early labour and Henry was born at just over twenty-three weeks. They said it was a miracle that I'd carried him for so long really, considering the equipment I had. He didn't make it, but he tried his best. And John didn't want to adopt. He said he could never accept a child that had been fathered by someone else.'

'That's ... that's rough, Pom.'

'On the day my son died, there was a freak heatwave. I wanted it to rain so hard it knocked down buildings. *How dare the sun come out today*, I thought. How dare it. How dare people smile and say how gorgeous it is and have barbecues and parties in their gardens.'

'Oh, Pom.' He could hear the pain in her voice. There was a well of it still left inside her, full of stagnant waters.

'It's a taboo subject for me, I won't let it be used even if it would – quote – "make me appear more human".'

'Surely that wasn't said to you?' said Elliott, incredulous.

'Oh yes. And more than once. But I've always stood firm.' On that, at least.

Elliott shook his head. 'I think a lot of people have done you a great injustice, Pom.'

'I stopped believing in God when that happened to me, so you see, you have a heathen in your midst,' she said, after a pause that indicated she knew she was about to reveal something he might find contentious.

'Did you stop believing or were you just angry at Him, Pom?'

'You have no idea how angry.'

'I can imagine. Did you tell me that expecting me to evangelise?'

'I wanted to be straight with you, Elliott. I felt I owed it to you to say. Especially because it's the church that is giving me sanctuary and so I feel hypocritical enough as it is.'

'Thank you, I appreciate your honesty, though it won't stop Him loving you and trying to guide and protect you. And I will not be throwing you out on the street.'

'If I'd said what I just have to the resident priest at St Saviour's in Cherlgrove, I'd have been strung up until I begged for his forgiveness.' Sophie shuddered at the thought.

'It's not up to us to forgive anyone,' said Elliott. 'That's His job,' and he pointed upwards.

'I won't lie and say that I was particularly religious before, but to be told that "God doesn't give us anything more than we can cope with" made me angrier than I think I've ever been.'

Elliott winced at the insensitivity of those words, however kindly they'd been meant, as he put a bowl down in front of Sophie.

'I didn't want to believe in a God that could take my baby away from me. I wanted to scream that at the idiot priest but I couldn't. Inside I was raging, but I was too far gone in my grief to have the energy to tell him what I wanted him to do with his religion and his very considerate God. Is that what you would have said to me, Elliott?'

Elliott nudged a jug of cream over to her.

'No. I would have told you that I was so sorry about what you were going through and that I couldn't hope to under-stand it. I would have told you that it wasn't God to blame but just life, circumstance, that it is not part of His design to make anyone suffer like you were, that what had hap-pened was not because of some unchangeable blueprint. And I would have told you that God is there for you, even though you think He isn't. I would have told you that grief does not last for ever but your love for your child will. Then I would have stuck around and tried to help you to live alongside it so it wasn't blocking your way forward. I would have tried to help you work through the anger.'

'I'm not angry now,' Sophie said.

'I think you must be, Pom.' His voice was soft but firm. 'Anger is a huge part of the grieving process: you feel it and it gives you energy to survive, then you let it go. But the longer the anger stays with you, the more destructive it is, it can settle inside your emotional make-up like concrete. Anger can become a cloud that blocks out the sunshine.'

'Angry people scream and shout. I don't do that.'

'Not always,' replied Elliott. 'Sometimes they hold it up as a shield so nothing gets in or out. Shadows have filled you and anything that tries to alter the status quo is immediately rejected from fear because you cling to a consistency you can cope with. It's a defence mechanism that is in place to stop hurt getting any worse, but at the same time it stops it getting better too, it fixes you in the moment.'

That was exactly what it was like. She couldn't do anything about it, but she could recognise it for what it was.

'I've seen it quite a few times. Grief is different for everyone. There is no textbook on how to deal with it. There is no marker in the sand that says you have grieved enough now and should snap out of it. Oh, the most useless expression in the English language,' Elliott went on. '*Snap out of it.*'

Her mother's words: '*You're becoming maudlin, trapped in the past like a fly in aspic, Sophie. Time to rally. Three months is more than enough to get over the worst of anything.*'

Sophie gave a small swallow, a nod. 'I couldn't cry. I tried.'

'Did someone hold you, Pom? Did someone make you feel safe enough to let all your pain out?'

Her eyes flashed to his. He could see inside her, she was sure of it, see the deep canyon of emptiness within her. She didn't answer him. If she had, she would have said no, no one did, but she thought he would know that anyway.

'I wish I'd heard your words then instead of the priest's at St Saviour's. I think it might have made a difference.'

'It would. Now eat your pudding.'

She smiled and obeyed.

'I make a really good dessert, don't I?' said Elliott. 'Maybe I should have been a chef rather than a vicar. Maybe that's my true calling.'

'I think you're in exactly the right job.' Sophie licked the spoon. It was better than anything that even Margaret could come up with. Maybe because Margaret's cooking was a result of duty rather than pleasure. *Or maybe you're just being indulgently fanciful, Sophie*, she told herself.

'Does Luke talk about his mother ever?' she asked. 'Tell me to mind my own business.'

'I shall do nothing of the sort. I presume that Tracey has told you a little of our history. She finds you easy to talk to, which is quite a compliment if you knew my sister. Alas, the subject of Joy is one that we butt heads on, so we tend to avoid it unless we have to speak about her.'

'She didn't tell me much.'

'Joy and I first met when I was in Whitby hospital visiting a parishioner. She was in the next bed. She'd been beaten up by an ex-boyfriend. The image of her stayed with me for a long time, this little, fragile, broken thing but I didn't see her again until a year later. I was trying to get out of Slattercove but there was a protest march about the new road. I spotted her immediately, holding up a banner. Things had started to turn ugly and I managed to drag her out of the way before she was trampled underfoot or arrested. We went for a coffee. Things progressed very quickly, too quickly. She was like no one I'd ever met before, a force of nature: I was enraptured by her. We were married six months later, under the impression that we knew each other better than we did . . . big mistake. She felt trapped, she said, and left me the day before our first anniversary. I was understandably devastated, even though our differences were glaring by this stage. Joy always had to have a cause, a fight; she was high, she was low, everything was extreme. We'd fallen into victim and rescuer roles: she lurched from one drama to the other, manically; it was exhausting. Then she came back because she had found out she was pregnant. I was reeling with shock but I was happy to try again and things seemed to settle. Is this boring?'

'Not at all, go on,' encouraged Sophie.

'Luke was born but Joy had difficulty bonding with him. I thought she was post-natally depressed but then she took off again, weeks later, without any notice at all or any contact afterwards. I was worried sick, I didn't know her state of mind. I tried to trace her, looked everywhere, did eventually find her in Wigan, and I wrote – no response at first. I drove there but the person at the house said she'd moved and left no forwarding address. Then out of the blue she wrote back, saying she'd consider meeting up if I left her to think about it for a month or so, which I did. Then she filed for divorce. Obviously we never did meet up.'

'Wow.' Joy sounded anything but a joy. 'And ... how did you feel about that?'

'Honestly? Shocked, bewildered ... relieved. But at the same time, I wanted to build a bridge between us – for Luke. I had hoped she would decide to be part of his life. I have difficulty getting my head around the fact that a parent wouldn't want to be involved in bringing up their own child. Especially a mother, who carried him for nine months and then gave birth to him.'

'And if she scrapped the divorce and came home, would you try again?'

'I don't know. I really don't. I've tried to imagine giving myself advice as if I were giving it to someone else and I have no idea what to say. Would I like a stable family unit for my son? More than anything, yes. Do I think it is possible to have that with Joy? I have no idea; but she's his mother so would I give it another shot, for him? Do I still love her? I don't know that either, because I don't even know if it ever was love: it was like being caught up in an exhilarating storm where I could barely catch my breath. I suppose

I must have loved her, but I can't remember being anything but unhappy, desperate, consumed, at the begging end in our whole relationship. It was all such hard work.'

Sophie had the feeling that he hadn't poured any of this out to Tracey, that it had been sitting inside him for a long time, festering.

'I suppose you're going to let God guide you,' she said, hoping she didn't sound too sarcastic.

'Yep, exactly. And He will. Coffee?' he asked. 'Parsnip wine loosens the tongue too much, I think.'

'I'd love one, thank you.'

'I have some decaf pods. You can't tell them from the caf ones.'

'Perfect.'

Elliott put a pod into his coffee machine and it sprang to very loud life. 'And what about you, Pom? Do you think you can fit back into your marriage?'

'I don't know,' said Sophie, although she did. She'd have to. Like a car that had pulled off the motorway for an emergency pit stop, she'd have to join a slip road, ease back into the traffic of her familiar life. What else was could she do? 'I can't hide for ever, can I?'

'Some do,' said Elliott. 'I used to sort of admire people who upped and left a life they didn't find suited them, the guts it must take to start from nothing. Until I realised the devastation they often leave behind. The families who have no idea where they are or if they're safe, alive even. The mental torment they go through.'

'I did send John a message to say that I was fine and needed some space,' Sophie assured him hurriedly.

Elliott came back at her, equally quickly, 'I wasn't implying . . .'

'I know, but I wanted you to hear that from me.' It was important he didn't think she was a Joy, that she hadn't left a pile of mess in her wake. It sounded like currying for sympathy to say that she doubted her family would be worrying about her welfare more than they would be annoyed at her desertion of her post, so she didn't. 'Although I'm not sure that space is helping; if anything it's making me think too much.'

'That's what space has a tendency to do.'

Sophie's eyes fell on his hands, large and square as he handed her a cup. The sort of hands that caught you when you fell, tender and strong. He was still wearing his wedding ring, she noticed.

'I met John at university,' said Sophie. 'He was unfaithful to me there. He totally smashed my heart into little pieces. Four years later we got back together. He swore to me that he'd never hurt me like that again, so I committed the past to history.'

'The only way forward if you are going to start over,' agreed Elliott.

'The week ... well, two days ...' began Sophie, feeling as if she were standing at the top of a cliff, about to dive into waters that might be full of rocks, '... before I went into labour with my baby, a woman turned up at our London flat. Someone who worked for John. She walked in, she had a key. She told me that she'd had an affair with him and wanted me to know what a total bastard ... sorry—'

Elliott cut in. 'No need to apologise, Sophie. We have to be men of the world to know how to deal with the world's problems.'

Sophie nodded, continued: '... what a total bastard he was. Then she left. I had good enough reason to believe that she was lying. But I went into early labour and I didn't want to connect the two because if I did, I'd blame John for his son's . . .'

A single rogue tear dropped onto the table. She didn't even feel it leave her eye.

'Oh, Pom.' She watched Elliott's large hand stretch across, close over hers, felt its heat travel up her arm. Felt things zapping and fizzing in her head. One single squeeze, that's all it took for Elliott Bellringer to take root in her heart, like a splash of warm rain and a wink of sunlight quickening a barren lonely landscape. Her head dizzied; what the hell was going on with her that she should be so affected by someone touching her so briefly and so innocently to comfort, to convey support with a mere press of fingers against flesh. It felt beyond intimate.

He felt it too, she could tell. His hand sprang away from hers as if it had delivered an electric shock and she read puzzlement in his expression.

She picked up her drink in an attempt to appear unaffected, consign whatever weirdness had just happened immediately to history, recover the situation.

'Nice coffee,' she said.

'Funny how sometimes it tastes better than others, as if the occasion impacts upon it.' He was doing the same; stamping normal back onto them.

She drank fast. 'I should be going,' she said.

'There's nothing to rush for, take your time.'

'Thank you for the lovely supper. And for introducing me to Plum. I hope you all have a peaceful night.' She stood and Elliott followed suit.

'Let me see you home at least.'

'No, I'm good. I'll go out of the back door and hop

over the fence. I'll avoid the curtain-twitchers that way.'

Elliott smiled, nodded. The ship had been steadied. 'Thank you for coming, Pom. Luke was desperate to show you the kitten. Even more so than he was Tracey, though never tell her that.' He smiled again and elicited the same from her. 'You know where I am if you need me. To talk or if there is anything I can do.'

'Likewise,' she said. 'I'm not sure if I can help you but if I can . . .'

'You have. By listening to me. Two-way traffic. I've told you things I haven't told anyone else. I'm a great listener, not so good at baring my own soul. At least I didn't think I was.'

'I'll pretend your kitchen is a confessional booth and everything you've said stays within it.'

'Reciprocated, of course.' His eyes were so blue, so kind, telling of the gentle soul behind them.

'Goodnight, Elliott.'

'Goodnight, Pom.'

She slipped out of the back door, down the garden, over the fence into the now neat garden of the almshouse. The bedsit was warm when she walked in, cosy, inviting, safe.

I can't hide for ever, can I?

Some do.

Oh, if only. If only she could wake up every morning, go for a run on the beach, work on the almshouse garden then spend the evening chatting to her new friends over pasta and parsnip wine. But *Shirley Valentine* was a play and though people saw hope in it and a dream made true, they went home when the curtain fell, because that's what people did in real life.

Chapter 30

The next day was gloriously sunny. Perfect weather for tidying up the borders at the front of the almshouse after a wonderful run along the beach. Why had she never had this level of satisfaction pottering around the grand garden of Park Court? Maybe because she never plunged her hands into the soil, felt the brambles protest as she wrestled them into submission. She'd titivated what the landscaper had established, not really gardened, not made it her own.

She broke for a late lunch: toast with grilled cheese, tomato and spring onion. She'd found an allotment special on the doorstep waiting for her when she'd come back from the beach: tomatoes, spring onions, sprigs of mint, a box of six eggs fresh from the hen's bottom, a lettuce wrapped in newspaper. You didn't get that on Cherlgrove Avenue.

She was writing a list of what she needed to buy on her next trip to Slattercove when there was a text from Elise.

Need to talk to you urgently. When's best to ring?

Now? Sophie replied.

The phone rang immediately.

'Sophie, how are you?' A voice full of rounded vowels, a voice from a distant world.

'Good. I'm good.'

'Marvellous. Now, I wasn't sure if I should tell you this but I'm going to anyway. I've just had lunch with Dena Stockdale. You were the main topic of conversation of course.'

'Of course,' echoed Sophie.

'Anyway, the wine flowed and Dena entrusted me with a little drunken confession, trying to impress, I suspect. Turns out that she once had a knee-trembler in the House of Commons. *Une liaison dangereuse*, in Emily Davison's broom cupboard, of all places.'

Elise let that sink in, leaving a pause that was pregnant with octuplets. Sophie waited for her to continue and then laughed when she didn't.

'You really aren't suggesting she had this with John are you?'

'We were discussing how much of the allegations of Rebecca Robinson were likely to be true and I asked why John should even think of being unfaithful to you and she replied that he had *form*. Apologies for not sugar–coating this, Sophie, but Willy Wonka I am not.'

She was right about that at least, thought Sophie. 'Dena Stockdale? John despises the woman.' Okay, so that was indiscreet but she was allowed a day off.

'My dear girl, I wasn't inferring a Dena and John coupling, not even he would be that stupid. But I did feel duty–bound to ask what "form" meant. Dena refused to expand on it.'

'I have no idea,' replied Sophie, but it could only mean that Dena had somehow heard about Crying-girl – Malandra Moxon. There had to have been rumours about her circulating, even if they had been quashed like a resting fly with a rolled-up newspaper. And as Chief Whip, Christopher Stockdale would have been party to even the barest whiff of scandal. John really did seem to have a thing about becoming entangled with women with alliterative names, which was another reason why Dena Stockdale was probably safe. Eileen Eveleigh ought to watch out though.

Sophie was vexed that Dena was acting like a gossipy tabloid. It was one thing divulging her own indiscretions, but to jump on the *let's kick the Mayhews in the bollocks whilst they're down* bandwagon was bad form.

'Elise, whoever Dena had her liaison with, I can assure you it wasn't John.' Sophie was adamant about that.

'Ah, I did wonder if she was telling the truth. It did cross my mind she was trying to insinuate a desirability,' sighed Elise, disappointedly. 'I mean she's hardly Uma Thurman. Then again, a man's penis is blind. A creature with one eye and a single basic need which it continually seeks to satisfy. Two if you count urination, I suppose.'

No one could criticise Elise for being short on detail.

'Obviously I swore to her that I would not tell a soul. I did not swear on Monty's life before you ask, only Gerald's. I do hope it all swims to light if it's true. Christopher is a thoroughly decent man, if hardline. John has certainly had a slaughtering in his office, according to Gerald.'

John would not have liked that. He considered Christopher his inferior in every way possible.

Elise carried on in full flow. 'We were also speculating on your whereabouts because there's been a leak that you are not ill in the family home at all. John apparently has sacked your housekeeper for gross misconduct, blaming that rumour on her.'

'Margaret? Margaret's worked for the family for years. She's as trustworthy as they come.' Sophie blew out two lungfuls of exasperation.

'Yes well, that's rather backfired because her loyalty has been kicked in the face, so newspapers are chasing her to sell her story about life in the Mayhew inner camp. The *premier cru* of backstairs gossip will be unleashed unless Len Spinks can put a stop to it, but she is by all accounts very, very cross.'

'Oh, the stupid man,' huffed Sophie. 'I can't say I blame her. She must be so terribly hurt.' Margaret had witnessed John speaking to his wife as if he had just wiped her off his shoe on quite a few occasions. He would not want his house-keeper's jaw to wag.

'I don't know if you are reading the papers but Rebecca Robinson is haemorrhaging public sympathy. Once you persist in kicking a horse after it's dead, one's appetite for viewing wanes considerably; it all becomes rather boring and distasteful. Have you made your point now, darling? Are you going to come home?'

'Not yet,' said Sophie defiantly.

'Come home now,' said Elise. 'Come back to what you know and rebuild. John has been an idiot, but it can strengthen a marriage, make you realise what you were in danger of losing – trust me, I do know – and I think that John has learned his lesson. If you rescue him from this, he will worship the ground you walk upon for the rest of your life. Demand anything and you shall have it. That's certainly what Gerald thinks, and he is wise. If he had been blessed with a Mayhew face, we would have had our stint in number ten. It won't happen, but I would rather like you to have it.'

'I'll think about it, Elise,' said Sophie.

'Playing devil's advocate, Sophie, I do have to ask if any side is entirely blameless when an affair happens. Think on that. Even when Gerald had his momentary madness with Sheila Crabtree, it did make me realise that our marriage had drifted off course without us realising it. We had to readjust our sextant. Maybe it was a *cri du coeur* from John?'

Sophie clicked the phone off. That conversation had given her too much to think about. The mere suggestion that John and Dena had . . . *no, impossible.* Then again, is that why she'd smirked so much that last time, when Sophie had seen her at the Charity Ball? Sophie tried to remember that comment Dena had made about men liking different cuts of meat. Was she comparing herself to a tenderloin there? Or brisket? She tried to picture John and Dena having *une liaison pornographique* in Emily Davison's broom cupboard – but that really was stretching her imagination way too far. It had been too easy to picture John and Rebecca the Red though. Was it a cry from John's heart as Elise had suggested? An attention-seeking exercise *par excellence*? Had she fallen short on supporting him, loving him? Had she missed signs that their marriage was veering off track and, in doing so, had played a part in what had happened?

*

Over in his Westminster office, John was pacing about the room in a state of high agitation whilst Len Spinks was leaning back in the captain's chair at John's desk, hands steepled, supercilious grin fixed firmly in place.

'Relax, John. We are over the worst of the storm. Tides have a tendency to turn and whirlpools calm to wimpy little swells. Your ship has negotiated the roughest waters now and is heading for calmer seas. How was your meeting with Christopher Stockdale?'

'Vile,' snarled John. 'He drowned me. Told me to get my house in order, which is ironic.'

'Ironic how, hmm?' asked Len, nose lifted to a possible scent of scandal.

John shook his head as if momentarily annoyed with himself for mentioning it. 'I heard a story in Strangers' bar about his wife and her propensity to keep her ankles warm with her knickers.'

'Really?' Len's interest was piqued. 'Well, those rumours have certainly bypassed my finely tuned receptors. How odd.'

'Talking of which, what are you doing about the rumours that I've killed my bloody wife? I can't believe that stupid cow of a housekeeper blabbed to someone *in confidence* that Sophie was not recuperating in bed and her family are all running around like headless chickens wondering where the fuck she is.'

'No one thinks you've murdered Sophie,' Len answered impatiently. 'Rumours without substantiation are easy to deal with but you flew off the handle, John. You shouldn't have sacked her, because that has given a weight to her words that they didn't have before. Now . . .' he reached down, opened up his briefcase, took out an envelope. 'I have negotiated a sweetener for Margaret. Total reinstatement—'

'No chance, Len. Not a fucking chance.' John crashed his fist into the top of his desk.

Len's smile stayed in place. 'I'm afraid you have little choice, John. Not unless you want this pitiful saga to carry on ad infinitum. Margaret Reynolds *will* be reinstated and compensated for hurt feelings. And she'll receive a pay rise and a week's paid holiday. This was all a terrible misunderstanding brought about by a very, very stressful situation. Margaret of course was quite right in that Mrs Mayhew is not in the house. She is in a secret location having the best of care. It's perfectly understandable that you avoided reportage saying as much, seeing as the press have a tendency to hunt and find and Sophie's recuperation is paramount. Margaret Reynolds has not done any harm at all; in fact if anything it makes you look even more considerate.'

'If Sophie doesn't come back, I'm going to end up being investigated for a crime,' John growled between his teeth like a mad ventriloquist's dummy. 'She can't have disappeared into thin air. Someone must have seen her. She must have told somebody where she's gone?'

In the corner, making coffee, Edward huffed. 'Like who? Those maggoty siblings of hers? Her loving family?'

John and Len swung their heads round to him. They'd forgotten he was even there.

'What?' said Edward, answering their look. 'I'm not saying anything that isn't true. There's no love lost between them is there? It's like the ugly sisters and Cinderella setup. Sophie – the only one of them all who has any human qualities – is treated the worst. How the bloody hell she grew up to be so ... so superlative, I will never know.'

'Bit like us. isn't it,' said John, narrowing his eyes. 'The eldest couldn't quite make the grade so the youngest had to. Face it, you're just the *first draft,* Edward.'

Edward took a step towards him, fist bunched. John didn't flinch but laughed.

'Oh, come on, big brother, really? Okay – do your worst if you must.'

'This truly isn't helping the situation, is it?' said Len,

pressing his hands down on the air as if the gesture would relieve the room of tension. 'We need to find Sophie. We need to winkle her out, bring her home. And you, John, have to practise some humility.'

Edward snorted. Len ignored him and carried on.

'I think a bouquet of flowers to Margaret in the first instance.'

'What about a statement to the papers, my side of the story?' asked John. 'What's the hold-up on that?'

'Rebecca Robinson is becoming a bore,' said Len. 'She's also contradicting herself quite a lot. Best to let her petrol run out and then we can blast everything out of the water with one definitive explosive interview, with your wife at your side looking fragile, beautiful and fully reinstated to the team. You need Sophie. *The Magnificent Mrs Mayhew.*'

'Just make this go away, Len. Whatever you have to do, whoever you have to pay.'

'Of course,' said Len, his voice caramel smooth. 'Rebecca might be proving a little more difficult than Malandra Moxon, but we will get there in the end. Trust me.'

Chapter 31

The next morning Sophie washed her clothes in the sink and hung them on the line to dry whilst she walked down the hill to buy some bread and milk. Three people said good morning to her and in Loste Things, the shopkeeper once again gave her a free breadcake. She protested, feeling guilty because she was a rich fraud, but he told her that she'd insult him if she didn't take it and, as she could hardly tell him why she was resisting so much, she accepted his kindness and thanked him.

She had lunch sitting in the garden on a deckchair that she'd found in the shed. After a scrub it was perfectly usable. She made herself a cheese sandwich and read one of the Mills and Boon books. This one featured a dark-haired hunk with very blue eyes. He was a doctor, but annoyingly he kept appearing in her imagination wearing a clerical collar and with featured sunray pleats at the corners of his eyes. As he kissed the heroine in the book, Sophie let herself wonder what Elliott Bellringer's lips would feel like pressed against her own, how he would hold a woman, what he would look like naked.

As Sophie climbed out of the bath that night there was a

knock on the door. She slipped on her robe, peeped through the curtains and saw Elliott. She held up her hand to indicate that she'd be a minute, then threw on some underwear, jeans and a top.

She hadn't noticed that Luke was with his father until she opened the door. He had his *Thomas the Tank Engine* dressing gown on and matching slippers.

'I am so sorry to trouble you, Pom, but could I ask you the biggest favour. I have an emergency. Talking someone down off a ledge. Is there any chance at all that you could look after Luke for an hour. If you can't I'll take him to the pub but there's a party on and—'

'No worries. I'll walk back with you,' said Sophie, interrupting Elliott's flow.

'You've obviously just got out of the bath.'

'It's fine, so long as the sight of me with no make-up on and wet hair doesn't scare you.'

'Not at all, you look . . .' He stopped himself and Sophie didn't get to find out what word he would have used, but she felt herself blushing slightly because she knew it would have been something charming, complimentary, something straight from his heart.

She locked up behind her and as soon as she started to walk towards the vicarage with them, Luke reached for her hand. The effect of that small action was ridiculous, totally out of proportion. He felt so little, so precious. She'd wondered before what it would have been like to hold her baby boy's hand as they walked along. She'd imagined him reaching for her, his protector – *Mummy's hand*. Her son would have been four now, the same age as Luke. *This* is what it would have felt like to hold his hand. She didn't want to let go.

'Luke's ready for bed now. In fact he's late and I'm hoping he won't be fractious.'

'I'll settle him with a story, how's that?' said Sophie.

'Yaaayyy,' cheered Luke.

'I'm sorry, I have no idea how long I'll be.'

'Don't worry. Be as long as it takes.'

Elliott pushed open the vicarage door. 'Raid the fridge and cupboards. Watch TV, make yourself at home.'

'It's fine. Just go.'

'The kitten might plop.'

'I'll clean it up. Go.'

Elliott leaned down, kissed Luke on the head. 'Be good for Pom. Sleep after one story – that's one, Master Bellringer. Thank you again, Pom.'

Elliott darted to his car, Sophie closed the door on him, turned to Luke. 'Okay, show me to your bedroom.'

'Can I kiss Plum goodnight first?'

Plum was in the kitchen doing a huge poo in his litter tray and the smell took over the whole room. Sophie and Luke held their noses and giggled.

'How can one small cat make a pong like that?' asked Sophie, scooping it up as Luke picked up his kitten very gently and kissed him.

'Daddy flushes the poop down the toilet,' said Luke, putting Plum back in his bed and showing Sophie the way to the downstairs loo. That duty done, they went upstairs and along the landing to the end. Luke's bedroom was a proper little boy cave, with a train-shaped tent in the corner, shelves full of toys and boxed games, *Thomas the Tank Engine* wallpaper, quilt cover and a wardrobe that looked like the front of a train. There were stars stuck on the ceiling that glowed with a soft light in the semi-dark.

A bedside lamp at the side of Luke's single bed was also in the shape of a train.

'I'm seeing a theme here, Luke,' said Sophie. 'I'm guessing that trains are a thing.'

'That's Thomas,' said Luke, pointing to his quilt.

'Is he your favourite?'

Luke nodded. 'I like Percy second.'

'He's the green one, isn't he?' Sophie knew because she'd bought a book. For Henry. A lift-the-flap book. She knew at thirteen weeks that it was far too early to start buying things but it made it all seem real. She had no idea what had happened to it. She vaguely remembered stuffing clothes and baby toiletries into a bin liner when she came home from the hospital, dismantling the part-finished nursery, ripping up the carpet like a mad thing.

'Come on then, in you get.' She helped Luke take off his robe, then he climbed into bed. He passed her the book that was on his bedside cabinet: *Scary Edwin Page.* Sophie flicked through it warily. It was about the scariest kid in the world. 'Won't this give you nightmares?' she asked.

'He's not real,' whispered Luke, which made Sophie chuckle.

'Okay then, here we go. Are you sitting comfortably?'

Luke was as wide awake at the end of the story as he was at the beginning. But one story was all his father had allowed and Sophie didn't want to deviate from the instruction.

'That's it. Time to sleep,' she said, expecting a protestation, but none came. 'Do I leave your bedside light on?' she asked.

'If you do this, it goes off by itself in a bit,' said Luke, reaching over and pressing a button on its base.

'Right. So, goodnight then.' Sophie stood.

'Kiss goodnight, Pom.'

Sophie leaned over, kissed his cheek, inhaled that little

boy smell of minty toothpaste and post-bath talc. His arms came around her neck just as she was about to pull away and hers wrapped around his body. He felt so sweet and small and she felt her breath catch in her throat.

''Night, Pom.' He shuffled down the bed and she tucked the quilt around him, wanting him to be toasty warm.

'Goodnight, darling.' Under her breath she added, *bonne nuit, dors bien, fais de beaux rêves.*

She shut the bedroom door, eyes clouding. She had wanted to be a mother so much. She had shut those feelings away into a trunk, but the merest scent of Johnson's baby powder had threatened to break the lock.

At the top of the stairs, she gave herself the hard word: *pull yourself together, Sophie. Rally.* By the time she had reached the bottom, she was back in control. But she didn't want to be, she wanted to howl and let everything go, be totally out of control, cry and grieve and scream that it wasn't fair.

She went into the kitchen and made herself a cup of tea, checked on the kitten who was also snug in his bed, then carried the mug through to the lounge. The room was dominated by a very long squashy sofa and an equally squashy armchair. There was a coffee table with a sensible A4 black Moleskin notepad and a Parker pen set on it, a colouring book and a pot of pencils, a holder full of remote controls. The TV was large but not super-massive and there was an impressive collection of DVDs and CDs in a cabinet at the side. It seemed the Reverend liked rock and retro: The Who, the Stones, Heart, Nirvana, INXS, Bowie. But on the shelf below, Schubert, Beethoven, Handel's *Messiah*. And he liked box sets too: *Line of Duty, The Tunnel, Sherlock, The Office.* This was a room where you could snuggle up quite happily and binge on them.

She pressed a few buttons on the remote, eventually finding the one that switched on the TV. There was a
programme on about the death of Stalin, which was as good
as anything, she supposed. Sophie was fascinated by Russian
history. She'd picked the wrong subject to study at university: she was channelled into doing French because she was
very good at it, but she'd learned over the years that what
you were given as a gift wasn't necessarily the thing that
made you the happiest.

She toyed with the idea of looking in the notepad just to
see what Elliott's hand-writing was like. That was too nosy,
she decided. Then she did it anyway. She didn't know anything about graphology but she did know that if she had to
guess which sex had written on the pad, she would have
presumed it was a man. Not too precise, not too regi-
mented – she would have said that the writer was open,
friendly, easy-going. Notes about a sermon and PAYING
IT FORWARD in pressured, underlined capitals. A cleverly
drawn cartoon of a wide-eyed kitten on the next page and
underneath it an instruction:

Worm every month until 6 months, then 3 months.

Then she turned the page and saw her name in elaborate scroll:

Pom

Squiggles and swirls around it, as if he had been absently
doodling it whilst he was on the phone. She gulped, closed
up the notebook quickly, replaced it on the coffee table,
hoping she had positioned it so it wouldn't look as if it had
been interfered with. Then she sat back on the sofa and put
all her efforts into watching Stalin's demise.

Chapter 32

The last thing Sophie remembered about the programme was Stalin dismissing all his guards the night before he died. She presumed, when she heard her name being called softly, that she had dozed off for a few minutes and Elliott had returned. She did not expect to see the TV off, light seeping through the curtains and find herself under a blanket. Elliott was standing there holding a mug of coffee.

'I didn't have the heart to wake you when I came back,' he said, putting the coffee down on the table.

Sophie sat bolt upright, Elliott held up his hand.

'Don't panic. Take the time to come round, you were in a *very* deep sleep.'

What did that mean? Oh *no* – she was snoring.

'Ah,' she said.

'I wouldn't have had you down as a noisy sleeper,' he grinned.

'How embarrassing,' said Sophie, ripping her eyes from his. 'I don't sleep well usually. I have tablets to help me. I don't know what it is about this place but I'm out like a light most nights.'

'Maybe you're just stress-free here,' said Elliott, parking himself on the arm of the chair.

'I don't have that much stress at home though,' replied Sophie.

'Really? You don't think that being in the public eye, being constantly on display as you are is high pressure?'

'Well, not compared to the pressures some people have,' replied Sophie. 'I wouldn't equate . . .'

'Forget other people and comparing, we're talking about you and your life.'

She felt whacked. As if she had risen too quickly through water and had some strange sleep version of the bends.

'Is your whole life about duty to others?' he asked.

'Well, isn't yours?' she threw at him, slightly defensively.

'I enjoy what I do.'

'I should go and let you get Luke ready for nursery.'

'I dropped him off there half an hour ago.'

'Oh my goodness. I'm so sorry.'

'It was past one when I came in last night,' said Elliott. 'Crisis averted. Thank you for babysitting.'

Sophie tried to sit up and then flopped against the back of the sofa.

'This is far too comfortable. I could fall asleep again,' she said. She couldn't relax like this on the sofa at home. 'I should like to bottle this air and take it with me when I leave. I'll miss it.'

Then don't leave.

The words were so loud in her head, she thought for a moment that Elliott had spoken them, but he was drinking his coffee.

'Luke was no trouble last night, I hope,' said Elliott eventually.

'Nope. One story—'

'*Scary Edwin Page*, I presume? His particular favourite at the moment.'

'Yes. I did wonder if that was okay.'

'He's like his father, nothing fazes him,' said Elliott.

Sophie smiled. 'One story and I never heard a peep out of him. I did watch TV for a while. I didn't just blank out straightaway. The rise and fall of Stalin.'

'Sounds riveting.' A crinkle of lines appeared at the corners of his eyes as he grinned at her. His eyes were far too unholy for a vicar. Whoever became the next Mrs Bellringer was a very lucky woman.

She made a concerted effort to sit up now, pulled the woollen blanket from her and folded it up.

'I think I'll go for a walk and blow the cobwebs away.' Even the coffee was good, working its magic to boot her up and chase away the lethargy.

'If you walk on the beach to the right, you'll come to a path that takes you into Briswith. There's quite a breeze today, perfect for cobweb-ridding.'

'Not sure I dare go to Briswith,' replied Sophie. 'I have this idyllic picture of it in my head and I don't want it desecrated.'

'It hasn't changed that much over the years. It's like most of the places on this stretch of the coast, pretty unspoilt.'

'Okay, you've convinced me,' said Sophie. 'Thank you for the coffee, Elliott. Once again, I'll use the back door. I wouldn't want anyone spotting me leaving the vicarage in last night's clothes.'

'Oh my, that would never do.'

Just at that moment, the front door opened and in walked Tracey. 'Only me,' she called and then stopped dead, eyes swinging from Elliott to Sophie and back again.

'Well, hello?' she said, eyes wide with amusement. 'Ding Dong.'

Sophie's mouth opened to protest.

'Oh, Pom, take that expression off your face,' Tracey chuckled. 'I know my brother too well. Whatever it might look like, I know it isn't that.'

'I'll leave you to explain, Elliott,' said Sophie, taking her cue to go. 'But I will still use the back door. See you later, Tracey.'

'See you later, Pom.'

Tracey waited until Sophie had left before speaking.

'Nice isn't she?'

'She is a very nice woman, yes,' replied Elliott.

'She fits in here, doesn't she? I think whatever happens, a couple of weeks in Little Loste will have done her some good.'

'I hope so,' said Elliott. 'I can't say I ever took much notice of Sophie Mayhew but when I did, I always wondered what must be going on behind that dispassionate expression. I never did think it would be something happy. Anyway, are you here to work on Jade's dress?'

'I am,' said Tracey. 'The prom is two weeks today so I need to crack on.'

'I'll make you a coffee and some toast and then I'll crack on myself with Sunday's sermon.'

'Oh, you'd make someone a proper little housewife.' Tracey winked. She was joking but he really would. Someone who respected him and supported him and loved him and wasn't anything like Joy bloody Bellringer. Someone that made her brother's eyes dilate – like Pom did. Oh yes, she'd noticed that. What a bummer that her new friend was married because Tracey would have match-maked her socks off and wouldn't have stopped until they were standing at the altar together.

The sun was shining but the breeze was cool, blustery and perfect for blowing the last vestiges of her very deep sleep away. Sophie hadn't thought about her life being pressurised until Elliott mentioned that it must be; she didn't worry about money or have a debilitating illness, stuff that turned people's hair grey, but the quality of her sleep at home was never brilliant. If she woke up at four a.m., there was little chance she would drop off again afterwards because her head would start to mull over all manner of things. Duties, correspondence she needed to answer for John's constituents, dry-cleaning to arrange – usually John's suits – information she needed to find out for John's surgeries. And then she would begin to dissect herself, what people had been saying about her in the press and online, what they *would* be saying about her in the press and online. How they criticised what she wore, how she looked, how she spoke, how she breathed. Vile and vicious comments from people she had never met, ripping into her because they thought she was too southern, too slim, too tall, too blonde, too rich, too quiet, too out of touch, too frigid. Being Pom with none of that cluttering up her head, no wonder her brain had space and was free to flop and wander and think about vicars' eyes.

A seagull swooped down to her, considered whether or not she was important for a moment, concluded she was nothing of interest and soared off – how brilliant to be so indistinct. The sea lapped gently at the sand and Sophie considered kicking off her trainers and socks and walking along to their meeting point but decided that would be her treat for the way home. She found the path, helped by a weathered wooden sign pointing to it that had 'BRISWITH UP HERE' scratched into it. The way was steep enough to challenge her calf muscles but the view from the top was wonderful and well worth the burn.

Elliott was right, the village hardly seemed to have changed in essence. She passed by the hotel where Tina's best friend had lived. It looked so much smaller than it had back then, or maybe her mind had distorted the dimensions over the years. The Sea View Hotel, it was called now, not highly imaginative. It had been Sandcastles the last time she'd seen it; a nicer name. The gift shop next door looked exactly as it had eighteen years ago. Bunches of buckets and spades were hanging outside along with toy flags and fishing nets, bags of candy floss and sticks of rock. The window was crammed full of cheap souvenirs that had faded in the sun. She remembered buying a pen from here that had a mermaid floating in some water set in the barrel, and a box of clotted cream fudge for them all to share on the beach. Their gang had made a massive sand-castle once, complete with moat. The sea had flattened it overnight and they'd all been gutted after all their hard work.

She walked down the road and came to Mrs Ackroyd's cottage and something inside her gave a little sob of delight. A conservatory had been built at the side of it and a door had replaced the pantry window, but those were the only differences. Whoever lived there chose that moment to open the front door to come out and Sophie recalled walking inside with as much familiarity as if it were her own home. She noticed there was a blue carpet on the floor now where there had been old polished floorboards and a busy-patterned dark pink and green rug that Mrs Ackroyd had bought in Tunisia. Chintzy curtains had hung at the windows and the sofa was made up of a similarly busy-patterned material; the overall effect had been chaotic and cosy. Sophie looked up and saw Tina's old bedroom window. There was a two-foot-deep window seat below it where they used to sit, applying make-up to each other's faces, talking about teenage girl things. It had been a beautiful summer; even the few days confined inside because it was too rainy to go out had had their charm. Sophie decided that when she did go back to Cherlgrove she was going to make it her mission to try and find the Ackroyds in Australia, say hello, connect.

The fish shop wasn't there any more; it was a café now, but the wall outside where they used to sit and dangle their legs as they ate was still the same. How she hadn't been the size of a house for the amount of times she had parked her bottom there as she gobbled up haddock and chips was anyone's guess. She went inside and was sure that the woman who served her was one of the girls who was friends with Tina. She didn't go through a long, convoluted 'Hello, can you remember a girl who went to St Bathsheba's who once stayed with the Ackroyds whilst her teacher was mid-emotional crisis?' but she did ask if she had known the family.

'I used to go to school with Tina,' the woman answered, 'but they all moved to Australia and we lost contact, like you do.'

Maybe some friendships were only ever meant to be transient and not last the course of time, Sophie thought as she made short work of a plate of vinegary fish and chips, for old times' sake. Maybe the purpose of meeting the Ackroyds had been solely

to add some colour to her grey existence, show her a different sort of family to the one that had formed her standard
template, give her something to aspire to. Instil in her a love
of creating via the medium of material and thread. Introduce
Sophie Calladine to Pom No-Surname.

She had quite fancied Charlie Ackroyd with his sandy-
blond hair and soft grey eyes. She had derived a lot of
pleasure from knowing that he liked her, even if it was quite
obvious that he didn't fancy her. His attention had thrilled
her younger self, given her insides the sensation of warm
honey spreading over them whenever his smile found her.
She could see him now, tall and lanky, his smooth young
skin tanned, hands in his shorts pockets, kicking stones idly
as he waited for his friends to come racing down the hill,
chasing a football. The Ackroyd family had no idea what
happy disorder they had brought to her life. Then again,
maybe if she hadn't met them, she would have accepted her
lot and never dreamed of eating meals around a table where
a family talked and laughed.

Sophie paid the bill and decided to head back to Little
Loste because this visit to Briswith was digging up too many
sun-soaked memories, causing an ache deep inside her. She
desperately wanted to climb through a portal in time, knock
on the cottage door, walk in and kick off her shoes. She felt
incredibly sad that those days were gone and nothing could
ever bring them back. She'd truly lived that summer. She
wasn't sure she'd lived as much since.

She took off her trainers and socks on the beach, trod
along the seam of the sea, felt the sand squish up through
her toes, such a simple pleasure but wonderful. Running in
the fields wouldn't feel as good as being able to walk out of
the house and straight onto the beach. But the clock was

ticking and its beat was getting louder every day and soon a great big fat alarm bell would sound and tell her it was time to wake up and smell the coffee. The coffee that came from the percolator that stood in the corner of her kitchen in Cherlgrove and not from the noisy pod machine on Elliott Bellringer's worktop.

Chapter 33

Sophie had been in the house a matter of minutes when there was a rap on the front door, an insistent, impatient knock. She opened the door to find Tracey there, her usual smile replaced by a downward arc.

'Can I come in, Pom?'

'Of cou—'

Tracey didn't wait to be answered but barged straight into the hallway and then into the bedsit. 'You okay?' Sophie asked her.

Tracey burst into tears. Her hands covered her face and her shoulders juddered with the weight of whatever it was that was troubling her.

'What on earth's wrong?' asked Sophie, pushing her towards the small sofa. 'Sit down and tell me. Can I get you a drink or something?'

'No thanks,' said Tracey, removing her hands to reveal a face so wet that one might be forgiven for thinking her cheeks had sprung a leak. 'Pom, I've cocked up. I don't know what I'm doing. Elliott sent me over, he said you might be able to help me.'

'What is it?' asked Sophie.

'It's that sodding dress,' she said. 'It's a mess. Jade is going to hate me. I've butchered it and I'm going to wreck her prom and she'll never forget it. Elliott says you're really good at sewing, please tell me he hasn't got that wrong.'

Sophie trotted off into the bathroom to fetch a toilet roll, though a bath towel might have been more appropriate. She snapped off a python-length of tissue and handed it to Tracey. 'No, he hasn't got it wrong, I am very good at sewing,' she said. 'I'm sure I can undo the damage and Jade will have her dress.'

'You haven't seen what I've done to it,' said Tracey.

'Well, let's go and have a look at it then, shall we?' returned Sophie.

Luke's face almost split in two when Sophie walked into the house. He cannoned into her legs, considerately holding his kitten to the side so that he wouldn't get squashed.

'Long time no see,' said his father with a smile in his voice. He was sitting at the kitchen table with his notebook open, the notebook in which he had doodled her name, and as if he were on that actual page, he closed it as Sophie neared.

'It's been ages,' replied Sophie.

'I told you Pom would help you,' said Elliott to his sister, before addressing Sophie again. 'She was afraid to ask.'

'The word is *ashamed* to ask,' Tracey corrected him. 'Pride goes before a fall, as they say.'

Sophie bent down to Luke. 'And how's Plum today?'

'He's just done a really enormous poo,' replied Luke with glee. 'It was that long.' He stretched his arms to capacity as if he were much older and bragging about the fish that had got away.

'Not quite,' said Elliott, 'but not far off.'

'Are you reading me a story at bedtime again?' asked Luke.

'Not tonight, mate. I need Pom all to myself,' said his Auntie Tracey then.

'Come on, Luke, we'll make Auntie Tracey and Pom a coffee and you can be biscuit monitor,' said Elliott, rising from behind the table.

'Yaaayyy,' replied Luke, putting Plum down on the rug and running over to the cupboard to get out a plate.

Tracey strode off into the erstwhile sewing room and Sophie followed. There she was met by the sight of a mannequin wearing a deformed satin dress. One shoulder was longer than the other and there was a seam running down the front like an abdominoplasty scar. It was worse than Sophie had imagined, and that really was saying something.

'I think I've put the back where the front is and sod knows what I've done with the sleeves.'

'Do you have a picture of what it should look like?' asked Sophie.

Tracey scrabbled around on the table until she found a printed-out sheet. 'Here you go, this is the photo that was up on the eBay site.' The dress looked very nice, but didn't resemble what the poor old mannequin was wearing one bit.

'What's this?' asked Sophie, picking up a drawing, a very good one too.

'That's what she originally wanted, but she couldn't find anything remotely similar, at least not with a price tag Steve could afford. I was going to try and alter the one she bought so it was more like it.'

'Really?' There was no disguising Sophie's disbelief.

'I know, I know,' Tracey winced. 'It was ambitious but I thought I could do it.'

Ambitious was not the word Sophie would have used. Lunacy came closer.

'Right,' she said. 'How long do we have?'

'The prom is two weeks tonight.'

Sophie bit off an expletive as Luke came in, carrying a plate of biscuits as carefully as if he were walking down an aisle behind a bride with them. Instead she said, 'Well, let's get the bad news over with first: I think you're better off starting again from scratch.'

Tracey gulped. 'Okay, if I must.'

Sophie's eyes came to rest on the curtains with the wonky swags and tails and the hems that were so far away from the carpet, they looked as if they'd had a serious row with it and were no longer on speaking terms. 'Did you make the curtains here by any chance?'

'Yes, why do you ask?'

They had a big problem.

'Ah. Right. Do you have Jade's measurements?'

'Only her waist, bust and hips. Do I need more?'

'If you want her dress to fit her like a prom princess, you do.'

'No, I don't have them. Oh farts, I've really cocked up. I can't do this.'

'Maybe not, but I can. I can sew the dress that Jade drew.'

That claim landed like a massive rock in a pool. Tracey's smile spread as she was joyously splashed with relief. 'No way! Can you? Would you?'

'Yes, I will. Let's have a coffee . . . and a delicious biscuit of course,' Sophie said for Luke's benefit, 'then I suggest that we go and measure Jade properly. I'll pretend that . . . I'll think of something that explains why I'm helping.'

'When?'

'The sooner the better, really.'

'I'll ring Steve, make sure she's in,' said Tracey, crossing her brother's path as she dashed out to the kitchen and he came into the study, carrying two coffees.

'So did you go to Briswith then?' he asked.

'I did.'

'You find it's changed much?'

'Yes, but it also felt the same, if you know what I mean. It was lovely to be walking around it again. I have so many wonderful memories of the place, but it was bittersweet, too. It made me realise how much time has passed since I was there last.' *And how I've never managed to be as happy since.* 'I shall go and look up my old friends when I . . . when I get back on the internet.'

'You can always use my computer,' offered Elliott.

'Thank you, but no. I've enjoyed being away from the world wide web and I'm no rush to get back on it.' *Web* being the operative word, because sometimes she felt caught up in the internet, trapped in it as if it were a real net.

'It's a mixed blessing isn't it – all this technology?' sighed Elliott. 'I sometimes wonder how much further it can go. Kids today seem so much more outwardly confident, but inwardly insecure. I worry for them.'

'Yep, she's in,' said Tracey, bouncing back into the room.

'Right, then,' said Sophie, taking a long glug of coffee then whipping a jam ring from the plate whilst winking at Luke. 'This sea air is making me eat like a horse as well as sleep like a log.'

'Just as long as it makes you sew like a machine,' said Tracey, gathering up a tape measure, pad and pencil. 'I will owe you my life if you get me out of this pile of sh— . . . cat poo.'

'Auntie Tracey nearly said sh—'

'Luke Bellringer, do not use that word,' warned Elliott, lifting up a finger. 'Auntie Tracey is a naughty lady.'

'Auntie Tracey knows that only too well,' said Auntie Tracey.

Jade stood with her arms outstretched, pout firmly in place.

'How come I'm having all this done again?' she asked.

'Because Tracey's worked out a way to give you the exact dress you want, from the drawing that you did,' said Sophie, noting down Jade's waist measurement. 'And she wanted me to 'elp because I ... I know the way of material.' Spoken with a French accent, the deliberately nebulous phrasing passed muster.

'What happened to the eBay dress?'

Behind Jade's back, Tracey and Sophie traded glances and Tracey blurted out, 'It's not good enough for you.'

'I'll send it back and get a full refund.'

Tracey made a horrified face. There wasn't much chance of that in its present condition.

'I'll buy it off you and save you the hassle. I'll slim into it. It'll give me something to aim for when I'm dieting,' she said, knowing that, even if she could restore it to how it was, she had more chance of getting into the SAS than she did that gown.

Steve, in the kitchen, called Tracey's name and she excused herself from their company.

'She's leaving it a bit late, isn't she?' said Jade to Sophie when they were alone.

Sophie shrugged nonchalantly. 'If you know what you are doing, it won't take a long time. It will be ready. Are you sure about the colour?'

'Yeah, why? What's wrong with red?'

'Nothing,' said Sophie. 'But with your name being Jade, I wondered if you had thought about green. Especially with your beautiful hair and your grrreen eyes. It would be your colour, I know. Now stand up straight, with your arms down.'

'I hadn't thought about green,' said Jade, thinking about it now.

''Ave you bought your jewellery and shoes yet? Red is very hard to match. So many different shades.'

'I was going for black accessories anyway. I'm off shopping to Whitby with my mates tomorrow.'

'Black would look very nice with green. Dark jade green, I think. Trust me, I am very good at putting colours to people.'

'I didn't know until I'd ordered it that this posh girl in my class has got a red dress. Her parents took her to London for it – some big designer place. It cost over a thousand quid. I started worrying people might compare us but Tracey said mine would be better than hers by the time she'd finished altering it.'

'Why set yourself up for a comparison? You both should feel like the only princess in town. Hair up or down?'

'Up, I thought.'

'Yes, I think so too. Make sure all your accessories are the same black. There are variations of that colour too.'

Jade was seriously mulling over Sophie's suggestion. 'I don't think anyone else I know is wearing green.'

'There you go, then. I will take a measurement of your length but we will not do the 'em until we 'ave your shoes. I presume you want the dress to the floor?'

'Yep.' Jade's eyes narrowed with suspicion. 'Is Tracey making this or you?'

'Tracey, of course,' returned Sophie, as if that were the most stupid question in the world. 'She is going to make you the queen of the prom. I am only here in an 'elping capacity. She wanted to double-check everysing because she knows 'ow important this is.'

Jade bent to whisper in Sophie's ear. 'You haven't told anyone about you-know-what, have you?'

'Not a soul. Living or dead. Although Kitty 'Enshaw probably knows already. *Entre nous,* as I promised.' And Sophie tapped her nose.

Half an hour later and back at the vicarage, Sophie studied the dress on the mannequin, shuddered then stripped it off and put it down on the desk.

'Jade has decided on a green dress,' she announced. 'We will go and find some material tomorrow. Where's the best place?'

'Slattercove, probably,' suggested Tracey. 'There's a market on Saturdays. You'd think with the popularity of proms these days that someone would have opened up a shop around here where you can buy dresses for them from; I mean, there's loads of schools in this general area. There's only a stuffy old bridal place in Slattercove and failing that you have to go miles to one of the big cities for a gown shop. One of the girls in Jade's class went down to London for hers, but then her parents are loaded so it'll have the designer tag in the back. It's a lot of money to pay out when you don't have it to spare, especially just for one night. What do you suggest doing with that?' She nodded towards the Frankenstein-patched red dress.

'Dusters?' said Elliott which made them all laugh.

'Remind me to stick to what I'm good at. Pulling pints and selling crisps. I always knew my English Lit degree would come in handy. I'd better go and relieve Dave of his duties. I asked him to stand in for me for a bit. What about a pattern for this super-dress then?'

'I'll make one,' said Sophie. 'Leave it to me.'

'You can do that as well?' Tracey's mouth was agape with admiration.

'I've had a lot of practice. If I can see it in my head, I can sew it. If Elliott will let me use the desk in his study for an hour or so now, I will have it ready so we know how much material to buy tomorrow.' She looked expectantly at Elliott.

'Be my guest,' he replied.

'And if you have any large sheets of paper, that would be good, or some A4 and a roll of Sellotape.'

'We've got some spare wallpaper lining,' he replied. 'Luke uses it to draw on.'

'Perfect.'

'Please don't leave and go back down south until you've done this, Pom,' said Tracey, suddenly serious.

'I can promise you that at least,' replied Sophie.

Eventually Sophie had a pattern which would make Jade's design a reality, with a few enhancements of her own thrown in. The dress would be sleeveless, halter neck, to make the best of Jade's perfect shoulders, with a ruched bodice and a fishtail skirt to lend her slender frame a more shapely silhouette. There would be some sparkling detail: she had no idea what, yet, but she would know the right thing when she saw it.

Luke had long gone to bed when she walked into the

kitchen to say she was finished for the night and found Elliott working at the table there.

'I told him not to disturb you,' said Elliott. 'I had quite a battle about it.'

'I wouldn't have minded,' said Sophie.

'Thank you for doing this for Tracey,' said Elliott. 'She would have been in a proper mess if you hadn't been here.'

'I haven't made it yet. I might have been lying to you both about my sewing prowess.'

'I trust you,' said Elliott. He was smiling, but then Sophie rarely saw him without a smile. Even if it wasn't a full-blown one – as now – there was always merriment dancing around the corners of his lips, lifting them. It was a different sort of smile to John's, a smile that came from the heart, not from the brain.

'I'm writing my sermon for Sunday: The Prodigal Son,' said Elliott, indicating his notebook. 'We haven't had that one for a while. Can I get you a drink? Hot chocolate?'

I'd better go, she said in her head but somehow it came out as 'Yes, why not,' because as welcoming as the almshouse was, she wanted to stay and have a hot chocolate and sit at the table and chat to him. Just for five minutes. She should have bid him goodnight because although the voice in her head was now saying, '*Why shouldn't you have a hot chocolate?*', she knew exactly why she shouldn't. Because this man touched her hand and awakened something in her that she didn't even know existed and his eyes were blue and beautiful and warmed her like the sun. That was why.

'Do you have sisters – or brothers?' Elliott asked her as he waited for the kettle to boil. 'And if so are they as exhausting as my own?'

'Two sisters,' replied Sophie. 'And I wish they were more

like Tracey but they're sadly not. They're entitled and con-descending and, in case you haven't gathered, we aren't close. They wouldn't have done what I did.'

'No rebellious streak then?'

Is that what she had? A rebellious streak? She wouldn't have thought that she had one of those. Apart from risking exclusion by throwing Irina's gang in a pool all those years ago and standing on a doorstep to tell a bunch of micro-phones thrust in her face that her husband was a total shit, she'd always played the game. That's why her actions two weeks ago had shocked everyone so much, because they came crashing in from left field. Miss Palmer-Price had said to her after the pool incident that she was going to 'quench that fire within her for her own good' and she hadn't had a clue what she was talking about.

'I would hardly class myself as a serial mutineer. Maybe running channels away my insubordinate tendencies, keeps me from boiling over.'

Elliott had his back to her as he poured the water over the chocolate powder but she could sense that her answer amused him.

'When did you start running?' he asked.

'At school. Ah.' She made a face, remembering the exact day. Maybe she had more of that rebellious streak than she'd given herself credit for. 'One of the PE teachers held a run-ning club after lessons and I was forced to join it for a week as a punishment for writing too short an essay on St Bathsheba of Whitby. Myself and my nemesis Irina Morozova, who was sentenced to two whole weeks of run-ning club for referring to the saint in none too flattering terms.' *A boring old fart* had been Irina's verdict, as she remembered.

'I would find it very difficult to write anything interesting about St Bathsheba myself,' said Elliott, bringing over the mugs.

'Thank you. And precisely. She was an absolute doormat, wasn't she?'

Elliott nodded. 'Not the most inspiring of the saints, I'll give you that.'

St Bathsheba was a woman who sacrificed everything in her life – and ultimately her life itself – for her husband and was rewarded by being canonised for her devotion, although she was little known. She certainly wouldn't have gone down well with any feminists, but then St Bathsheba's was not a school that encouraged women to smash through glass ceilings.

'I pretended that I'd misread the question and wrote about the biblical Bathsheba, who had far more appeal.' Sophie cringed at her youthful arrogance. She'd been fascinated by that Bathsheba, a very beautiful (married) woman whom King David saw bathing and desired. He impregnated her and then called her husband Uriah back from the war to sleep with her so he would think she was carrying his baby. But Uriah didn't want to violate the code of war and insisted on staying with his soldiers. So David engineered it so that Uriah went on the front line in battle where he would surely be killed – and he was. Then David married Bathsheba and their second son – Solomon – acceded to the throne, rather than David's older sons, which led to all sorts of trouble and civil war.

'We had a debate about Bathsheba – the unsainted one – in a philosophy lecture,' said Elliott, remembering. 'Was she powerless or powerful? David found himself quite helplessly attracted to her beauty, which started a train of events that ultimately corrupted him.'

'Was her pregnancy an unplanned-for consequence of his lust, or designed by her to install herself as queen? Victim or agent?' Sophie lifted up her hands as if they were scales, weighing the possibilities. 'She definitely manipulated David on his deathbed to put their son on the throne, thus securing herself the potent position of queen mother. Was she then the power behind the throne or the throne itself? My school would have believed the former, but I'm not so sure.'

'She certainly is a very interesting character, who has divided opinion for centuries.'

'Compared to St Bathsheba, who makes a wet blanket look dynamic.'

Elliott gave a hoot of laughter. 'I totally agree.'

Sophie took a sip of the hot chocolate before speaking again. 'This is all a bit deep and academic, isn't it?'

'Maybe. But it's also very thought-provoking.'

'I never get the chance to talk to anyone like this,' said Sophie. 'The women in my circle only ever want to gossip about each other, the press want to know whose dress I'm wearing and everyone else thinks I'm just a vacuous arm decoration for John.' Despite her first class degree from Cambridge, she knew that many people didn't consider her to have a working brain and that included her family. It felt good to be having a proper meaty conversation, a scholarly one with someone she felt respected her opinion and didn't try to dismiss her as the equivalent of candy floss, totally out of her verbal depth.

'That's a shame,' replied Elliott. 'I love a good intellectual discussion, which is handy when you're in my line of work because there are always a lot of questions thrown at you for debate.' He took a drink and when he lowered his mug, he had a perfect Rhett Butler hot chocolate moustache that made Sophie snort with laughter.

'Have you heard of the Bathsheba Syndrome?' she asked him when he had wiped it away. She'd found that a very intriguing concept when she'd read about it.

'I have indeed,' replied Elliott. '*The seeds of a man's downfall are sown in the very ground of his success.* An ethical man made successful, abusing the power he wields. The unstinting desire to win at all costs because knowing one has power triggers psychological changes, bad changes. Power leads to greed as leadership leads to entitlement.'

Sophie gulped. He could have easily been describing John; she hadn't thought until that very moment how much power might have corrupted her own husband.

'Really it should be called the David Syndrome though, shouldn't it? Poor old Bathsheba gets the blame for leading him to the dark side when it's his own weaknesses that do that,' Elliott continued.

'You're right of course. Poor Bathsheba.' *Yes, blame the easy target.* 'Being surrounded by yes-men who substantiate his feelings of supremacy and have fed his ego until it's bloated. I imagine all that led him to believe he was coated with Teflon.' She was talking about David, yet thinking of John. If ever there was a living, breathing example of Bathsheba Syndrome, he was it. Sophie sighed heavily.

As if Elliott felt the dip in her mood, he dragged the conversation back to its origin.

'You were telling me about your running, and how it started off as a punishment. So how come you got hooked?'

'Ah, yes, well one thing that life at St Bathsheba's did teach me was that it took only a little more effort to do a good job than a bad one, so I thought I might as well do my best for Miss Geraint because I really liked her. Plus Irina was flopping and pretending to be exhausted and out of breath and it annoyed her that I appeared so enthusiastic. I did as Miss Geraint taught me: alternate walking and running, building up my stamina. After the week, I asked if I could carry on. I liked the feeling of pushing myself, feeling my lungs working to capacity, my heart thumping. Irina thought I was a masochist. I even started getting up half an hour earlier and running around the grounds, sometimes in the pouring rain, sometimes in the first showing of sunlight. When I ran I felt my head clear of everything, respite from exam stress' *and from feelings of inadequacy and loneliness* '. . . so, thanks to St Bathsheba of Whitby being a total non-entity, I discovered something wonderful; a valve, a survival mechanism. I run when I want to be alone with my thoughts, when I'm sick up to here with political phrases and jargon . . .' *When I'm tired of being savaged by the media, disregarded by my family, ignored by my husband.* Sometimes, when she set off running for the fields behind Park Court, she imagined leaving them all behind in her wake, feeling the air grow clearer the further away from them she got. Running helped her to breathe.

When Henry had died, she had to force herself to wash, eat, put on her shoes and take steps outside, because all she wanted to do was curl up into a ball, around the memory of him being safe and growing inside her. Running helped her to rejoin the world again, when she didn't want to but had to because John needed her and her mother was admonishing her for bringing everyone down with her depression.

Sometimes she dreamed that she ran to the edge of the earth and jumped off into the inky star-filled blackness, her

feet continuing to power through the oxygen-less atmosphere. But in those dreams Sophie was always running away
from and never towards anything. There was nothing
to run to.

'Miss Geraint was forced to resign the year after, when
Miss Palmer-Price discovered she lived with a woman,' said
Sophie, shaking her head. 'What a horrible, horrible place
it was. So intolerant and hypocritical. The head of Religious
Studies was the most unchristian woman I ever met. I once
commented in class that I thought Mary Magdalene was
probably very much in love with Jesus and Miss Egerton
went ballistic.' Talking to Elliott was making Sophie realise
she really had been quite the renegade. 'I was going through
a romantic – with a small "r" – phase at the time, I think,'
she went on. 'I never meant it was a consummated relationship, just that I thought they must have been very fond of
each other.'

'And I would be inclined to agree,' said Elliott.

'She reported me to the head as insinuating they were
friends with benefits. Sex hadn't even crossed my mind, but
she wouldn't listen. She said I was disgusting for suggesting
there was anything other than a spiritual connection
between them.'

'Your teacher sounds grim.' Elliott said, a growl lacing
his words. He'd met far too many people who purported to
be Christians when they were enemies of decency and
compassion.

'She made me believe my soul would be damned. I was
terrified. I daren't tell her that I harboured a secret hope that
they *were* madly in love with each other and wanted to get
married. She'd have blown up and redecorated the assembly
hall with her intestines.'

'You aren't on your own in believing that Jesus and Mary Magdalene had a more than platonic relationship, though I personally don't,' said Elliott.

'When I got a little older, I preferred to think of them as close friends who loved each other so much that sharing each other's orbit was enough to make them happy. Nothing more complicated than that.'

'And now?' asked Elliott, but the clock in the hallway interrupted any answer she had been about to give. It chimed over and over and Sophie realised how late it was.

'Elliott, I am so sorry, I'm keeping you up.'

'You're not, I'm often up until the wee small hours anyway.'

'Even Cinderella didn't leave it until the last stroke of midnight.'

Elliott picked up her mug just as she was reaching for it to take over to the sink.

'Cinderella would have washed her own cup, too,' said Sophie.

'Not if she'd been in my house. I'd have made her feel like an honoured guest.'

Of that, Sophie had little doubt. She felt very welcome in this house; not merely tolerated, but valued for who she was, not for her connections or how beneficial she could be to someone.

'Cinderella had decidedly better shoes though.' Sophie lifted up her foot with the cheap sneaker on it.

'Good tight laces,' Elliott adjudged. 'She was a fool not to favour a strap in my opinion.'

Sophie wagged her finger. 'Then again, if she hadn't lost her shoe, she might not have married the prince.'

'Do you know, I hadn't thought of that.'

'I'll go out of the back door . . .'

'. . . to avoid the curtain twitchers, I know,' said Elliott, finishing off her sentence.

The moon was a perfect disco ball of bright silver tonight, lighting up the bay of Little Loste, making the wave-tops glitter. The world looked monochrome, like something from a 1930s movie where the hero grabbed the heroine and kissed her passionately after a half-hearted protest from her.

'Goodnight, Pom. Let me see you to the bottom of the garden.'

'No, I'm good, don't worry,' said Sophie, stepping quickly away from him in case he was thinking along the same lines as she was. Because if Elliott Bellringer seized her around the waist and pulled her towards him, Sophie didn't know if she would have resisted or not.

Chapter 34

The next morning, Tracey picked Sophie up at half-past eight. She was in a state of high trepidation.

'Don't laugh,' she said, 'but I started thinking in bed last night, what if Pom lied as much as I did about being good at sewing. Then I had this dream where you made a dress out of really cheap material and it was awful. I woke up in a right old panic at half-five and I couldn't get back to sleep.'

'That might happen,' said Sophie.

'Please don't joke.'

Sophie yawned. She hadn't exactly had a restful sleep herself last night. It had taken her at least an hour to drop off because thoughts of 'Ells Bells' kept trespassing into her brain. She could have happily stayed at the vicarage for hours more, talking to him – no, talking *with* him. John talked *to* her or *at* her, they didn't really converse much: there was a difference. Then, when she did eventually drift off, something had woken her up in the early hours, a feeling that she was being watched. Her eyes had sprung open but there was nothing there. She'd called out, but no one had answered her. Not that the sensation had been scary; just odd. Almost as if something were checking on her as a mother might check on a sleeping new baby, putting her head close to assure herself he was still breathing.

'Sorry,' said Tracey. 'I bet I've turned you into as big a stress-head as I am. Did you get a shit night's sleep because of all the trouble I'm causing you?'

'On the contrary, I sleep better here than I have done for years,' said Sophie, which was true – apart from the previous night. Too much talk about Mary Magdalene and Jesus and orbits. And love.

Slattercove market was in full swing when they arrived there.

'This is the best place,' explained Tracey, leading her over to a stall. Sophie locked down into material-hunting mode, shifting bolts of cloth aside to view others. Nothing there. They moved on. Nothing there either. She found the right colour but not the right material; then she found a right-ish material but not the right colour.

'Where else could we go?' asked Sophie, after they had exhausted all the stalls without success.

'Whitby? Although we'd probably be better going to Nunbury, but that's an hour's drive away.'

An hour and ten minutes later they were in Nunbury.

'I hope Jade flipping Darlow realises how much trouble we are going to,' tutted Tracey.

'If you want this dress to bond you together, then it has to be right,' said Sophie. 'I trust my instincts and they weren't coming up trumps.'

'Do you ever make dresses for yourself?' asked Tracey.

'Yes ... but John doesn't ... The thing is, newspapers want to know whose outfits you're wearing, and it wouldn't look good to say that I'd made them myself.'

'Why not, though? You'd think in this day and age that making your own would be respected. Even Princess Anne gets mega brownie points for putting on the same outfits a few times, cutting costs. Some of those designers charge an absolute fortune, don't they? The most expensive thing I have in my wardrobe is a leather jacket. I paid three hundred quid for it after my divorce as a treat.'

Sophie didn't say what she must have paid in her lifetime so far for clothes. *Clothes maketh the man* had been a familiar mantra both for her family and for John's. She'd felt, though, that a lot of her own creations suited – and fitted – her much better than those she'd bought.

Nunbury had a sizeable prom and bridal shop not far from the multi-storey car park and just for interest, they went in to look. The place was full of teenage girls rifling through the racks. Sophie wasn't that impressed by the selection.

'They're all so samey,' she said. 'Drab. As if they've been made by people who've churned out uninspiring brides-maids' dresses for fuddy-duddies all their lives and can't quite adapt to the whole idea of the prom. These are not designed for teens.' She picked one off the rail and held it up. 'Dreadful, insipid, cheap,' she said.

'I beg to differ,' coughed Tracey, pointing to the price tag.

Something danced at the side of Sophie's brain: an idea; but when she tried to focus on it, it slid away.

'They're certainly making their money today though,' remarked Tracey as more teenagers and their mums walked in through the door as they walked out. 'Yep. It's an expensive time of year. And a worrying one for a lot of parents, I shouldn't wonder.'

'You can always get your dad's girlfriend to make you a dress,' put in Sophie, tongue firmly wedged in her cheek.

'Oy, cheeky,' Tracey said, then shook her head slowly from side to disgusted side. 'All that cash, just for a few hours' wear and then it's totally redundant. It'll sit in a wardrobe for years before eventually being donated to a charity shop. Madness. Thank goodness we didn't have them in my day. My dad couldn't have afforded five hundred quid for a frock.'

'The thing is, we do have them now and every girl wants to look like Cinderella at the ball,' said Sophie. The Cinderella image was fresh in her mind from last night, holding up her sneakered foot to a man who could easily be a lucky woman's Prince Charming. Dena Stockdale's father's firm, Daisy Shoes, must make a killing at this time of year, she thought, maintaining the Cinderella theme. Some kids probably didn't even go to their proms because they couldn't afford the outfits. And if they could, there was all the other stuff, for girls anyway: shoes, bags, jewellery, nails, hair, spray tans . . . it was never ending.

They found a large material shop in the precinct selling dreadfully overpriced stock, but – as luck would have it – on the sale rack was a bolt of cloth that was the perfect colour and quality for Jade's dress. Sophie gathered up all the other things on her list from various shelves in the same shop: cotton, boning, tailor's chalk, interfacing. She also found a beautiful strip of jewel-encrusted ribbon that would make the perfect embellishment for the neckline and the waistband.

'How much?' shrieked Tracey, blanching when the shop assistant told her the total cost. She took out her Visa with a sigh. 'Me and my big mouth,' she said. 'This'll teach me a lesson I'll never forget. It would have been cheaper to feed Jade a load of pies until she filled that red frock out. In fact, why didn't I think of that first?'

'Wait till I hand you *my* bill.' Tracey's jaw dropped and Sophie laughed. 'Let's go for lunch,' she suggested then, pointing to an Italian bistro. 'I'll pay. I think we need to eat to combat the shock.'

'No, I'll pay. I owe you,' insisted Tracey, but Sophie insisted back.

Over lasagne, buttered mangetout and a bucket load of French fries, Sophie and Tracey traded information and chatted like friends who had known each other for far longer than they had. It was different to being with Elise, filtering every mouthful in case she said something indiscreet that Elise could ferry back to Gerald. Tracey told her more about her ex-husband and how controlling he'd been, how everything had to be done his way or he blew a fuse, even down to how their house was decorated. Sophie didn't say how much Tracey's marriage seemed to mirror her own.

'I saw a photo of you in the paper and you look so very different with black hair, Pom,' said Tracey, finishing off the last of her small rosé wine. 'It's going to be a hell of a job trying to get it back to your natural colour when you go home.'

'That's the least of my worries,' said Sophie.

'I can't call you Sophie. You don't look anything like her. I can't believe you're one and the same person.'

We aren't, Sophie wanted to say to her. *Pom's happy.*

She picked up the dessert menu because she didn't want to think about going back to Cherlgrove and having to face all the Mayhews and the Calladines again.

Over tiramisu Tracey told her that she wished Elliott could meet someone who wasn't a twat like his ex-wife. 'I'm so worried that Joy is going to come back and disrupt Elliott's life – and Luke's, I've got a gut feeling about it. He was never as content with her as he is now without her. I want him to find someone who—' She stopped in mid-sentence, and Sophie prompted her to go on. 'Okay then, who he talks to like he talks to you. He tends to keep his barriers up with women. I mean, imagine what could happen if he invited Miriam Bird for lunch? She'd consider that an engagement. He's aware of her feelings and wouldn't lead her on. It's too easy for people to fall in love with some-one like Elliott, someone strong and good and kind; but with you, he's totally relaxed.'

'Maybe that's because I'm married and out of bounds,' replied Sophie, even though she suspected it wasn't that.

Tracey knew it wasn't that either. 'There are plenty of married women in the congregation and he doesn't open up to any of them like he does you.'

Sophie tried to look bemused but her heart was betraying her with an excited tattoo. It would be wrong to think of herself as special to Elliott Bellringer, but her brain was not in control of her feelings. It needed to seize the reins from her heart – and fast.

Chapter 35

Sophie sat in church the next morning and listened to Elliott's sermon about the prodigal son and her thoughts started to wander. She tried to envisage rocking up at Park Court, walking into a hallway full of Calladines and Mayhews who threw up their hands in joy and immediately instructed Margaret – or whoever was employed in her place – to go and kill the fatted calf; but she couldn't conjure the scene. Even in her imagination, which she was supposed to be able to direct, all she could see was them standing in a disapproving crescent. Her father would be shaking his head, unable to look at her; Clive would be regarding her as if she were a black-haired alien. Celeste, in that horrible mink coat, wearing the expression of someone who had just had a bad smell released under their nose and her mother, Annabella and Victoria in a tight judgemental knot, like the three witches of *Macbeth*. Edward might smile, she thought, but his smile would quickly vanish again for fear of recrimination. She didn't even want to contemplate what John's reaction would be.

She turned her attention back to the pulpit. 'You see, God

is kinder than we are. We would probably get really annoyed if our brother or sister ran away and then turned up again and was treated like a king. But God doesn't give up on us when we do something wrong,' Elliott was saying.

'I wish I were going home to God then.' Sophie thought she'd said this to herself, but from the way the people seated in front of her whipped their heads round, it seemed she hadn't. She felt herself growing hot with embarrassment as Elliott's mouth quirked with amusement as he continued to speak, his blue eyes lingering on her for a long moment. She wished he would go on to say, 'What this story is really telling you is that if you ever run off, don't go back. There's no point because it will be awful, give or take a roast dinner. So why not stay where you are and be happy?' But he didn't. And fatted calf or no fatted calf, she would have to go and face the music at some point and risk her siblings kicking up a stink just like the prodigal's did. Maybe God was sending her a clear message after all, via Elliott's sermon. Maybe He was telling her to go home and everything would be okay, after they'd all given her a piece of their minds. Best to get the turning up part over and done with, sooner rather than later, find some semblance of normality.

Sitting there, watching Elliott hold court in church she thought again what a lovely man he was. Solid and steady, and kindness shone out of him. She couldn't think of him as the sort of person who might use her heartache to score him points with the general public. She couldn't imagine him tricking her into visiting a hospital ward knowing that it would slice her up inside. She could imagine, however, what he would look like first thing in the morning with his dark hair tousled and his eyes sleepy. And looping his arm around her in bed, pulling her close, finding her lips with his own and that was a big problem. Little Loste was binding her to it with tendrils as strong as the weeds she had hacked at to free the flowers in the almshouse garden. She had a place in life, duties, responsibilities, a man and none of them were here.

Tracey had insisted Sophie join them for Sunday lunch again. She had agreed on condition that as soon as she'd had her last mouthful, she would be starting on Jade's dress. She wanted to get all the pieces cut out today so she could begin sewing tomorrow. Even when it was all put together, there would be lots of little tweaks in order to make it the perfect fit and they were already on a tight schedule. The sooner it was hanging up in Jade's wardrobe, the better.

She didn't go with Tracey to pick up Luke from Sunday school; she didn't want to see Miriam Bird spontaneously combust because she was still on the scene. In any case, Miriam wouldn't have long to wait before she was gone for good, she thought as she waited outside the church.

'Look what we made in Sunday School,' said Luke, running to Sophie, holding aloft what looked like a ball of scrunched-up white paper. Because it was a ball of scrunched-up white paper.

'It's the rock that was in front of Jesususes cave and that got rolled away,' he explained. 'But it's also a toy for Plum.'

'They could at least have used grey paper,' said Tracey quietly. 'Jade ought to thank her lucky stars that Miriam Bird isn't making her frock. She'd make me look like Vera Wang. Oh, Pom, I'm so nervous about that dress. Jade's going to hate me, knowing I failed her.'

'Jade will know only that you made it. But do me a favour

and tell her that it was such an ordeal it's put you off sewing for life. Do *not* volunteer to make her wedding dress in the future.'

Tracey slipped her arm inside Sophie's as they wended their way on, which surprised but also touched her. It was the sort of thing she'd always thought sisters would do. Hers didn't, obviously. The Calladines were not an affectionate or a demonstrative family. She'd often wondered if Annabella had become pregnant by osmosis.

Plum was mewing pitifully when they walked into the vicarage.

'Look, he's missed you, Luke,' said Tracey.

'Awww I'm here, Plum, don't worry,' said Luke, smothering the kitten with kisses and taking him into the lounge.

'Funny thing, isn't it – love. Do you ever stop to think about it?' asked Tracey, turning the hob on. 'What makes us love one person and not another? Why have I known Steve Darlow all of my life and yet one night across a crowded – well, an empty pub, it was like a switch went on and I suddenly thought *phwoar*.'

Elliott Bellringer squeezed my hand and turned on a light inside me.

'Er, no idea. It's strange, isn't it?'

'And then it can go the other way, as quick as that.' Tracey clicked her fingers. 'Once I thought that if Barry and I ever split up I would die. Now life is a non-stop party because I'm divorced from the horrible bastard. Why is that?'

Sophie couldn't answer. She had no idea why love rushed in, what made it choose to stay, or why it decided to leave. All she knew was that she had just heard the front door of the vicarage open and her heart had skipped at the thought of Elliott Bellringer being a few steps away.

'Hi, girls, sorry I'm late. Mrs Braithwaite wanted a few hundred words.' Elliott crossed to the oven, took out the pork joint, turned up the heat in readiness to cook the Yorkshire puddings. 'I'm going up to change, I won't be long.'

'I have no idea what he ever saw in Joy, or what she ever saw in him,' said Tracey, when he was out of earshot. 'The biggest mismatch in history. I think Cupid must be a really screwed up, vindictive, nasty individual.'

'People don't always marry for love though, Tracey. My eldest sister married for money, without question. And I'm pretty sure the other one married for prestige, because she'll be a Lady when her in-laws shuffle off this mortal coil. I've never detected a lot of love between them. Even when they were first going out together.'

'Opposites attract sometimes, that's what it was for me and Barry, i.e. I was human and he was an alien from Planet Knob. It was certainly the case for my brother and that hippy cow. He felt protective and she wanted a change from her usual scabby boyfriends. Trouble is, she likes scabby men. If Luke hadn't looked so much like the Bellringer side of the family, I would have been very suspicious, if you know what I mean.'

There was no mistaking that Luke was his father's son though. That hair, the summer-blue eyes, the form of his lips when he smiled.

'Do you love John?' asked Tracey then, but the subject was cut off before Sophie could answer as Elliott walked into the kitchen, wearing tracksuit bottoms and an AC/DC T-shirt.

'I thought you were heckling me today, Pom,' he said.

'I am so sorry,' Sophie replied. 'I was thinking aloud. About the prodigal son and returning home and what reception I'll get.'

'Presumably not a full roast dinner then,' said Tracey, taking some apple sauce out of the cupboard.

'Not even a parboiled carrot.'

'They won't be pleased to see you?' asked Elliott, eyebrows dipping in disbelief.

'I expect they will really,' replied Sophie, because to admit anything otherwise would be humiliating.

'I'm sure they will. How could they not?' said Elliott.

Clearly, Elliott had no experience of belonging to families like the Mayhews and the Calladines, thought Sophie. *Lucky him.*

Chapter 36

Over at Glebe Hall, the Mayhew seniors' residence, a pretentious, draughty Georgian pile that was originally designed for a Lord with more money than sense, Sunday lunch was being served to the immediate and extended families. The Calladines had been invited over, seeing as this dratted business involved them too.

'I mean, where the bloody hell has the girl got to?' said Angus Calladine. 'The trouble she has caused us all!'

'I hear your housekeeper is firmly back in the ranks, John,' said Alice. 'At least that's some good news.'

'He's had to give her a monster pay rise to reaffirm her loyalty though,' said Robert, with more glee than he intended to expose.

'Robert!' admonished his mother. 'Revelling in the misfortunes of others is not what we do.'

A sarcastic snort from Edward, followed by an 'ow' as Davina gave him one of her infamous elbow digs.

'This is delicious, Mother,' said John, after swallowing a chunk of lamb.

'Thank you.' Celeste took full credit even though their housekeeper had prepared, cooked and served it.

'Anyway, back to this ridiculous situation, what's the full SP,' barked Angus, who was too cross even to taste what he was eating.

'PM's behind me all the way,' said John. 'I have a legal team sifting through every word *that woman* has said and will be suing at least two tabloids and possibly a broadsheet.'

'I heard she was on *Loose Women,* if that wasn't meant to be ironic,' chortled Davina. 'And she didn't go down very well.'

'Not what I heard,' muttered Edward, which prompted yet another elbow jab. The sexual reference went over the elders' heads, clearing them by at least six foot.

'Someone must know where Sophie is, she can't have just vanished into nothingness,' said Alice with a haughty trip of mirthless laughter. 'I am totally ashamed of my daughter and when she does eventually turn up, I will be telling her exactly what I think of her.'

'Aren't you worried about her?' The words tumbled out of Edward before he could halt them. They transformed the whole table to a silent, frozen tableau. His natural instinct would have been to apologise for the remark but on this occasion he overrode it. 'Sophie went through a terrible humiliation which she didn't deserve. Isn't anyone con-cerned that she might have harmed herself?'

'Of course she hasn't harmed herself, don't talk rot, Edward,' said Clive. 'She's stamping her foot and—'

For the first time in his life Edward spoke over his father. 'It occurred to me last night how many conversations we've had since Sophie left about who could possibly know where she's gone. Who could she turn to? Who were her friends?

And no one can answer those questions because she has nobody, she was entirely devoted to John and his career. She is both condemned and revered in the press at the mob's whim, all because John *has* to court publicity. She puts up with being thrown to the lions day after day, not for herself, but for her loving husband, a man who can't keep his own dick in his trousers.'

That threw the cat amongst the pigeons, but Edward was not to be shushed, not even by another vicious elbow from Davina.

'Oh yes, John F. Mayhew, family jewel. Has Britain at his feet. Has wealth, has charm, looks, is married to the most magnificent woman but is it enough for him? Nope. God's Gift here with his best fillet steak at home has to go and shop in the abattoir for a bag of rotting giblets. And don't you dare . . .' He turned to Davina after seeing her arm draw back. 'Don't you bloody dare.'

John burst into laughter. 'Eddie, I register your stress, we are all stressed here, so let's just bring this down a couple of levels. This is not the Roman Senate.'

But Robert decided to poke the beast with a stick rather than offer it a conciliatory banana. 'Seems Eddie has a bee in his bonnet that he's not the family jewel,' he smirked.

'Funny word, *family*, isn't it?' said Edward. 'Implies trust and love and care, but listening to this diatribe today I have no doubt in my mind why Sophie didn't turn to anyone around this table when she was obviously desperate enough to abscond over a six-foot wall. Aren't you supposed to run *to* your family, not away from them as if your rectum was on fire?'

'Now steady on there, Edward,' warned Clive.

'John comes running to me when he needs help. Mainly

in a professional capacity, of course, because he pays me to watch his back,' continued Edward. His flow could not be stemmed because the banks had broken and it felt very *very* good to let out what had been pent up behind his internal dam walls for too long. 'You would think that Sophie might have approached her siblings for advice, succour, perhaps? I wonder why she didn't. Could that be because one of them looks like a bullfrog and is so hideously jealous of her sister's beauty that it's almost tangible, and the other is so twisted that she finds it acceptable to wave her ability to produce a child in Sophie's face like a point-scoring sheet.'

'How dare you speak like that of my family,' said Alice Calladine, throwing her napkin down onto the table like a gauntlet.

'Apologise immediately,' roared Clive and Angus together, perfectly synchronised both in their fury and in rising to their feet.

'I will not,' said Edward, standing also. 'I'm the only person around this table who is hoping that wherever Sophie is, she's actually with people who don't want to use her, who don't want to show off in front of her, who don't want to punish her for having the gall to be selfless and bloody lovely. I hope she's with people who are caring for her, being nice to her. In fact – I hope she's so happy that she doesn't come back.'

John couldn't take his brother seriously. Especially not this version of his brother with his Y-fronts in a twist. He'd never seen him so ballsy – it was hilarious.

'She will come back, Edward. Despite what you think, Sophie has an enviable and easy life and I know her, she will be missing her home comforts. And she loves me.'

'I don't think you know the meaning of the word,'

Edward rounded on him. 'I mean what sort of husband actually considers locking up his wife in a psychiatric hospital in order to get out of all the shit he caused himself? How very loving and considerate of you.'

'Edward, sit down now or we are finished,' growled Davina.

'I'm not sitting down and we *are* finished.' Then Edward gasped; he hadn't intended to say that, then he realised that he'd meant it. 'Yes, we are finished. Davina, you are one of the coldest women I've ever met in my life, so you might fit in with everyone around this table; but seeing as I don't fit in with them, we should call it a day. You look down your nose so much at everything I'm surprised your eyeballs haven't migrated to your nostrils.'

'Edward!' Now Celeste was on her feet as Davina's face started to crumple.

John once again called for peace. 'Come on, this infighting isn't helping any of us. Eddie, apologise and eat your lamb.'

But this went far beyond an uncharacteristic outburst for Edward. He'd been thinking so much about Sophie since she ran off, thinking about how scared she must have been to go to the lengths she had.

Four years ago, he'd not only known all about Malandra Moxon, but he'd enabled the affair by covering John's tracks for him. Then he'd been party to his brother and Len putting the frighteners on the woman with the result that she had confronted Sophie and whatever the doctors said, no one could be absolutely sure that there had been no correlation between Malandra's visit to the London flat and Sophie's miscarriage. Maybe if she could have carried the baby for one or two more weeks, he might have lived. If only Edward, as a brother, as soon as he'd known what was going on, had taken John to one side and told him not to be so bloody stupid, to end this before it had properly begun. He hadn't, because he knew that John did what he wanted, when he wanted and with whom he wanted. But he *should have tried*, John just *might* have listened. That was why Edward had never been able to mentally untangle himself from the tragedy that unfurled and why he'd sworn to himself that he would always be Sophie's invisible knight from then on.

So far as the Rebecca Robinson episode went, he hadn't known about her until the day before the story hit the papers, and he'd worked harder than Len Spinks to try and halt the leakage. Len was spinning to save John's reputation, Edward to stop Sophie getting hurt again. They'd all stood in that room on the morning before she absconded, listening to John's arrogant affirmations that everything would be all right because Sophie would back him up. He'd watched his parents – and hers – clucking around John, bolstering him, pandering to him and he'd noticed too late that she was alone, ignored. He'd felt disgusted with them all – and himself. He'd let her down again; it would never happen a third time.

Edward gave his mother a dry smile. 'Thank you for lunch, Mother, but leave me off the invitation list in future.'

'Well, I'm not going anywhere,' humphed Davina, recovering quickly from her loud – and tearless – sobbing.

'Stay or go, I don't care,' said Edward. 'I will not be marrying you. If you're adamant about wanting to be a Mrs Mayhew, I suggest you try and cop off with Robert. You'd make an excellent match.'

'What?' Robert was confounded by this doppelganger who looked like his brother but was behaving nothing like him today. 'Eddie, are you on your period?'

'Enough is enough now,' said John, his patience fraying.

'I'm sick of clearing up your effluent, John. You're a human version of a muck-spreader. Well, I say "human"...'

'That really is enough, Edward,' said Clive. 'Get out of this house until you can behave yourself.'

'I'm going, don't you worry, Father.'

'He'll be back,' chuckled Robert. 'Or maybe not. Maybe he'll start up an estate agency.'

Davina gave a hoot of laughter, offsetting her humiliation by savouring Edward's.

Edward, who had reached the door by this stage, turned slowly, gleefully.

'I already have,' he said. 'Remember the "to be recommended" estate agency your neighbour used, Angus? I handled that sale. My new estate agency. At least, I say new but it's been up and running for a year. I just wanted to make sure it was on course for succeeding before I told you all, because you'd expect me to fail; but then I sold a Saudi Prince's apartment in Knightsbridge for ten million, so I'm really not going to. I was planning to leave your employ when Sophie returned, but I think this is as good a moment as any to tell you to stuff your job right up your sanctimonious, faithless, selfish arse, John Effffff.'

The sea of open mouths was a bigger reward than this week's commission for Edward. And with that, the eldest Mayhew brother, newly single and smiling, flounced out of his parents' house and experienced a little of what his sister-in-law Sophie was feeling: that a tight band across his chest had snapped and he could breathe properly at last.

Chapter 37

Tracey watched Sophie cut, the newly sharpened scissors slicing through the material like a hot knife through butter. She was fascinated by the ease with which she operated, as if every movement were instinct rather than design.

'Don't mind me noseying, do you?' she asked. 'I'm not putting you off am I?'

'Not at all,' replied Sophie.

'I am so worried.'

'Don't be. The one thing I do know about is dressmaking. You're in safe hands. Especially when I haven't had any parishioners' home-made wine with my lunch.'

Tracey sipped on her beetroot wine. She was standing at a safe distance so she couldn't possibly spill anything on the lovely green cloth.

'I can't believe you're doing this for me.'

'It's a pleasure. I love sewing, I'm looking forward to making it.'

'Jade will never believe I've done it. And I don't feel comfortable about lying.'

Sophie grinned at her. 'Let yourself off the hook this once and don't beat yourself up about bending the truth.'

'Bending it? Not so much bending it as smashing it to bits and cremating it.'

'I feel at peace when I'm sewing. I think I would have gone mad sometimes if I hadn't been able to shut myself away in my own room and make things. John thinks it's just a "little hobby" but it's much more than that to me. I feel as happy surrounded by cottons and materials as he does in his arena. Not that he'd equate them as having the same importance.'

'You ever thought about leading classes or becoming a designer?' asked Tracey.

Sophie laughed. 'Who, me?'

'Yes, you. Why not?'

'Because . . .' Sophie considered her answer. 'Because I don't have the time for a start. I already have a job.'

'Being John's assistant?' Do you enjoy that?'

Sophie opened up her mouth to say that she did – stock answer. Tweaked it to the truth.

'It's what I do.'

How weak does that sound, she thought then. She was hardly a shining example of the modern world, thanks to the indoctrinations of St Bathsheba's. Her sisters were more like women in a Jane Austen book whose sole purpose was to snare a husband before they withered on the vine, and they'd just managed it, but what a pair of cold, arrogant plonkers Giles and Pearson were. Her mother Alice had gone there too, any warmth pressed out of her out by the strict Bathsheban practices, then she'd gone on to hook a rich duck in Angus Calladine. Thinking about it, she'd never witnessed any tenderness between her parents either,

other than a dry kiss on the cheek on birthdays and anni-
versaries. She'd never known them not to have their own
bedroom each.

'What a shame that you have this talent and don't capitalise on it. Sorry, ignore me, I'm lecturing, change the
subject. It's been lovely having you here, Pom,' said Tracey,
sitting down on the chair at the other side of the desk. 'I
know that when you go back, you won't keep in touch so
I'm not even going to pressure you by asking, but I will
miss you.'

'I'll miss you too, Tracey,' smiled Sophie. 'It's been wonderful to talk and have lunch and shop and not have to
worry about anything I say. I do have a friend at home –
Elise, but her husband and John have a rivalry and our
friendship doesn't run very deep.'

'I had a really good friend,' said Tracey. 'Jess wanted to
be an artist. She always had a dream to open up a studio and
she could have, she was really good at watercolours. And I
mean *really* good.'

'What stopped her?' asked Sophie, interested.

'She killed herself last year. No one had a clue how
depressed she was, not even me, not until I read the letter
she left for me. It took me a long time to forgive myself for
not having spotted it. I really miss her, it was such a waste
of life. She should have thrown herself at her dream instead
of being so scared of failing that she never tried and ended
up that unhappy. Life's too short for not taking chances. I did.'

'People can be expert at hiding inside themselves,' said
Sophie, who knew. She'd struggled after Henry had died
because she was expected to carry on as normal and not
mope but sometimes she'd felt as if she couldn't go on, didn't
want to go on. She'd stood on a clifftop once watching the

Red Arrows at a memorial service and thought about kicking off her shoes, running forwards and jumping off, hoping the rocks below would smash her to a blessed final unconsciousness. The newspapers had printed a photo of her the next day berating her lack of emotion when meeting the veterans. She wished they could have seen inside her head.

'Elliott will miss you too. It's been good for him to speak to another woman who doesn't have a vested interest in getting into his vestments or isn't his stroppy sister. I can be a bit too opinionated where Joy is concerned and so he won't talk to me about her. I do worry about him and Luke, only because I want the best for them.'

'That's totally understandable. He's a good man. I'm sure that someone will come along who is perfect for them both.'

Tracey yawned, stretched, apologised. 'You're not boring me, honest. I've been worrying about this dress so much I didn't sleep well last night.'

'Go and get yourself some rest,' said Sophie. 'You don't have to stay here with me. I'm just making a start and then I'll be back in the morning. Once I get stuck into a project, I'm like a machine.'

Tracey nodded. 'I think I will. Thanks again, Pom. I'll say my goodbyes and see you tomorrow, most likely.'

After she had gone, Sophie played back part of their conversation. *She should have thrown herself at her dream instead of being so scared of failing that she never tried and ended up that unhappy.* Tracey might as well have been talking about her as her friend Jess. *It's a shame you have this talent and don't capitalise on it.* Sophie treated her ability to sew like an embarrassing ailment. John also scoffed at his brother Edward's secret ambition to open up his own estate agency. He'd wanted to do it since he'd been a boy apparently, yet they were both destined to be planets who rotated around the sun that was John F. Mayhew rather than occupy their own solar systems. That was their place in this universe.

Life's too short for not taking chances.

As she carried on cutting, she started to think what it would be like to be able to sew all day, every day. To own the shop that she'd built in her imagination, the one with the huge bowed front window and racks and racks of dresses inside all with her trademark accoutrement which was . . . well, she didn't know, but something that was her signature. Every dress would fit perfectly because she could nip and tuck at will to make sure that it did. Someone would saunter in with a picture and say, 'Can you make this?' and with absolute certainty, Sophie Mayhew would answer, 'Of course.' She wanted it all so much. There had to be a way of getting it: she had the money, the skill . . . what was really stopping her, other than herself?

Later, as she was folding away the dress pieces, the door flew open and Luke barrelled forward in his dressing gown.

'Pom, will you read me a story before I go to bed,' he pleaded. In close pursuit behind him was Elliott.

'You cheeky thing, Luke Bellringer. What did I tell you about disturbing Pom's concentration?'

'Oh, it's okay,' said Sophie, stretching a creak out of her back. 'I'm packing away for the evening. I don't mind meeting Scary Edwin again.'

'Yaaayyy,' said Luke, bouncing up and down and Sophie smiled, knowing that there was no artifice with the little boy; he really was that pleased that she had agreed to read him a story. What he wanted from her was out there and obvious, no hidden agenda.

'Come on, then.' She held out her hand and he took it

and something kissed her heart when his small, soft fingers closed around hers.

Sophie was aware of how intently Luke was looking at her as she read to him. At the end of the story he snuggled into her and she savoured the scent of his freshly washed still-damp hair and it brought a sensation to her chest that felt sharp and deep and she wasn't sure if it was painful or pleasant because it felt like revisiting a memory she had never had.

At the bottom of the stairs, she gave herself a mental shake before going into the kitchen for her key. There was a smell of chocolate in the air and Elliott was stirring two mugs. 'Non-alcoholic nightcap,' he offered. She couldn't refuse. She didn't want to refuse.

'Thank you,' said Sophie, sitting wearily down at the table.

'You can go through into the lounge if you'd rather?'

Not a chance, she thought. *And fall asleep on that sofa again? Be observed dribbling and snoring?*

'I'm good here.'

'Once again, thank you,' said Elliott. She wasn't sure if he meant for lending his sister a hand or reading his son a story, so she gave a one-size-fits-all answer.

'Happy to help.'

'So you'll be back in the morning, I presume?' She read the hopeful note in his voice and it both concerned her and thrilled her a little.

'If I'm not disturbing you.'

'Of course not. No point in trying to drag Mum's sewing machine over to the almshouse. I'll be out from nine but I'm sure you won't mind being here by yourself.'

'Not at all,' said Sophie. 'The sooner I get the dress finished the sooner your sister will be able to sleep properly.'

'Are you sleeping all right over there?' asked Elliott. 'Not too cold is it? I have a portable heater . . .'

'Honestly, I don't need it.'

'I know it's a bit basic. It was only meant as a place for the desperate, really.'

'I was desperate, so it's a perfect fit. It was very odd early yesterday morning. I felt as if someone was in the room watching me,' said Sophie, remembering that strange sensation. 'Not unpleasant; caring. if anything. It only lasted a second or two and it could have been the fallout from a dream but . . . I don't think so.'

'A few people who've stayed in the almshouse have reported similar. I knew Kitty Henshaw who owned the house and she didn't entertain fools gladly, but when she liked someone she was very kind and she loved young people especially. She was certainly very gracious in leaving the house to the church, although it had fallen into a lot of disrepair by then.'

'Well, it's been a sanctuary for me,' said Sophie.

'You must be missing your home comforts, though,' said Elliott, leaning forward. His large hand circling the mug made it look small.

'Not as much as you'd think. I sleep so much better here. Okay, I miss the shower, I admit that, but even the food is tastier. Oh my, those bread rolls from the shop down the hill! And I love running on the beach; the air feels so bracing and cleaner somehow.'

He was clearly amused by the passion in her voice.

'Honestly, Elliott, I've adored being here. It's changed me. I don't quite know what I mean by that really, but I feel different.'

'You'll be missed when you leave,' he said.

'Not by Miriam Bird, I bet,' she chuckled.

'Maybe not, but Tracey will miss you, Luke certainly will and . . . so will I.'

Silence hung between them like a thick, warm cloud. Neither breathed for a long moment.

'I'll miss you as well.' It sounded too heavy, she scrabbled around for something to whisk into the conversation to lighten it. 'I've never spoken so much to a vicar before. I used to think they were quite intimidating.'

'I hope I'm not,' said Elliott. 'When I was in the police, people – even innocent ones – were quite scared of me sometimes, of the authority. And now I'm a vicar, a lot still can't be themselves with me because they think I'll disapprove of them, which I don't.'

'For the record, I'm neither nervous nor wary of you.'

'Good.' He smiled.

'There should be more vicars like you.'

'Thank you, I'll take that as a compliment,' said Elliott. 'I do the best I can and I hope I'm good at it. It can be challenging sometimes, it's not all judging jam at the summer fair. I'm nothing special, though; just a normal man who happens to wear a selection of fancy vestments for his job, a job he loves very much.'

'It's quite obvious to me that you're a normal man under your clothes,' said Sophie. Then she realised what she'd said as Elliott's eyebrows raised, and she tried to amend her words. 'I do apologise, that came out totally wrong. Life should have a rewind button, shouldn't it?'

Elliott laughed. 'I know what you meant, so don't take it back. Yes, I'm an earthly creature. I have been known to drink too much at weddings and hit the dance floor – I do a great Night Fever. I love listening to rock music and

watching box sets. I love my God, who made this life possible, and I love to be in love. Luke is the result of a sexual
relationship; vicars have sex. I miss sex. I miss the intimacy,
being part of a couple, of having someone to come home to
and cook with or for – and although I always seem to have
Tracey on my doorstep to do some of those things with –
not the sex that would be weird – yes, I am a normal man,
with likes and dislikes, faults and needs.'

Sophie tried not to think about Elliott Bellringer having
sexual needs but it was difficult because the air between
them was charged with a dangerous energy.

'You're very easy to talk to, Pom. Too easy.' Elliott took
a deep breath. 'I think maybe we should call it a night before
I say something I regret.'

'Yep,' said Sophie, standing quickly. 'I totally get it. We
are both vulnerable people and because of that, the mem-
brane between sense and foolishness is very thin.' She
pinched her finger and thumb to demonstrate, held them up.

'Even thinner than that. And we are good people who
like each other, I think. Friends.'

'Yes friends.' Like Jesus and Mary Magdalene. They could
only ever be friends.

'Goodnight, Sophie. Back door?'

'To avoid the curtain twitchers, of course.' She smiled at
him and he smiled back and she thought she really ought to
get out of the vicarage and away from him as soon as was
humanly possible.

Friends or not, she was going to find it especially difficult
to get to sleep tonight.

Chapter 38

'Hmm, I think it's time we tried to smoke Sophie out,' said Len Spinks the next morning. Which of her family is she closest to?' he asked.

'Er . . .' John thought. It certainly wasn't her sisters, that pair of hideous gargoyles. Angus had been the least critical of her absconding, which wasn't quite the same thing, but in the absence of any other suitable criteria, probably he'd be the one. 'Her father, I'd say.'

'We'll have to clear it with him, of course, but a rumour pushed out there that he isn't in the best of health . . . possible stress-related chest pains. Nothing too dramatic. Nothing in the newspapers either. I think that if we beat a quiet drum in our court, the sound will be picked up and carried on the wind somehow to Sophie. Going to the press might make her suspicious that it's artful manipulation. I'm sure she's poring over every article, hence why she's staying away in a grand huff, so it needs to be subtle, a puff of Pied Piper juice in her general direction. I am not convinced that she is an island, there is an open channel somewhere that we don't know about, so you can start by saying something to Gerald Penn–Davies and Christopher Stockdale.'

'Not the Stockdales,' said John quickly. 'Dena and Sophie are definitely not in contact.'

Len's radar swept over the words and left him with an unpleasant tickle.

'Something you haven't told me?'

'Don't be ridiculous.'

'Question answered far too fast, John F. I can't help you if you don't help me.' He smiled a smile that was oily and fixed and impatient. 'Let's not have another Rebecca Robinson debacle, shall we. I. Need. To. Know.'

John opened his mouth to issue a further denial, then shut it again. He sighed resignedly, and then said:

'All right, I admit, there was a ... an incident. With a female. Not Dena Stockdale, I hasten to add.' He shuddered. 'Big mistake. It was nothing. A silly, impulsive episode.'

Len didn't react. He sat there in silence and waited for the rest of the story to roll from John's tongue.

'A one-off. And it wasn't penetrative.'

Len closed his eyes. 'Are we possibly looking at a stored item of clothing with a splash of indisputable evidence?'

'Ugh. Well ... I shouldn't think so. It was all over very quickly.'

'All over what? Her skirt? Top?' asked Len, dryly, without humour.

'She made all the moves,' said John. 'She would not want this known. I feel secure in that. A brief erroneous encounter. She won't say anything. She has as much to lose as I do; more, in fact.'

'Once?'

'I absolutely swear.'

Len nodded. He had no choice but to take John at his word but knew he was an extremely practised liar. 'Swear' was nothing more than five letters of the alphabet: John was the master and truth merely a slave that he bent to serve him. 'Where the hell is Edward, by the way? I've been ringing him all morning.'

'Sulking because he doesn't feel loved by Mummy and Daddy,' said John, his nose crinkled in disdain. 'I don't know why that should come as a surprise to him. None of us were. I'm not sure my father loved anything that didn't have a front sight and a recoil pad.'

Len's shaggy eyebrows dipped half in disbelief, half in sympathy which made John hoot.

'Don't look like that, it didn't do us any harm, Len. Prepared us for this tough world. Attention was given to us in relation to our accomplishments rather than personality when we were growing up. Attention which we mistook for affection, seeing as it was the closest we ever got to any. Robert did quite well on the leadership board, although I obviously headed it. Poor old Eddie . . . an also-ran. Had he been a racehorse, they'd probably have had him gelded and put him out to grass. Quite the sensitive one, my big brother. He told us yesterday at lunch that he'd started up an estate agency and I really didn't believe him but . . . it's all true and he seems to be doing very well. I shan't hold him to his notice period. Maybe we could give him some advertising? One brother helping out another.'

'How very philanthropic,' burred Len. He admired the Machiavellian Mayhew as a statesman, an orator, a leviathan but he didn't like him very much as a person. Len saw things as they were, he had to in his job. He saw the stick, not the candy floss spun around it. He saw John F. Mayhew for the cold-blooded, calculating self-serving lizard that he was. Definitely on the psychopathic spectrum. There were plenty of those in high-powered jobs, they didn't all go out and murder people, at least not physically, but they had no compunction or conscience about figuratively taking out the opposition, locking their jaws down onto the jugulars of people like Malandra Moxon. Rebecca Robinson thought she had been victorious, but the spotlight was fading on her fifteen minutes of fame, maybe twenty given an appearance on a reality TV series where she would be feted as the tramp she was. She'd been a fool playing the short game and would now never realise her ambition to work in a fast-tracked position connected to the government because she was totally blacklisted. No one could trust her. She was already reduced to a hissing, toothless grass-snake who contradicted herself more and more in her pursuit of publicity, casting doubts on everything she had revealed to the media and exposing herself to litigation. John's lawyers were going to have a field day crucifying her; he could more than afford to attack her, she couldn't afford to defend herself. Money paid for the best barristers, the best barristers won. Stupid girl, she'd have been better doing a Malandra and taking a pay-off. John would come out on top, if he held firm. And he would.

Len flicked from contemplative mood to action. 'So, back to Sophie. Let's start a little ripple in the water shall we?'

'I'll ring Angus and set that up,' said John, reaching for his mobile.

Chapter 39

After a sprint on the beach, Sophie had a long soak in the bath, though she would have preferred a cold shower this morning after the dream she'd had about Elliott last night. She wasn't sure she'd be able to look him in the face after what they'd been up to. It had felt very real, his hands on her body, his mouth . . . She'd needed a cigarette rather than a coffee when she sprang awake.

John had been an attentive lover, at least in the early days, but she'd always had the feeling that once she was 'in the bag' he hadn't needed to try as much. He didn't like her initiating sex either, said it put him off. Sometimes there had been months between intimacies which frustrated her because it wasn't just about the act, but the closeness, the words, the love, the exclusive connection. She hadn't felt connected to John F. Mayhew in private for a long time though, despite their very public united front. And as for 'exclusive' . . . Why had he gone elsewhere when it was 'on tap' for him at home? But she couldn't recall the last time she and John had made love; she didn't count the night they'd had sex after the Rebecca Robinson story had broken because that wasn't love, it was stamping her ownership on her husband on her part, and keeping his wife onside on his.

The John F. Mayhew that Rebecca Robinson described in bed was a man she didn't recognise. *Insatiable lust*? *'At me like a hammer drill'*? Was she lying or was that was it was like for them? Those details hurt, whether they were sensationalist lies or not, because the images of her husband with another woman were born from the words and real enough to torment her.

She set off for the vicarage and spotted a pink VW Beetle with eyelashes on the headlights – Miriam Bird's car – parked outside it, so she did an about-turn. She waited until she heard the car start up and drive off before vaulting over the back fence and knocking on the kitchen door. Elliott answered and she tried not to stare at the mouth that had done all manner of ungodly things to her last night in her dream.

'Come on in,' he said.

'Is the coast clear? I noticed you had a visitor.'

'Miriam volunteered to take Luke to nursery this morning. I have a funeral to conduct at the crematorium in Slattercove. The old lady from whom my sister bought the inn. I say "old" but seventy-seven isn't really these days, is it?'

'No, it isn't. We should enjoy life whilst we have it, shouldn't we?' *You're a fine one to talk*, said a voice inside her.

'Can I make you a coffee before I go?'

'No, I'm good thank you. I just want to get in there and sew.'

Elliott had his clerical collar on, a black shirt that showed off his broad shoulders, smart black trousers, shiny black shoes. He looked like a cross between a man of God and a vigilante in a spaghetti western. A sexy hero in black who liberates a whole town from outlaws, and with whom the whorehouse madam in the saloon falls in love but has to wave him off because their worlds were too far apart.

'*Mi casa, su casa*,' said Elliott, reaching for a long black tailcoat. He put it on and something inside Sophie wolf-whistled. 'You know where the kettle and biscuits are,' he continued. 'Help yourself to what you need. Tracey's going to pick Luke up after nursery and take him to hers. I should be home about four. If you leave before I get back, take the key with you, then you can let yourself in tomorrow morning because I have a really early start. A breakfast meeting with the bishop in Whitby.'

'Hope today goes well.'

'Me too.'

She ran a brief video clip in her head, as if she were Mrs Bellringer and he bent at this point to kiss her. She'd say, 'I'll have dinner waiting for you. We'll open up a bottle of wine and watch a film.' He'd say, 'Sounds great, we'll have an early night, shall we?'

John didn't want her to cook, he'd told her to leave that duty expressly to Margaret. 'Why keep a dog and have to woof yourself?' was a stock phrase of his. Maybe she should have insisted, maybe she should have said, 'I have sent Margaret off for the evening and I've made a lasagne. And you are not going in your office because we are going to curl up on the sofa and watch TV and share a bottle of red.' Trouble is, he wouldn't have done. He'd push the food around on his plate, then sit on the sofa for five minutes, tense, straight-backed, drumming his fingers impatiently at the side of him, then tell her he was just going to check

something in his office and that would be the last she would
see of him for the evening. He might as well have kept her
on ice until he needed to roll her out for a glittery function,
a constituency surgery or a PR call.

She sewed for most of the morning and when she took
a coffee break, she noticed yesterday's Sunday newspaper
in the recycling bag in Ells' kitchen. A picture of John on
the front, walking across Parliament square, mobile to his
ear, grim expression on his face. She reached out and
touched it and felt inexplicably confused. That man was
her husband. She had been in love with him since she was
eighteen years old and *he was hers*. They'd created a child
together, so why did she feel as if she were looking at
a stranger?

She'd been interrupted before she could answer the question that Tracey had asked her the previous day: 'Do you
love John?' The honest answer was that Sophie didn't know.
What she did know was that she wanted to. That love she
had for him in the beginning was still inside her, wasn't it?
Lost in the brambles and weeds of their disparate lives and
it was up to her to find it again and free it so it could grow
and blossom. It had to be there. Somewhere.

She made sure she left the vicarage before Elliott returned.
She slipped out of the back door and locked it even though
her instinct was to stay, have a coffee, ask Elliott about his
day. But it would have been wrong to do that, too cosy, it
wasn't her place, it was pretending and stupid. It was like
taking a glass of water after a harsh thirst from the first
person who offered it to her. She was mixing up affection
with gratitude, and who could blame her for those wires
being crossed?

She had an early night, closed the curtains, turned off the lights so that if Tracey – or Elliott – thought about calling in, they'd get a clear signal she did not want to be disturbed. At about eleven o'clock she was woken by that peculiar sensation of being watched once more, and again it disappeared as soon as she snapped to full consciousness.

Chapter 40

Sophie took only a short run the next morning, because the clouds were low, lumpy and dark – warning of a storm. She found three missed calls from Elise on her phone when she got back to Seaspray, just before raindrops started falling heavy and fast, turning the view from the bedsit window into a Monet painting. She rang her straight away.

'Hello, my dear friend,' said Elise, the concern in her voice putting Sophie on alert. 'I don't mean to worry you, but I have heard a trickle of a rumour on the grapevine that your father is a soupçon out of sorts.'

'Dad?' Sophie stiffened. Then suspicion raised a wary finger. This had Len Spinks written all over it. She could imagine him steepling his fingers, sitting back on a chair in John's office and suggesting they throw out some bait. Which member of Sophie's family would she be more likely to walk towards the trap for?

'How did you find that out, Elise?'

'Gerald had a conversation with John last night, in the Strangers' bar. He asked him how you were doing, obviously, and he said you were bearing up, but that your father wasn't doing too good and he was worried about him. He told Gerald to keep that to himself, not even to tell me. Gerald, however, does not keep anything from me these days. Not if he wants to remain attached to his testicles.'

Sophie wasn't convinced. 'But John knows that Gerald would tell you, even if he said not to.'

'I have thought of that, but Gerald said that he sounded genuinely concerned.'

John could have out-acted Leonardo DiCaprio. Then again, this might have Len Spinks tattooed all over it, but also there was a very small chance it wasn't a bluff.

'If there is any way you could do some more discreet digging, I would be very grateful,' asked Sophie.

'Leave it with me, mum's the word. Or rather dad,' Elise promised. 'It's the Old Lions monthly dinner tonight so Gerald will be able to find out the lie of the land. I'll be back to you tomorrow with more detail.'

Sophie let herself into the vicarage through the back door. By tonight, the dress would be ready for Jade's first fitting. It was beautiful and she was delighted with it and she knew that Jade would be too and she'd credit Tracey for making her the belle of the prom. But Sophie's father was on her mind as she sewed today. He was the same age as the woman whose funeral Elliott had conducted yesterday. Apart from some arthritis in his knees and shoulder, he was fit and well and she wished she knew for sure if that was still the case. John had always got on with his father-in-law, enough to be genuinely worried about him if he was ill.

She could no longer keep the tide of her other life back;

it was starting to seep into this one. It was always going to. Her father couldn't be seriously unwell, she argued with herself, because then John would have risked saying more to Gerald in the hope the news would reach her. Or would he? Her father would have forbidden it, not wanting to add to any scandal. That John had been careful in what he said to Gerald, scant with detail, was the biggest indicator that he was telling the truth ... wasn't it? Sophie tapped her forehead with the heels of both hands, hoping to summon an answer. Life in Little Loste was so much less complicated, and she loved that it was so.

She took a coffee break when she heard Plum crying outside the door because he was aware that she was around and craved some company. Maybe she should try that when she was back in Park Court: cry outside John's office and hope that he'd rush out, gather her up and soothe her, just as she was doing now to Luke's little kitten. Plum really was sweet. He climbed up Sophie's T-shirt and snuggled under her neck, purring like an engine.

'You can't stay there,' she said to him. 'I have work to do.' But she sat for longer than she had planned, the scrap of black fur pressed against her skin, trusting her, snug and safe. *How could he not feel protected here though*, she thought. This house was the brick form of Elliott Bellringer, big and warm and calm. In the same way that Park Court was a representation of John: bright, showy, cold. However high the central heating was fired up, it never warmed up properly. That was why Edward was so interested in houses, he had once told her. He could walk into a building and instantly feel the personality of the owner reflected in it. Out of all the Mayhews, she liked him the best. He had a genial vulnerability that the others didn't have. She hoped that he wouldn't marry the dreadful Davina, but she suspected that he'd never have the guts to finish with her and would carry on being railroaded along a track he didn't want to follow.

Eventually, she put Plum in his bed and returned to the machine, buried her attention in the dress. She hadn't a clue what time it was when she heard the front door open, Luke's and Tracey's voices calling, 'Hello, anyone in?' Luke's small footsteps padded across the kitchen floor and then the study door was thrown open.

'Hello, Pom,' he said, proudly holding up a picture. 'I've drawed this for you.'

It was a crayon portrait of four people, all with a hundred fingers each. The figure on the left had a giant head, large circles on its chest and mad brown curls. Next: someone tall wearing a cross, then a small stick figure and a black blob with a tail – presumably Plum – then, on the end, someone with very dark hair and pink lips and a red thing hovering near her head that looked like a floating kidney.

'That's Auntie Tracey, that's Daddy, that's me, that's Plum and that's you.' Luke was grinning, his smile as large as a croissant.

'And what's that?'

'It's a love heart between you and Daddy.'

'Ah, I see.' Behind Luke, Tracey pulled a face. 'That's fabulous, Luke,' said Sophie. 'Can I keep it?'

He nodded excitedly.

'Okay now, Luke, I think we need to think about a bath and then bed, don't you?' said Tracey. She turned to Sophie and said, 'I took him to a play centre, he's whacked. I'll be back with you in about half an hour. How's the dress going?'

'Nearly done.'

'No way – really?'

Tracey was back in twenty minutes.

'I read *Scary Edwin* in "Flight of the Bumble Bee" mode,' she said. 'Can I see it?'

Sophie held the dress up against herself. 'I'll need Jade to try this on as soon as possible so I can do the hem. Then, I just have the sparkles to sew on the collar and the waistband and I think you can deliver this to her by end of play tomorrow.'

'Shall I ask her to come over now?'

'Please.'

'Trouble is I need to go and take over from Dave in the pub. As soon as Elliott gets here, I'll have to shoot straight off.'

'Which is the excuse I shall give to explain why I'm fitting her dress and not you?' It was a statement asked as a question.

Tracey gave her a hopeful look.

'Go and ring her, then.'

Sophie studied the crayon drawing whilst Tracey was on the phone. That heart bothered her. The little boy was falling in love with her, and it was reciprocated because her smile was like a croissant when she saw him too.

'She's on her way,' said Tracey, glancing at her watch. 'I can stay for five minutes, just so I can see her face.'

Sophie got up from her chair at the machine. 'Get into position, then.'

'I can't.'

'You can. Go on.'

Elliott arrived at the same time as Jade Darlow did, apologising profusely to his sister for being late. As he strolled into his study, his scent came to Sophie like a gentle whisper: *fougère*, and foresty. He smiled at Tracey positioned behind the sewing machine, pretending to be putting the finishing touches to the beautiful green gown.

'Ah, been working on Jade's dress, I see, Tracey,' he said, giving both her and Sophie a secret wink and a grin that would have dwarfed the world's biggest croissant.

'Yep, nearly there now,' trilled Tracey. She held it up. 'What do you think, Jade?'

Jade's eyes said it all. And the way that her mouth moved silently forming the word 'Wow'.

'Tracey 'as to open up the pub, so she's asked me to mark up the hem, is that okay?' asked Sophie, adopting the accent once more now that Jade was here. 'Did you remember to bring your shoes?'

'Er, yeah.'

Tracey gave a pained smile. 'I'm going to have to go, sorry,' she said. 'So I'll leave you in Pom's capable hands.'

'And I'd better leave too, hadn't I?' said Elliott as Jade stood there, arms folded, waiting for the room to empty so she could undress.

'Thanks, Tracey, it looks great,' said Jade, her words pulling Tracey back from the door.

Tracey hesitated, torn between telling a lie and accepting the compliment. 'Oh, it's . . . so long as you like it,' she said and hurried off before an all-seeing entity in the sky boomed over an invisible tannoy that she hadn't put a single stitch into it.

Sophie helped Jade put on the dress. There was just the smallest tweak that needed to be made at the neck; the bodice fitted perfectly, the skirt flowed over her slim hips. Then, using Sophie's arm for support, Jade got up on a stool wearing her new heels.

'I'm actually gobsmacked,' announced Jade. 'I didn't think she'd pull it out of the bag. I've been panicking like mad.'

Sophie marked the hem with a pin, measured the distance from the waistband.

'She wouldn't have let you down,' said Sophie with all certainty. Tracey would have totally broken her bank buying a dress for Jade if this project hadn't happened. 'She thinks a lot about you and your dad. She lost her mum at the same age as you were, so she knows 'ow 'ard it is.'

'I do want my dad to be happy. It's not that I don't. I'm not a bitch.' Jade's tone was defensive.

'I'm sure that Tracey—'

'She's a nice woman. It's just that ... I'm scared I'll be letting Mum down. Being disloyal. I feel ... I feel ...' She stopped and Sophie prompted her gently.

'What do you feel?'

Jade blew out her cheeks. 'I see her and my dad laughing together sometimes and it makes me mad. I mean that's really bad of me, isn't it? That my dad's happy and I don't want him to be.'

Sophie gave her a soft smile. 'Your feelings are all mixed up and that is natural. You want your dad to be happy ... with your mum.'

'I do, that's it.'

'But your mum is not here any more, and nothing can bring her back. And he deserves a little happiness himself, do you not think? Would you rather he cried and was miserable for the rest of his life or would you like to see him smile again? It does not mean that he will ever forget his lovely wife. He has you to remind him of her every day.'

'He said that,' said Jade, wiping her eye surreptitiously.

'You only ever have one mum. Tracey is not trying to replace her. She knows what you are going through. She was a young girl herself once, you know.'

'It was different then.'

Sophie laughed. 'No, not at all. There was still 'ormones and exams and puberty and all that stuff to go through. And then throw in your heart being broken in the cruellest way possible. She has been through that pain.'

Jade shrugged and Sophie noticed the swallow in her long delicate throat. She changed the subject, lightened the tone.

'So, do you have your bag and jewellery?'

'Yeah, got all that.'

'I like your shoes.'

'They're cheap ones from Whitby market. And illegal. No one is going to believe they are real Louboutins.'

'They are very good copies,' said Sophie, though they weren't. 'And why would they not believe you?'

'Are you kidding? Because *I've* got them on, that's why.'

'But you should walk in them as if they are. That is how a lot of impoverished grand people convince you they are wearing Chanel and diamonds, because they believe it. They are full of swagger.'

'Get out of here.' Jade laughed.

'It's true,' Sophie smiled at her. 'Confidence works like magic.'

'Yeah, maybe for some people. I shouldn't have bought them. Even if they fool other people, they don't fool me.'

'What size are you?'

'Five and a half.'

That was too much of a coincidence to be ignored.

'Wait 'ere.'

Sophie dashed out of the back door, over the fence, into

Seaspray, opened her suitcase and returned with the real McCoys.

'I 'ave only worn them once. They're size six but they pinch and you can get those inners to make them fit smaller feet if you need them,' she said. Jade couldn't speak, her jaw was hanging somewhere down by her knees. 'Would you like them?' Sophie asked her.

Jade's hands came out to take them, reverently, as if they were about to cradle a Fabergé egg.

'These are real, aren't they?'

'Yes they are.'

Hopefully Jade was in too much shock to ask why a French woman relying on the kindness of the church for a roof over her head was giving her a pair of seven-hundred-pound shoes.

'Oh my *God*,' she said.

'Someone gave them to me. What do I need with them?' Sophie said by way of explanation.

Jade slipped off the fakes and put on the real ones. They were a little loose, but nothing a heel insert wouldn't sort out.

'Oh my *God*,' she said again. 'I feel like Cinderella.'

'Yes, well, don't lose one on your way 'ome,' warned Sophie.

'Sod Cinderella, I'm going to feel like Beyoncé.' Jade did an excited shimmy.

'Jade, please, stand still. You do not want an edge that is not even.' And Sophie carried on pinning the hem.

After a minute's silence, Jade asked her,

'Is your mum still around?'

'Yes, she is,' replied Sophie.

'You close?'

'No.'

'My mum was lovely. Really kind,' said Jade. Sophie wasn't looking at her, but she could feel the heat of the smile in her voice.

'Lots of good memories for you then?'

'Loads. When I was little we were always making things out of clay and paper together, sticking things, glitter, glue, all that messy stuff . . . and baking. We once made Marmite and banana biscuits just because we wanted to know what they tasted like.'

'Not good, ah?'

'Surprisingly, not as bad as you might think.'

Alice Calladine would have gone through the roof if Sophie had put glue and glitter anywhere near a table surface. She couldn't recall one instance of her mother ever doing anything like that with her. Children were meant to be seen and not heard.

'I could always talk to my mum. About anything. I miss that,' Jade went on.

Sophie had never felt able to take a problem to her mother. Hence why she was sporting a black bob, pretending to be French and living off the charity of others in a bedsit by the sea.

'I get jealous of other girls who still have their mums. I can't help it.' Jade's voice cracked.

'Oh, *chérie,* just because someone has a mum, it does not mean they have the special relationship you had with yours. You were very lucky to have a woman who loved you so much. Not everyone who has a child gives them time and affection.'

'Why bother having them, then?' asked Jade. It was a question that Sophie couldn't answer.

Sophie didn't want to leave Little Loste, but that wonderful peace inside her was dissipating. The call of duty was beginning to crank up its volume. As soon as Jade's dress was finished, there was nothing to keep her here. Then again there was everything to keep her here and that's why she had to go.

She had lost track of time when there was a soft knock on the door and Elliott walked in with a coffee and a plate of hot buttered toast that scented the whole room and made her stomach keen in response. She couldn't even remember eating anything that day.

'I thought you might fancy a midnight snack,' he said.

'Midnight? Goodness, is that the time? I'm making a habit of this.'

'Well, it's eight minutes past if we're going to be pedantic. Would you prefer to eat it here by yourself or in the kitchen with me?'

'I don't want to get butter all over this dress,' she said, nicely avoiding the real truth that she would rather have shared the supper with him.

Sophie stood up and her bones cracked with stiffness as she stretched. She dropped into the chair at the kitchen table, only then realising how tired she was.

'It's decaf,' said Elliott, watching her rub her eyes. 'You look worn out.'

'I could do with a rest, my eyes are sore.' And running now, too; she hoped he wouldn't think she was crying.

He passed her a square box of *Thomas the Tank Engine* tissues and she pulled a couple out.

'Is the toast making you emotional?' he asked with faux seriousness.

'That's it in a nutshell. Dear me.' She couldn't remember if she had put any mascara on. If she had, she must look like Kung-Fu Panda by now. She crunched into a buttery triangle, chewed, swallowed. 'Why does midnight toast always taste so good?'

'Our dad made the best toast,' said Elliott. 'I have no idea what he did with it – and we couldn't afford the expensive stuff so it was always margarine – but for some reason, when Dad made toast, it was perfect. Golden, just brown enough, buttered right up to the edge. I even ate the crusts and I hated crusts. I didn't want curly hair.'

'And you got your wish.'

His hair wasn't curly but it was thick and dark and starting to go grey at the front in a romantic Mallen streak.

'I'll have finished the dress by lunchtime tomorrow latest. You'll be able to have your office back,' said Sophie, wiping a drop of butter from her lip.

His notepad was at the end of the table and she wondered if the doodle of her name was still inside it.

'I don't mind working at the kitchen table,' he said. 'You don't need to rush it for me.'

'A friend rang me and said that she'd heard my father wasn't very well. I'm not sure if it's true or not but it's made me realise that I need to go back to Cherlgrove sooner rather than later.'

Elliott sat back in the chair, folded his arms, tilted his head.

'Is that what you want to do?'

'It's what I have to do.'

He asked the question again, with emphasis. 'Is that what you want to do?'

Sophie lifted her shoulders, dropped them heavily. It sounded pathetic to say that she had been so used to doing what was expected of her that what she *wanted* was way down at the bottom of her priorities.

'What is your heart telling you to do, Pom?'

'Go home,' replied Sophie. She didn't tell him that the reason it was screaming at her to leave was because it didn't want to.

She thought she heard his breath snag in his throat, before he spoke again.

'Then you must. Do you have a date in mind?'

'The weekend, I think,' she said, forcing a lightness into her tone that she didn't feel. She bit into the second slice of toast and thought that toast would never again taste so good anywhere else made by anyone else. 'I'm so glad I came here though. Being in Little Loste has given me so much to think about. Probably too much.'

'In what way?'

Sophie ate quickly to clear her mouth before answering. Hardly sophisticated. Hardly what Sophie Mayhew would do.

'It's made me realise all the things I don't have that I need.'

'Like a beach?'

She smiled. 'I wish I could fit it in my suitcase. I need to trace the people I've lost contact with, find some friends I can trust.' *Love.* She had been shown more affection in the two and a half weeks she'd been here than she had in years. From croissants and pickles on her doorstep, to a shopkeeper who insisted on giving her breadcakes, a woman who gave her a roof and a flask of soup, a man who helped her tidy the garden, a little boy who needed a kiss goodnight, a vicar who loved to cook and smelled of cedarwood and set her heart in a strange, skittish rhythm. She needed to relocate the love in her marriage because it had become a casualty of work, of John's ambition.

'You know, you have an extraordinary gift that I'm not even sure you're aware of, Pom,' said Elliott. He answered her quizzical look. 'People find you incredibly easy to talk to. I could hear you with Jade through the door; I don't think she's opened up like that about her mum before. And Tracey, she's always been quite guarded about her feelings. And as for Roger, I don't think he's ever spoken above a dozen words to me.'

'Yeah, right.' She found that hard to believe. She'd always thought people found her aloof, cold, unapproachable.

'And me, too. You've taught me something very important in the short time you've been here.'

'Never give your house key to a woman using your study as a sewing room, because she'll eat all your Jaffa Cakes?'

'That my heart is ready to love again.'

She hadn't been expecting that. She felt her mouth drop open. He smiled at her reaction.

'Oh, don't worry, I'm not about to leap across the room and throw myself on you . . . but what happened with Joy scarred me, irreparably I thought, and I was quite sad about that. But you . . . ' His eyes were full of something that kept hers locked to them. She felt magnetised, held in the grip of something powerful and then he switched it off, broke contact, shook his head as if to clear it. 'Thank you for waking up my heart, Pom.'

She smiled, tentatively, giving him no clue of the tornado of feelings swirling inside her in response to his words. 'I'm glad if I did that for you.'

He gave a very weighty sigh, a little laugh, muttered something she couldn't quite catch but it sounded like, 'Oh boy, did you.'

She dragged them back to the normal, the everyday, before she leapt across the room and threw herself on him. 'Is it okay if I carry on sewing a little longer, Elliott? Say no if you want me out of the house.'

'You carry on as long as you like,' he said. 'You have a key.'

'It's kind of you to trust me. I could have run off with all your valuables.'

'Take the valuables, leave the Jaffa Cakes. Luke and I cannot survive without those. Goodnight, Pom. And thank you.'

'Goodnight, Elliott.'

She had turned a light on inside him. She wondered if she'd ever had that effect on her husband.

She let herself out an hour and a half later, wended her way down the garden and struggled over the fence, because she was truly worn out. She walked into the quiet of Seaspray's hallway and just for a second imagined it as it was in its heyday. Light from the massive moon had filtered through the fanlight above the door and given the reception area a temporary monochrome makeover; much of the disrepair was smoothed out by the low, silvery hue. She thought of Kitty Henshaw living here by herself and surmised that she wouldn't have felt lonely, despite the size of the place. She would ask Tracey to show her the downstairs rooms before she left, so she could think of them when she was back in Park Court, when she lay in bed unable to sleep and let her mind return to this other place, this other time.

Sophie pushed open the door to the bedsit. She didn't want to draw the curtains tonight, she wanted to drift off looking at that lovely big moon hanging like a bauble over the sea. Wearily she stripped off and climbed into bed, closed her eyes, listened to the silence. No creaks or cracks tonight as the house settled.

'If you're there, Kitty, and have any words of advice for me, please let me know before I go,' called Sophie. But there was no reply.

Chapter 41

She was awoken by her phone going off. Elise. She snatched it up and answered it.

'I've been investigating subtly, as you asked, and as you know I am not very good at subtle. What a total waste of energy subtle is,' Elise said with an impatient note in her voice.

'And?' asked Sophie, dreading what her probing might have unearthed.

'Firstly Edward is no longer working for John. He quit his position with immediate effect on Sunday.'

'Really?'

'Apparently he's been running his own estate agency. He didn't want egg on his face so he didn't announce anything until it was up and running and doing rather well, if what Gerald says is true.'

'That's some welcome news,' said Sophie, shocked to the core – in a good way. 'I'm glad for him.'

'And . . .' Elise paused and Sophie read not so much good news into that. 'Gerald went to the Old Lions golf dinner last night and your father wasn't in attendance.'

Sophie frowned. Her father always went to the Old Lions monthly dinners. That was beyond odd, and worrying.

'I was furious because I specifically asked Gerald to dig deep. I told him that I was worried because I hadn't heard from you in over three weeks and I suspected something odd was going on and then tagged on that he should ask John about his father-in-law as well in case the two were connected, but he didn't get the chance, got hijacked by the bloody treasurer.'

'Well, thank you anyway, Elise,' said Sophie.

'On the positive front, if there had been any bad news then there would have been some gossip circulating at the Old Lions dinner, surely?'

Her father never missed those dinners, though.

'I'll be home by the weekend.'

'Oh, wonderful,' said Elise, with true delight in her voice.

'I want you to promise me. . .' Sophie began, hardly able to believe that she was about to ask this, '. . . that if I really do disappear, if you hear that I have gone into hospital for my own good, you must go to the newspapers because I'll have been dragged there kicking and screaming, Elise. You must promise.'

'I absolutely swear on Monty's life that I will.'

A sigh of relief escaped through Sophie's lips. She would trust Elise to do that for her.

'Thank you.'

'We shall have lunch at your earliest convenience and you can tell me all about where you've been. Oh, and – guess what – I had a very contrite phone call from Dena, trying to make a joke of what she told me at lunch last week about her indiscretion with person or persons unknown. I imagine she is in a state of high alert and vowing never to drink alcohol again.' Then she laughed at Dena's misfortune. That circle took much entertainment from the mortification of others.

As much as Sophie did enjoy Elise's company, the thought of slipping seamlessly back into her old life and listening to a full report on who had been bitching about her this week didn't excite her one bit. The prospect was as bad as the last night of the school holidays before she had to return to St Bathsheba's, when her heart had sat as heavy as a rock within her chest.

She didn't go for a run that morning; she needed to get the last tweaks on the dress done, then a gentle press and it would be completed. And she'd had an idea about a calling-card embellishment, two tiny pom-poms to hang from the ties at the back of the collar. That's what she'd put on her dresses. If she ever made another.

There was no one at the vicarage when she got there but it didn't feel empty. Like the almshouse, it was warm and solid – a house that embraced its visitors, made them welcome. There was an oak clock on the wall that tocked a slow beat, adding to the calm. She fancied that everyone who had ever lived here must have been happy, and had left a little of that happiness behind. Give or take Joy Bellringer.

Tracey arrived just as Sophie was pressing the lovely green gown.

'Hi,' she greeted Sophie nervously. 'How's it going?'

'Five minutes and then all that needs to be done is for you to deliver it.'

'Did she like it when she saw it last night? Steve said that when she got home, she told him it was nice. Nice! But I don't know what he meant by nice. Or if that was his word or her word or—'

'She really liked it,' said Sophie, interrupting her panicked waffling. 'Massive brownie points.'

Tracey gave a strange hybrid of a hiccup and a sob. 'Never again will I lie. Never. Not in my whole life. I'll make us a coffee whilst you finish off.' She slipped away quickly as though worried she would make Sophie lose concentration enough to burn a big hole through the dress. By the time she had returned with two mugs, Sophie was putting it on a hanger.

'Is it done?' asked Tracey.

'All done.' Sophie twirled it around and Tracey's face broke into a grin of delight.

'Have you got a plastic cover or something to put over it?' asked Sophie.

'I'll go and look in Ells' wardrobe. He's bound to have a suit cover or something.'

She returned with one a few minutes later and Sophie slipped it over the top of Jade's gown, ready for transporting down the hill. It had been intensive work making it in such a short time, but worth it. Jade would out-Cinderella the girl with the red London dress. Especially with her genuine Louboutins on.

Tracey opened up her arms and gave Sophie a very squashy squeeze. 'I'm not a hugger normally but on this occasion I think this says everything that is presently clogging up my throat and unable to come out.'

'It was a pleasure, really. I'm rather proud of it, I have to say.'

Tracey then flopped onto the sofa as if she were a marionette and someone had just cut her strings. She drank her coffee as if it were celebratory champagne.

'Jade was talking about you yesterday,' said Sophie, sitting down also. 'She does like you, you know. She feels disloyal letting you in, I think.'

'I'd never try and take the place of Jenny. She was a lovely woman.'

'I think she knows that deep down. But putting it into practice is another matter.'

'I'll make sure I tread extra carefully.' Tracey looked down into her cup and fell silent. When she raised her head again she was wearing a smile that looked sad rather than happy.

'I hope everything works out for you when you go back, Pom. Will you be able to forgive John? I couldn't, I'll be honest.'

'*I have no idea* is my answer,' replied Sophie. She didn't say that she had to go back because she didn't know how to go forward. 'I'll give it my best shot. Love can't just die, can it?'

'Mine did for Barry,' said Tracey. 'I thought I'd love him for ever, but then for ever ended.'

'You're a strong woman. Much stronger than I could be.'

'I don't think I am,' countered Tracey. 'I didn't exactly have a plan of action when I walked out of my marriage. Other than not staying in it.'

'You were incredibly brave.'

'Maybe, but I was also crapping myself. You can be brave and frightened, you know.'

Sophie hadn't thought about those two qualities co-existing. But you needed to be extra brave to go through with something when you were scared. Tracey had more guts than she thought she had. More than Sophie would ever have.

'Could I ask you a favour, Tracey? Would you show me the rest of the downstairs of the almshouse before I leave?'

''Course,' said Tracey. 'The keys are in the kitchen here, hang on.' She got up and returned moments later. 'Want to look now?'

'Well, after I've tidied up all the bits of material and put the machine away.'

'Don't be daft. The least I can do is the tidying up,' said Tracey. 'Come on, but don't expect to wow much.'

They walked out of the front door and a small red car zoomed past them. Arms annoyed and akimbo, Tracey watched it drive on down the hill.

'That thing nearly ran me over when I came up here,' she said, calling out 'Knobhead' after it. Then she turned to Sophie. 'I bet you don't hear language like that in your world.'

'Are you joking?' she replied. 'There's more name-calling in the world of politics than you could ever dream of here. It's all smiles to the face and daggers in the back.'

'I wouldn't like to swap you then,' said Tracey.

In the almshouse, Tracey unlocked the first door and pushed it hard, then had to put her shoulder to it as it was too comfortable in the jamb and didn't want to part company with it.

'Welcome to the kitchen,' she said, when it eventually gave.

'Wow,' said Sophie, following her in.

'Wow? Are you looking at the same thing I am?' said Tracey, with a hoot of disbelief.

The kitchen was long with two enormous picture windows letting in a view of the newly cleared-up garden. Dust motes danced in the air as if playing to an audience.

'Why is it so warm in here?' asked Tracey. 'The pub isn't this warm when the heating's on full blast.' She rested her hand on the cast iron radiator, but it was cold to the touch.

Wooden doors were hanging off the kitchen units and the dark red walls and ceiling added nothing by way of charm, but the scrubbed oak floorboards were beautiful.

'There's a massive pantry there,' said Tracey pointing to the corner. 'People were taking them out of their houses and now they're putting them back in. Dining room next, follow me.'

Sophie tried to imagine the kitchen painted in light colours: pale lemon maybe. A dresser, like the one in Elliott's kitchen, covered in photos and knick-knacks; souvenirs from holidays, postcards from friends. She pictured a table in the middle of the room, a bright green Aga with an old-fashioned whistling kettle sitting on top of it. A cat basket with a large, fat, sleeping black tom, or a white cat like Deaf Jeff. Or both, curled up like Yin and Yang.

She trailed after Tracey into the next room, separated from the kitchen by two oak pocket doors that slid into the wall. Sophie's eye was immediately drawn to the magnificent plaster ceiling rose. A door with a stained glass panel led out to the side garden. Both women stood still for a few moments to admire it.

'I'd forgotten about that. Pretty isn't it? About the only thing that is in here. Come on, next is the study. Get ready for your eyes to be assaulted.'

Tracey went in first and opened the thick, dark curtains to let in the light. The study was at the front of the house and had the same deep bay window as the bedsit. The décor was dodgy: the ceiling and two walls were painted snot-green and the other two very dark brown. It was like standing inside a giant chocolate-lime sweet. Quite a lot of floorboards had been removed, leaving gaping holes. Not a room to traverse safely in the dark.

'One of our temporary residents was under the illusion there was treasure hidden in the house. Bad trip I think,' sighed Tracey. 'He broke in here and caused quite a bit of damage but found nothing except a few dead mice and some dodgy wiring. Sadly not everyone respects a free shelter.'

'But it didn't stop you offering it to me, did it?' replied Sophie.

'The house is a bit of a white elephant now to be honest. Fancy buying it from us?'

Sophie chuckled. 'Don't tempt me. I could use it as a secret bolthole and escape here for two weeks out of every four.' Split her life: be the dutiful wife for half of it and Pom No-Surname for the other. Recharge her batteries by running on the beach, sewing to her heart's content and eating lasagne at the vicarage. A dual existence to keep Sophie Mayhew sane and able to cope with the spotlight.

'So there you have it. Seaspray. Needs a lot of work from someone who loves it enough,' said Tracey.

I love it enough, thought Sophie.

They stood looking out of the window, beyond the sand and the sea to the horizon and then that small red car caught their attention flying past on the road again.

'Someone's lost,' Tracey said. 'A little lost in Little Loste.'

Ironic, thought Sophie, as here in Little Loste, she'd found herself.

Chapter 42

There was something Sophie needed to do though before she left. That afternoon, she rang for a taxi to drop her off on the High Street in Slattercove and headed straight for the toyshop. The large blue teddy bear that had previously stood in the window had gone and recently so, by the look of it, as the place he had occupied had not been filled and this was the sort of shop she imagined would pride itself on an immaculate front display.

A delightful tinkle of bells above the door heralded Sophie's admittance and she walked into yesteryear. The quaint exterior of the shop perfectly matched the inside with its floor-to-ceiling wooden shelving and old-fashioned counter, complete with a massive ornate silver cash register.

'I'll be with you shortly,' called the shop assistant, tending to a female customer who was holding the big teddy bear at arm's length and studying it. He wasn't wearing his guard's uniform. Clearly the customer wasn't interested in buying that also.

'It's okay, you can serve someone else whilst I think about it,' the customer said.

'Thank you. I'd like the sit-on train that you have in the window. And do you have the train guard's outfit as well. Small boy size?' asked Sophie.

'Yes to both. I'll get you ones out of the back. All fresh and boxed.'

'He's gorgeous, isn't he?' Sophie said to the bear-holding customer. 'Looks like someone's going to be a lucky boy or girl.'

'My son. It's his fourth birthday today,' replied the woman, then the volume dropped from her voice. 'I know he'll love it, but if I appear to be tempted and then suddenly change my mind, I bet they drop the price. Especially as it's the last one.'

'Ah, I see,' replied Sophie, surprised that the woman was a bargainer. She had a henna CND hand tattoo and little beads in her choppy ash-lilac hair. She looked more like the type who would have supported the survival of small independent shops and not tried to hack at their profits. But then Sophie more than anyone knew that appearances could be deceptive.

The shop assistant reappeared carrying the train and the costume, both in boxes.

'That train's heavier than it looks,' she said, explaining her huffing and puffing. 'Big solid toy this one. We've sold it for years and years.'

'How old is your little boy?' asked bear-woman.

Sophie opened her mouth to reply that it wasn't her little boy, but what came out was 'Four. And mad about trains.' She was caught up in her lie because it was too easy, too tempting to be a mum, in a queue with another mum, talking about their children. For a short snatch of time.

'Perfect present then,' said the woman.

'It's a lovely age, isn't it?' Sophie went on. 'You can have little conversations with them at four.' She thought of Luke in his train-rich bedroom leaning forward to inform her that Scary Edwin Page was not real.

The woman nodded in agreement. 'Yes it is. Birthday present?'

'No . . .' *A goodbye present. An 'I will miss you so much' present. An 'I have to leave you before you break my heart' present.* '. . . just a whim.'

'My girl was train mad when she was little,' said the assistant. 'Wasn't interested in dolls, but trains – oh my. They tried to stop her liking them at school, they said it was weird for a lass. I had a right set-to with a male teacher about it. She drives a tube train in London now and she loves it. I've always wanted to bump into that dreadful man and tell him that.'

'Good for her,' said Sophie.

'He nearly ruined my girl's dream. Luckily for her she was made of strong stuff.' The assistant shook her head with annoyance. 'No one should take your dreams away. Having a toy shop was mine. I suppose I could have aimed higher, but I never wanted anything else as much. I was never interested in travelling or writing a book or being famous. My dream fits me fine. No law that says they have to be massive, is there? Want me to gift wrap this for you, love?'

'No, but I'll take a gift tag if you have one, please.'

She had a vision of Luke spilling into the almshouse and seeing the train in front of the fireplace. She could imagine his dear face frozen in a shock of delight. She wished she could be there to see it in person.

'I hope your little boy likes his teddy,' Sophie smiled at the woman on her way out.

'He will,' came the reply.

*

As she stood waiting for a taxi back to Little Loste, Sophie's mind idled on the lady in the toy shop and what she had said about dreams. Her own was so small that she would have been laughed at, ridiculed for it in school. Girls at St Bathsheba's, Calladines and Mayhews did not serve the general public in *shops*. She'd had to pretend that her aspirations were as lofty as those of her academic peers: to marry a rich/powerful/titled man, drive an Aston Martin/ Porsche, live in a grand house, have a holiday apartment in Monaco/Rome; and not that she wanted to sew dresses and sell them in her own shop. So her dream had remained packed tightly in her heart like an unopened parcel tucked under a Christmas tree, becoming dustier and harder to get to with every year that passed. *My dream fits me fine. No law that says they have to be massive, is there?* was what the lady in the toyshop had said. The smiling, happy-looking lady.

*

Tracey took the dress over to Jade before she opened up the pub that evening.

'Ta-da,' she said, nervously, placing it across her out-stretched, waiting hands.

'Oh my *God*,' said Jade and rushed upstairs with it, leaving Tracey loitering in the hallway. Should she stay or go? She didn't usually hang around when Steve wasn't in because there was a less welcoming vibe. She was about to go home when Jade called down the stairs.

'Want to see it on?'

'I'd love to.' Tracey padded upstairs. Jade was on the landing, looking like a billion dollars.

'My hair will be up and I've got an arm bangle but what do you think?'

Tracey's eyes were blurred. She thought that it should be Jenny Darlow standing here staring open-mouthed with wonder at her beautiful daughter, not her, and she was so sorry for Jade that it wasn't.

'I think you look perfect,' she said, with a voice that was stripped of volume by emotion.

'You did such a great job, thanks,' said Jade, swishing the skirt from side to side, like Belle from *Beauty and the Beast* on the dancefloor.

'Jade, I've got something to tell you ...' said Tracey, unable to stop herself. 'I didn't make it, Pom did. I started to and I made a total arse of it and—'

'Tell me something I don't know.'

There was a pin-drop silence, then Jade shattered it with a laugh.

'What?' Tracey's eyebrows shot up her head.

'Well it was obvious. Doesn't matter. You promised you'd sort the dress out and here it is. So thanks.'

'Oh, right.' She felt as shocked as if she'd just been tasered. 'I'm sorry. I really wanted to do it myself.'

'I know that. Are you going with Dad to watch us all arrive? Sarah's mum's hired a pink stretch limo for us.'

Tracey gulped. 'I'd really like to.'

'Okay.'

Jade disappeared into her bedroom to take off the dress and Tracey attempted to push a flurry of tears back into her eyes. Tears that were happy and warm and were pouring out of a grateful heart. All she'd wished for was that the dress would change things between them and her little dream, it appeared, had come true.

Chapter 43

Elliott Bellringer looked down at the page in his notebook. What a ridiculous teenage thing to doodle a woman's name – how old was he? The thing is, he didn't feel any of his thirty-six years at the moment because his heart was skipping around in his chest like baby Bambi in the forest and he had no desire to try and stop it because it was the most alive he had felt in years.

Pom would be gone soon and that was probably for the best, given that he was experiencing a riot of emotion which was both wonderful and awful at the same time because he would miss her so very much. A few shared coffees and conversations, that's all it had taken to make him realise that it was okay to want something for himself. Something outside the job, outside the duties of being a big brother and a father. He'd closed off a part of himself after Joy had left. Like the almshouse: locked it up apart from the main functioning aspect. Then *she* had walked in and made him see the potential in himself to live fully, to love fully.

Sometimes people gravitated towards you for a small but important time before moving on, but they left something of themselves behind, like a gift. If his life had not entwined with Joy's he would not have had Luke; if he had never met Sophie Mayhew, he might never have realised how deeply he could feel for another woman. John F. Mayhew was a lucky man and Elliott would pray that he quickly came to realise that, if he didn't already.

The front door bell rang. He wasn't expecting anyone but he was a vicar and surprise visitors were par for the course. He opened the door with a ready smile of welcome, but on this occasion he could not hold it up because there, holding a giant blue teddy bear, was his wife.

Chapter 44

Sophie put the presents down in front of the fireplace. She had written on the gift tag: 'To Luke, with love from Pom xxx'. She wondered if he would remember her in time. He would have memories of a woman who didn't exist – the French Pom, who was really the English Sophie Mayhew. He would never realise how fond she had grown of him or what an effect his lips pressed against her cheek in a good-night kiss could have on her aching heart.

She had a sandwich for supper before starting to pack a few things in readiness. She sat at the table and read an old newspaper whilst she ate. Ironically, the middle pages were taken up with the story of four women who had all decided to 'Reach for the Stars', as the article header described it. Rosemary, aged fifty-seven, had gone to university after a life of caring for her disabled parents and bringing up seven children and was now a criminal psychologist. Rachel, aged sixty-two, had been a nurse until she retired – and then opened up a burlesque dancing school. Katrina, aged forty-one, had changed from being a barrister to owning a garden centre. Jamaica, aged twenty-nine, had been a drug-using tearaway, written off by teachers, and now ran the Alice in Wonderland Tea Rooms in Doncaster, which looked magical. They'd all reached for their varying-sized stars and the beaming smiles on their faces said everything the words had missed out. She turned over, to a less interesting article about the rising sea levels; read half of it before getting up for a glass of water. When she returned to the table, she found that the newspaper was once again on the 'Reach for the Stars' page.

'This a message from you, Kitty?' Sophie called, as a draught breathed on her from behind and fluttered the page. A rogue wind channelling down the chimney and visiting the room, nothing more supernatural than that. No message from Kitty. Sadly, Kitty no longer existed.

Afterwards, Sophie tidied around, leaving the bedsit as clean for someone as it had been left for her. She was taking the rubbish out to the bin when she heard her name being called.

'Pom, Pom ...' Luke's unmistakable excited voice. He was on his swing. She waved. He scrambled off it and ran down the garden towards her.

'Pom, guess what?' he said, his face almost split apart by the grin he was wearing. 'My mummy's come back.'

Sophie had been expecting him to say that he'd had crunchy pie for tea or maybe some news about Plum. Maybe another story about a massive poo in the cat litter tray, but not that. Her head exploded with prickles as if someone had thrown a full bucket of cold water at her.

'Your mummy?' Why was that word having such an effect on her?

'Daddy said I could play in the garden for five minutes

until Auntie Tracey comes for me.' He leaned forward as if about to tell her something very secret. 'They're talking.'

Right on cue, Tracey came storming up the road on foot. Seeing Sophie and Luke outside, she halted, her expression speaking volumes. She plastered a smile on her face for her nephew's benefit. 'Lukey,' she waved to him. 'How do you fancy staying with me and Deaf Jeff tonight?'

'Yaaayyy,' he cheered.

'Right, tell your dad to pack your bag.'

Luke scurried up the garden towards the back door of the vicarage. Tracey turned to Pom, dispensed with the smile and threw her hands up in the air.

'I was having the best day. Jade invited me to the big prom dropping-off ceremony and I've been smiling like a loony since . . . and then this bites me on the bum. I wondered who that idiot in the red car was and now we know: bloody Joy Cowface, that's who. She's probably been driving around all day trying to build up the courage to wreck his life again. Elliott just rang and asked if I'd look after Luke for an hour or so because *she's* decided she wants to talk. Apparently she doesn't want to get divorced now, wants to be a mother and a dutiful wife and settle down and . . .' she growled. 'I should have known she'd do something like this. I tell you, I will murder her given the opportunity.' Tracey nodded towards the vicarage. 'She'll have been in trouble, I bet you anything. She uses him like a first-aid kit and then as soon as she's mended, off she trots to another disaster. I'd better go and get Luke. I think it's best if he stays with me tonight, so they can . . . do what they have to.'

'Of course,' said Sophie. She felt inexplicably numb.

Tracey began to march towards the front of the vicarage.

'Wish me luck keeping my hands off her,' she shouted over her shoulder.

'You'll manage,' replied Sophie.

She walked back into the house then and resumed her packing. All of it now. The message from the cosmos was clear. It really was time to go home.

Sophie

Chapter 45

Sophie managed to drop off to sleep at just after one a.m. and woke up at four-thirty a minute before the alarm on her phone went off. She stripped the bed, folded the sheets, placed them with the towels and a note apologising for not having had time to wash them. She also thanked Tracey for her friendship, hoped Jade would have a fabulous prom and sent everyone in the village her best regards. Then she wrote to Elliott and Luke, thanked them for their kindness, told Luke to take good care of Plum, wished Elliott luck – a word that had a container-load of connotations. In her heart the letter was much longer. In that version it said, *I have fallen in love with you all and so it is time for me to leave because it feels too right to stay.* She put the note on top of the presents in front of the fireplace, turned off the light and walked out of the bedsit for the last time.

The hallway felt uncommonly eerie, chilled. She had the crazy notion that the house didn't want her to go. That made two of them then.

'Goodbye, Kitty. Thank you for your hospitality,' Sophie said to the dark. Her voice crumbled on the last word. She heard the noise of a car getting closer – her taxi. 'Goodbye,' she said again, before locking up the front door, putting the key through the letter box, forcing her fingers to let it go.

She glanced up the road whilst the taxi driver was loading her case into his boot and saw Joy's red car parked outside the vicarage and she wondered where she was sleeping now. They passed the Little Loste Inn and she blew a kiss towards it, felt a pain prickle behind her eyes, blinked it away. Time to be Sophie again.

In Slattercove railway station, Sophie glanced at the headlines on newspapers outside a kiosk: an actor accused of a racist slur at an awards ceremony, a warning about an invasion of ladybirds, some massive company accused of not paying enough taxes. No John F. Mayhew gossip, not on the front covers at least.

In York she called John's mobile. Her mouth was dry with anxiety as it began to ring. He picked up a split second before it switched to voicemail.

'Hello.' His voice, its tone wary. She was strangely unmoved to hear it; shock, she presumed.

'It's me. I'm on my way home.'

'Sophie? Oh, thank God, where the fuck are you?' He sounded relieved more than cross, despite the invective.

'I'll be home by two o'clock at the latest.'

'Right, okay.' She imagined him pacing up and down as he spoke. 'Let me know when you're at the station, I'll come and pick you up.'

'Don't worry. I'll get a taxi.'

Then she put down the phone.

The gates to Park Court opened on her taxi's approach, which told her that someone in the house was watching out for her in order to operate them. She saw her father's and Clive's cars parked in front of the house and she tried to swallow the ball of dread lodged in her throat, but it was too compacted to shift.

'Nice house,' said the taxi driver. He had no idea who she was. 'Friends or family?'

'Just people I know.' The door to Park Court opened and John rushed out. Her John. His arms closed around her.

'I didn't recognise you,' he said, pushing her out to arms' length then, looking into her face as if her eyes would give up her secrets. 'Oh, Sophie. Where have you been?'

He paid the taxi driver, picked up her suitcase with one hand, put the other around her shoulder, walked her into the house. There was a family welcoming committee. But no one had told their faces of their purpose.

'We've all been so concerned,' said John. Four stiff trees confronted her: a furious-looking Clive and Celeste, her father – fit and well – and her mother, whose displeasure was evident in her avoiding eye contact with her errant daughter.

'Sophie, feelings are running high. It might not look like it but we *all* have been so worr— '

'Haven't you got anything to say for yourself?' barked Clive Mayhew, his tone brittle, demanding.

'Let's go home, Angus,' said Alice. 'I've seen enough.'

John began to plead with Sophie's parents as they stepped towards the door. 'Alice, Angus, please, remember what we said, this isn't the time—'

Her mother again, throwing the words over her shoulder. 'Utterly selfish. No consideration for anyone else. She never had.'

'Go upstairs, Sophie. You look shattered. Let me talk to them,' said John.

Sophie headed towards the stairs, heard John's low remonstrations with his parents and in-laws, heard the words: *Preposterous. Outrageous. Unforgivable.*

Home sweet home.

The bedroom looked the same but also not the same and she couldn't explain why. Everything was in the place it should have been but it felt oddly unfamiliar. Had she really only been away for three weeks? It felt like much longer.

Sophie sat on the edge of the bed and caught sight of herself in the dressing-room mirror. That woman with her choppy black hair, in cheap jeans and needing-to-be-washed T-shirt, did not belong in this bedroom. She was a trespasser. Sophie stared at her, trying to read what was going on in her hazel eyes. Nothing. There was nothing going on in them. She felt numb, dazed by lack of sleep, adrift.

The door opened by slow degrees minutes later. John came in carefully, soft cautious smile playing on his lips.

'It's good to have you home,' he said. 'Don't take too much notice of the old ones. Whatever you might think, take it from me they've been extremely upset. We all have. I didn't have any idea where to start looking for you. Where were you?'

'I wasn't with anyone you know,' she replied. 'I wasn't with anyone I know for that matter.'

He sat down tentatively on the bed next to her, reached for her hand. His fingers were long and cool. 'We need to talk, obviously, but not today. I'm just so glad you are here, back where you belong. I've been thinking, maybe after what happened with Henry, we never really addressed it properly. I've been thinking a lot actually . . . about so many things. But' – he waved that away – 'later. You need rest.'

Rest. The word came with an unpleasant tingle.

'If you think I need *rest* in a hospital, John, let me warn you that I have put measures in place to stop that happening,' she said, summoning up the energy to be firm from a reserve stored deep within her. She saw the small swallow in his throat before he spoke again, his features uniting in an expression of confusion.

'There's no question of you going into hospital, I meant here at home.'

He leaned over, kissed her head, his hand cupping her face. At the door he turned, smiled again. 'Can I get you anything? Tea, a sandwich, hot milky drink?'

'I'm fine,' she said.

He closed the door behind him. He still hadn't said sorry.

Chapter 46

'You look different,' adjudged Elise the following Monday. 'It's not only the hair, which gives you more gravitas, I think. What else has changed? I can't work it out.'

Sophie's hair had been stripped of the black two days previously. She'd kept the bob and had a very expensive trim but in her opinion Betty of Slattercove had cut it as adeptly for a fraction of the price.

Elise looked around them to see who was gawping in their direction and eyes everywhere pretended they hadn't been, quickly switching their focus.

'So, first public trip out, then?'

'Apart from to the hair salon, yes.'

Elise clicked her fingers at the wine waiter, who had had the audacity to pass by the table when her glass was standing empty. He apologised and poured for her from the bottle.

'And how are things at home?'

'Don't even ask.'

'I have every intention of asking.'

'I feel terrible.' She was back to not sleeping well. 'Everyone is so cross with me. My parents aren't speaking to me.'

'And John?'

'Too nice.'

'I see.' Elise wasn't taken in either. 'I presume you're going to do a press release.'

'When I'm ready. I don't think they can afford to push me, considering what happened before. Len and John are in consultation as we speak, preparing.'

Elise was incredulous.

'He's gone to London and left you?'

'I told him to.'

He'd offered to not go but she could tell that it was a very half-hearted bid. She knew that he would want to consult with Len now that his 'asset' was back home.

Elise's 'Huh' said much more than the sum of its three letters.

'Yes, no doubt I will be rolled out in front of a sympathetic glossy in full Vivienne Westwood. Len will secure editorial control. It will be perfectly stage-managed.' Sophie knew she would be expected to deliver the speech she'd been instructed to when, instead, she had called John a shit, and to admit that the stress Rebecca Robinson had put her under had led to a momentary madness that she bitterly regretted. And when the magazine came out, people would bitch ad infinitum about her new hairstyle.

Elise made a grumbling sound. 'Has anyone acknowledged why you were driven to do what you did? Has John apologised?' When Sophie didn't answer immediately, she pressed her, 'Well, have they?'

'No.'

'Bastards.'

'I'm going to London later to join him for a few days. Maybe we'll talk properly then. I don't think either of us knows where to start.'

Elise sat back in her chair, studied the younger woman.

'You know, Sophie, when we first began having our lunches and brunches, my primary concern was networking, even spying for Gerald. They were pleasant enough occasions but you were never very forthcoming where gossip was concerned, never seemed to enjoy the intrigue – it was all frightfully disappointing. I was starting to think about extricating myself from your company. I judged you shallow, of little substance, all beauty and no brains.' She broke off to drink, leaving Sophie stunned into silence by her honesty. Then Elise continued. 'I realised eventually that you weren't shallow at all, quite the opposite in fact; you were intelligent, loyal, principled, a true friend. I must admit, I have fed you the odd line over the past couple of years, like a diagnostic dye, hoping to trace where it turned up, but it never did. And I have come to prize that more than I actually realised until you ran away. I'm not sure I've ever had a friend before whom I could truly trust, Sophie, or valued enough to care if they trusted me. I was quite surprised that keeping your secret was more important than the prospect of spreading insider news.'

Elise smiled and it was totally different to her usual smile, as if Elise had let her into an inner sanctum of herself. Sophie was touched.

'That's lovely of you to say so, Elise. I was exceedingly grateful for what you did for me.'

'Oh, that was nothing,' A flick of Elise's hand dismissed the suggestion that her actions were special. 'Whilst you were away, I met Gerald's Welsh daughter Fennie, the secret one that I thought was his mistress. He had a short fling with her mother before I came on the scene. He never knew she existed until recently, and she didn't know about him either until a deathbed confession enlightened her. Delightful girl, I took to her straightaway. She has her own business. It's only a tiny one, she makes soap and those bath bomb things and sells them at fairs. She lives in a house the size of a shoe-box, but she cherishes everything she has, appreciates life in a way I can't quite manage, enjoys ridiculously simple pleas-ures. Don't get me wrong, I wouldn't want to swap places but I envied her all the same. I couldn't stop thinking about her in the car on the way home and how she reminded me of you. A free spirit.'

Sophie dropped a wry laugh at that.

'But I'm not, Elise.'

'Oh, Sophie, I think you are. We've all wondered what lay behind that beautiful mask you wear and when you stood on that doorstep and declared John a shit, I saw the real you for a trice, a trapped bird with a throatful of song and no space to sing it, suddenly finding the door to its cage open. Where did you fly to, Sophie Mayhew, because you look like her but you aren't. Not the same Sophie who took wing.'

'I went to Yorkshire. Near St Bathsheba's school.'

'Yorkshire? Yorkshire! Of all the places on the planet, you went back to *Yorkshire*? After everything you told me about it?'

Her disgust was so evident that Sophie had to laugh.

'What I never told you was one summer I was forced to spend my holidays there doing extra study with a teacher, but she entered a secret pact with the school cook to look after me because she needed to chase a man halfway around Europe.' She acknowledged Elise's look of disbelief. 'I know what it sounds like, but it happened exactly like that. I had the most brilliant few weeks. Probably the happiest of my life. That's why I went back.'

'And what did you do in the three weeks you were there this time?'

'I stayed in a bedsit in a dilapidated house, I ran on the beach, I served beer in a pub, I pretended to be French, I went to church, I made a prom dress for a teenager ...' *I fell in love with a little boy and his auntie ... and his father.*

'Sounds horrific,' decided Elise, then she sighed, 'but I suspect it wasn't, was it?'

'No. It was wonderful.'

Sophie felt Elise's hand on hers.

'I hoped you'd come home for purely selfish reasons, because I really didn't want to be starved of your company for too much longer, but ... but ... dear Sophie, don't let them force you back into the cage again. In the nicest possible way ... I don't think you belong here.'

*

In the London office, Len was taking John step by step through his grand strategical plan. Now that Sophie was back on board, things should be pretty straightforward. But this time they must all be aware that Sophie Mayhew was the queen on the board, not a pawn. They'd underestimated her when the Rebecca Robinson story had broken, trusted her to stick to the script and play the loyal wife, never even contemplated that she might rebel. John had not been best pleased to discover that his popularity had depended so much on her standing by his side. He'd counted on Len successfully spinning the public's sympathy towards him: deep-rooted problems in his marriage caused by tragedy, wife unreachable and icy, husband had no choice but to seek warm harbour – no wonder he had strayed from the path of righteousness; and was genuinely surprised – and annoyed – to find that it hadn't gone that way at all. He'd been branded with the insalubrious title of 'Love Rat', pigeon-holed with adulterous brattish footballers and F-list celebrities. Rebecca was mesmerising at first but her spicy revelations had cast her as a far more cold-blooded creature than Len was trying to paint Sophie as: in fact, there had been a tsunami of public sympathy for the wronged wife. Columnists who had crit-icised her viciously in the past came out fully on her side. Her outburst on the doorstep of the morning of 1 June had shown everyone she was anything but frigid, especially coming only three days after she had broken down in a neonatal unit. This woman was suffering terribly and it was her husband's job to mend her, not crush her further into the ground using his mistress's heel. The British public, feeling a teensy bit rotten about their previous lack of under-standing, wanted to throw its arms around Mrs Sophie Mayhew and make it all up to her.

'I trust you greeted her lovingly, without reproach upon her return, hmm?' said Len.

'I did,' John answered him, 'even though I wanted to grab her by the fucking throat.'

Len bet he did. He knew that John had been boiling with rage ever since he found his wife had vanished from their house; John F. Mayhew reacted badly to not being in con-trol. Luckily for him, men with psychopathic tendencies were expert at pretending, because they had to study human behaviour and ape it in order to blend in. Len had no doubt that he had played the considerate husband role to perfection since Sophie had returned to the fold, give or take actually apologising for his role in the drama. People were objects to John, blocks to be positioned where they served him best.

It was a condition Len found fascinating and admired on an intellectual level but he wouldn't have wanted not to feel a full spectrum of emotion himself.

'Her cretinous parents nearly had her running off again. Bloody hell, I thought the Mayhews lacked feeling but the Calladines – they'd make Caligula look gushy. God forbid anything gets in the way of Angus's future knighthood. One day I'll inform Sophie how it was her mother's idea to have her own daughter hauled off towards a waiting straitjacket.'

It might have been Alice Calladine's suggestion that Sophie be hospitalised but John had leapt on it with zeal, Len thought, but he didn't inflame the situation by mentioning it.

'All that matters now is that Sophie feels valued and loved and safe and most importantly, unthreatened.' They'd all had Sophie categorised as a pet mouse rather than a potential velociraptor. Len's own possible inclusion on a future honours list depended on restoring John's popularity levels too. He'd earned it more than John F.'s doddery old father-in-law.

'So, the schedule. This week, of course, you and Sophie will be seen around London. Dinner, theatre, ease yourself back into the public domain as a couple, a show of strength. When Sophie is ready – let's not push her and risk another meltdown – *My Home, Your Home* will feature the exclusive. You and Sophie photographed in Park Court: domestic scenes, particularly the kitchen, eating together, cooking together. I want a few shots of you relaxed watching TV, and in the bedroom, Sophie fastening your tie for you whilst you hold your briefcase; putting her earrings on at the dressing table, you standing over her fondly smiling. A nice mix of business and pleasure.'

'Doable,' mused John.

THE MAGNIFICENT MRS MAYHEW

'*My Home, Your Home* are tame, we will retain full editorial control of course. You need Sophie to open up about your son. Have you discussed Rebecca Robinson with her yet and if so, what was the outcome?'

John grimaced at the prospect. 'No. I wanted to hear from you what I should say for the best.'

Len gave a small laugh. He certainly couldn't coach John F. Mayhew in shelving blame. He should have held masterclasses.

'My suggestion is the sooner you approach the subject the better, John. Say what you have to in order to get back on track. This is perfectly recoverable. Sophie may even have done you a favour. Voters do like to see a little human frailty. If a poppy grows too tall, they will cut it down. Then, when it's looking all pitiable and broken, they'll try to regrow it.'

Professionally, Len Spinks was congratulating himself in anticipation of what would surely be a *coup de maître* in PR, but in his heart – and Len Spinks did have one away from the job – he was thinking: *Poor Sophie.*

Chapter 47

When Sophie got back from her lunch with Elise, she set up a Facebook account in the name of Pom Calladine and searched for the Ackroyds in Australia. Her best bet was Charlie, as Tina could have married and changed her surname, but there were quite a few Charlie Ackroyds on the site. She checked them all and found four in Australia who were male. She wrote them each a private message:

> Hi, I'm trying to contact Tina Ackroyd who lived in Briswith and will be 31 now. She had a twin brother called Charlie and her mum was a cook at St Bathsheba's school. I spent the summer with them 18 years ago and I'd love to trace them. Best wishes, 'Pom'.

She sent the message and immediately regretted it. What was the point of keeping Pom alive and kicking? Pom had no place in the world to which she had returned. At best Charlie or Tina would reply, there would be a couple of 'how are you' emails pinged between them and then contact would cease again. It would only complicate things in the long run. The past was gone, she should let it lie.

But still, with any time at all to think, her mind strayed to Little Loste. As she packed a jade-green silk blouse into her suitcase for her forthcoming London trip, she wondered how excited Jade would be now in the build-up to her prom on Friday, and if she would feel like Beyoncé in her beautiful dress and designer shoes. And she wondered how Elliott was, if he was attempting to rebuild his family as she must attempt to rebuild hers.

She and John were going to spend a few days in London together so she could introduce herself back into the social whirl: lunch, theatre, dinner, sending out a clear message that she was restored to health and standing behind her husband one hundred per cent. She was dreading it.

The sound of the doorbell disturbed her thoughts and she hoped that her caller was no one related to her by either blood or marriage. She walked down the stairs to find that Margaret had let in the only exception to that hope – a beaming Edward.

'Sophie, I am so glad to see you back safe and sound,' he said, bounding over, enclosing her in a very un-Mayhew-like hug. 'Are you all right? Have people been kind to you? I was passing on my way to an appointment and I had to call in.'

'Yes, I'm all right,' she answered. 'Can you stay for a coffee?'

'Of course I can,' he said.

'Come through.'

He followed her into the kitchen and threw himself down on a chair. He looked smilier than she could ever remember him being, like a man in tune with himself.

'It's so wonderful to see you again, Sophie. Are you alone in the house?'

'Apart from Margaret.'

'John's gone to London?' he asked, puzzled.

'He had an early meeting, I'm going to join him.'

He made a breathy sound of relief. 'Ah, I see. Good. I had to risk that he'd be here with you when I knocked on the door. I'm not exactly flavour of the month with the family.' He made a face. 'Did you hear?'

'That you have a new occupation? Yes, I heard. How's it going?'

'Bloody brilliant. I've found my niche. Of course I've been building up the business for a year on the side, splitting myself in half, but it's been worth it. I was aiming for the mid-price market but after an old contact of mine who now works for a Saudi prince asked if I'd handle a top lot, I've been inundated with those.'

'So you won't miss life in governmental chambers then?' She asked it, but she already knew what his answer would be.

'Absolutely not. I've bought myself a new pied à terre in London. Bachelor pad.' He puffed out his cheeks. 'I expect you've heard about my change in relationship status too.'

'I'm so sorry to hear you'd split up with Davina.' Sophie brought the coffees over to the kitchen table.

'Don't be. I feel as if I've been let out of jail.'

Sophie gave a soft chuckle. 'For the record, I never thought you were a match.'

'I'm better at matching people to houses than I obviously am to other people, including myself.' He slurped his drink and she smiled. He was so very un-Mayhew.

'Was she terribly upset?'

'I expect she was over me by the time I'd reached the front door.'

'Find someone who makes you laugh next time,' said

Sophie. 'Someone who you enjoy being with and coming home to. With no elbows.'

Edward guffawed. He had a deep, genuine laugh that came right from his belly, like a posh, slim, balding Father Christmas. 'Will do. But for now, I'll enjoy my freedom. So what's on the agenda for you now? I suppose you'll have a lot lined up, won't you? I expect Len will be on a PR offensive. Piece of advice, Sophie, you take things at your own pace, not theirs. You've been through a lot. I hope John's bloody well made it up to you.'

She didn't answer. She wouldn't lie to Edward.

They passed the length of time it took to drink their mugs of coffee talking about the Mayhew clan blacklisting him. 'I don't believe I ever fitted in with them, Sophie. My own family, isn't that strange?'

'More common than you think,' replied Sophie pointing at herself.

'Yes, you too, you're right. We stand out like sore thumbs, don't we? I think we'd have made a much better pairing. Two black sheep standing in the same field, we'd have been good company for each other.'

Sophie nodded. 'We would.' She'd always known her brother-in-law was a little in love with her. His choice of women were all of a similar physical mould to her: long caramel hair, slim, over-composed. She hoped the next one would be very different.

Edward gave Sophie a lift to the train station. After he had wheeled her case to the barrier for her, he pulled a few business cards out of his shirt pocket to give to her.

'*Forwarding Address*, estate agency, that's me. If any of your friends are selling their properties or buying, tell them to give me a call. I'm very good at what I do.' He gave her a hug and held on to her as if he wanted to transmit something through the embrace that might relieve him of saying the actual words. Then he decided that she should have those words; he needed her to hear them. He took a deep bolstering breath before he spoke.

'I owe you an apology, Sophie. That day when we were all gathered in the hallway about to face the press, no one asked if you were all right. Everyone was buzzing around John like bees around the proverbial honey pot and when I thought about it all afterwards, I was ashamed. I was ashamed that I didn't stand with you. I should have been there for you.'

'No, Edward, you shouldn't have. John should.'

'Don't settle for anything less than you deserve, my dear Sophie,' he said.

She waved him off, then looked at the cards in her hand and for a moment it was as if a highlighter pen had swept over the two words: *Forwarding Address*. Most odd.

Chapter 48

The Mayhews' London flat was small but incredibly chic with a fabulous view over the Thames. Sophie had always liked this place, although it had never quite felt the same after Crying-girl had barged into it and dumped the key. That incident had tarnished it indelibly with a memory she had tried to sponge away, but vestiges of it remained like the faintest pink bloom of wine on a white dress – almost but not quite gone.

She unpacked her suitcase, made herself a coffee and went out onto the veranda with it. The panorama never became any less impressive; London was equally beautiful during the busy day as it was at night with all its Christmas-like coloured lighting. Whenever she had been here before, she could sit for ages just watching London life happen; she adored its energy. So why now, if she could have snapped her fingers and teleported to another place, would she have done so in an instant: to the view of a quiet Yorkshire beach where the sea rocked backwards and forwards contentedly under a vast moody roof of sky.

She needed to rally, as her mother said, move on. No good ever came of something that had been cast into a mould and then tried to change its shape when set. It warped at best; shattered at worst.

When John came home, they ate a simple pasta meal that Sophie had prepared for them. Then John opened a bottle of wine and they sat on the sofa. It wasn't big or squashy with black kitten hair on it. It was stylish and terribly expensive and uncomfortable as hell. But they were together, in the intimate scenario she had wanted for them. Except that they weren't about to cosy up and watch a film.

'I suppose we should talk, if you're ready,' he said. 'About why it happened. Blast it open. Get everything out there so we can draw a line in the sand.'

'I suppose we should,' replied Sophie.

'Sounds a cliché but I . . . I didn't feel loved. And in no way am I blaming you for this' – his open palms in remonstrative pose – 'but somehow, we lost *us* along the way, didn't we? And I want us back so much, Sophie. We are a team, a brilliant team.'

She nodded, smiled encouragingly, but felt nothing. She presumed she was numbed by the events of the past month, the equivalent of novocaine in a dental surgery. It wore off, allowing one to feel again, eventually. Given time.

'Why her?' she asked her husband.

'Because she was there. There was nothing special about her, Sophie. There were a lot of lies in the press. *It* only happened a few times, I swear to you, and I didn't know about the pregnancy, whatever she says. I don't even believe it. I think her PR lot knew that would really hit home and make the story even bigger than it was.'

'Did you love her, John?'

'God, no. It wasn't about love, it was something primal and idiotic.' He committed *primal* to a memory chip, it was definitely the word to use in an interview. It almost removed the element of choice. He reached for her hand. 'One thing I did realise whilst you were away ... I thought ... thought maybe we could think about adopting.'

He watched her reaction and he knew that she was hooked, lined and sinkered.

'Adopting?' Her voice barely audible.

'I resisted the idea for stupid reasons, Sophie. I love you and I want to have a family with you.'

'Really, John? Is that what you truly want?'

'Truly it is.'

She looked into his eyes and there was no hint of a lie there.

He went on. 'This whole episode has taught me a lesson about what is important, Sophie. And it's family, it's you and me and the job comes second, not first.'

Her head was whirling. *Her own baby*, because it would be her own if they adopted. It didn't matter that someone else had given birth to the child, it would be she who picked a son up when he fell, or read to a daughter before she went to sleep. *Scary Edwin Page*. A child would breathe life into Park Court, and into her.

She glanced over at John to find him smiling and she felt a glimmer of a flame in her heart.

'John, one more thing. I need to know. Have there been any more women, any more indiscretions? Ever? Tell me now because I need to know if we are to move on from this. Just tell me the truth, it has to be the truth.'

'I swear to you, no.'

'Swear on Henry's memory.'

'I swear on Henry's memory.'

She looked into his eyes and there was no hint of a lie there.

Chapter 49

The day after, she walked into the Palace of Westminster having arranged to meet John in the Strangers' bar. She bought herself a small red wine and picked a corner table at which to wait, aware of eyes everywhere, nudges, gasps, and some smiles too cast in her direction. She felt the nip and bite of words uttered in quiet gossip but remained composed and cool as always. Sophie Mayhew was back on the scene.

She was early so she took a book out of her bag, made herself look unavailable for chat. Whatever Elliott might have said about Pom being approachable did not apply to Sophie Mayhew, with her impenetrable and alienating air which, today, she was more than glad she had. She'd read five pages when someone sat in the chair opposite bringing with her a pulse of floral perfume. Sophie raised her eyes ready to combat any Dena Stockdale-style rounded vowels of disingenuity. *'I'd just like to say I was so sorry to hear . . .'*

'I thought it was you. I've hoped to bump into you so many times burra never 'av. I made up my mind that if I got the chance, I'd bite the bullet and say hello.' A wonderful Scouse accent that stripped back the years. In front of Sophie sat the mighty oak of a figure she had never associated with the little acorn she had known so well. 'I'm Lena Sowerby. We went to school together forra bit. I was Magdalena Oakes then.'

She held out her hand, which Sophie ignored.

'Magda!' she shrieked instead, rising from her chair and throwing her arms around the chic, elegant woman. That would set tongues wagging. *Let them,* she thought. 'Oh my goodness, I can't believe it.'

'I've never dared to talk to ya in case you told me to piss off,' said Magda, holding her old friend as tightly.

'You should have. Oh, you really should.'

'I was only ever called Magda at that bloody school and I didn't want to ever be her again. What a difference a name makes.'

Sophie knew that for sure. 'You look amazing.'

'I'm a bit different to what I used to be, aren't I?' Magda grinned. 'My eyebrows were like two morbidly obese slugs until you got hold of 'em.'

Sophie grinned back.

'If it hadn't been for you, I'd still be shovelling on the blue eyeshadow like they did in Abba. Okay to sit here? I presume you're waitin' for John so I'll shoot off as soon as I see him.'

She sounded like Magda but looked nothing like her. It was beyond odd.

'It's so good to see you, Magda.'

'And you. Well, properly, because I've seen you loads of times from a distance.'

'Maybe if I'd known Lena Sowerby went to St Bathsheba's it might have set me thinking.'

'You are jokin' aren't ya? Do you think I'd ever admit I went to that educational abomination? How the hell it

existed in this day and age I have no idea. It was like something out of a Hammer horror film, wasn't it? Miss Egerton
and that bloody cane.' She laughed, a tinkling Magda laugh,
a sound that made Sophie's heart soar.

'I can't tell you how happy I am at this moment,
Mag— ... Lena.'

'Oh, don't worry about the name thing. You've got permission to call me Magda, but don't let on to anybody else.
We'll have to have a proper catch-up one day.'

'I'd like that very much.'

'Just don't tell your other half. He won't like you consor-
tin' with the enemy.'

That was true. John would totally forbid it.

'Where are you living now, Magda?'

'We're in between houses. We sold ours but the one we
were buying fell through at the last minute so we're renting
at a stupid price and I need to find somewhere permanent
as soon as poss. Looking for somewhere in the St Katharine
Docks area. Always thought I'd be a country girl, but I've
fallen in love with the London vibe and my husband's from
the East End. He's a big lad in the city. Funny how life turns
out, isn't it? I was on course to be an English teacher living
on the Wirral with a house full of kids, and here I am in the
shadow cabinet; couldn't make it up, could ya?'

'Nope.' Sophie couldn't have closed up her smile if she
tried. 'That's quite a change. How did it all come about?'

'I found I didn't care about the Brontës or Byron any
more, it was as simple as that. They weren't enough for me
to get my teeth into. So, in my first year at uni, I looked to
change to another course and History and Politics was suggested. I didn't even know what the House of Lords was
when I started, but I became fascinated by it, and by all the

people who got into the game because they wanted to better things for everyone else. And all the dickheads who got struck down by the old Bathsheba syndrome, of course. I hoped I'd never become one of those.'

So many did, though. So many were intoxicated by the drug of power and it toppled them in the end.

'Do you have any children, Magda?'

'No, just a Cornish Rex cat who is my baby. I'm sorry to hear about the . . . what happened to your son. I wish I'd reached out then . . . not that it was the right time to . . . plus I didn't know if you'd want to be associated with me.'

'Why ever not?'

'For a start it was my fault you ended up having to stay at school through the whole summer. I always felt really guilty about that. No wonder you never replied to my letters.'

Sophie was confused. 'What letters?'

'Letters I sent to you at the school. I wrote and told you that I wouldn't be coming back but asked if we could be penfriends.'

Sophie shook her head. 'I never got them, Magda. Did you get mine?'

'No. Did you write?'

'I did. None of the teachers I asked would give me your address but said they'd forward them to you. When you didn't reply I presumed that you'd left me behind with everything else.'

Magda scowled and just for a moment, Sophie recognised the Magda of old. 'The rotten, stinkin' bitches. Probably saw the Liverpool postmark and burned them.'

'Bitches indeed,' agreed Sophie. She wondered how her fate would have been altered for not receiving those letters, because lives were changed irrevocably by such things.

'When we eventually get a place, I'll be having a house-warming. You'll be first on my invite list,' said Magda, reaching across the table and squeezing Sophie's arm, her affection evident.

Sophie opened her handbag and drew the zipper on the inside pocket. 'I know a very good estate agent in London. He matches people to property. He might be able to help you. It's my brother-in-law. He's a Mayhew but he's a good sort. His company is called Forwarding Address.' She handed one of his business cards over and Magda read it.

'Ah, Forwarding Address. Thanks for this. Right, I'd better go and get back to the red corner.' She stood, gave Sophie another hug. 'Google me and my website comes up top, there's a contact form on there. Let's arrange something soon.'

'Very soon,' said Sophie as Magda disappeared into the throng hanging around the bar and wondering why – again – the words 'forwarding address' had a weight to them and a meaning that she couldn't quite put her finger on.

Chapter 50

When Sophie returned to Park Court at the weekend, it was to find four messages waiting for her on Facebook. Two Charlies had replied and said, 'Sorry, not me.' The third had replied:

> That'll be me. I remember you! I've sent you a friend request and so has Tina. She's called Tina Turner now (she's heard all the jokes!) We are all delighted that you got in contact, Pom. Mum says are you still making pom poms?

The fourth message was from Mrs Tina Turner.

> Oh my GOODNESS I cannot believe it is really you, Pom. I have thought about you so much over the years and wondered how you were, where you were, what you were doing. You must tell me EVERYTHING.
>
> All good here. Mum got married five years ago to a really nice man. He moved out here twenty years ago from WHITBY – can you believe? All that way and she

meets someone from virtually around the corner from where she was born. Such a small world. I'm married with a ten-year-old son. Hubby is a cameraman. He shoots Neighbours. Obviously not shoots the neigh-bours, you know what I mean. You married? Kids? Tell all and soon!

Pom it would be great to see you. Please please, we must meet when I'm next over, not sure when though as we came over last year. Here's my address, email, telephone number, mobile. I can't tell you how much you have made us all smile by getting in touch.

Sophie accepted the two friend requests, scrolled through Charlie's and Tina's photos. Charlie was taller, balder and wider but unmistakably the man of the boy she remembered. Married to Darryl, who was a fireman. She smiled at that and thought no wonder he'd been impervious to her girlish charms. Tina's pictures showed her as a glam, sleek, cheerful woman. Her husband was a bear of a man, her son a mini image of him. And there was a photograph of her cuddling a plump lady with grey curly hair – Mrs Ackroyd. Tina's occupation was listed as 'Multi-award winning make-up artist to the stars'.

Whilst she was on Facebook, she clicked on search, put in the name Jade Darlow; last night would have been her prom. The top picture that came up was of a girl in a jade-green gown posing at the side of a pink limousine, leg cocked behind her, hint of a red sole showing. She looked stunning, full of far more sass and swagger than Beyoncé could hope to conjure up. There were a lot of images from the prom: Jade and her friends in their coloured gowns and obligatory teenage pouts; Jade and various boys in suits; Jade and presumably her teachers and one of Jade standing in between her dad and Tracey, all three with their arms around each other. Sophie didn't even know she was grinning until she felt her face muscles ache.

She closed her eyes, tried to imagine that she was back in Seaspray, that beyond the window to her left was sand and sea and if she walked outside and turned right she would come to the front door of a vicarage where there was love and laughter and lasagne within the walls and a little boy who loved crunchy pie and trains.

Chapter 51

Two months later

Life for the Mayhews was smoothing. Rebecca Robinson's fire had petered out and 'doing a Becky' had slipped into modern parlance as an analogy for sleeping with a high-profile figure, doing one's best to savage him in the press and in the process ending up as a charred, spitting, bitter, pathetic figure that had a certain novelty appeal on low-grade TV shows where the desperate and fame-hungry congregated. Just as 'The Spink Doctor' himself had predicted.

Sophie totally confused a nation that had been expecting a PR whirl following her return to the public eye, by giving them nothing. Her refusal to be interviewed had frustrated John, who was a natural 'fight fire with fire' man, but Len had expressly forbidden him to push her. Len himself had been initially confounded by her 'invoking of the fifth amendment' but when he started to monitor polls and reactions he quickly became convinced she had played a blinder. Sophie's popularity points appeared to have gone up by a zillion per cent. And when hers went up, they pulled John's up with them.

There were, of course, many who disparaged her decision to return to her husband after such a cruel humiliation but they seemed to be grossly outnumbered by those who admired her unassuming decorum and determination to rebuild the shattered castle of her marriage brick by quiet brick. Sophie Mayhew had somehow become the poster girl for dignity. In this age of washing grubby laundry in full view of the masses, she was a blast of fresh air with immaculate white sheets.

'Sophie the Trophy' had transmogrified into 'Sophie the Toughie', a woman with bearing and loyalty, strengths but also the best sort of weaknesses. The PM Norman Wax came out in full support of the Mayhews. He even named John as the man he wanted to succeed him.

In short, all was good.

Nearly all. Because something wasn't quite right. As much as Sophie tried to be the same self she had been before she had bolted to Yorkshire, she no longer fitted precisely into the space she had left behind her, however much she tried to cram herself back in. It was too small – she had grown, expanded and it pained her to try.

She went into the dressing room and took out her suitcase, the old faithful one she had taken with her on her adventure. She and John were going to a wedding that weekend in Dorset. A Labour backbencher was marrying a Conservative frontbencher and Sophie had heard that Madga would be there. She hoped she would be able to sneak off and chat to her at some point. Even if it happened to be in the ladies' loo.

She hefted the case onto the bed and opened it up,

unzipped the inner pocket to place some underwear in it and saw paper. She'd forgotten she'd put them there: the newspaper article about the women who had reached for their various-sized stars, and the picture that Luke had drawn for her with the disembodied kidney hanging between herself and Ells Bells. The smile on her crayoned face was a deep curve of happiness and she felt herself mirroring it. She had only smiled like that once since she'd left Little Loste and that was when she encountered Magda in the Strangers' bar. Tears started to pour from her eyes so fast that she couldn't wipe them away as rapidly as they flowed. What the hell was wrong with her? She almost never cried. Her mother's voice in her head with that word she detested: *Rally.*

She packed a blue taffeta dress for the wedding which had cost an arm, two legs and a head and still it wasn't a patch on the one she had made for herself that John had forced her to change out of for Clive and Celeste's golden wedding lunch. The dress was the same blue as Elliott Bellringer's eyes. And Tracey's. She wondered how they both were, wondered if Tracey's and Jade's relationship had changed gear in the two months since the prom. She wondered if they laughed at the eBay dress saga and thought of her sometimes.

*

The wedding was being held in the private chapel of a stately home, which was now an exclusive hotel, and most of the guests were staying in the rooms.

'I don't bloody believe it,' said John, as they entered the reception area to find Magda booking in. '*Her.*'

'Oh, Mr Mayhew, how great to see ya,' said Magda, pausing to speak to them on her way to the grand staircase.

'Lena,' said John, with a strained smile.

'And Mrs Mayhew, how good to meet you at last in person.' Magda held out her hand and Sophie shook it, noticing the twinkle in her eye. Then off she swept, leaving Sophie trying to appear innocent and John's lip pulled back over his teeth.

Their bedroom was outrageously large. One of the most expensive rooms at the top of the hotel with a view of the sea. It was the first time Sophie had been near the coast since she had returned from Yorkshire. She stood in the window and stared out at it, thought of herself walking barefoot in the warm shallows as she had on the day when she'd visited Briswith, until John told her to get a move on because they were due downstairs for pre-wedding drinks in half an hour.

They dressed. John looked strikingly suave in a Tom Ford navy suit, pristine white shirt, handmade shoes; an outfit that cost more than Elliott's entire wardrobe probably. *Elliott Elliott Elliott.* All roads insisted on leading her thoughts back to him. She had tried so hard to push those three weeks to the back of her mind for the sake of her sanity, but they were too rich, too loud, too colourful. She hoped he was happy, she hoped that Joy had finally got the wildness out of her system and appreciated what she had.

They went down to the bar. John made a beeline for Chris Stockdale, leaving Sophie lumbered with Dena who once again said to Sophie that they 'must do lunch'. Sophie excused herself from Dena's scintillating company after Magda pushed past her, apologising profusely for almost knocking her over. A far from subtle message to follow her, Sophie thought with an inner snigger. Thank goodness, Dena didn't decide to tag along.

The ladies' powder room was enormous and full of chaise longue seats and dressing tables. Inside it a delighted Magda was waiting for her. She looked stunning in an Everton-blue suit and a matching hat with an upturned brim.

'I was hoping you'd taken me banging into ya as a gentle hint.' They threw their arms around each other.

'It's so brilliant to see you again,' gushed Sophie. 'I'm sorry I haven't been in touch yet about meeting up, I've been finding my feet.'

'Oh, don't worry,' replied Magda. 'I figured as much, plus I've been dead busy myself. I used your brother-in-law's services by the way. He found us a fantastic place. I've passed his name around a few times since.'

'He's a good egg,' replied Sophie.

'I was up in Yorkshire last month. Showed my hubby Colditz.' She shuddered. 'Called in to see friends whilst I was up there. I was at uni with someone who lives in the next village. Little Loste, it's called. Isn't that lovely?'

Sophie felt a rush of longing. 'It is,' she said. *It really is.*

'She runs an inn so we stayed overnight.'

Sophie wanted to ask questions, so many questions.

'Her brother's the local vicar,' Magda went on. 'He's absolutely gorgeous as well. One of those annoying people that gets better-looking with age.' She hooted. 'He once came to stay with her at uni and my eyes started pumping out cartoon hearts.'

Sophie was desperate for detail. 'He must be married, then.' Was that too obvious a question?

'Yeah, he is, but he's going through a divorce apparently.'

Sophie's heart stopped. She had to kick-start it with a large gasp.

'He's single?'

'Far as I know.' Magda gave her a quizzical look. 'Got a thing about vicars, have ya? He's got a lovely little— ... ah ... sorry.' She broke off and admonished herself. 'Stupid.'

'Child.' Sophie filled in the missing word for her. 'Magda, you can say it. Little boy or girl?' *Luke.*

'Boy,' said Magda. 'He's four, going on forty-four.'

'Did you take any photos when you were up there?' *Please say you did.* '... I'd like to see the school again.'

'Oh yeah, hang on.' Magda took her phone out of her glittery silver bag, keyed in her passcode, clicked on photos, scrolled.

'This is my other half and me, a selfie in front of Colditz ... Colditz again. Still grim, isn't it? Skip through the boring scenery ones. Ah, this is my mate's pub and this is me and her ...'

Tracey and Magda, arms around each other. Two beautiful women.

'This is her and her fella. He asked her to marry him the day after his daughter's prom.' The next picture was a blurred close up of a ring on a finger. 'We took this when we were pissed on celebratory champagne, hence the quality. This is her cat, he's deaf and old and gorgeous if you like cats, which I do. Here's her nephew, isn't he cute?'

Luke, in his guard's uniform, sitting on the ride-on train. His eyes bright blue, his hair in his face and her hand came out of its own accord, before she could stop it, as if to smooth it back. She swallowed, her throat felt blocked with tears, smiles, love.

'And this is the vicar. Isn't he a looker?'

Elliott and Tracey together. Dear Elliott with his dark hair and dimple in his chin, broad shoulders, heavenly eyes, unholy sexiness pouring from his image.

'How can someone who looks like that be single?' asked Sophie.

'He won't be for long though, will he?' replied Magda. 'According to his sister his wife was a bit of a twat. Messed him about a lot. Turned up a couple of months ago with a big teddy bear expecting to play happy families but she couldn't even remember when the little boy's birthday was.'

A sob escaped from Sophie's mouth, surprising her more than Magda.

'You all right, girl?'

'Hiccup,' said Sophie. 'Go on, Magda, you were saying.'

'Well . . .' A little confused why Sophie was so interested in people she didn't know, Magda nevertheless indulged her. 'So he kicked her to the kerb. Tracey said he'd been feeling really low, but obviously my sparkling presence cheered him up.'

Elliott and Joy hadn't got back together. He was single. None of that altered anything in Sophie's life, so why was she feeling as if her emotions were on a fast spin in a washing machine?

'You'd better go before John sends out a search party,' Magda nudged her affectionately. 'Come over to the flat the next time you're in London. We need a proper natter with gin. Give me a couple of minutes' head start out of here so John doesn't see us together.' Magda embraced her again. 'Oh, Sophie, you are so lovely. I just hope after all you've been through that you're happier than you look.'

And with that telling observation, she was off.

*

The Chapel of Mary Magdalene was a short walk down a path from the back of the stately home. It was narrow inside with a long red-carpeted aisle and ornate stone pillars, friezes of biblical scenes painted on the walls. A magnificent stained glass window faced the congregation, featuring a resurrected Jesus outside the sepulchre, a woman standing in front of him, arms outstretched in greeting. The Magdalene herself. Now there was a woman who split opinion. Sophie thought of the verbal assault Miss Egerton had given her for implying Mary Magdalene had been in love with Jesus and yet in this depiction there was no doubt of her adoration. Their affection for each other was clear, their happiness at being close again. She heard Elliott's voice whisper to her: *And we are good people who like each other, I think. Friends.*

Sophie knew exactly where Mary M. was coming from.

The chapel began filling up. Magda and her husband walked past them and sat on a pew at the other side. He looked a nice man: very tall, solidly built, salt-and-pepper curly hair. Sophie noticed how he took her hand when they sat down, cradled it, and she tried to remember the last time that John had taken hers, but couldn't. The sense of unease she always felt at being in church revisited her; she half expected a figure from the wall to swivel his arm around to her and point her out as a heretic. She hadn't always been, she would have replied. But sometimes it was easier to hate than to love.

Sophie's eyes settled on the window again and she remembered the rolled-away stone that Luke had made in Sunday School. She suppressed a small giggle thinking of Tracey's incredulous expression on seeing it. And the pipe-cleaner lion with no head. *Let's call him Salvador.*

The pew behind them filled up, a drift of aftershave filtered forwards. It must have been the same one that Elliott used because her body responded to it: something sighed deep within her, something happy and sad at the same time.

The chapel was heaving at the gills by now and just before the guests impatiently started exchanging glances or checking their watches, the organ muzak gave way to the staccato opening bars of the Wedding March. A tiny flower-girl scattering petals preceded the bride and her father, bridesmaids and pageboys followed behind. The vicar in sumptuous robes began his address.

'Dearly beloved, we are gathered here today to witness the union of Vanya and Paul in holy matrimony . . .'

Sophie thought back to her own wedding which had been hijacked by her mother and Celeste. She'd battled to have any say in the arrangements but it had been such hard work and so unpleasant that, in the end, she'd given up and let them get on with it. Her day had been outwardly perfect but it hadn't been the one she had pictured in her imagination. She had wanted to make her own wedding dress which obviously hadn't been allowed to happen. The gown she had picked had been expensive and showy as befits the bride of a political Titan-in-the-making, but she didn't feel half as much of a princess as she would have in the one she had designed for herself.

'Do you Vanya take Paul . . .'

Vanya was looking at Paul with eyes full of love. Had she looked at John like that at the altar? Did Vanya, behind her smiles, have alarm bells ringing that she really should have waited longer, made sure, not been seduced by the flamboyant proposal in the middle of a family gathering where the cheering began before she had even said 'yes'?

Paul mispronounced Vanya's middle name and the congregation chuckled; jollity warmed the chapel by degrees.
Sophie remembered standing at the altar trying to stop her
teeth from chattering, not just from the chill of the abbey
or nerves but the atmosphere had been so austere and
sombre, a vacuum of seriousness as if it were a business
arrangement instead of a happy celebratory occasion.

'I now pronounce you man and wife.' A merry burst of
applause, but Sophie's thoughts had wandered from the
nuptials taking place in front of her.

She should have stood firm on so much. She had never
quite rebelled *enough* in life. She might have kicked Irina
Morozova into the pool and written an (accidentally)
contentious piece about a biblical woman, but she'd
hardly gone down in the annals of the school as being the
Boudicca of St Bathsheba's. Visions bombarded her of all
the times she had 'played the game' when her heart was
screaming at her to stand up and be counted. *Rallying*
when she knew she was nowhere near ready to face the
world after she had given birth, taking blame for John's
constitutional cock-ups in order to leave his reputation
shiny-white, not digging deeper into Crying-girl's story,
absorbing all the snidey comments her sisters decided to
throw at her, putting up with being invisible to her close
and extended families ... until they wanted to roll her
out in front of a baying mob of press and decry her as the
cause of her husband's faithlessness. Even when she had
broken ranks and run away, and found what was missing
from her life – what had she gone and done then? She'd
come back. *I hope you are happier than you look*, Magda had
said to her. She wasn't. She wasn't happy at all. *Let's adopt*,
John had said. Two months later, he was avoiding any

mention of that promise. Had she really expected anything less?

Light streamed through the stained-glass window as if the
volume on the sun had suddenly been turned up to max.
Mary Magdalene's smile seemed to widen as she beheld
Jesus. Her friend. He would have made her hot chocolate
and talked to her over a kitchen table, Sophie thought. This
was love, whatever Miss Egerton argued, love born from
respect and friendship, trust and tenderness – and it would
have been enough to sustain them both.

'I have found the one whom my soul loves.' The priest's
voice broke into her reverie. 'This, from the beautiful Song
of Solomon. A man who understood the true meaning of
love. His book is written from the point of view both of the
woman and the man, and of the love held equally between
them. Marriage is not a contract empty of affection but one
of fond attachment as we see in friendship, but with that
added sprinkle of romance and desire . . .'

The priest could read her heart, Sophie thought.

I have found the one whom my soul loves.

Of course, that was it. That was why she hadn't been able
to fit back into her life with John F. Mayhew, because she
had found the one whom her soul loved and he wasn't her
husband but a vicar with blue, blue eyes who lived with his
son in a house by the Yorkshire sea.

Those words were the key to a door that led to another
life. Words from the Song of Solomon, the son of Bathsheba
whose life continued to weave in and out of her own, influ-
encing her destiny. Words from the Bible, the book of a God
she had turned her back on four years ago.

Chapter 52

Sophie didn't get to see Magda again at the wedding other than a discreet goodbye wave when they were booking out of the hotel the following morning, but it didn't matter, she would see her soon without having to skulk around, she knew that. During the night, her head had been weaving words into a plan: *Bathsheba, Yorkshire, love, happiness, prom gowns, Magda and Mary Magdalene, Edward and estate agencies, reaching for the stars articles, floating kidneys and forwarding addresses.* Words that lay behind the door opened by that beautiful quote which had crashed into her heart, jolted it into action, made it realise what she had to do. Sophie needed to get home, and so when John suggested they set off at first light, she readily agreed. She was euphoric and terrified in equal measures. *You can be brave and frightened, you know,* as Tracey had said to her.

As soon as John left for London on Monday, Sophie went into her sitting room, switched on her laptop, opened up a notepad, picked up her phone and engaged a solicitor and an accountant. Then she spent the rest of the day alternating between taking command of her life and falling to pieces. Doubts came often, firing into her head like poisoned arrows: *You won't be able to go through with this, Sophie. This is not how St Bathsheba girls act, Sophie. You have duties and responsibilities, Sophie.* What the hell was she doing, dismantling everything she knew? She had no idea – but it still felt right so she kept on with it. She was looking at a different future to the one that had stretched before her only two days ago. This time she would not let bravery be eroded by fear.

*

The next day, whilst Len was planning a Christmas PR offensive featuring the long-awaited 'At Home with the Mayhews' article that he was sure he could get Sophie to agree to with some artful manipulation, Sophie was standing outside a primary school in Kent. It was the start of the new school year and uniforms were pristine, shoes were shiny. The smallest children were a mix of apprehension and excitement: she knew how they felt because she was full of both herself. She was certainly more of the former as she waited until everyone in the playground had funnelled through the school doors and they had shut behind the last of them. Today she would close her own door on something too. There was a matter she needed to clear up, so she would never wonder about it again, could stop it taking up space in her head which could be filled with thoughts of greater value.

Malandra Anderson, Moxon as was, walked into the vacant classroom, registered who was waiting there for her and took a step backwards. 'What the . . .' She stopped short of what she had been about to say, though it was obvious it would have been an expletive.

'Hello, Malandra. Do sit down.'

'What are you doing here? They said you were from the Inland Revenue.'

I lied,' said Sophie, crossing her long, slim legs. 'Please sit down. You once invaded my space without warning and so you will afford me the courtesy of letting me do the same to you.'

Cautiously Malandra sat down on one of the small desks, a safe distance from Sophie.

'What do you want?' she asked. Her neck was mottled red from an immediate eruption of unease.

'I just want to ask you something. We didn't really have a lot of time to speak when we last met,' said Sophie, calm, her mien neutral, unreadable.

'Look, why are you dredging this up now? It's a long time ago and—'

'Four years, four months and six days ago; trust me, I know exactly how long it is. That week is one I will never forget.'

Malandra lowered her head as if it were weighted with shame. She knew what had happened to Sophie in that week and it had stayed with her ever since that she might be partly responsible for the tragedy that had befallen the woman now sitting in front of her. That was why she had bowed out at the first sign of pressure when Len Spinks had borne down on her like a psychotic eagle.

'I want to ask you a couple of questions that I hope you will answer honestly and then you will never hear from me again, you have my word. What you tell me will remain between ourselves, but I have to know the truth.'

'I'm not sure I'll be able to,' said Malandra, hiding her stress not too well.

'I think you will. I think you may even feel better for it.'

Malandra jerked nervously, as if it were the last movement allowed before she was forced into a straitjacket.

'Firstly,' began Sophie. 'What you told me about having an affair with my husband, was it true?'

'I can't possibly say either—'

'How much did he buy your silence for?'

A pause, then Malandra gave a heavy sigh followed by a small, hard laugh. Sophie Mayhew was right about one thing, she would feel better for saying it aloud. This had been sitting inside her like a lump of lead for four long years. 'Ten thousand. I had no choice but to take what he offered because I didn't want to be blacklisted. Contrary to what he thought I'd do, I wouldn't have gone to the press. I'm not like that. I do have some morals. . .'

Her voice trailed off. It was rich really, purporting to be honourable to the wife she had wronged.

'How many times did you sleep with my husband?'

'I didn't keep a tally. Quite a few.'

'Did you ever sleep together in our London flat?'

'Always in the London flat. I more or less lived there at one point. It was me that broke the clock in the kitchen. I was trying to straighten it and it fell off and smashed. I got another one to replace it. It wouldn't hang properly so I attached a piece of string on the back to wrap around the nail and hold it in place.'

Sophie had no doubt the detail would check out if she ever went back to the flat. John had told her the cleaner had knocked the clock off the wall whilst dusting it and he'd bought another.

'Did you love him?'

'Yes, very much, but I honestly wouldn't have looked at him in that way had he not made the first move.' She shook her head at her apparent weakness. 'It sounds stupid I know but . . . but I couldn't resist him. I felt . . .' she studied, searching inside herself for the right word, found it: 'consumed.'

Sophie recalled John's romantic assault on her when she had worked at *Mint*. The wildly expensive meals, the flowers, the jewellery, the eloquence dropping from his lips like warm Elvish honey. He had taken her breath away with his attentions, made her feel like the only woman in the world.

'He made me feel like the only woman in the world,' said Malandra, and Sophie knew she was telling her the truth.

'Did he say that he loved you?'

'Yes. I'm not sure I believed him but I wanted to.'

'Did you ever talk about me?'

'He spoke about what was wrong with his marriage and why he was looking outside it for . . .'

'What did he say was wrong with it?' Sophie fired the question at her like a bullet.

'That there was no love between you. That he married you because you were the ideal partner on paper.' Malandra apologised then. 'I'm sorry if that hurts you, I'm trying to give you the truth.'

'It's fine. Did you know I was pregnant?'

Malandra broke eye contact, she swallowed, tapped her fingers nervously on the desk before replying. 'Not until I walked into the London flat and saw you. And I was totally thrown by it because John said he never wanted children.'

Sophie saw a dark spot appear on Malandra's skirt; she was crying.

'I swear I had no idea. If I'd known, I would have resisted

him. I'd have resigned, I'd have gone.' She sniffed, dried her tears on the heel of her hand. 'He never said.'

It had been Sophie who insisted they keep the news of her pregnancy out of the public domain, until after the baby had been born. A superstition she'd thought would protect them from anything going wrong this time.

'For the record,' Malandra then continued, 'it was me that finished it because I discovered he'd been seeing someone else. I had the cheek to feel aggrieved that he was being unfaithful to me. It made me realise what a ridiculous situation I was in, so I walked out. I threw some false threats at him about exposing him as an adulterer but it was just wounded bluster. I shouldn't have, but we're all a lot wiser in hindsight.'

Malandra's disclosure hit her like a blow from Miss Egerton's cane. 'Someone else? Who?'

'I don't want to say.' There was a moment of internal struggle that showed on Malandra's face and then she blurted out, 'Oh, fuck it, the Chief Whip's wife. That snotty Stockdale woman.'

'Ah.'

Shock gave way to a surprising emotion.

'Why are you laughing?' asked Malandra, viewing Sophie as if she was mad.

Sophie stood. 'Thank you for being so candid, Malandra, I appreciate it. I will keep to my word, you won't hear from me again.'

She strode out of the classroom, then out of the school and back to her car without looking behind her.

Sophie's brain was sparking with activity all through the drive home. *Dena Stockdale, who would have thought?* So it was true after all. Behind all those sweet and innocent let's have lunches, Dena was secretly relishing getting one over on Mrs Mayhew. Sophie made a hands-free call to Elise.

'Where would you usually choose in London as a suitable venue for a private gossipy lunch?' she asked.

'Raul Cruz's place in St James's is perfect and my personal favourite: Toro.'

Bull. How fitting, thought Sophie. 'Would you do me a favour and arrange a table for two?'

'Absolutely. What day and time do you want to meet me there?'

'I don't,' Sophie replied.

*

Two days later, Sophie sat in a quiet booth in Raul Cruz's dimly lit restaurant waiting for her guest. It was decorated like a bordello with dark red walls and scarlet lighting which was appropriate, she thought. A little shiver of anticipation snaked down the middle of her back. She was owed this moment. It had come as an added bonus and slipped into her fast-forming plan like an unexpected windfall.

She noticed the waiter leading over her lunch companion whose eager smile withered as soon as she spotted Sophie.

'Dena, how good of you to come. Do sit down. I'm so looking forward to this.'

'I . . . I thought . . . where's Elise?'

'Oh, last minute, she couldn't make it. I figured it would be nice just for you and me to finally have that overdue lunch. And a lovely chat. About shoes.'

Chapter 53

Two weeks later

Both sides of the clan always convened at Glebe Hall on the last Sunday in September to celebrate Clive's and Angus's birthdays, which were only two days apart. They were all looking forward to Christmas, this one sure to be a true celebration after such a turbulent few months. But the storm had been weathered and they were all set to sail into a calm new year, bolstered by fair winds from behind. John F. Mayhew's career was back on track thanks to some more foolish decisions by Norman Wax, which were alienating at best, deranged at worst. Norman was starting to make Oswald Mosley look like Gandhi and 'concerned officials' were blamed for leaking sensitive documents into the public domain, questioning his fitness for duty. John F. Mayhew had struck a perfect balance between toeing the party line and being true to his conscience; looking worried and pained in media photos had drawn a lot of support to him. Thanks to Len spinning positive PR like a spider on speed, John's troubled star was once again on a rapid upward trajectory, forcing

Norman's down in the direction of inter-galactic hell. Strangely enough, details of Norman's affair had somehow trickled out to the press too so he was fighting for survival on all fronts, plus it was generally agreed that the deputy leader was as much use as 'a fart in a wind tunnel', as a member of the opposition had been heard to say. Oh yes, the new year was set to be a very successful one for the Mayhews.

This was the first time both families had all been together since the weekend before doorstepgate; bar Edward, of course, who was still in the cold hinterland of rejection. At least Sophie could do him a favour there, she thought, because today she would turn him into a saint by comparison. Lunch was chateaubriand with a red wine jus. There were no home-cooked Yorkshire puddings or beetroot wine, nor a black kitten in a furry bed in the corner. There was, however, a lot of forced politeness and good behaviour. Dessert was panna cotta; individual portions, each turned out of its own precise mould. Not crunchy pie with a smash of raspberries on top. Would she miss these gatherings at all, she asked herself? The answer was a very easy no. She felt fear clamp its hand around her jaw, then bravery prise off its fingers and tell it to get lost because it wouldn't change anything with its unwelcome presence.

As soon as her offer had been accepted, she had started packing. Elise's garage now boarded the boxes and bags and cases she would take with her into her new life: bolts of material and all her sewing paraphernalia, her wardrobe of dresses that would constitute her first stock, jewellery which she would sell, all her shoes – with the prospect of many other shoes to come when she was ready to take possession of them. In the boot and passenger side of her Mercedes sports car were a few suitcases of essentials that would cater to her immediate needs, and in the tank enough petrol to take her where she wanted to go. She had been expecting something at every stage to stop her, been prepared for a head-on battle, but nothing had interrupted the smooth flow of her planning. As if it were meant to be.

'So, don't you think it's about time we saw some articles in the press about you both as a couple?' asked Clive, directing the question more at Sophie than John. His tone was casual with a hard edge. This was something that had long been niggling him, thought Sophie.

John answered for them. 'Absolutely. It's all in hand. A wonderful Christmas feature, we thought. "At Home with the Mayhews".'

The 'we' was Len and John, not Sophie and John. John had broached the proposal: mistletoe-covered inglenook in the drawing room, Everest-sized tree in the hall, fake snow on the lawn. He was probably planning to dig up Perry Como to sing about chestnuts roasting on an open fire too. She'd listened to what he had to say and hadn't said no, which John had taken for a yes. She was slipping more and more into insignificance with every day that passed; Sophie the Trophy, the puppet on a string.

'About time,' Clive huffed. 'People want to see evidence of family life when your husband is Secretary of State for Family Matters, Sophie. They don't want his wife to be hiding away. She should be there at his side where she belongs.'

Something reared inside her. Something that would have raised its hand to make a small protest in times past and then decided against it; but not now.

'They might see much more of a family soon, as John has suggested we adopt a child.'

The result was a silence bomb which thudded onto the table in the middle of them all.

'Sophie, we ... er ...' John wiped his mouth with his starched linen napkin, smothering his annoyance. 'Shouldn't really have said anything until we've actually started the process, darling.'

'Well, that is a surprise,' said Celeste, in the manner of one who had just been told that her son and his wife were about to renounce Conservatism in favour of Marxism.

'It is, but of course it won't happen,' said Sophie, an imp of mischief sitting on her shoulder, handing her verbal weapons of mass destruction. 'It was merely something John said to keep me onside.' She carried on eating her panna cotta, but the others had frozen mid-pudding. Annabella's husband made a small choked-off sound as if he were responding to a joke that he didn't quite understand.

'Now why would you think that?' John's clipped response.

'Probably because you aren't capable of telling the truth, John,' Sophie returned, with her sweetest smile on display. 'And that's why I'm leaving you. That and the fact that you don't love me, of course. Did you ever, John?'

It was a rhetorical question; he never had. Love went hand in hand with respect and there was none of that in their relationship. She was a first-aid kit expected to come to the rescue when he self-harmed.

Margaret had unfortunately picked that moment to check on how the desserts were going down and reversed out at speed as if this were a film and someone had just hit the rewind button. An awkward laugh – from Robert, Sophie thought; for once reduced to a state of no sarcastic comment.

This was not how it had played out in her mental

rehearsal. She had planned to have a civilised lunch, say a polite goodbye and then skedaddle.

Annabella's plummy voice now: 'Sophie, is that a joke because if it is, it isn't very funny.'

'Totally uncalled-for behaviour,' said sister number two. 'Especially since you caused—' She cut off her words.

'Oh, don't stop; please continue, Victoria. Especially since you caused what? Caused a furore by not letting you all section me in a hospital because I wouldn't take the blame for John screwing a fame-hungry political aide? Sorry, political aides, because there was more than one, wasn't there, John? Two I know of for certain, plus someone's *stocky* little wife, which makes three. And God knows how many others. Even though you swore to me that there weren't. Swore on our baby's memory.'

'John, what is she talking about?' snapped Celeste.

Angus ripped his napkin from his collar.

'Not this madness again,' he said.

Sophie stood up and rounded on her father.

'No, there's no madness here, only cold, clear, sanity. Mum, Dad, I'm sorry that I've been such a disappointment to you. Celeste, Clive, unfortunately it's not my fault that John has jeopardised his career and any future honours for you by not being able to keep his genitals in his trousers. You should look up the Bathsheba syndrome. It may explain a few things.'

Angus and the Mayhew seniors joined together in a choir of outrage. 'Well really!'

'John, say something,' screeched Alice, but John remained abnormally silent. Outmanoeuvred. A king piece on a chessboard, brought down by the queen of the same colour.

Sophie wasn't finished. 'Annabella, Victoria, we've never

got on, have we? Sometimes blood isn't thicker than water, is it? Sometimes it's simply red stuff. But do look after that little boy, Annabella, because all children need love, otherwise they grow up . . . well, like us.'

'For God's sake, Sophie,' snarled her mother and for a split second she felt a spike of real gut-wrenching fear, fear that this time she was about to close a door that could not be opened again. Then it segued into the wonderful realisation that she was about to close a door that could not be opened again.

Sophie picked up the handbag at her side; there was nothing more to be said, she was done. She turned to the now puce-faced John who seemed for once unable to dredge up any fitting response. 'I'll take the car, I'm sure someone will give you a lift, and I'll be gone by the time you get back to the house. I'll be in touch about the divorce – play fair and I will too. You wanted me to give interviews to the press – well, I'll be happy to . . . if I don't get what I want.' Then she swept her eyes across the roomful of people and said, '*Au revoir*' in an accent worthy of Pom, although in her heart, she knew that it was far more likely to be *goodbye*.

Chapter 54

'*Excusez moi*, do you have a room for the night?' asked Sophie in an exaggerated accent that belonged to someone in a beret with a necklace of onions around their neck.

'Oh my goodness, it's you,' shrieked Tracey, bouncing out from behind the bar to embrace her friend. 'What are you doing here? Couldn't keep away, eh?'

'I could, but I really didn't want to,' replied Sophie.

'Hello, lass.' Old Marshall nodded from the corner. 'Nice to see you back.'

'Hello, Marshall,' smiled Sophie. 'It's good to be back.'

'I do have a room and it's all yours,' Tracey said.

'Well, if you hadn't, I'd have taken the bedsit in the almshouse,' said Sophie, as Tracey embraced her for the second time, unable to contain her delight.

'Can you believe, it's been sold?' said Tracey. 'Subject to contract of course. A company from down south gave us the asking price and didn't even try and negotiate or even request a viewing. Mad idiots.'

'Solomon Holdings by any chance?' asked Sophie.

Tracey's mouth was pulled open by surprise. 'How did you know that?'

'Because it's me. I'm Solomon Holdings.'

'Fuck a duck.' Tracey hurriedly went back behind the bar, poured out two glasses of wine: rosé for herself and red for her guest. 'What are ... did you ... why?'

'I want to be a woman who lives out her dream, however small it seems to anyone else, that's why,' said Sophie, picking up her glass and chinking it against Tracey's. 'I want to own the biggest centre for prom outfits in the north. I'm going to buy up all those prom dresses and suits that are worn once and forward them on to a new wearer.'

Forwarding Address. She hadn't realised why the name of Edward's company persisted in sticking to the inside of her skull until the night of the wedding in Dorset. *Forwarding A Dress.* The idea was as simple as it was brilliant. And if Edward could break free from the Mayhews and make his dream come true, so could she.

'That's bonkers,' said Tracey.

'Isn't it.'

'You're off your nut. It's fantastic.'

'I can but try.'

It was time to be the sun in her own solar system.

'Luke will be thrilled to see you. He wouldn't take his guard uniform off for six weeks. It threw itself into the washing machine in the end.'

Sophie smiled. The inside of her bloomed with warmth at the mention of his name.

'I'm sorry that I didn't say goodbye last time,' she said. 'I thought it best I should go when I did. When I knew Joy was back.'

Tracey huffed. 'She turned up on what she thought was Luke's fourth birthday, which he'd already had the month before, which tells you everything. With a bloody enormous blue *bear* which traumatised me, never mind him. She tried everything to get back with Elliott: crying, pleading, threatening, pretending the brakes on her car were faulty and she couldn't drive anywhere. It was late so Ells let her have the spare room in the vicarage and I stayed with her to make sure she didn't chain herself to the bannister or something, whilst he went over to the pub to stay with Luke. I had Steve come over and look at her brakes first thing the next morning and guess what – nothing wrong with them. Elliott sent her on her way but it wouldn't have worked between them because he was in love with you. Obviously I couldn't tell you that; your life was complicated enough.'

Sophie's whole body froze; she felt as if she had forgotten how to breathe.

'I'm not daft, I know why you left here when you did,' said Tracey. 'I guessed you felt the same about him. I'm hoping that you haven't come back just for Kitty Henshaw's old house?' She looked hopeful.

'No,' replied Sophie, a rasp of emotion in her voice. 'Not just for the house.'

Tracey grinned. 'Why don't you pop along to the vicarage and see Elliott? If you chuck me the car keys, I'll take your cases upstairs. How many have you got?

'Four and a sewing machine.'

'Blimey, planning on staying a while?' snorted Tracey.

'Yes,' came the reply. 'For ever.'

Sophie knocked on the back door of the vicarage. Elliott opened it tentatively, not expecting to see *her* there.

'I wanted to avoid the curtain-twitchers,' she said, trying not to laugh at the look on his face because it was the sort of expression a small football-mad kid might wear finding Cristiano Ronaldo on his doorstep.

'Pom. Come in. How lovely to see you.'

She crossed the threshold into this dear kitchen. It smelled of baked potatoes and grilled cheese; it smelled like a home. There on the table was his large notebook and she wondered if her name still sat on the pages. Luke's kitten was running madly around the kitchen playing with a ping-pong ball. He'd grown. Time didn't stop for anyone, that's why sometimes it was important not to wait for it, but to jump onto the train, ride with it.

'Can I . . . can I get you a coffee?'

'Thank you, that would be nice.'

He didn't know what to say to her, that was clear as he put a pod into the machine, pressed a button, waited for something to happen.

'You need to switch it on at the mains.' She leaned forward, did that for him.

'Oh yes, of course.'

'And I'd put a cup under the spout as well.'

He was flustered, almost dropped the cup. Sophie smiled. She wondered if she would ever stop.

'Luke will be sorry he missed you, he's in bed obviously at this time,' said Elliott as the machine started to growl and deliver.

'I'm sure I'll see him tomorrow,' Sophie replied.

'You're staying for a while?'

'Yes. I've bought the almshouse.'

Elliott's head snapped round to her. 'You? It's you?'

'Yep. It's me.'

'What are you going to do with it?'

'I'm going to turn it into a prom outfit paradise.'

She made a quick mental note to contact Dena Stockdale now she was in situ. Daisy Shoes was supplying a huge consignment of footwear suitable for proms for the price of her silence. But she was probably wiser not admitting blackmail to the local vicar.

'How will you manage the business from down south?' asked Elliott. His eyebrows had pulled together in the middle, his brain must be tumbling with questions, she thought.

'I won't. I'll be moving in with Kitty. I'm an outcast. I don't mind, I've had some of my happiest times as a pariah. I reckoned it was time to start living for myself, rather than for someone else. I'm expecting a very generous divorce settlement.'

He took the cup from the machine, placed it on the work surface at the side of her. She noticed that his hand trembled as he did so, sending the coffee over the rim.

'Why?' he asked. 'Why here?'

'Because I have friends here and the shopkeeper down the road gives me free breadcakes.'

He smiled. 'Any other reason?'

'There's a little boy that I'm a bit in love with.'

'Anything else?'

'The beach.'

'And?'

She swallowed down the fear, prepared to launch. 'Elliott, I have no idea if I'm here because of the cosmos sending me messages on business cards or Kitty Henshaw turning pages over or God talking to me at a wedding or maybe it's all of them, maybe it's a three-pronged attack ... Sorry, I know this makes absolutely no sense to you at all but what I'm trying to say is . . . is that . . . if you want me . . . '

Tumbleweed. He didn't answer. She'd got it wrong. She was here because she'd followed a Norwegian sea-full of red herrings. Her damage-limitation auto-correct cranked up.

'But . . . if you don't, that's okay, we can be friends. I can live with that. I'd rather have you in my life as a friend than not and . . .'

He was looking at her with his beautiful blue eyes. She wanted the floor to open up and drag her down – this woman who had just made a complete fool of herself.

Elliott took a breath, began to speak slowly, calmly.

'I can tell you now. . . that even as a non-believer, you are witnessing an actual moment where a prayer has been answered.'

His hand came out, captured hers, lifted it to his lips. The kiss flew to her heart, landing there with a contented sigh and even as a non-believer, Sophie Mayhew knew she had found her heaven.

The Magnificent (Ex-)Mrs Mayhew Revisited

By Gina Almonza for South Counties Magazine

Sophie Mayhew has changed since I interviewed her over a year and a half ago. Then she was designer-preened and polished and beautiful, now she is in jeans and sneakers and if anything is even more stunning, plus there is a light dancing in her eyes that was not present at our last meeting.

We are in the homely, bright kitchen of her grand, but not grandiose, house, delightfully named 'Seaspray', and drinking festive hot chocolate with a shot of egg-nog. My mug features the name of her business, *Prominence*. Hers features the wording, 'Best Mummy in the World'. There is a sewing machine on the table and a pair of pinstripe trousers. Clearly Sophie, as she insists I call her, is mid-project.

Sophie has been divorced from John F. Mayhew for seven months now and has happily turned her back on the limelight, whilst the limelight has unhappily turned its back on her ex-husband. Following the general election which saw the Conservative Party ousted, Mayhew did not find himself elected party leader as expected, thanks to the surprise rise of back-bench whizz-kid Barclay Freemantle. Meanwhile his old rival Lena Sowerby – ironically, an old school friend of Sophie's – has become the new deputy Prime Minister. Still, John F. Mayhew has his many millions from his increasingly successful business portfolio to compensate him. Do Sophie and John ever speak? There is no reason to, she answers.

They belong to two very different worlds now and it is easy to see in which one Sophie is most comfortable.

The front rooms of the gorgeous Seaspray are filled with shoes and accessories, fabulous gowns and suits, most of them ready to be tweaked and altered to fit their new owners like the proverbial glove, although some are made to measure from scratch, too. 'I want my young clients to have their Cinderella – or their Prince Charming – moment,' says Sophie, 'and without their parents having to sell a kidney to supply it.' Any profits are ploughed back into *Prominence*, which is less of a business and more of a service.

Her home, which had been standing empty for many years, has been lovingly restored to all its former glory and more. Presently Sophie has guests staying with her – old friends from Yorkshire who are now living in Australia. She introduces me to Mrs Ackroyd who was once the school cook at Sophie's boarding school, the controversial St Bathsheba's, currently being converted to a hotel and conference centre which should bring a lot of welcome visitors to the area. 'It was Mrs Ackroyd who gave me my love of sewing,' says Sophie, though Mrs Ackroyd is insistent that the pupil left her teacher far behind where skills are concerned.

In one of the upstairs rooms is a cover over a dress that I am not allowed to see, although I do get a sneak preview of the material: snow-white velvet. Next week, on Christmas Eve, Sophie Mayhew will exist no more. She will walk down the aisle of the local St George's church where she will marry the incumbent vicar Reverend Elliott Bellringer, known affectionately to his parishioners as 'Ells Bells'. She will then officially move next door to the vicarage with her new husband, son Luke, cat Plum (It is very important I mention him for Luke, says Sophie) and five-months-old Rose, whom the couple have been fostering and hope to adopt in the not too distant future.

Sophie has made her own wedding dress, one she has had in her head for many years, she tells me. Her own personal princess dress: her 'Cinderella at the ball' moment is nigh.

She employs two staff (and has just advertised for two more): one a lady who arrived in the village a year ago having escaped an abusive relationship who has found a new life in the community of Little Loste. And – part-time – Jade, the step-daughter of Tracey Darlow, who is Elliott's sister, 'and my best friend', Sophie is keen to add. Jade is a local A-level student hoping to go to university to do a Fashion and Textile degree who, Sophie says, reminds her of herself under the tutelage of Mrs Ackroyd. 'Jade has shown an amazing flair for the craft' she says. Jade, apparently, wore the very first of Sophie's bespoke prom dresses. 'That's a whole article by itself,' she laughs. I make a note to come back and ask her about it one day.

So no repeat of the three hundred guests-plus wedding that she had when she became Mrs Mayhew? Is it true her family will not be there? 'Sometimes you have to make your own family,' Sophie replies. 'Mine is cobbled together from the best of people. Those who truly care about us will be there to share our big day.'

Sophie Mayhew, Sophie the Trophy is no more, that much is clear. She has blossomed and changed into a woman lit from within by happiness and contentment and, if not too sentimental to say, by love. My prediction is that Sophie Bellringer will be more magnificent than Sophie Mayhew ever was.

I have found the one whom my soul loves.

Song of Solomon Chapter 3: Verse 4

Acknowledgements

As always I have a few people to thank for helping get this book to the shelves because it's a big team effort. I might have my name on the front, but in the background there are a whole host of talented, clever and proper nice souls holding me aloft to absorb the limelight.

Firstly my copyeditor Sally Partington who has to take top billing with this one. I love working with her because she is the wand that sprinkles the magic. What she doesn't know about grammar is not worth talking about. And horses and the Song of Solomon. She should be on *The Chase* as a Chaser.

Thank you to my publishing team at Simon & Schuster: 'God', Suzanne, SJ, Laura, Emma, Dawn, Dom, Joe, Rich, Gill, Hayley and the indispensable Alice and last but by no means least – my wonderful and supportive editor Jo Dickinson. My amazing agent Lizzy Kremer at David Higham Associates and all the lovely lot there. My brilliant team at Ed PR: Emma, Sian and Annabelle. All of these FAB people help me keep living the dream whilst I give them nightmares.

Thank you to my mate Tracey Cheetham, who gave me a crash course in politics – any mistakes are mine. Her fee was a breakfast and she is always well worth the price of the sausages. I love you, Cheeters. Not only because you rescued me from political ignorance but because you are you. Also her other half Tim for his invaluable contribution to the old Whitehall detail and whose words of encouragement when I needed them most – 'Write Bitch' – are pinned on my wall and never fail to motivate.

Thank you to our lovely vet Keith Bellringer at Churchfield Vets in Barnsley for lending me his superb name which I absolutely had to use for my vicar.

Thank you also to Dianne Core who is my go-to lady for matters ecclesiastical. She is a member of the spiritual care team at St Leonard's Hospice in York and her wonderful words are channelled by Ells Bells.

Thank you to Stu my website designer who is a marvel and a thoroughly nice bloke, even if he thinks I look like Uncle Bulgaria. Tell him I sent you if you use his services: www.nm4s.com.

Thank you to my greetings card mucker, the very talented Alec Sillifant for allowing me to refer to his book *Scary Edwin Page*. He was the first of us dreamers to get published and it gave me the kick up the backside to get cracking.

Thanks to my lovely friends: Traz and Kath, my Sun Sisters: Karen, Pam and Helen. McStables, Deb, Cath, Rae, Maggie, Sara, Jen, Paul, Nige, Chris, Andrew. And all my brilliant author mates – in particular Debbie Johnson, Catherine Isaac and Carole Matthews, who are helping me sail my rust bucket of a ship through menopausal waters. Where would we be without friends – especially ones who put up with authors constantly having to change plans because of deadlines.

Thank you to my family who take this crazy job in their stride, mainly to my other half Pete who organises a constant stream of coffee when I'm in head-down mode, walks the dog, does the shopping, makes fires (in the grate, not just randomly), cleans out Alan, acts as a taxi, produces a bottle of red from behind his back like the best sort of Ali Bongo. You're a keeper, love. I'm so lucky to have you.

Apologies for taking a liberty and inventing St Bathsheba who does not exist. Nor does her horrible school. Just in case you were hunting for their prospectus.

And lastly, dear readers, for keeping me in the job, for sending me your emails, for writing me gushing reviews, for taking the time to support me and turning out to get your books signed ... the biggest thank you that my little Barnsley heart can muster.

Milly Johnson is a *Sunday Times* Top Four author, joke-writer, newspaper columnist, after-dinner speaker and poet. She is a Vice President of the Yorkshire Society, an organisation that promotes and celebrates God's Own County, proud patron of Yorkshire Cat Rescue and the Well, a complementary therapy centre for cancer patients in Barnsley.

She loves nice stationery, cruising on big ships and flying birds of prey. She does not like marzipan. Not even from Godiva.

She was born and bred in Barnsley where she lives with her fiancé Pete, her teenage sons, cats, dog and rabbit in organised chaos. She still lives around the corner from her mam and dad.

The Magnificent Mrs Mayhew is her sixteenth novel.

FIND OUT MORE ABOUT

milly johnson

Milly Johnson is the queen of feel-good fiction
and bestselling author of sixteen novels.

To find out more about her and her writing,
visit her website at
www.millyjohnson.co.uk

or follow Milly on

Twitter @millyjohnson
Instagram @themillyjohnson
Facebook @MillyJohnsonAuthor

All of Milly's books are available in print and eBook,
and are available to download in eAudio

Milly Johnson

The Mother of All Christmases

Eve Glace – co-owner of the theme park Winterworld – is having
a baby and her due date is a perfectly timed 25th December. She's
decided that she and her husband **Jacques** should renew their wedding
vows with all the pomp that was missing the first time. But growing
problems at Winterworld keep distracting them . . .

Annie Pandoro and her husband **Joe** own a small Christmas
cracker factory, and are well set up and happy together despite life
never blessing them with a much-wanted child. But when Annie
finds that the changes happening to her body aren't typical of
the menopause but pregnancy, her joy is uncontainable.

Palma Collins has agreed to act as a surrogate, hoping
the money will get her out of the gutter in which she finds herself.
But when the couple she is helping split up, is she going to
be left carrying a baby she never intended to keep?

Annie, Palma and Eve all meet at the 'Christmas Pudding Club',
a new directive started by a forward-thinking young doctor to help
mums-to-be mingle and share their pregnancy journeys.
Will this group help each other to find love, contentment
and peace as Christmas approaches?

AVAILABLE NOW IN PAPERBACK, EBOOK AND AUDIO

SIMON &
SCHUSTER

Milly Johnson

The Perfectly Imperfect Woman

'With mystery, romance and humour, every page
of this enjoyable tale is glorious' *heat*

Marnie Salt has made so many mistakes in her life that
she fears she will never get on the right track. But when she 'meets'
an old lady on a baking chatroom and begins confiding in
her, little does she know how her life will change.

Arranging to see each other for lunch, Marnie discovers
that **Lilian** is every bit as mad and delightful as she'd hoped –
and that she owns a whole village in the Yorkshire Dales. When
Marnie needs a refuge after a crisis, she ups sticks and heads for
Wychwell – a temporary measure, so she thinks.

But soon Marnie finds that Wychwell has claimed her
as its own and she is duty bound not to leave. Even if what she
has to do makes her as unpopular as a force 12 gale in a confetti
factory! But everyone has imperfections, as Marnie comes to
realise, and that is not such a bad thing – after all, your flaws
are perfect for the heart that is meant to love you.

The Perfectly Imperfect Woman is a heart-warming and hilarious
novel of family, secrets, love and redemption . . . and broken
hearts mended and made all the stronger for it.

AVAILABLE NOW IN PAPERBACK, EBOOK AND AUDIO

SIMON &
SCHUSTER

Milly Johnson

The Queen of Wishful Thinking

'A glorious, heartfelt novel' Rowan Coleman

When **Lewis Harley** has a health scare in his early forties, he takes it as a wake-up call. He and his wife Charlotte leave behind life in the fast lane and Lewis opens the antique shop he has dreamed of. **Bonnie Brookland** was brought up in the antiques trade and now works for the man who bought out her father's business, but she isn't happy there. So when she walks into Lew's shop, she knows this is the place for her.

As Bonnie and Lew start to work together, they soon realise that there is more to their relationship than either thought. But Bonnie is trapped in an unhappy marriage, and Lew and Charlotte have more problems than they care to admit. Each has secrets in their past which are about to be uncovered . . .

Can they find the happiness they both deserve?

AVAILABLE NOW IN PAPERBACK AND EBOOK

**SIMON &
SCHUSTER**

Milly Johnson

Sunshine Over Wildflower Cottage

New beginnings, old secrets, and a place to call home – escape to Wildflower Cottage for love, laughter and friendship . . .

Viv arrives at Wildflower Cottage, a tumbledown animal sanctuary, for the summer. Her job is to help with the admin, but the truth is she is here for something much closer to her heart.

Geraldine runs the Wildflower Cottage sanctuary. She escaped from her past to find happiness here, but now her place of refuge is about to come under threat. Can she keep her history at bay and her future safe?

Back home, Viv's mother **Stel** thinks she might have found a man who will treat her right for once. Ian is kind, considerate, and clearly head over heels for her. That's what she has wanted all along, isn't it?

AVAILABLE NOW IN PAPERBACK AND EBOOK

SIMON &
SCHUSTER

Milly Johnson

Afternoon Tea at the Sunflower Café

'When it comes to creating characters that
are believable, loveable and engaging, Milly strides
comfortably to the head of the pack' *heat*

When **Connie** discovers that Jimmy Diamond, her husband
of more than twenty years, is planning to leave her for his
office junior, her world is turned upside down. Determined
to salvage her pride, she resolves to get her own back.
Along with **Della**, Jimmy's right-hand woman at his
cleaning firm, Diamond Shine, and the cleaners who meet
at the Sunflower Café, she'll make him wish he had never
underestimated her.

Then Connie meets the charming **Brandon Locke**, a master
chocolatier, whose kindness starts to melt her soul.
Can the ladies of the Sunflower Café help Connie scrub
away the hurt? And can Brandon make her trust again?

AVAILABLE NOW IN PAPERBACK AND EBOOK

SIMON &
SCHUSTER

booksandthecity.co.uk

the home of female fiction

BOOKS | NEWS & EVENTS | FEATURES | AUTHOR PODCASTS | COMPETITIONS

Follow us online to be the first to hear from
your favourite authors

booksandthecity.co.uk

books and the city

@TeamBATC

Join our mailing list for the latest news, events and
exclusive competitions

Sign up at
booksandthecity.co.uk